After service in submarines in WW2, Alexander Fullerton learnt Russian and was employed in Germany as a naval liaison officer with units of the Red Army. In the course of this, after a conversation with a somewhat inebriated Soviet officer, he predicted the lowering of the Iron Curtain – a prediction that was firmly rejected by Intelligence in London. Consequently, when the curtain did crash down, the Allies had only days instead of weeks in which to mount the Berlin Air Lift. It was several years before Fullerton realised that the desk on which his report had landed had been that of Kim Philby, then a ranking colonel in the KGB.

Staying Alive is Alexander Fullerton's forty-ninth own-name novel.

Praise for Alexander Fullerton

'His action passages are superb and he never
puts a period foot wrong'
Observer

'Has the ring of truth and the integrity proper
to a work of art'
Daily Telegraph

'The prose has a real sense of urgency and so has
the theme. The tension rarely slackens and the
setting is completely convincing'
Times Literary Supplement

'The most meticulously researched war novels that
I have ever read'
Len Deighton

'Impeccable in detail and gripping in impact'
Irish Independent

'You don't read a no‍vel... You live it'

Also by Alexander Fullerton

The Everard series of naval novels

The SBS Trilogy

The Merchant Navy Series

The Rosie Series

STAYING ALIVE

A novel by

Alexander Fullerton

sphere

SPHERE

First published in Great Britain in 2006 by Time Warner Books
This paperback edition published in 2007 by Sphere

A CIP catalogue record for this book
is available from the British Library.

ISBN 978-0-7515-3976-9

Papers used by Sphere are natural, recyclable products made from
wood grown in sustainable forests and certified in accordance with
the rules of the Forest Stewardship Council.

Typeset in Bembo by Palimpsest Book Production Limited,
Grangemouth, Stirlingshire
Printed and bound in Great Britain by
Mackays of Chatham plc, Chatham, Kent
Paper supplied by Hellefoss AS, Norway

Sphere
An imprint of
Little, Brown Book Group
Brettenham House
Lancaster Place
London WC2E 7EN

A Member of the Hachette Livre Group of Companies

www.littlebrown.co.uk

For Priscilla
– with love and appreciation of what a lot she's put up with – come to think of it, almost Rosie-fashion, in fifty years and books. Could be that's where Rosie sprang from?

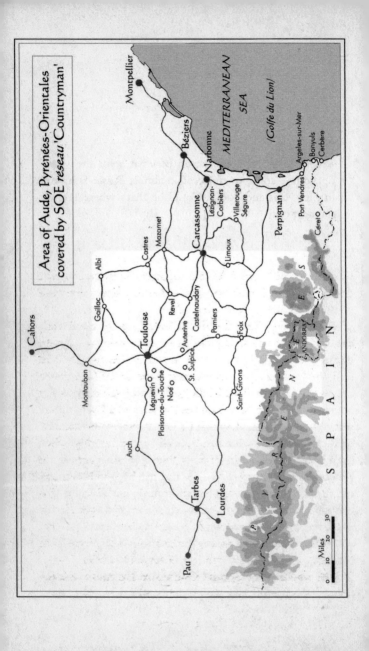

Area of Aude, Pyrénées-Orientales covered by SOE réseau 'Countryman'

I said, facing her across a marble-topped table in the Brasserie des Aviateurs, 'Still can't believe it – that I'm sitting here with you. With Rosie – *the* Rosie . . .'

Who allegedly had vanished in Australia quite some while ago, and about whose exploits in German-occupied France during World War II I'd written several novels: which she'd read, she'd told me, and which must more or less have passed muster with her, or she'd hardly have invited me to meet her here in Toulouse to hear from her the story I had *not* written, that of her first mission, which I'd had no way of researching. I'd kicked off with what had been her second outing, when she'd been put ashore in Brittany from a motor-gunboat, on a moonless night in 1943. But her first had been in November of '42, not long after her twenty-fourth birthday; on that occasion, by the light of a near-full moon, she'd parachuted into open countryside somewhere near Cahors and made her way down to Toulouse, where she was to join the local SOE network (or *réseau*) as its radio operator and courier.

SOE standing for Special Operations Executive. Exceptionally courageous men and women who'd had the nerve for that kind of thing: as well as certain specialist skills and of course fluent French.

Now, in October of 2002, Rosie had to be eighty-four. Although if one had been guessing one might have said twenty years younger than that. Mid-grey hair with what looked like natural waves in it, *lovely* eyes, and skin a much younger woman wouldn't have been ashamed of; trim figure elegant in silvery trousers and a grey silk shirt with a ruby brooch at the throat, studs in her ears that matched it. While a ring on the appropriate finger of her hand resting on the marble prompted me to ask her – needing to know, and not necessarily anticipating a *happy* answer, her husband had after all been six or seven years older than her – I tried gently, 'Ben not with you? Left him in Australia, or –'

'Ben's long dead.' Small smile, shake of the head, I suppose at my own reaction. Not shock, I'd at least half expected it, but sadness, for her. Sadness anyway: if I'd got Ben Quarry even half right in the novels he'd been a great guy, really tremendous, and the pair of them had been deeply, desperately in love. She was saying, 'Long, *long* time ago. More than forty years. So in that sense I'm inured to it, although in quite another I'm very definitely nothing like inured and never will be. The bloody awful truth is he was murdered.'

'*Murdered* . . .'

Meeting her calm but sensitive brown gaze. My own I dare say showing some degree of shock.

'Forty years ago – about 1960, would have been – but where, how, who –'

'In Aussie, is where. Queensland. Nineteen fifty-eight. And it was me they were after. *Who* – well no, that's something else.'

Blinking at her. Repeating what she'd said – '*You* they

2

were after . . . Whoever *they* may have been. Sounds like it's two stories you'll be giving me?'

'All one, really – 1942, resurfacing 1957.' A glance beyond me: 'Here come our martinis.'

She'd written to me three or four weeks earlier, in care of my publishers and writing from an address in Paris – smart address, 16th *arrondissement* – introducing herself as

the original of the person you've called Rosie in several novels that I've read, having been introduced to them by a friend who'd happened to pick one up and found herself astonished by what struck her as similarities to me and to 'Ben' and as much as she knew of our earlier lives. And in the last of those books, the Paris one, I must admit that the woman you called 'Marilyn Stuart' is an easily recognizable portrait of her as she was, which makes the source of all four stories obvious enough. 'Marilyn' was beyond doubt my SOE Conducting Officer, equally plainly she must have given you the facts out of which you built your fiction. I wonder how you came across her. But in that Paris book, where she tells you in the final pages that my darling and I had done a disappearing act into the Outback – basing this on her allegedly not having had Christmas cards from me over a period of a few years – well, to put it plainly I found myself admiring her bloody nerve – I'd gone on sending cards maybe two or three years after hers stopped coming!

That's going off the track a bit, but it was when I was reading the end of the Paris story that I had the idea of getting in touch with you, or trying to. I haven't done so until now because – well, laziness is one factor, but another is doubting whether you'd want yet more 'Rosie' history, whether it wasn't only vanity making me think you might be interested. I admit I've enjoyed reading about myself – or your version of myself, at times a somewhat glorified version of me as I see me. How's that for syntax? I should in fairness add that all the stories as you tell them come close enough to

3

the truth, despite the odd embellishment or wild fancy here and there, what I suppose might be called novelist's licence; and of course one might have expected as much, since 'Marilyn' was supplying you with the details. She really did get to know it all, and obviously her memory was unimpaired at any rate at that stage! It's equally a fact that she wouldn't have known anything much about my first trip, because although she saw me off from the airfield at Tempsford, she was then despatched on some SOE business which kept her out of London – one assumes, in France – until quite some while after I got back. In-house gossip had it that she'd nagged them into giving her a trial in the field, and they eventually pulled her out of it on account of her dangerously English accent. I know she'd had a theory that she'd get away with it by claiming to be Belgian: I guess that in practice this didn't work out, and as she didn't actually come to grief it would have been the Organiser of her réseau who had her shipped home. And the file on my Toulouse adventures wouldn't have come her way at all; whereas after each of the other excursions, as my Conducting Officer she sat in on the routinely lengthy and detailed debriefings, she'd have had no business in that one.

However – circumstances have now arisen which I think justify my throwing caution to the winds and offering to bend your ear. There's to be a three-day reunion, on the face of it BCRA but with SOE section 'F' and 'RF' also invited – although it seems unlikely there'll be many other takers, from our side – and it's to be in Toulouse, of all places, where on that first jaunt I worked as pianist/courier with the Countryman réseau. The last BCRA/SOE get-together was in Paris ten years ago, and what's special about this one, apart from its location, is that it's almost certain to be the last, as survivors who are both mobile and in their right minds are getting to be rather thin on the ground. The organisers are the French Fédération Nationale Libre Résistance, the invitation came to me through the Special Forces Club in London – and I've accepted.

4

A break here for some interpretations, since not all readers of this will have read the earlier Rosie books, and even those who have may not remember a lot of detail.

BCRA, standing for Bureau Central de Renseignments et d'Action, was General de Gaulle's London-based equivalent of SOE, employing only Frenchmen – Gaullists, naturally. He – characteristically – resented SOE's existence, taking the view that any secret army in France should belong to him. This view was in fact held and implemented more stringently at Free French command levels than in the field, where agents whose lives were at constant risk tended to help each other out when necessary. And BCRA had to rely on SOE in any case for such essentials as transport and radio communications, which in itself must have irritated Monsieur le Général no end. But that's BCRA. 'F' Section SOE was simply the department of SOE that dealt with France, British through and through although employing some French agents, while Section 'RF' was still part of SOE but had its own management and employed *only* French agents, French nationals who for instance weren't keen on working for de Gaulle. And a 'pianist' – Rosie mentioned having served as such – was SOE/Resistance slang for a radio operator. This had been her occupation even before 'F' Section took her on as a field agent. Part of the set-up was a signals establishment in a large country house near Sevenoaks in Kent; signals received from agents in the field were received there and rushed up to Baker Street (or in 'RF's case, to Dorset Square) by despatch riders on motorcycles. And it was at this Sevenoaks establishment that Rosie worked. She and her first husband, Squadron Leader Johnny Ewing, had a flat nearby, and he was based at RAF Biggin Hill, until his Spitfire with him inside it was shot down in flames, within a day or two of which she'd got herself on to the agents' training course. Actually her first application was turned down, the interviewer deciding that as a brand-new widow she had to be suicidally inclined, whereas the truth was that by this time she hadn't even *liked* her husband, for various reasons including the fact he'd frequently cheated on her. And being already a skilled radio operator as well as speaking fluent French – her father had been French – she was an ideal recruit; had only needed to be taught to parachute, live rough in the open, shoot with all types of handgun, fight with knives, handle explosives, blow safes, resist interrogation, and so on.

Back to her letter, though.

The reunion's scheduled for October 4th, 5th, and 6th, Friday to Sunday, and the venue is the Hôtel l'Ambassade on Boulevard d'Arcole. I've been offered a bed-and-breakfast reservation, which I'm now accepting, but although it's a biggish place I'm told it's going to be very full, with our bunch of superannuated thugs occupying a whole floor, apparently. So I'd suggest that if you did feel inclined to come, and could make those dates, you might book yourself – or yourselves – into some other hotel in that vicinity or at any rate not too far away. Could be wet in October, couldn't it. Although I know you spent your war in submarines, and a submariner shouldn't mind getting wet? Sorry. One thing your stuff about me does not reveal is that I have a rather childish sense of humour. Bring an umbrella, anyway. I'd say the reunion itself will consist of speeches and discussions between sessions of food and booze; I'd introduce you to the committee as the writer you are, with special interest in SOE and the Resistance generally, and I'm sure they'd be only too pleased to let you sit in on whichever events may appeal to you. Much of it's likely to be fairly boring, I dare say – and a lot of it will be simply old friends meeting again and swapping memories, so forth. In fact a lot of the people who attended last time, ten years ago, were only relatives of former agents. Odd, but there it is. Spreads the cost of such junkets, I suppose. Anyway, the great thing would be for you and I to get together in peace and quiet in our own free time – don't you agree? Suppose we were to get there the day before it starts — Thursday the 3rd, spend that evening together and then play it by ear — if you're on, that is?

By the time I'd read her letter I had no doubt that this truly was Rosie, the one and only, and I felt real excitement at the prospect of just meeting her, let alone getting the story of that 1942 deployment straight from her own mouth and memory. All I remembered Marilyn Stuart telling me about it — all she herself would have known, according to Rosie — was that the Toulouse *réseau* was penetrated by the Gestapo, and Rosie escaped over the Pyrenees 'by the skin of her back teeth'. In *Into the Fire* I'd written that this happened about seven months after Rosie had joined the *réseau*; whether this had been misinformation from Marilyn or simply my own wild guess, the truth is that Rosie had been there only a few *weeks* before everything went up in smoke. I'd guess it would have been simply Marilyn's assumption: if *she*'d been away that length of time, and Rosie might have been on what one might have called survivor's leave, returned to Baker Street only a week or two ahead of her. Something like that. Anyway, I'd be hearing all about it now, and was thrilled at the prospect. As I say, even just to meet and speak with Rosie Quarry . . . So I telephoned, and the ball was rolling — to the extent that I'd flown into Toulouse around noon on this Thursday 3rd October 2002, transferred by taxi to the Hôtel Mermoz on Rue Matabiau, called Rosie at her conference hotel, l'Ambassade, at five-thirty, met her there at six and settled down with her in the Brasserie des Aviateurs, which was situated at the hotel entrance, all plate glass and marble.

2

Rosie admitted, 'It was scary, all right. I suppose setting out on trips *always* was, but that first time – oh, crikey . . . And the parachuting itself – the prospect of it, mostly, the waiting around and thinking about it. When the moment came it all happened so fast you barely knew it *had* – you were on the ground suddenly, maybe a few bruises here and there but mainly thanking God you hadn't broken a leg or your neck, whatever. But I'll tell you – our para training was at Ringwood, near Manchester, and the first thing that happened when we got there was they took us out to the airfield for a demonstration to show us how easy and safe it was, some old aircraft flying over dropping dummies – sandbags – and believe it or not half the 'chutes didn't open. I mean literally half: sandbags just hurtling down and bursting. And this was to give us confidence.'

'And when you did it?'

'Oddly enough, there were no casualties, in training. Were some in action. Oh, there had been one earlier that summer, a Section "RF" pianist – male. I was only the second female to be sent in, did you know that?'

I'd asked her about her departure from Tempsford that first trip, how nerve-racking it must have been. As in fact I knew already, there was an SOE hut on the airfield, where her Conducting Officer, my latter-day friend Marilyn Stuart, had put her through what she, Marilyn, had referred to as 'the last rites'. Checking on clothing and contents of pockets, ensuring there were no give-aways of British origin – even laundry-marks for instance – that every item had originated in France, and that her papers – identity documents, authorities to travel, ration cards and so forth – matched her cover story. They'd have been checked and treble-checked before, of course – and forged by a team of geniuses or ex-criminals in a villa on the Kingston bypass in Surrey; Rosie's cover on this outing being that she was Suzette Treniard, born in Paris in September 1918 and now widowed, her husband Paul, a young *lieutenant de vaisseau*, having been killed in the British attack on the French fleet in Mers-el-Kebir on 3rd July 1940. He'd been serving in the battleship *Bretagne*, which had capsized; she'd had a letter about it from a friend of his, Arnaud Dupré, who'd been in the battleship *Provence*, which although damaged had managed to get itself to Toulon. She'd had this letter in her bag, crumpled, even tear-smudged, along with other items including a snapshot of Paul in a swimsuit at a picnic on a beach near Le Palais on Belle Ile where they'd spent their honeymoon just before the war; background features were easily identifiable, by anyone wanting to check on it. She also had a bitter hatred of the British, especially of their Navy. SOE interrogators had rehearsed her in all this, and Marilyn had her run over it again in the Tempsford hut; it was essential of course to have it all off absolutely pat, believe in it, *be* Suzette Treniard, not for instance to have to think twice when asked what were her late husband's parents' names or where they lived – they came from Nantes – not all that far from Belle Ile – or in the case of her own parents the de Gavres (with whom she didn't get on well), St Briac-sur-Mer, near Dinard and St Malo.

She'd had her radio transceiver with her, of course, a B Mark II supposedly boosted for long-distance transmissions – as would be essential from the Languedoc – in a suitcase sixty centimetres long and weighing about fifteen kilos, with its battery and twenty metres of thin, dark-coloured aerial wire. Rosie's individual, easily-breakable crystals were packaged separately, inside her clothes. The set's heaviest item was the battery; and a priority she'd had in mind when starting out was to have a couple of spare sets and several batteries either dropped or shipped in to her, for the purpose of setting up alternative transmission sites. She'd been assured that this would be treated as urgent. Pianists had been having a rough time of it lately: there was a nasty rumour that their operational life in the field had been averaging out at only about six weeks.

Wouldn't apply to her, of course. She'd simply see to it that it didn't – she *thought* – and one basic precaution was never to transmit from the same place twice. Use of batteries, as distinct from plugging in to the mains, allowed one to tap out one's messages from open countryside – or from ruins, farm buildings, church towers and the like.

Marilyn had asked her, 'Got your one-time pads?'

For cyphering and decyphering purposes. She'd nodded, touched the small of her back. 'Along with the cash.'

Half a million francs: to be handed over to her boss, the *réseau*'s Organiser, as soon as she established contact with him.

She told me – looking across the now crowded brasserie at three elderly men who'd just come in and were goofing around for an unoccupied table, Rosie frowning slightly as

10

if unsure whether or not she might know or have known one of them – and then giving up, starting again . . . 'Felt as if one had everything except the wash-house mangle. Really *stuffed* with bits and pieces. Including a battered cardboard suitcase with one's personal gear in it. That was hooked on externally, same as the transceiver. I was wearing an overcoat as well as the jumpsuit, mark you. Skirt, blouse, coat, and a scarf covering my hair. Which, as I think you mention here and there in the books, *used* to be brown with coppery lights in it.' She'd smiled; *was* a little vain, I realised for the first time. And had a right to be, must have been startlingly attractive, at that time. In fact still *was* attractive. Shaking her head: 'Imagine it. Jumpsuit trousers pulled up over the skirts of the topcoat, parachute harness over that – the two cases slung on it, and my handbag on a cord round my neck, hanging inside the suit. Could barely stagger, and looked like God knows what, and when one landed – intact, please God – and hid or ideally buried the parachute, harness and jumpsuit, one had to reorganise the rest so as to look as near-normal as possible. Catch a train for instance without attracting any particular attention, especially that of gendarmes. Oh, I say gendarmes, as distinct from more sinister elements such as Gestapo, because this was the non-occupied zone I'd be landing in. Pétain's police and snoopers – the DST, Vichy security police, Direction de Surveillance du Territoire, as well as the gendarmerie – well, those had comprised the main opposition, up to this time there'd been no Boche soldiery or overt Gestapo presence; but *now*, at this precise moment they were flooding in. In response to Operation Torch, you see, our invasion of northwest Africa. On 8th November, Torch was launched, Boches began their move on the 11th, and I was flying in on the night of the 12th/13th. From that point of view you might say I couldn't have timed it worse.' A shrug and a movement of the head that was entirely French. 'On the other hand, looking on the brighter side, in the Western Desert our Eighth Army had smashed through the Africa Korps at El Alamein, and Rommel and his boys had their tails between their legs. It was a relief to know something *somewhere* was looking good at last. Don't you want to make notes at all?'

'I'll do that later. I've a laptop in my room.' I asked her, 'Did you take a pistol in with you on this trip?'

Headshake. 'Could have, of course – and later as you know changed my mind on this – but at that stage I was accepting advice that if one was to get into shoot-outs one couldn't expect to last long thereafter, and meanwhile it was an item which – well, if one was searched, would guarantee being arrested and no doubt shot or – whatever. As with the transceiver of course, but one wouldn't normally be toting that around. Not if I could help it, one wouldn't. No, the only item of significance I haven't mentioned, and which Marilyn handed to me last of all, was your regular standard issue poison pill – little gelatine capsule of potassium cyanide which if the worst came to the worst – well, I'd been told that if I bit on it I'd be dead before my teeth had actually come together.'

'Handy.'

A smile, and the shrug again. 'In some circumstances, a convenience.'

'Convenience.' I liked that. Suggested, 'How about we bite on another dry martini?'

Our third, that was, and waiters were trying to pressure us into ordering food, but we'd been in that place long enough, were ready for a change of atmosphere. I suggested a small restaurant I'd noticed on my way here and thought looked promising, Rosie was amenable and had no alternatives in mind; in fact she wasn't familiar with twenty-first-century Toulouse, hadn't patronised the better (i.e. black market) restaurants in 1942, and none of them would have been recognisable to her now in any case, even if they still existed.

The place I'd seen was called the Colombier, and wasn't far from l'Ambassade. Just along Boulevard Arcole to where it becomes Boulevard de Strasbourg, along there and up to the left a bit.

Arcole pronounced with a hard 'c', incidentally. Should perhaps have mentioned that before. But I asked her, while on the subject of towns and their topography, whether she still knew Paris as well as she had in 1945, the year of her SOE swansong as recorded in my last Rosie novel, *Single to Paris*.

'Darned well should do. It's my home, for God's sake, has been since 1961!'

The brasserie's blue-tinted glass door hissed shut behind us. Wet paving and cool night air but no rain falling at this moment.

'Nineteen sixty-one. So you didn't stay long after Ben was killed. I'd wondered.'

'Remember what we'd been expecting to do out there, in Aussie?'

'An Australian governmental land-clearing scheme Ben had reckoned to go in for, wasn't it. Returning ex-servicemen being offered some enormous acreage, and as much again if they cleared the first lot on schedule?'

'Right. He was really set on it. *Would* have gone in for it if they'd accepted him, but as you know he'd had two smash-ups in motor-torpedo boats, and he was really too lame for that hard labour. He swore black and blue that he was perfectly all right, went through agonies trying not to limp, and so on, but they still wouldn't have him. Obstinate bugger, he was bloody mad at 'em, although the alternative was so simple and obvious – his father had been asking him since God knew how long to join him in his timber business; Ben saw this as the "soft option", which in principle he was against, had to make it on his own. Well – you know this, I think – the old man had started it in the early thirties, he'd been in the Merchant Navy, had his master's ticket, left the sea when he married Ben's Aussie mother, and had the intention of building boats – yachts – but got diverted into timber. Which was a success right from the start. Yes, you mentioned it somewhere – how just before the war when Ben was adrift in Paris chasing girls and trying to get to be an artist, keeping himself alive by washing dishes in the big hotels, and so forth, the old man writing letter after letter calling him home by the next boat, Ben saying yeah, yeah, coming – got as far as England and joined the RNVR in September 1939.'

She'd stopped, pointing up to the left, where we were about to cross at a major intersection. 'Place Jeanne d'Arc, right?'

'Is it? I'm sure you'd know, Rosie. Yes – must be. So we take the next left after this. You're saying he did finally go into the timber business?'

'He'd've been crazy not to. It was going like a bomb and the old man really did need some help. He'd obviously counted on Ben seeing sense eventually, he was tickled pink and Ben of course having made up his mind went for it hell for leather, like he did everything. He certainly earned his keep – bloody *good* keep, and – you know, everything coming up roses.'

'Until 1958.'

'Fifty-seven actually. The two of us were lunching in the MHYC – Middle Harbour Yacht Club. One of the biggest and most successful in the country, although this was before they built the smart new clubhouse. They were a great crowd. Ben's father had been in on the start of it, and Ben like him was mad on sailing. He'd done a lot of it as a boy, there in Brisbane before leaving to seek fame and squalor in Gay Paree.'

'At lunch, you say. Just like that – out of the blue, whatever it was?'

'Just like that.'

'A year before they killed him, meaning to kill *you*.'

'That's – yes . . . Is this where we turn?'

'If it's Rue Bayard –'

'Beginning to rain.'

'Hang on.' Umbrella, large enough for two. It was only a bit of drizzle, actually. I asked her, to get this into perspective, 'In 1957, you'd have been thirty-nine, Ben forty-five, and his father – what, sixty-five or seventy?'

'More like seventy-five. He was eighty in '62, the year I left. Fit as a fiddle, but – you know, sad. He'd made himself rich, and Ben would have been too. I came in for that, of course – inheritance I mean. Truth is, the old man and the company did me proud.'

'Good for them. Better than bush-clearance, eh?'

'Well, there'd have been a hell of a lot of land and several million sheep. And then again, if we'd been doing that, more than a thousand miles away, we wouldn't have been in the yacht club that lunchtime, huh?'

'Consequently you'd still have Ben, still be living there?'

'I'd still have Ben.'

'Maybe a crippled Ben.'

'Or who knows, maybe dead. I mean without – assistance. He was a few years older than me, you know.'

I was suggesting we might cross the road, at this point, starting over right after the passage of an ambulance with a screaming siren. I could see the restaurant on the other side, only a short way up. I was thinking that the subject of Ben's death was overdue for dropping – thinking this as the ambulance and its spray rushed by and she repeated, 'Still have old Ben. That truly *is* a thought. Hey, rain's stopped . . .'

We drank a bottle of good wine with our excellent meal, booked a table for the next evening, Friday, and agreed that I'd handle evenings while she'd pick up daytime tabs – in the Brasserie des Aviateurs anyway, where from Friday on we'd most likely be mingling with former BCRA and/or SOE stalwarts and it would be easier for her to treat me as her guest. In the evenings, she said, she'd 'sing for her supper'; and I pointed out that we were going to need all the song-time we could get, especially as we'd be covering happenings not only in Toulouse and the Languedoc in 1942 but also Brisbane in 1957/8. Maybe she'd play hooky from some of the reunion's daytime sessions? She promised me she would; probably from most of them. And the Brisbane stuff would take no time at all. As little as half an hour, maybe, it was the build-up to it that was going to keep us busy.

I took her word for that. Over supper she'd only talked about the para drop and how she'd got from Cahors to Toulouse. I tried to push it along a bit, but was realising we'd cover more ground much faster in daytime sessions *without* attentive waiters; and I'd need to be a little cunning, if not ruthless, in getting her well away from the conference hotel and its brasserie – i.e. from what had brought her here in the first place.

We summoned a taxi to take her back there now. I'd walk, the Mermoz being really very close. It wasn't far short of midnight, and I was reckoning on spending an hour or more at the laptop; a little fresh air and exercise now couldn't do any harm. In the morning we were to meet for coffee in the Aviateurs at ten. Now, outside the restaurant, I kissed her on the cheek.

'Rosie. Can't even begin to tell you how grateful I am, or how much I'm enjoying your company. It was a wonderful idea.'

'As you've mentioned a few times. But I'm enjoying myself too, I really am. Honest truth, would've been a bore to have been here on my own. Give my best to your wife.'

'I will. Ten o'clock, then.'

'Don't work *too* late . . .'

It was too late to call my wife in Ireland. Although midnight here was only eleven there – eleven-twenty by the time I was back at the Mermoz. She'd gone over there to spend a few days with her sister, whose husband was in hospital and (we thought, although no one was saying this) unlikely to come out of it; I doubted whether either she or her sister would appreciate being woken in the middle of the night, just for a chat.

In any case, time now to focus on twenty-four-year-old Rosie in her parachuting gear in a Lancaster bomber of the Special Duties Squadron, droning over France towards Cahors. Not far to go: they'd dropped a pair of male French agents somewhere near Limoges, spewing them out through the hole in the deck about a quarter of an hour ago, and at the Despatcher's suggestion she'd now moved into their place on the trembling cold metal, a couple of feet for'ard of the hatch. You went out feet-first and facing the tail: more a matter of pushing off than jumping. Hatch still shut at this stage: round hatch, whereas in the old Whitleys from which she'd done her training jumps they were square.

'OK, Missus?'

Missus, indeed. Well, she'd look to him like a tub of lard with two eyes at the top under the tight dark headscarf. He was a flight sergeant, Polish, high-voiced to be heard over the general racket, small man in a wool hat. Big ears, crooked smile. She'd answered, 'Fine, thanks.' Feeling like a triced-up sack of spuds and very, very nervous, but actually drawn *towards* that hole in the deck, thinking of it as an emergency exit, her only way out of this.

'Crazy, but how it was.' Rosie sipping wine as she'd told me this. 'Sack of spuds I said, but more like jelly, internally bloody *shaking*. Smiling at the Pole and telling him "Fine!" while shivering and sweating in the cold, and the aircraft shaking even harder. Probably somewhat over the hill: SD Squadron didn't get first pick. But don't get me wrong, I was probably more het-up than I'd ever been, but I never thought *my* number would be up, I was going in there to do this and that and then get out again, I doubt it even occurred to me as conceivable I wouldn't.'

Still was scared, though, she'd admitted. Actually, terrified. Hardly surprising to me, however contradictorily or confusedly she'd put it, when one recalled that fifty per cent of them did *not* come back from their various jaunts. Despite that irrational faith in one's own survival. How you *had* to feel, to have gone in for it in the first place. Anyway, I'll tell it *my* way now, the way I'll write it, my interpretation of her recollections as condensed that night on the laptop. The Despatcher opening the hatch as the machine dropped lower: she'd be jumping from only 600 feet, and that was moonlight out there as well as a howling rush of wind. No doubt if she'd peered over the edge, looking down, she'd have had a view of the ground – woods, fields, maybe a river or two – the Lot, for instance, the big one that ran right through Cahors, looped around its city centre, but she wasn't inclined to look down – 'having no head for heights', she'd said – in any case she'd be down there *on* it in a minute. On it or in it – field, please God, not tree or bloody river, and pasture preferable to vineyard, on account of posts and wires. Despatcher urging her to shift forward, to the brink: he hooked her rip-cord to the static line and pointed at the red light which when it turned green would be the pilot's signal to her to jump. Machine settling lower and banking now, she guessed adjusting its approach to line up on the torches or lanterns, of which there should be four in a straight line with a fifth set off at right-angles to the top end of that line, this one flashing a pre-agreed morse letter.

If the reception party was in place, it would mean they'd heard the BBC's confirmation, broadcast of some prearranged *message personnel* telling them she was on her way.

They *were* in place. Light switching to green. Despatcher's gloved hand on her shoulder, a short, sharp shove and a scream of 'Go-o-o!' trailing into the howl of wind as she went out and the rip-cord did its stuff, canopy opening to arrest her flight in a fantasia of moonlight, stars, fields and hedgerows, and a welcome reduction of noise in her immediate vicinity. The Lanc would hold on for at least a few miles, rather than turn back soon enough for anyone on the ground to guess this had been its target area. Rosie swinging through dark sky and reminding herself about landing with knees bent: then she'd hit turf, rolled with the smell of it in her nostrils and the thought in her head. *Now what?* Knowing perfectly well *what*, though, already doing it, gathering in the cords and billowing silk, on her knees and then at a crouch, pleasantly surprised at having suffered no injury, and getting it all in more efficiently than she'd ever done in training jumps, thanks to the lack of any wind; not letting up on the effort even when a rough male voice called 'Bienvenue! Mais parfaitement, madame!' Madame Suzette Treniard, widow, back on French soil again at last – and *two* of them now, relieving her of the mass of parachute material while she unhitched the two suitcases from the harness and then divested herself of both harness and jumpsuit. Standing again – headscarf loosened, strap of the handbag over one shoulder of her tatty old coat, seeing that the man who'd got to her first, the taller one who'd been first on the scene, was stuffing her discarded gear into sacks. Earthy smell of potatoes, doubtless the sacks' previous contents. He'd shouldered the load, growled to the shorter, noticeably broader man, 'See you again all too soon, Alain, I dare say.'

So this would be Alain Déclan, right-hand man to the *réseau*'s boss. He'd said to the tall one, 'Count on it. And thanks.'

'For nothing. Adieu, madame.'

'Perhaps au revoir, monsieur.'

Déclan watched him go, trudging off with the sacks over his shoulders, then asked her in English, 'All set, Lucy?' Stooping to pick up the larger of her cases; she'd taken possession of the smaller one, the one that mattered enough to give your life for. Peering at him, making him out as quite short – five-seven or eight maybe – but very solid. Sweater, and peaked cap, face black-looking in the moonlight. Not so much bearded as maybe hadn't been shaved for a week or so. She'd nodded to his question, asked him, 'Should I take it you're Batsman?'

Wrong way to have put the question *Should* have asked him, 'What's your code-name?' He knew it *now* – even if he was an imposter and hadn't before, in which case he'd be glad of the information. Sloppy of her: he'd started it, of course, by calling her Lucy, which was *her* code-name, the only name she or SOE in England would ever use in signals. He'd grunted an affirmative anyway, adding 'Come on. First thing is pick up the lamps.'

'And then?'

'My *camionette*'s not far.' *Camionette* meaning truck or pick-up. 'We'll sit it out till daylight, then I'll drop you at the station.'

'In Cahors?'

'Where'd you imagine?'

'Conceivably, Toulouse.'

'Daft, would that be. I'm on that road night time, chances are I'm stopped. OK for me, they know me – if they're locals that is. I've a wife at Léguevin – west of Toulouse, that is – *I'm* local, near enough. But who do we say you are – middle of the night, suitcases an' all, including you know what?'

'I can account for myself, Alain.'

'Not for that radio you're carrying, you can't. Besides, supposed not to be seen together more than we bleeding have to – right?'

It was one of the principles instilled in the course of training. One *réseau* member gets arrested, others move away fast and lie low, while the one that's caught is counted on to hold out against interrogation for at least forty-eight hours before leaking anything that might earlier have led them to his or her *confrères*. Whereas if the Gestapo had prior knowledge of any such associates, chances are the arrests would have been simultaneous.

Instructors had admitted that not to be seen together was a principle, not a blanket instruction. Very often you *had* to be together in public places. Just a matter of common sense, she guessed, in practice. She wondered whether Déclan knew she was a greenhorn, still had practically everything to learn. Following him now – along a hedgerow, for the advantage of its shadow, then after casting around a bit he stooped to pick up a bag containing the lamps – bicycle lamps probably – from where he'd left it among what looked like nettles and docks. Telling her as they went on, 'Proper bastard now. Boches taking over from bloody Vichy. Last couple of days, this is, truck convoys an' trains full of 'em. Won't make our lives easier, will it. Like as not you'll have a few on whatever train we get you on. I got you a ticket, by the way.'

'Well, thanks.'

'Save having to show papers at the *guichet*. But there'll be guards, bet your life. Account for yourself, you say – so why're you in Cahors, for a start?'

'I'm moving house from Paris to Toulouse, I've a cousin married to a farmer near La Capelle, took the chance of stopping off with them for a few days.'

'*They* know about it?'

'No. They exist, but – who'd bother checking?'

'Gestapo would, if they thought they had reason.'

'So I don't give them reason. I'm coming to Toulouse to find myself a job and because I was sick of Paris. I'm a widow – husband drowned by the bloody British. Needn't worry, that's cast-iron. And there's an aunt of my late husband's in some village somewhere – whichever way I'm going, I'm hoping to locate her. What's *your* story – French wife, you said –'

'Long an' short of it is I'm a local. Make my living fixing borehole pumps and suchlike. "Agricultural engineer" is what I have on my papers, what my wife calls it is "odd-job man". But look – stay put a minute, while I do a recce?'

He left the suitcase and the bag of lamps with her, vanished towards a dark confusion of buildings, ruins of some kind. The moon was obscured by cloud at this moment and it was a jumble, not easy to make out. Ruins of a small farmstead, must have been. No truck visible, anyway not from here. The ground was rutted, though, no doubt by farm traffic. Well – narrow ruts, so carts . . . Déclan had disappeared. She moved closer to the ruins, dumped the suitcases amongst long grass and rubble, went back for the lamp bag then sat herself down on the larger case. Not all that visible, and she'd be in the shadow of this nearer lot when the cloud shifted. Déclan's truck presumably somewhere amongst all that, or behind it; he'd be checking that there were no foreign bodies lurking in the immediate surroundings.

Wise enough, at that – if the truck had been standing there for an hour or two, as it most likely would have been. Déclan was obviously in his element, knew what he was about – and had worked with that other one before, was what he'd call a mate of his. Whereas she'd had her antennae and/or hackles up, to start with, for some reason. Instinct – or just nerves? One of the things you dreaded – well, there'd been cases of agents parachuting into traps, resulting either from bad security, radio interception or plain treachery – informants on the ground here being by no means rare and leading, in cases one had heard of, to reception parties composed of Germans or gendarmes instead of colleagues or *résistants*, agents like herself landing virtually into their arms then handcuffs, leg-irons, torture-cells and/or firing-squads, and nothing more heard of said agent, nothing known, except – another thing that *had* been known – messages tapped out on his or her transceiver and individual crystals, such messages having been coded on his or her one-time pad, and at least on one occasion a complete disaster scene developing quite swiftly – other *réseaux* penetrated and blown, multiple arrests and disappearances as tongues wagged and the ripples spread.

The nub of it all being that one couldn't – *shouldn't* – ever relax completely or take any set-up, individual or outfit, as sure-fire, *safe*.

Although one would, she guessed. Distrust had been strongly recommended as what one might call a proper initial attitude, but for one's own peace of mind, even sanity –

'Lucy – come on . . .'

'Alain — my field name's Suzette. Suzette Treniard.'

A grunt as he joined her and waited for the case on which she'd been sitting. 'Suzette. Sure. Just happens I've a weakness for "Lucy".'

'Nice for her, I'm sure. What's your wife's name?'

'Oh. Monique.' Rosie was on her feet; he picked up the suitcase. 'Watch out for brambles. Tell me — name of the people you're supposed to've been visiting at La Capelle?'

'D'you need to know?'

'If we got stopped on our way into town, need to know where I'd picked you up, wouldn't I?'

'Suppose you would. Sorry. Their name's Lafrenière.'

'Don't know 'em. About Monique though, I better mention she's not concerned in our business, only in my legit work, the farm stuff. This other I never talk to her about.'

'I'm not likely to meet her, then.'

'If I was with her and we ran into you, I wouldn't know you. Here's the old bus, though.'

A dark-coloured *gazogène* — charcoal-burning vehicle, the burner and tall funnel behind the cab. It was parked in the angle between what must have been a farm cottage and a roofless barn. Déclan told her, 'Converted her meself. Sunbeam Talbot she was once.' He pulled open the passenger door. 'Hop in, if you like.'

'First *gazo* I ever saw.'

'Dare say it would be.'

Gazogènes had come into being through petrol being virtually unobtainable, except by Germans, Vichy officials, or those rich enough to patronise the black market. Who'd more or less have to be collaborators or high-priced Pétainists.

'Did you know this was my first deployment?'

Asking him this as he climbed in on the driver's side of

24

the truck. Odour of charcoal, oil, cigarette smoke. He said, 'Jean did mention it. You'd know who I mean by Jean?'

'Jean Samblat.'

'Yeah. Big white chief. Captain. Whereas yours truly, you may not be surprised to hear, attained the dizzy eminence of sergeant, no less. Still be that, I dare say, if they hadn't like poached me from my outfit.'

'But to be an agent in the field you have to be commissioned?'

'You do, an' all – what I'm saying, on paper I'm a Second Loot. And *you*, now let me guess –'

'Fanny.' First Aid Nursing Yeomanry. 'D'you get on with Jean?'

'Poor lookout if I didn't!'

'And the other courier?'

'Sure. Don't see a lot of him, mind you.'

'Code-name Raoul.'

'Name on the ground, Marc Voreux. All we've wanted for is you, might say. Jean'll be over the moon, getting you. Good at it, are you?'

'I was a radio operator for a couple of years before they let me into training as an agent. What happened to the pianist I'm replacing?'

'They didn't brief you on that, eh?'

'Nothing beyond the fact I'm his replacement.'

'That's about all *we* know. Bugger should've been in a place where I'd pick him up, and wasn't. So if they got him – caught him on the job's the likely thing, eh? – least we know is he wasn't talking.'

Rosie thinking, *maybe* wasn't. Or *was* and they're leaving us in the open where they can keep tabs on us and whatever we may be up to – including what's done about replacing him. One had heard of *that* dodge, even if Déclan hadn't, or preferred not to take it into account.

One thing they'd know for sure was that he *would be* replaced. They'd be waiting for you, direction-finders ready to beam in on your first transmission; then no doubt they'd have their ways and means. She broke a silence with 'What sort of man was he?'

'Nice enough. Quiet, like. Supposed to be writing a book, was his cover. *Toulouse and its Environs*, he was thinking of calling it. Historian, he was supposed to be.'

'Would you have put him down as capable of holding out against Gestapo-type interrogation?'

'Oh. Oh, well . . . Tell you the honest truth, Suzette, wouldn't know *who* to put down as capable of that.'

'One more question?'

'Uh?'

'Not having a pianist, how did Jean set it up for me to join you here?'

'Ask *him* that, if I were you.'

'Used some other *réseau*'s pianist, I suppose.'

'Could've.' A shrug. 'Well – I mean, how else?'

'So d'you think *I*'ll be expected to take in work from other *réseaux*?'

'That I *don't* know. Another one for the boss, eh?'

The principle as taught in training was that *réseaux* received their orders from Baker Street and reported back to Baker Street, had no contact with each other in the field. On which basis one might hope that no other *réseau* would even be apprised of one's existence.

Déclan stretched and yawned. 'Don't have a smoke on you, do you, Suzette?'

'OK to light up, is it?'

'Oh, anyone close enough to spot it'd have us on toast already. And we'll be here an hour or so yet, by the look of it.'

The moon was low, behind cloud a lot of the time, and

would be down well before dawn arrived from over the distant Alps and the nearer Cevennes. An hour *would* about do it, she thought – rummaging in her bag for the crumpled pack of Gitanes which Marilyn had produced at Tempsford, when she'd confiscated the Players Rosie had been carrying.

'Gitanes.'

'Bless your heart. Duck down, light two while you're at it? Got a match?'

'Yep.' French ones, too. 'Are fags in short supply?'

'Anything smokeable's in short supply. *And* pricey. But I left mine with old Fernand.'

The farmer, she guessed. She passed Déclan his, then pushed herself back in her seat, head back, inhaling greedily. 'Boy . . .'

'Yeah.'

'When you were a sergeant, were you regular army? No, can't have been, can you. But –'

'Joined up in '39. I'd been third engineer in a cross-Channel packet, married Monique in Cherbourg and settled there like. Then when this lot started, thought I'd try the Army – reckoned I'd seen enough salt-water. And – hell, cutting a long yarn short, after Dunkirk, seeing as I was at home in French – and SOE having scouts out like –'

'And Monique?'

'Hung on in Cherbourg a while, then she moved down near Bordeaux where her folk are.'

'And you joined her – after SOE training, I suppose. Was she expecting you?'

'Was by that time, yeah, I'd got word to her. It was in Léguevin I joined her, though. She had a half-sister there – still has – and the pair of us was supposed to've come from Bordeaux. Not bad, eh?'

'Just about perfect. But if Léguevin's west of Toulouse, you're a long way from home?'

'Often as not I am. Go where the work is, near or far. Big country, eh?'

Tapping this out in note form on my laptop in the Hôtel Mermoz after that first session with old Rosie, I was tired – in fact about ready to drop off. It was gone 1 a.m., now, the hotel and the street outside dead quiet. In any case I could afford to call it a night now, remembering clearly enough her description of arrival in Cahors – enough to work on anyway, converting it into some kind of narrative form as I went along. Déclan for instance piloting his old *gazo* into the station forecourt, stopping between a farm-cart and a charcoal-powered motor-bus from which country passengers were alighting, and telling her, 'Get in that crowd, none of 'em's going to look twice at you.'

'Well, *thanks*.'

'Oh, don't get me wrong . . .'

At our table in the Colombier a few hours ago she'd put her hand on one of mine and confided, '*Nice* man, was Alain Déclan. A bit rough, in some ways, but absolutely genuine, the real McCoy.'

'*Was*, you say. Sure it's *was*?'

'Oh yes – sadly, quite certain. But for instance, there at Cahors he must have realised how shaky I was, just at that stage, and although he'd been going to drop me there and leave me to to get on with it, he changed his mind, saw me right on to the train – didn't say anything, just came along – through the station building and on to the platform, bringing the larger of my cases. The platform was crowded, not only with new arrivals but with Germans, soldiers who'd come off the train – milling around, goofing at the stacks of freight – farm produce including crates of

28

eggs and – oh, rabbits, chickens, pigeons, cabbages . . .'

Then she'd seen the Gestapo, her first ever. First *gazo* earlier, now first *Geheimer Staatspolizei* – and exactly as she'd envisaged them, in belted raincoats and soft hats. Cartoon characters, almost, but none the less loathsome for that – not in the least difficult to believe what one had been told, that a lot of them had criminal records. There were uniformed Boches who were *not* off the train, too, mostly *Funkabwehr*, security police. She and Déclan had stopped, looking up and down the train to see where there might be room, windows and/or doorways where it might not be absolutely crammed; and in the course of that she'd perhaps unwisely watched one of the uniformed Germans disdainfully handing an elderly woman back her papers. It was his manner that appalled her – as if, if the old girl hadn't been quick to take them, he'd have dropped them, let her scrabble for them. But glancing away from her as she snatched at them, he'd seen Rosie's interest in him, was staring at *her*.

'Alain – aren't these sweet?'

'Uh?'

A crate of piglets – pink, squiggly, squealy. She was crouching beside it. 'Poor little *darlings* . . .' Looking up at Déclan, with the transceiver in its small, heavy case on the stone flags beside her, her left hand resting on it but her attention back on the piglets, Déclan gesturing towards the train – soldiery reboarding, peasants crowding in where they could, Rosie rashly allowing herself to look past him in the direction of that German, who fortunately had lost interest, turned away.

I had that scene in mind, didn't need to make a note of it on the laptop. Nor of the train journey itself – Rosie jammed between two large women on the slatted wooden seat, avoiding the smirks of a group of Boche soldier-boys

29

who until they fell asleep persisted in eyeing her, whispering and sniggering amongst themselves. Sixty kilometres to Montauban, another fifty from there to Toulouse.

3

I had one breakfast at the Mermoz – why not, I was paying for it anyway – and got to the Brasserie des Aviateurs shortly before ten, prepared for Rosie to buy me coffee and, if she insisted, another croissant. But she wasn't down yet. The place was quite full, predominantly with senior citizens who for all one knew might be former *résistants* of one kind or another. I might even have written about some of them. Anyway – conveniently – a group of three *vieillards* were vacating a side-table from which there'd be a direct view of the blue-glass entrance, and I got to it ahead of a middle-aged man and two girls who might have been his daughters. He looked disappointed at having been beaten to the post, and asked me whether I'd be prepared to share; I told him that regret-tably it would not be possible, and as luck would have it, Rosie made her appearance at that moment.

'Am I late, or were you early?' She looked charming, in a pale-green linen suit with that same ruby brooch on it. Victorian, I guessed. And precious to her. Another guess was that it might have been a present from old Ben and she'd never be seen without it. She was saying as I shifted along the banquette seat to make room for her on my left side – the ear that works best – 'Had to call Paris, and the darn line was busy. Did you get through to your wife?'

'Did indeed. And all's as well as it could be in the circumstances.'

A waitress with red hair was clearing away those old men's litter. Rosie suggested, 'Coffee and croissants?'

'Well – why not. But *one* croissant, if that's obtainable.'

'From which I deduce you've already breakfasted.'

'Well –'

'Burn much midnight oil?'

'Got it all noted anyway. It's left you on the train from Cahors with the young Germans ogling you. You'd have got here – Toulouse – about mid-morning?'

'Yes. Two and a half hours, roughly, with a stop at Montauban.' She broke off to ask the redhead, who'd returned with her order pad, for croissants with café au lait, and gave her a room number in the hotel. The Ambassade owned this brasserie, apparently. Rosie told me, 'We're having an opening session of our conference at eleven. General get-together, introductions, speech of welcome by Monsieur le President, and a meal of wine and cheese served up there in the conference room at twelve-thirty or so.'

'Only wine and cheese?'

'Because our guest of honour can't get here until tomorrow at the earliest, maybe even Sunday. He's coming from – oh, from Réunion, and missed some connecting flight, they think.'

'Who is he?'

'First question, though – d'you want to attend this eleven a.m. session?'

'Not unless you think I should.'

'Or the wine and cheese part?'

'Not really. I'd only be in your way. You'll have to, won't you?'

32

'I think so. Yes, I will. So maybe – if we got together early afternoon? Meet here at say two o'clock?'

'Fine. I'll have a look round the town and a snack of some kind, back here at two. Unless you'd rather make it half-past – time for a rest after all that wine?'

'All right. Yes, might be as well. Two-thirty . . . As for our guest of honour – you'll have heard of him, read about him, I'm sure – André Brussaud, the famed Resistance hero?'

I thought for a moment, drew a blank, shook my head. 'Don't think so.'

'You wouldn't from your researches into *my* shenanigans, but – well, try this – heard of Jean Moulin?'

'Well, sure, him, but –'

'Tell me what you remember about him?'

'Key figure in the Resistance, wasn't he, and the Gestapo killed him, in the course of interrogation. Yes – first time they had him, he tried to kill *himself* – in his cell I suppose, between torture sessions – broken bottle, glass of some sort anyway, tried to cut his own throat, and – well, did it a lot of damage, but survived, and – afterwards, got away somehow? Don't remember how, they wouldn't have *let* him go, would they – but he actually got to London. I suppose once he was on the run, your lot must have shipped him out. He was in London, seeing de Gaulle and others – wearing a scarf to hide his lacerated throat – right? He was BCRA, wasn't he – nominally head of it in the field then, de Gaulle's top man in France?'

'He was Chief of the National Resistance Council. Enormously respected. But then betrayed. There was to be an important, highly secret meeting of the Council, and some rat brought the Gestapo in on it. They surrounded the house, smashed their way in, killed some of the delegates, arrested others including Jean Moulin.'

She'd broken off, to wave and call 'Amélie, hello!' to a

33

tall woman to whom she'd introduced me the day before; continuing then after a pause, 'So they had him again. June of 1943, this was, and this time as you say they tortured him to death. In Lyon, Gestapo headquarters, SS Leutnant Klaus Barbie's stamping-ground at that time, uh? But the man we're expecting here shortly, Brussaud, was one of Moulin's close associates. I don't know if he was at that meeting, but if so he must have been one of the few who escaped. He swore revenge – well, was supposed to have – and went on to make a Resistance legend of himself. According to stuff that was passed around at the time he kicked off by catching the traitor who'd led the Germans to that meeting and had him incinerated.' A smile, small gesture. 'Which even in those days and circumstances would have got him noticed. Then managed to keep it up *and* remain at large, over some period of time attracted such a following that a lot of them wanted him installed officially in Moulin's place – logically enough, you might think, but de Gaulle wouldn't have it.'

'Any particular reason?'

'Well, Brussaud was missing no chance of killing Germans and French traitors – actually specialised in eliminating Gestapists – while Gaullist policy was *attentiste* – wait, train, equip, prepare for the big day – invasion and post-invasion. I think that must have been it, mostly.'

'De Gaulle with a keen eye for what you might call the main chance, his own position and authority post-invasion.'

'Not far wrong *there*. Aren't you going to eat your croissant?'

'Oh –'

'Anyway, that's the man we're waiting for.' She checked the time. 'Look, we have about half an hour. Like me to start on as much as I can remember of my arrival here – making contact with my new boss, for instance, if that's of interest?'

'Unless you'd rather leave it until after lunch. If we're meeting at two-thirty, rest of the day at our disposal?'

'All right. Yes, *might* be better.'

'That's a lovely brooch, Rosie. Present from someone, was it?'

I was back at the brasserie by two-thirty, having reconnoitred the general layout of the town, especially the ancient parts, and had lunch at a bistro just off the Place du Capitole. I thought Rosie might like it, as a change from the Aviateurs, and it wouldn't be all that much of a hike for her. At the Aviateurs, though, there she was waving at me from a table not far from the one we'd used at breakfast: I headed for her – not overjoyed at the fact she had people with her – elderly male, middle-aged female.

Inevitable, of course. This was a reunion she was attending, after all.

'Afternoon, Rosie.'

She introduced me to Monsieur et Madame whatever their name was, asking me did I remember the person I'd called Guy Lannuzel. I looked at him more closely; idiotic, of course, there was no question I'd ever have set eyes on him before: and my memory wasn't reacting to that name. Then Rosie prompted: 'Chicken farmer?' and I got it, told them after a moment's further thought, 'At Châteauneuf-du-Faou, of course.'

Delight all round. Rosie said, 'Full marks. Fascinating, to find fictional characters turning into flesh and blood; and 'Lannuzel' cut in with 'Most creditable, seeing that I must have changed a little, over the past sixty years.' Rosie breaking into the polite amusement with 'But Madame you wouldn't remember. "Guy" as you called him was a lonely bachelor in those days. His sister lived with him. Remember *her*?'

'Yes, of course.' Actually, barely remembering her at all:

except she'd made a more or less life-or-death bicycle ride at some stage. Middle of the night, to warn some Maquis group . . . 'Lannuzel' – tall, grey-haired, but plenty of it, and he'd obviously kept himself in shape – told me that Brigitte – the sister, I supposed – was in good health, had married a neurosurgeon in Paris but was now a widow; and that he himself had moved to Rennes, which as it happened was his wife's home town. Rosie interrupting him then, telling me, 'He *did* run Maquis bands in the Montaignes Noires. Remember?'

'I do indeed.' I did, too. Adding – as if there was nothing very surprising about this feat of memory, 'The attack on the Château de Trevarez.'

This made their day. In fact I began to wish I'd kept my mouth shut, since it was a subject that 'Guy' didn't want to leave, despite the fact that for poor Rosie the episode had ended with her in hospital under Gestapo guard and sentence of death. Actually, to be fair to 'Guy', he might not have known it. Anyway at this juncture she came up trumps, checking the time and squawking that she and I should have been on our way ten minutes ago, heavens above! Perhaps tomorrow – if time permitted . . . We were on our feet then, 'Guy' observing that as far as time was concerned, a lot depended on when guest-of-honour Brussaud might show up – and that *I*, as a chronicler of those momentous days, should on no account miss the chance of meeting and speaking with that quite exceptional individual.

He had a rather sonorous manner of speech. Touch of standard Gallic pomposity in the delivery. And as we escaped, I remembered something else about him – reminding Rosie as we emerged into the Boulevard d'Arcole, 'Made a pass at you at one stage, didn't he?'

She cocked an eyebrow at me. 'Are we perhaps confusing fact and fiction?'

'Could be – but fiction stemming – I'd *guess* – from your own account of the event – or anyway Marilyn's interpretation of that account. OK, so it's what you might call *raw* fiction here and there – in fact all through, really, but –'

'But in this instance something more like Marilyn's innuendo touched-up with novelist's licence?'

'Well – could be. But – but (a) it was only an indication that "Lannuzel" was interested in you, attracted to you – as practically everyone else must have been – and (b) you came out of it entirely honourably – turned him down flat, said yes, there *was* a man in your life. That one being I think your third deployment – by which time you and Ben were going strong?'

'Weren't we just!'

'Whereas on this first trip you wouldn't have been thinking about him very much, would you? You'd been at some pains to evade him, leave no tracks. He didn't even know your name – other than "Rosie" – or that SOE had changed their minds and taken you on. He'd done his best to find you, hadn't he – after that super-binge you and he'd embarked on?'

'Are we crossing here?'

Place du Peyrou. We'd passed the Basilique St-Sernin a minute or two ago; weren't exactly legging it, but had covered quite a bit of ground. Were lucky with the weather, we both had raincoats but didn't need them. I said, pointing, 'If we hold on *tout droit*, we'll wind up close to the Pont St-Pierre – gardens and a promenade along the river-bank, seats we could sit on if they're dry?'

'Wet or dry, might need one by that stage.'

'Although you're still noticeably sprightly, Rosie.'

'Well, one manages. Touch wood . . . You're right though in what you said then – it *was* a super-binge!'

'How do you feel about its culmination – or rather my version of it?'

37

It had worried me, since accepting her invitation – that having put them in bed together on that night of their first meeting, binge or no binge, I might have been overstepping the mark a little. Background to this being that on the evening in question she'd gone to Baker Street to offer herself for training as an SOE field agent – her husband having been killed only a day or two earlier, she having no great inclination to sit in her flat in Sevenoaks and grieve, also having the advantage of being already an experienced radio operator as well as naturally fluent in French – a combination which she'd thought they'd jump at. Whereas, in the event, the interviewer had turned her down. He was a major with Great War medals on his tunic, and suggested to her that she might try again in say a year's time, if she still felt so inclined. Well, Rosie being Rosie, this advice aggravated her no end, and she was rushing out in a fury, deciding to offer her services to SIS instead, when Ben Quarry – Australian, a lieutenant RNVR – had come busting in, almost flattening her. He'd had something to celebrate – as well as a keen eye for a startlingly attractive sheila – and after a few very brief exchanges they'd done the obvious thing, gone on a terrific bender.

'Culmination.' She'd repeated the word I'd used. '*Would* have been culmination too, if it hadn't been for – well, fate . . .'

Floundering, slightly. I tried to help us both with 'Better word might have been "outcome". Or "end result". Of that night on the tiles, I mean, the way I wrote it, or rather wrote *of* it –'

'A bit *much* of the novelist's licence there, as you obviously appreciate!'

'Except that for the sake of the story there had to be *something* of the kind. And Marilyn had I'm sure signalled that there'd been some fairly traumatic climax.'

'I wouldn't have described it as traumatic.'

'Well —'

'And my God — of all places, the Charing Cross Hotel!'

Shaking her head: peering across at a street sign then. I asked her — snidely, maybe, but unable to resist it — 'Would you have liked it better if I'd made it the Ritz or Claridge's?'

She'd glanced at me, and away again. We'd crossed a small square into — she murmured it — 'Rue Valade.' Voice up then: 'I remember this part. Church over there is the Eglise St-Pierre-des-Chartreux. You were right, straight ahead for the bridge.' Pointing again: 'Saw my first killing there. Car rammed that corner and turned over, one guy was sort of thrown out and ran for it, Gestapo in a grey Citroen that had been on their tail screeched to a halt and they shot him down — the running one — right on the church steps. There was another boy in the wrecked car, and they dragged him out, shoved him in the back of their Citroen, slung the dead one in with him and drove off.'

She'd stopped, gazing at that corner. 'I was with Jake, my Organiser, at the time. Don't recall where we were going or what for, and we had no idea who the victims were.' She shook her head. 'No — I *do* remember. We'd had lunch, and — why, like now, walked down to the Garonne . . .'

We were moving on now. I asked her, 'Jake meaning Jean Samblat?'

'That was his field-name. Yes, I should have called him Jean, not by his code-name Jake. Bad habit I got into — and he never seemed to mind . . .' Looking sternly at me then: 'But honestly — Charing Cross Hotel. Didn't think of the Savoy, I suppose?'

'Well, no, but —'

'Never mind.'

Could see the river now. Thinking of asking her, 'A single room, was it, by any chance?' Because that was what I'd given them, in the novel. And if she didn't react too violently to that question, might follow it up with 'And *did* Ben offer to sleep in the bath?' In the novel he'd denied having made any such offer, in fact had ridiculed the very thought of it, at some later stage. But Rosie herself must have given at least *some* of this to Marilyn. Mentioning no names, I guessed, only amusing her close friend with an anecdote that had had a strong appeal to her – as no doubt it would have, after she and Ben had met again and fallen in love and she'd got over being shocked at her own past frolics.

The Savoy, though. Why not? It was the area they *would* have been in. Staggering in the small hours through that fog, a real pea-souper that would also have been keeping Luftwaffe bombers out of London's sky, for once.

Must have been the Savoy. Make a note to change it, in any reprint or new edition? And send her a copy, with the page reference?

A couple of hundred metres past that church, I put an arm around her shoulders, pointed with the other one: 'Cross over when we can, turn down there, shall we?'

'If you say so. Yes . . .'

To get down to the riverside promenade, where the benches were, hoping to find a dry one.

On the train from Cahors, she told me after we'd put on our raincoats and settled down, she'd made a point of chatting to her neighbours from time to time – remarking on the weather, the overcrowding, the slowness of the journey, duration of the stop at Montauban, and so forth. No direct mention of this Boche invasion: but anything else one thought of – including, in answer to their curiosity, the fact she was a war widow and moving to Toulouse to look for work. Then shortly before arrival, breaking a silence to ask whether they happened to know if there was a tram or bus service from the station to the vicinity of – well, Port St-Etienne? One of them said yes, she'd show her where the buses left from – only a stone's throw from the station exit. Rosie in fact knew even the number of the bus that ran south past Gare Riquet and along the line of the Canal du Midi, to where she'd ferret around a bit and find a certain café. She hadn't exactly memorised the map but had studied it a great deal, knew the general shape of the town, main arteries and points of reference such as ancient buildings, *places* and major intersections; what she was really after with that enquiry was to have these women's company when leaving the station, passing not only ticket collectors at the barrier but as likely as not Germans, *Funkabwehr* if nothing worse.

To acquire company wasn't her own idea, or original, only one of the dodges they'd been taught in training. Approaching and passing through inspection points, to try to be part of a group, or at least to seem to be, rather than a 'solitary'. And they were happy to asssist: as a young widow – 'poor little thing, at *your* age!' – she already had their sympathy. They'd agreed wholeheartedly with her condemnation of the British Navy – for sheer brutality and trickery, directed against an ally who in any case had taken the brunt of this whole disastrous conflict – *sacrés Anglais*, running like rabbits when they'd had the chance!

It had got her out of the station, all right. First to the *consigne*, left-luggage office, where she'd left her larger suitcase, then into the tail-end of the crowd pushing out of the gates past not only *Funkabwehr* but a civilian with an unmistakably German look about him. The elder of the women had already said goodbye, embracing her and wishing her a full and happy life, but the other one came with her to the bus stop and pointed out the one she needed. All busy, noisy, crowded. In the square outside the station entrance, German soldiers were being embarked in trucks or fallen-in in their

41

platoons or squads, French children gathering to stare at them – wide-eyed, otherwise expressionless.

This time yesterday one had been in England – safe as houses. Now – this was the new, real world. The one you'd chosen and they'd tried initially to keep you out of. So get used to it, adopt protective colouring; for others to believe that you belong in it, first convince yourself, *be* Suzette Treniard – devoted Pétainiste with a personal hatred of the British.

And no fear of Germans. Not even awareness of their presence. Especially having come from Paris, where the streets and restaurants were crawling with them.

She got out at a stop opposite the Halle aux Grains – might have done better to have sat tight one more stage – hiked on down the boulevard and found Rue de Valenciennes. It was blowing half a gale. And time passing – would actually have saved a few minutes and some physical exertion by waiting for the next stop, the bus having moved on from *there* by now – and conscious that Jake – Jean Samblat – would be waiting for her call, might have been waiting an hour or so already.

Valenciennes had been wrong. Rue de Tivoli, God's sake. Meaning an extra few hundred yards. Correcting that – few hundred *metres*. *Think* in the right language, otherwise risk using the wrong one in your sleep. In that train, for instance, might easily have dropped off. To the right now: and the wind really hitting her on that corner. But there it was – Café Fleurance. In sight of the Grand Rond, all that greenery up at the top end – the Rond itself and the wooded *allées* and – beyond, not visible from here – the Jardin des Plantes. The café looked smaller than she'd anticipated, and crowded. She paused inside the doorway; lunchtime, of course, it would be busy. Madame – scrawny, black-haired, desperate-looking – was doing the legwork, aided by a young girl. Daughter, maybe, or niece. The *patron*, behind the zinc bar – red-faced, with very white, fat arms, in a sleeveless vest – was pouring beers.

Glancing at her – impatiently. 'Uh?'

'Use your telephone?'

He slid a *jeton* across the bar – she had a coin ready – and pointed with his head. The phone was on the wall, no barrier between it and the general racket, nothing to do but yell. She wove her way through to it, reminding herself of the number, one of several she'd memorised. No option, since one did not, ever, carry notes of numbers, names, addresses. Had to put the transceiver down then – the case on edge, flat against the wall below the telephone, with her toes against it. Her baby, almost – what she was *for*, here and now virtually ninety per cent of what she *was*.

'I was jittery, all right. I can just about feel them now, those jitters. Can you understand, how one would be – despite all the training and preparation?'

'I certainly can.'

'Could hardly overemphasise one's state of nerves. It's important, you know, for – well, your atmosphere. Me, complete novice, in a real state of nerves, much worse than I'd expected.'

'I'll bear it in mind. Rosie as *ingénue*, a long way short of the steely character she grew into.'

A smile. 'Never all *that* steely. Not even at the very end, to be honest. Even then one tended to get the inner shakes. Truly, my God, some of those long night hours, the three a.m. sweats as I've heard it called.' She expelled a short, hard breath, remembering it. 'Anyway, I dialled the number . . .'

'Yuh?'

Female, and hoarse, distant-sounding. Rosie yelled, as close

43

to the mouthpiece as she could get, 'May I speak to Marcel? It's Suzette, tell him.'

'Don't know you, do I?'

'What matters is Marcel does. Will you get him, please?'

'Would if he was here, but he ain't. Want him to call you?'

'D'you expect him soon?'

'Oh, I know better than to have *expectations*, with that one! What's your number – or does he know it?'

She read it from the card pinned to the box. Added, 'This is a café, so –'

'Could be quite a while!'

'Please, the minute he gets in?'

The woman had rung off. Rosie hung up, stooped to pick up the transceiver case; as she moved away a priest took her place without even glancing at her. There was a queue at the bar now: might order from Madame when she came by, there was certainly no hurry. She'd been heading for a vacant table beyond the bar, but on second thoughts turned back – to put herself reasonably close to the phone, as one would if one were actually expecting a call. As it happened she was not, it was now only a matter of appearances.

'Mind if I use this chair?'

A table for four, with only one couple at it – middle-aged, dowdy, had been eating sausage with *choucroute*. The man stared at her woodenly, but his wife smiled, shook her head: 'We're about finished.' Draining her cup, and the husband following suit with the last of his thin-looking, fizzy beer. Rosie explained with a nod towards the telephone, 'Expecting a call, don't want to miss it.'

The priest was still there – talking or listening, inaudible over the background noise – and the husband was checking his bill then fingering coins out of a purse. They were harmless enough, she thought. In fact it might be better if they stayed; when they moved she might well get something worse, was unlikely to be left on her own at a table that had chairs for four.

He'd got the money settled. Nodding to his wife. 'If you're ready —'

'Wait a minute.'

'Huh?'

Glancing at her, then looking where she was looking, at the entrance. Rosie too, craning round — seeing two men in the famed belted raincoats and felt hats. Hands in their pockets, staring round — from table to table, face to face, and meanwhile effectively blocking the exit.

The husband said quietly, 'Boches.'

'Police of some kind.' Looking at Rosie, then back at him. 'Best hang on. In no great rush, are we?'

'They seem to be looking for someone.'

'Not for us, at least.' A snigger, under her breath. Conversation elsewhere had virtually ceased. She murmured, 'And I'm sure they couldn't be after our young friend here!'

Rosie thinking, They *could*, though. A wire-tap — if like Jean they've been expecting me? Intercepted signal? She still didn't know what might have happened to the pianist she was replacing: and such horrors *had* occurred, in SOE memories. She had her back to the Gestapists, and didn't look round again — instinct telling her to show no interest in them, more essentially no concern for oneself in their presence. Not to push the transceiver's case further under the table even — when one of these two might somehow react to the movement, drawing attention to it. In the comparative quiet, hearing the priest say loudly into the telephone, 'I am much obliged, monsieur', and the clatter as he hung up — turning with a look of surprise — struck by the silence first, then seeing the Germans, mouthing to himself in surprise . . .

Prayer?

'Coming this way, one of 'em.' The woman had whispered it to Rosie. Picking up her empty cup, making a show of draining it, actually hiding behind it, peeping over it at the one who was on the move: towards them, but surely to pass them – en route to the bar, perhaps, the patron. Nothing to do with me – really can't be. Not this soon, God's sake there's no way it could . . . She had a back view of him as he did pass – and of the priest standing motionless, watching, the patron similarly transfixed – but certainly no suggestion of any challenge, and the German exuding – what, self-importance, conviction of his own supremacy? Not at all surprised, anyway, by the effect he was having on them all – which on its own would have been enough to arouse instant dislike – easily confusable of course with fear, or euphemistically anxiety. Although as it happened – surprisingly – there seemed to be a lightening of the tension elsewhere in the room – people resuming their conversations or looking round for service. The priest snapped out of his daze too, started towards the exit, while at the bar meanwhile the patron's voice was a high squawk, jowls wobbling as he protested, 'No persons of such description, monsieur. Not that I've seen, in any case. Mind you, one's been hard at it since mid-morning, so –'

Making common cause of whatever it might be – or trying to, and the German turning away contemptuously. Rosie turning away too, giving the husband a glance and asking his wife whether they'd always lived in this town: in order to be seen as belonging, one of the group, the German passing on his way back, the woman putting down her cup and muttering, 'Good riddance!' Her husband, startled, murmuring in alarm but she and Rosie exchanging smiles. Out of a sense of shame, collective cowardice? The German having by this time rejoined his colleague, barking something like 'No good, let's go!' in what to Rosie had always been an ugly, brutal-sounding language. At school in England years ago, when they'd realised they couldn't teach her any French she'd been allowed to switch to German, and had very soon thrown her hand in. The woman was shaking her head: 'Sort of thing we have to expect from now on, I suppose.'

'I dare say.'

'Now the barbarians are in our midst . . .'

'Oh now, shush!'

A flash of anger: 'Why shush? Aren't we in France?'

The *patronne* then, demanding, 'And for you?' Scooping up the man's assembly of small change and looking almost angrily at Rosie for her order. Rosie told her, 'Coffee, and a *galette* – cheese *galette*.' She'd seen one on another table and thought it didn't look too bad. The *patronne* scribbling briefly, snapping back to a question from the woman as she and her husband got up, 'I have no idea. But no doubt that they had good reason.'

One ready-made *collaborateuse*, one potential *résistante*. Maybe: at first showing, but in the longer term, maybe not. Maybe in the longer run they'd both – all – keep their heads down, play the three wise monkeys . . .

The coffee was revolting, but after half an hour or so she'd bought a second cup of it – which wasn't improved by having now gone tepid. Still had the table to herself, at least. There were plenty of empty ones. The young girl, daughter or niece, whatever – about seventeen, pudding-faced – was now doing all the waitressing that was required, madame having disappeared. *Patron* still present, sprawled at a table close to the bar. Rosie happened to be looking his way when he glanced up, disturbed by the street door swinging open for the first time in quite a while.

Man blundering in, pushing the door shut behind him against the wind. *Could* be him. Jean – Jake. *Could be*. Stopping there as if he might have come into shelter only to light a cigarette; match flaring in his cupped hands. Then straightening from it,

47

looking around – not at people so much as – well, he'd located it, the telephone.

Still wouldn't bet much on it, but it had begun to seem not improbable. He'd flicked the spent match away, was moving unhurriedly to the bar; beckoning the girl, asking for a *jeton*.

So far, he fitted the bill, all right.

He was wearing a leather jacket – soft-looking leather, well-fitting, no doubt expensive – over a chequered shirt with a thin, dark tie loosened at the throat. Thickset, about five-ten or five-eleven, and maybe forty, even forty-five. Hair grey and thick, and a short, blunt jaw. It matched the description Marilyn had provided except that for some reason Rosie had thought of him as younger. Exhaling smoke, nodding to the girl. 'Merci.' Growling as he turned and limped towards the phone – which meant towards Rosie too – 'Blowing like hell out there.'

Baggy, fawn-coloured trousers. The limp was noticeable. He'd given Rosie one slowish passing glance – evincing no special interest in her, but she guessed he'd have seen as much as he needed. As she had of him. Stopping now well short of the phone, looking back at the girl, screwing his face up and slapping his forehead – an effort to remember the number he had to call. Making a joke of it, presumably to amuse the child – and succeeding, but the *patron* looking up peevishly from his newspaper, growling something that sent her to clear a table recently vacated.

Oddly, that performance had seemed to age him, in Rosie's view. Forty-five at least, she thought. *Uncle* Jake . . . Marilyn might have said forty-five and she'd heard it as *thirty*-five?

She heard him lift the receiver and dial.

Ringing tone, presumably. Then sharply: 'Oh . . . But that's not Marie-Claire?'

Pause. Grunt of annoyance, and 'An *hour*, damn it!' Further pause: then, 'Look, have her call me here, will you. The number's –' Reading it out. 'Got that?'

He'd hung up – after talking to a dead line. She pushed her cup away, was checking the time. Looked round then; telling him, 'Good luck to you – I've been waiting at least an hour to have a call returned, and I don't think it's bloody coming.' Shrugging, seeming to make her mind up in that moment: adding in a mutter to herself, 'In fact, the hell with him!' Shifting her chair, reaching for the suitcase that hadn't until then been visible – but was now, all right.

Spreading his hands. 'Leaving? Giving up?'

'Regrettably, monsieur –'

'I'd just thought – hoped – I might be so fortunate as to have your company for a while. Being in the same boat, so to speak –'

'*Would* have been nice, but –'

'Well, look here – if I might suggest it – having an hour to kill and no inclination to sit here on my own –'

Rosie said, 'First pick-up ever. Unless you count Ben in the hallway at 62–64 Baker Street. But that was more of a collision than a pick-up. This one might have been more elaborate than it need have been, but at least – see, no names, real numbers or addresses, not a thing to give the game away, and there we were, *fait accompli* – he and I out into the gale, over the road and up towards all that greenery, the Grand Rond and its surroundings.' She'd pointed back over her shoulder, southeastward – a couple of kilometres from here, it would have been – and told me that the so-called Jean Samblat's first words when they were out of the café had been: 'Call you Suzie, may I – or Lucy? Welcome to Countryman. How's London looking, these days?' and she'd told him, 'More battered than when you last saw it. Battered and burnt, quite a lot of it. But life goes on.'

'Bloody better, hadn't it. Suzie, we'll talk French, from here on. And you must have more luggage than just that blessed object?'

'Blessed' because it was what he'd been waiting for – transceiver plus its handler, the essentials with which to start solving his *réseau's* problems. She told him yes, one other suitcase, which she'd left in the *consigne* at the Gare Matabiau, and he commented that that was about as convenient as it could have been, since he'd arranged for her to move in with a local school's headmistress, name of Berthe Devrèque, who had a house on Place Marengo in which she'd be glad to put her up. It would do to start with anyway, as long as the two of them got on, and was in easy distance from the station, which might have advantages other than just picking up the rest of her luggage by and by. Then he asked her how she'd got on with Alain Déclan, and she said fine, fine, nice guy, and – well, a great reception, having a lift to the station – train stiff with Germans incidentally – Déclan had seen her right on to it, marvellous of him! Jean had agreed that Alain was one of the best. Adding though, incomprehensibly, 'Touch wood.'

Then as she glanced at him in surprise, 'There's so much I need to tell you, *heck* of a lot to fill in, plus a situation in which we really need to have you hit the ground running, as they say . . .'

'Perfectly OK with me. But about Déclan – that "touch wood" – meaning you've doubts of him?'

'Not of *him*, no. The problem is – *could* be – his wife. Although I'm pretty sure we're OK. I mean that he'll see to it we remain so. Hell, *he's* OK, salt of the earth. He's a cool customer, and with that old truck of his and his work on farms, farm machinery, he's in a really marvellous position – as regards *parachutages*, for instance. The problem is that his wife, who in his view of it *acts* the part of a Pétainiste, almost certainly *is* one.'

50

'*Almost* certainly . . .'

Affirmative grunt. 'Best to be warned, that's all. Her value of course is she's his cover and in the light of what I just said a particularly good one – even though she doesn't know it, obviously *mustn't* know it. As long as he has it under control – *her*, that is, and maybe her friends.'

'From as much as he said to me, I'd say he does have, and was warning me. Makes better sense of it, in fact. Possible, I suppose, he doesn't *want* her involved?'

'Distinctly so. That's a generous thought, and – yes, pretty well in character.'

'You have another courier as well, a Frenchman?'

'Marc Voreux. Code-name Raoul. Frenchman of BCRA origins but assets/qualities no less useful to us than Déclan's. All in all it's a darn good team – and now with you joining us, we can get on with things that – well, none too bloody soon!'

'Things such as – specific operations, or –'

'One specific, important operation which has become more urgent in recent days, and more or less part and parcel of it, a *parachutage* or maybe two of them.'

'How *have* you managed, since you lost your pianist?'

'Well, I'll tell you all that. But first things first – number one, I very much hope you've brought us some cash?'

'Half a million francs.'

'Ah, now, that *is* a relief. Where exactly, at this moment –'

'Poacher's pocket inside this coat. Quite a wad, I'll be glad to be shot of it. Want it now?'

'At the house, better. Chez Berthe Devrèque, by and by. Wouldn't want that much cash blowing on the breeze.'

'Wouldn't, would we. Subject of Berthe Devrèque though – is she one of us?'

'She's a patriot, loathes Vichy and the Germans – at heart one of us, therefore, and I'd say she'd like to be. Time being,

51

she provides us with a *planque* – which is all I want of her. She doesn't have to know any more than the fact we need it.'

Planque meaning a safe-house. Rosie asked him, 'What sort of age?'

'Berthe – oh, middle forties. But let's take one point at a time now – OK? My agenda, all questions and/or elaborations to follow – right?'

In other words shut up now, just listen.

Rosie and I had been finding the bench a bit hard, so for a break after another half-hour we took a stroll southward along the river-bank almost to the next bridge, Pont Neuf, which was the best part of a kilometre, and found another – no less hard – where we sat down again, with the Eglise Notre-Dame-de-la-Daurade on our left and the open grassed space of Place Daurade behind us, and she continued on the subject of Marc Voreux, the Countryman *réseau's* other courier. In fact she'd been recalling her briefing by Jake, on which I'd already made a few notes – on his cover for instance as a civil engineer – *Ingénieur des Ponts et Chaussées* – and his having an apartment in a building on Place Victor Hugo, where as it happened a rather smart hotel called l'Ours Blanc was at that time – time of her arrival – being taken over by the Gestapo as their Toulouse headquarters. Jake had been in two minds whether to move elsewhere, there being a possibility that doing so might attract attention that would be best avoided; not that the Gestapo themselves were likely to take note of such a move by a businessman of whom they'd no reason to have any suspicions whatsoever, but that French neighbours or tradesmen might. There'd be plenty seeking to curry favour with their new lords and masters.

Marc Voreux, though. Code-name Raoul. French, aged at that time twenty-two, he'd been one of the prime movers in an escape-line that had folded – had been 'broken into' was old Rosie's phrase for it – by Abwehr (military intelligence) agents, a number of its operators arrested and no doubt either shot or sent to concentration camps in Germany. There were several escape-lines at work, most of them terminating in the south-west here and getting their evaders or escapers – which they referred to as *colis*, meaning parcels – away over the Pyrenees and through Spain to Gibraltar or Portugal to Lisbon. Not all, by any means. At least one escape-line smuggled their clients into Switzerland, while another delivered them to Resistance groups on the coast of Britanny – one such location being a mere niche in the rocks called l'Abervrac'h, where as it later transpired Ben's gunboat was to land Rosie on her second deployment. But Marc Voreux had operated to start with in and around Tours, and his sister Denise between Paris and Orléans. She, Denise, had set it up, the system being the same as in other lines, the *colis* often enough Jews but then – increasingly – shot-down aircrew, being transported/escorted across France from safe-house to safe-house with what were known as cut-outs at each stage, these ensuring that the transients would be passed from one escort to the next without overlap, i.e. without their escorts over one stage seeing those of the next or the previous one or knowing anything about them.

'For instance – you and I might have been parked in some boarding-house. Or if it was to be a short stop and quick change-over, here on this bench say. The agent who'd brought us would have some way of signalling that two parcels were awaiting collection and on-carriage. Could be some object in a shop window, a card on a 'jobs wanted' noticeboard or a message in a bar or barber's shop. We'd be picked up and moved on, by people we'd never seen before and wouldn't know from bars of soap. The shopkeeper or barman would be nothing but a middleman, he/she'd never meet us or the escorts; if we should be nobbled by Gestapo or Vichy police there'd be nothing they could get out of us, we'd – well –'

'Die screaming?'

'Oh.' A grimace. 'Conceivably.'

'You and your kind were extraordinary people, Rosie.' I corrected that: '*Are* extraordinary, I should say.' I'd noted down 'cut-outs' and 'colis', which would be enough to trigger all that stuff and the images it conjured up of Rosie and others like her; and asked her now, to restart the flow of reminiscence, 'So Voreux's escape-line was broken into, meaning *some* arrests, but obviously they didn't get to him – or to his sister either?'

'By that time he'd transferred himself down here to the south, end of the line, there'd have been dozens of cut-outs between him and his sister at the Paris end. But the Abwehr or Gestapo shortly afterwards got the pianist of a BCRA group in Montpellier, and that was another serious blow to him. From this end, you see, he'd have been sending evaders on the final stages of their journeys either via Narbonne–Perpignan to the border guides – *passeurs*, Spaniards, mostly smugglers – who'd take them over the Pyrenees, or he'd be escorting them to night-time pick-ups by feluccas that operated out of Gibraltar to and from various places on this coast. To the Riviera generally, I believe, but within our reach from here – Barcarès, for instance, or Canet-Plage. He took them there and saw them away himself. But as it happened, all of this had become rather

55

less than certain at the time of my own arrival, since with Boches taking over from the much less keen-eyed gendarmerie it was on the cards that the feluccas might have to pack it in.'

'Was Voreux still getting escapers out, then – that's to say after his line had been busted?'

'Call them "evaders" rather than "escapers". Shot-down aircrew, RAF and USAF evading capture, Jews evading round-ups and the gas-chambers. "Escapers" would literally have escaped – from prisons, Gestapo or Vichy police, so forth. The Pétain regime was extremely anti-Semitic, you know. And Narbonne and Perpignan had become dangerous places for anyone in transit long before the Boches took over.' Rosie shrugged. 'Anyway, that had been Marc's business until about the time I joined the *réseau*. There probably *were* a few stragglers still *en route*.'

'For whom he'd still have felt responsible.'

'Well, surely. Some from other BCRA operations maybe. There were incomers too – again, BCRA people, some of whom would have needed to be met wherever they were landed, guided to safe-houses or put on trains, whatever. Hence his need of external communications, i.e. the radio link – not with Gibraltar, only via London – well, Sevenoaks – which in fact was what brought him to us. Actually he went for help to a woman we knew by two code-names, "Germaine" or "Marie". American, correspondent in Lyon of the *New York Post*, worked I was told for SIS as well as SOE, knew everyone in Lyon including the police and – well, just everyone. Her apartment was a safe-house for agents on the run, and she had others at her disposal – flats belonging to her friends. She and Jake knew each other, from previous activities of his in and around Lyon; it was an important centre for us, you know, biggest city in the *Zone Non-Occupée*, Zone No-No as one called it then. Anyway, Germaine a.k.a.

56

Marie was on *her* skates too, a day or so before the bastards began moving in.'

'Got away all right, did she?'

'Yes. Over the Pyrenees, the route by which she'd sent God knows how many . . . Memory's stirring now, though – her real name was Virginia Hall, and before she set up shop in Vichy France she was the *Post*'s correspondent in Spain. She'd been there during the Civil War, I think.'

'Voreux went to her for help?'

A nod. 'She put him on to Jake – messages passed through London, so all above-board, bona fides vouched for and in any case guaranteed by her, Voreux presumably checked out with BCRA. And Jake arranged for the pianist he had then – man with the code-name "Wiggy" – to send and receive Marc's stuff as well as our own. In fact there wasn't all that much, most of it preceded or coincided with visits from the feluccas. Requests for pick-ups, dates, times, locations, numbers arriving and/or waiting. Freight too, on occasion.'

She'd paused, with a hand on my arm: 'I haven't yet mentioned how Marc Voreux had established himself as something of a specialist on the coast – as long as the feluccas kept coming. Guess what he dealt in?'

'Save time, tell me?'

'The answer's fish, which he bought from fishermen along that stretch of coast. He'd got to know them all and had acquired this van, supplied restaurants and hotels and had some private, well-off customers too, even Vichy establishment clientèle, gendarmerie barracks for instance. How he got away with it – well, you might say just his bloody nerve, together with a sharp eye for the main chance – source of excellent food in a hungry, rationed country – and having what you might call a way with him. Charm, I suppose – which he certainly did have – combined with a thick skin. Gendarmes seemed to treat him as a bit of a joke, a card . . . For instance, the fact he could live on his fish business – well, lobsters mostly, and crabs, and – oh, anchovies from Collioure – and ran a petrol-driven van, which meant the huge overhead of black-market petrol – well, he let them guess that he was into smuggling – Pyrenean, of which there was plenty, cigarettes and believe it or not saccharin being the prime commodities – also maybe by his friends the fishermen, their boats meeting larger ones a few miles out – that sort of thing. Gendarmes would stop him sometimes and search him and the van – and the place he lived in – forget its name – and he'd laugh at them, give them a crab or something to take home. They'd say "*Ah, c'est un gars, celui-ci*" – one with a heart, you know?'

'In fact he'd have been funded by the *réseau*?'

'Sure. By Jake. Partly by the lobsters etcetera, but Jake stumped up when he had to, apparently. Seemed worth it, after all, Marc's usefulness actually no less than Déclan's. In fact after a while Jake decided it was costing too much, and over Marc's protests he got Déclan to convert the van from petrol to *gazo*. So then, distance was no object – and in regard to *me* for instance, Jake's thinking was that both of them, but probably Voreux more than Déclan, would cart me around to suitably remote places from which to do my stuff. Not bad thinking either – in theory anyway – using both of them and places as far apart as possible, so that the Boche radio interceptors might get to think there had to be more than one of me – and no sound reason to assume either of us was based in Toulouse. Except – well, brings me back to what I was saying about Marc making use of Jake's pianist – name on the ground here Roger St Droix, code-name Wiggy. When he came to grief – vanished overnight, complete with his transceiver and bicycle – Jake then having no pianist and needing one quite badly, first of all to report Wiggy's disappearance and ask for a new pianist to be sent out, which of course is where I come into it – but also to arrange *parachutages* of weaponry for which certain Maquis bands were clamouring. So he – Jake – paid a visit to "Germaine" in Lyon, and she fixed up for his stuff to be handled for the time being by some pianist in that area. Which became Jake's only link with Baker Street until I dropped in, so Jake himself and then couriers Déclan and Voreux had a good deal of toing and froing over a period of – well, I *think*, several weeks.'

'Must have been glad to see you.'

'Sure they were. Toulouse to Lyon being more than five hundred kilometres, and even without Boches in the Zone No-No the train journey would have had its anxious moments. Checks not only at both ends but just about anywhere else along the route – and the Vichy security police, DST, weren't amateurs. For that matter there were Gestapo at work right there in Lyon. Shouldn't have been, but were; that bastard Laval colluded heavily with the Germans, of course – mainly through the Vichy chief of police, René Bousquet. Who as you may remember was a buddy of François Mitterrand.'

'And was admired by Himmler, I read somewhere. Anyone ever get to know what had happened to Wiggy?'

'Not in any detail, but broadly, yes. That night he'd been transmitting from somewhere near Albi, Déclan told Jake. Albi's about seventy-five kilometres from Toulouse; it's where Toulouse-Lautrec came from, also has a cathedral and a palace of great antiquity and it was going to feature in the book Wiggy was writing, a history of the area. First thing next morning he'd intended visiting the *Mairie* for purposes of research. Déclan, who the evening before had brought him from Montauban and dropped him and his bike a few miles outside the town, was going to meet him at noon and bring him back. But Wiggy didn't show up, hadn't been in touch with the *Mairie* either, they'd never heard of him or of his book, and Déclan found no clues or traces anywhere around the place he'd left him. All one can say is he'd somehow come to grief during the dark hours – and before you ask, Sevenoaks had no record of his having been on the air that night. Must've been caught or killed before getting down to it – which suggests they'd been on his tail, except that in that case they'd also have been on Déclan's – and weren't. Poor old Wiggy, though. Jake had become fond of him – a jolly, roly-poly character, he said he was. He'd come in origin- ally by felucca, by the way.'

'Met by Voreux?'

'No, silly. Marc wasn't anywhere near us at that stage, he'd still have been running his escape-line. No, Wiggy would have been put down on some beach, got himself here under his own power so to speak, and gone through a contact- making procedure with Jake, the sort of charade I was telling you *I* went through with him.' She asked me, 'D'you know what a felucca is, by the way?'

'The only ones I ever encountered were in Egypt – Alexandria and Port Said. Small craft with a lateen sail or two.'

'These weren't all that small. Twenty-tonners. Sails, yes, but an engine too. One of them had an engine taken out of an old lorry. And they were crewed and skippered by Poles. Two of them – I did know the skippers' names, but –'

'Sort of job one could imagine your Ben being attracted to.'

'Maybe. But that pair were described as being too rough even for the Polish navy.'

'What I meant was – you know, small, cranky ships, hostile coast – *bloody* dangerous –'

'Ben's *milieu*, all right.'

'Perfect match for you, Rosie, wasn't he.' I checked the time. 'Coming up four-thirty. How about we start back at five, and I collect you at your hotel again at – what, seven-thirty, then the Colombier again?'

'Using taxis for that bit?'

'*Certainly* using taxis!'

'You're on, then. Where was I . . . Oh, yes – Jake and I prowling around that wooded area, Jake limping along talking about – oh, everything under the sun. For instance I was going to need a bicycle – and bless him, he'd already got me one . . .'

Jake – whom she was going to have to get used to calling 'Jean', since that was his field-name, although 'Jake' for some reason sprang more readily to mind – Jake/Jean had told her, 'Haven't paid for it yet. Been a bit short, tell you the truth, and they're like gold-dust. Now I can use some of the cash you've brought. The bike's at Berthe Devrèque's house, did belong to one of her colleagues, has quite a large panier on it as well as a baggage thing at the back.'

'And I can receive from the attic, you said.'

'You'll want to confirm you've arrived on station, won't you – and establish a schedule for receiving – say an hour around midnight on certain days, two or three nights a week? You won't need skeds for transmitting, they'll be listening-out for you round the clock in any case – especially now, with these jobs pending, when you've something to send, just bung it out. From suitably distant locations, preferably, and using Voreux and Déclan when available – bike in the vehicle, transceiver ditto – stashed in Déclan's toolkit or Voreux's fish-boxes?'

She'd been waiting for him to draw breath. OK, she was a novice in the field, but she *had* learnt the rudiments of the business, and knew all the radio stuff backwards. She told him, 'I'll make my first transmission tomorrow or the day after, and independently – by which I mean I'll have a squint at the map, load the set on the bike and shove off, solo. Is whatever you've got encoded yet?'

'No, because –'

'I'll do it tonight. Either in the one first transmission or split up, depending on how much there is and where I am, how things look and feel. Mark your stuff according to priority? Because it has to be my decision, Jean – every time. What I mean is *I'm* not going to do a Wiggy.'

'We might do the encoding together this evening. Actually there isn't so much of it, I'm sure you'll make it in one transmission. But – do a Wiggy?'

'Get caught on the job. You're the boss, sure, but the radio's my business and I'm set on *staying* in business.'

'Glad to hear that, Suzie.'

Drily, as if humouring a child. She pressed on: 'Is any other *réseau* who may have lost their pianist likely to be leaning on us for help?'

'No question of it.'

'Good. All that stuff about Raoul and BCRA – frankly, I'd opt out.'

'Don't worry. That was a crisis situation that won't repeat itself.'

'What about Voreux's escape-line – if it got to be reactivated?'

'By the sister, you mean. Well, that might be tricky, but (a) it's not at all likely, (b) if anything of the sort was proposed I'd both resist it and discuss it with you.'

'And definitely no outsiders.'

'Count on it. Anything else?'

'Yes. I need two more transceiver sets, and batteries for them. Having to lump one set around from place to place really isn't on. OK for now, can't do anything else, but – you'll agree, I'm sure, three is really minimal, keeping one in Berthe Whatsit's attic for receiving?'

'*If* they'll give us two more sets.'

'They will. I nagged them about it before I left, and they promised.'

'Only bear in mind that when you're receiving you still have to put out an "OK, go ahead" and finally a "Right, message received" – so you're not *completely* detector-proof – huh?'

She smiled at him. 'Before I went into training for field-work, Jean, I worked in Sevenoaks as a radio operator for the best part of two years.'

A smile. 'So I'm teaching my granddaughter to suck eggs.'

'If the inward traffic ever got dangerously heavy, granddad, I'd have to shift elsewhere for receiving too.'

'Ask for the extra sets in your first transmission, will you?'

'And hope they'll come in the next drop. But what about this now. Wiggy had two sets – didn't he? One vanished with him, the other must have been stashed elsewhere – wherever he was living, or maybe in Voreux's keeping?'

'No such luck. You're right that he had two sets, but neither Déclan nor Voreux knew where the second one might be, and I visited his digs myself – two rooms over a greengrocer's shop – and the answer you might say was a lemon.'

She'd shrugged. 'Hidden in some cowshed. Anyway I'll ask for two.'

'If they do get them into this *parachutage*, won't be *so* bad – maybe no more than a week or so.'

He'd told her there were probably to be two *parachutages*, the first dropping-site and lists of contents already agreed, but that for the time being it was only possible to concentrate on the first – settle on a date for it, with time enough to warn the Maquis bands who'd be on the receiving end, then confirm to London. Ideally he'd have liked more of an interval between the drop and the operation – 'Hardball', Baker Street was calling it – for training purposes. 'OK, most of the boys in those Maquis bands have had military experience, but some not enough and a few none at all. There's also the fact British weaponry will be new to a lot of them.'

'These being people you've worked with before?'

'Yes. But they've had a lot joining them just lately – and with the arrival of the Boches, that's likely to speed up, if anything. In fact it's bound to. Actually one of the bands is led by a very experienced soldier, former *légionnaire,* so –'

'Who'd be doing the training, if there was time for it?'

'Well, I would. Assisted by Déclan, and if possible I'd use that guy too. It's mostly Sten guns and ammo they need. The nub of it though is that the job itself will be done by a visiting team of French commandos, Maquis as backup, while our part in it's to look after them – meet, accommodate, arrange transport, arrange the Maquis collaboration, then touch wood get the commandos away home again.'

'They drop in, do they?'

'That's not clear at present. They were to have come in by sea, but for one reason and another we can't be sure now. I'll go into it with you – as much as *is* certain – later, when we've more time. Point being, Suzie, that as you'll be handling the correspondence, so to speak, you've got to know it all – in fact be able to take over this end of it, if necessary. I mean if *I* should – er – 'do a Wiggy', eh?'

'Are you serious?'

'Entirely. *If* that happened. Touch wood it won't, but there has to be provision – right?'

'Well, *Christ* . . .'

'Hundred to one it won't happen. But a rider to your being in a position to handle things is that at this stage neither Déclan nor Voreux need to know any more than they do already. Voreux anyway. Déclan's a bit different, he has all the Maquis contacts, he'll be more involved in it than you will.'

'All right. I mean, good.'

Because what you didn't know you couldn't divulge, no matter what they did to you.

The hell. Telling herself then, *What you wanted – joined and got yourself trained for* . . .

But having – as it felt at that moment – more than enough in her head already. For instance the identities of 'Jake', 'Batsman', 'Raoul' – Berthe Devrèque even, whose storage of a bicycle on behalf of an enemy of the State would probably be enough to qualify her for a bullet; and inevitably others like her, soon enough. Those who'd be involved in the *parachutage*, for instance – yet more lives whose prolongation might come to depend on one's ability to keep one's mouth shut. Whether one *would* be able to, in circumstances such as she and Jake had been envisaging without actually mentioning, i.e. interrogation by Gestapists equipped with such old-fashioned devices as pliers for fingernails and red-hot skewers for eyeballs.

You *didn't know*. One subject in the SOE curriculum near the end of the training course had been Experience of Interrogation; they'd made it as tough as they could, but in a Beaulieu House classroom you'd known they weren't going to put your eyes out or take pincers to your nipples.

★   ★   ★

Rosie told me on our hard bench, which towards 5 p.m. was getting harder, 'That really is how one felt. Then, and to be honest in later deployments too. I'd say it's about the one thing you may have missed out on, now and then. I'm not saying it's how we all felt, only how I did. Although most of us must have felt it like that *some* of the time. Scared half witless wouldn't be putting it too strongly. You'd have to be fairly witless *not* to be terrified. Mostly of course not so much when you were on your feet and coping, as when – oh, in bed at night for instance.'

Looking at me as if inviting comment. I was thinking I *had* written at least once about the agonies of 'the three a.m. sweats', but OK, maybe hadn't done it justice. In fact obviously hadn't, if that was her impression.

Incidentally, when I call her *old* Rosie I'm only trying to make it clear where and with whom we are at that point in the narrative – *old* Rosie talking to me the (old) writer, as distinct from young Rosie in conversation with Jake, for example. The truth is, she was *not* old. May have had eyes that technically were older than they had been, but when you looked into them, you saw Rosie aged twenty-four looking back at you out of them. Simply *her* – as real now as she had been then.

Anyway, time to move on. I asked her, 'Didn't Jake tell you any more about Hardball at that stage?'

'May have. Memory's not all that hot, you know, you'll have to fill in the gaps here and there. But actually one couldn't work on the encyphering and so on without at least some notion of what it was about – so I dare say he did. There was the paradrop to discuss too. Truly basic uncertainties such as whether the team would come in by sea or *parachutage* couldn't have helped, and either way we needed a map in front of us to make much sense of it. I expect we'd have got down to the nitty-gritty when we were at Berthe's

66

house, later, when we were going over what I was going to send Baker Street. It was all tied up in that. Meanwhile there was stuff like the general background of the *réseau*, his administration of it – and his *own* background – which they'd most likely have filled me in on in Baker Street, come to think of it . . . I'm not sure; they may have. But *you* should know all that too – shouldn't you?'

I agreed. Notebook at the ready, therefore . . .

'Real name, James Kinnear. Contracting that of course you did more or less get "Jake". His mother had been French, father had some business or other in Lille, and James after schooling in England took a degree in civil engineering at Lille University, did postgraduate work someplace else and returned there as a lecturer – pre-war, this was – in the course of it making a close friend of a younger man – student, French – by name Jacques Jorisse. I'll come back to him in a moment. Nineteen thirty-nine though, Jake being a Territorial and also bilingual served in the BEF in some regiment or brigade, whatever, as their French Liaison Officer, was taken prisoner some time before the German breakthrough, escaped and was back with his unit in time for the Dunkirk evacuation; and back home, was roped in by SOE.'

'Similar background to Alain Déclan's.'

'Not really. Only in that they were both Army and both came out at Dunkirk. Déclan wasn't taken prisoner and wasn't commissioned – not until SOE got hold of him. Anyway Jake, after training, was sent as Jean Samblat first to Paris where he helped in setting up *réseaux* both there and in Lyon – which was when he and "Germaine" saw a lot of each other – then transferred himself here to Toulouse, walked in on his Lille University chum Jacques Jorisse at the offices of Mahossier, Jorisse et Fils, *Ingenieurs Civils*, and said more or less, "Here I am, what can we do about it?"

Jacques being the *fils* of Michel Jorisse, who as luck would have it – or Jake might have known this, known at least it was on the cards – was due for retirement and ready to hand over to his son. That's to say, as I undersand it or understood it at the time, hand over the official appointment as Toulouse's *Ingenieur des Ponts et Chaussées*, Jacques taking on Jean Samblat as an Associate, who'd handle most if not all of the private work that he'd been looking after and didn't want to lose. Mahossier was already out of it, well into retirement.'

'Jake must have been very certain of his man.'

'Must have, mustn't he. Especially as he'd sold the idea to Buck in SOE as a long-term project within days of being taken on for training, in that post-Dunkirk period.'

'What was he supposed to have been doing since '39?'

'Well – at Lille University, except for time in hospital. He was lame, you see, no question of being called up or on any reserve. Happened when he was still a student, bad fall from a horse. No – not a fall, he was following another rider and that one's horse lashed out and broke his shin-bone, drove it up through the kneecap. Hence the limp – and scarring as evidence, if required. Did actually happen just like that, only in England in the hunting field, although he had documentary proof that it was in some riding academy near Lille.'

'Impressive cover stories all round. Déclan's living, talking wife, for instance. What about Voreux?'

'He was half blind, wore thick glasses. Had had a job as a commercial traveller; and more recently of course the fish business, which he was struggling to make a go of and had somewhat exaggerated plans for, if and when he could only acquire the necessary finance, etcetera.'

'And *your* cover, Rosie – apart from the naval widow bit?'

'Apart from that, not so impressive. I was allegedly looking for a job, but not trying all that hard. The last thing I'd have wanted was to be tied down to regular working hours – shop or secretarial, whatever. I could go looking for my late husband's old aunt who was supposed to be living in some village – in the Cevennes, maybe, but anywhere else I needed her, you see, wherever I happened to be or it suited me to claim I was making for. As a cover story it was quite feeble, but somehow believable *because* of that – seemed so to me, anyway. I could be as vague as I liked – she didn't have to be in those mountains, I could have been mistaken . . . See what I mean, the vagueness gave it a kind of realism, how it *might* be for someone in my situation – lost, lonely, somewhat naive?'

She'd checked; glanced at her wristwatch. 'Knocking-off time?'

'So it is.' I moved, gave her a hand up: Rosie with her hands to the small of her back then, wincing: then a shrug and a mutter of 'Rotten design. That and/or overuse. Bloody frustrating, either way. Although the old memory seems to be working, in fits and starts. I've just remembered those Poles' names, the felucca skippers. Buchowski and Trajewski. That *is* extraordinary, seeing as I never met either of them. Wild men, they were said to be. By Voreux, I suppose, or Jake . . . Do *you* find walking's often easier than just sitting?'

'I'll grab a taxi when we see one. Around the Capitole maybe, if not before.' We were crossing the springy turf of Place de la Daurade, northeastward, which had to be about right for the Capitole and the Boulevard de Strasbourg; were sure to find a taxi well before that, I thought. Meanwhile – moment ago – I'd been distracted by the sight of a crazy-looking mongrel racing past us with what looked like a beret in its mouth and two children screaming in pursuit; Rosie had said something about Jake, his briefing of her that afternoon sixty years ago in the *allées* around the Jardin des Plantes:

she was telling me they'd started back at just about this time of day, caught a bus more or less where she'd got off hers earlier. 'Heading north up whatever that boulevard's called, runs up alongside the Canal du Midi – making for the station to collect my other suitcase, *en route* for Berthe Devrèque's house.'

'Pretty well exhausted by that time, I'd imagine. Having parachuted in the night before – no sleep, hardly any lunch?'

'Oh, a *galette* can be quite substantial. Might have had two, even. Dare say I'd have had some chocolate earlier on, as well. Any case, young and fit, and – you know, all geared-up, here at last. But listen now.' To my surprise, she took my arm. 'Here's a scene I do very well remember. When we got off the bus outside the station, Jake relieved me of the trans-ceiver, suggested I might go on and get the other case, then meet him back on that corner. He needed cigarettes and there was a newsagent/*tabac* right there which often enough had Disques Bleus, he'd try his luck.'

The station full of Germans, and a train at that moment pulling in. Racket of gushing steam, shouts and yells, long platform crowded with people – not *all* Germans but, she thought, more than enough. Gendarmes too, but it was the Boches one was most aware of. Well, think of it, having been safe at home in England only twenty-four hours ago. And this was the Paris train, she guessed, would have come through Cahors and Montauban as hers had that morning, and before that Limoges, Tours, Orléans. A certain thrill in naming the stops, at being here in France no matter what – and snatches of the language in her ears. *Her* language, as she thought of it – for the reason it had been her father's, whom she'd adored. He'd died when she'd been twelve; if he'd lived, she'd never have left France – her mother, with whom she didn't get on all that well, wouldn't have had a say in it.

There was a crowd around the entrance to the *consigne*; by the look of it, Jake was going to be kept waiting, poor man. She had the *fiche* ready in her hand, other hand for security on the handbag slung from her shoulder. But *was* actually moving forward – after only about a minute could actually see the baggage custodians – two men, and a woman who looked as if she might confidently have taken on Joe Louis. It was a big depository with a considerable length and spread of racks, most of them double-decker. Stacks of kitbags on the floor as well, although there were no soldiers in this throng, no Germans recognisable as such. Train doors slamming out there like artillery. Those embarking would be passengers for Carcassonne, Narbonne, Béziers, Montpellier, Nimes, she supposed, envisaging the map she'd studied. Others no doubt changing at Narbonne for Perpignan and points south to the mountains and the Spanish frontier.

'Next!'

The female custodian's yell – things having speeded up beyond one's expectations. Rosie pushed her ticket into the woman's hand, helped an overburdened old lady on her way, half a minute later had her own case shoved at her across the counter. Label on it reading S. TRENIARD and below that TOULOUSE – S. Treniard checking it was still locked, shouting 'Merci!' into the din, no one taking notice of anyone else or of anything but recovering their own possessions. Could really have left the transceiver here as well. Except its size and shape might conceivably have attracted an experienced eye. Which for that matter it might just as easily do when carried. Backing off, shouldering out against the continuous incoming stream – out and to the left, into the channel leading out to the station's forecourt.

Here however the crowd was near-solid: intermittently,

71

even static. Jake certainly *was* going to be kept waiting. Rosie immobilised now behind a large, white-headed man who with a view over most of the heads in front of him was telling a woman in a yellow hat, 'Searching folk an' their baggage *and* checking our damn papers.'

The immediate, choking question being how might they react to a poacher's pocket stuffed with half a million francs?

Just as well one had *not* left the transceiver here. Although that amount of cash on its own would be enough at least to arouse interest – leading to further searching and probably arrest, followed by interrogation. Wouldn't go all that well with her pathetic cover story either, that half-million. So – all right: she'd sold her flat in Paris, didn't trust banks; and an apartment or small house here was going to cost something, wasn't it? What'd they want, have her live in the street?

Bluster. Be stupid. Stupidity as refuge, camouflage.

At least one had no pistol. *One* small mercy . . . The woman in the yellow hat moaned, 'Could be here *hours* this rate. What *for*, heaven's sake, what can they want of us?'

'Looking for some person, or some object. Find the object, you got the person – right?'

Looking for anyone who might be a replacement pianist, for instance. Male, female, old, young: the *object* a leather suitcase sixty centimetres long, weighing thirty kilos. Heavy for its size. Could be inside a larger case, of course: carried by a rather scruffy-looking, obviously scared young woman with half a million francs in an inside coat pocket, as well as other items including the pads for coding.

As well as Benzedrine tablets for keeping one awake at night, and one capsule of cyanide. A game of some sort, call the one-time pads. Children's game, a present for some child. The aunt's grandchild, say.

'It's gendarmes doing most of it. Boches supervising, like.'

72

'*Sacrés* Boches . . .'

'Regrettably they're what we have now. Until they're beaten we *got* 'em, eh?'

'Do you believe, monsieur, they *can* be beaten?'

'Not by us, for sure, but – English, Russians, *and* the Yanks now –'

'Suzette!'

'Oh, *Jean!*'

Unbelievable, but thank God . . .

He had the transceiver under one arm, was reaching for this other case as he came thrusting, fighting his way through – from behind, how he'd got there she couldn't understand. Accept it as a miracle, was all: wonder-man laughing, obviously just as relieved at finding her, apologising to some people on whom he must have trampled or inconvenienced in some way, now back to her with 'What a scrum! God's sake let's get out of it – don't know about you, *chérie*, I need a drink!'

'Well, why not? Oh, *pardon*, madame –'

'Madame.' Big man addressing the yellow hat: 'Might be better than standing around here – if you'd permit me to offer *you* a drink?'

She wasn't having any: was late already, had a husband waiting for her. Jake talking into Rosie's ear as he piloted her away: 'Straight through and out – the way I came in – brasserie has doors to the forecourt. You all right?'

'Man saying they'd be looking for some individual – that tall man was. Could be right, d'you think – someone like *me*?'

'What would *he* know about it?'

'Sounded like a retired policeman. I don't know, maybe I'm talking rubbish, but they got Wiggy, and they know a pianist has to be replaced –'

'*Damn.*'

73

Nothing to do with what she'd been saying, only that a gendarme at the double doors leading to the street had just stopped a group of youths from leaving by it. Students, by the look of them – protesting noisily, gendarme insisting *that* way out, *this* exit temporarily prohibited – doors now locked – see? No, he couldn't say why or for how long, best just be patient, lads.

Jake suggested, 'Coffee?'

'Well – yes, I suppose . . .'

He dumped the two cases at the end of the bar, against the shiny brown-painted wall where the bar joined it. There was a space there beyond the flap that would be kept clear for the passage of bar staff, and the cases would be out of everyone's way, at least no one actually falling over them. Rosie couldn't see that any other customers had luggage with them in here. No reason they shouldn't have, she supposed, but the fact was they didn't. And although there were some unoccupied tables, out there the cases would be more conspicuous.

If anyone had any interest in them. She suggested, 'A glass of something might be easier than coffee.'

'It might, too. Beer? Or what's that – Framboise?'

She chose that – raspberry cordial – and he ordered a beer for himself. The barwoman told him, 'It's preferred that customers sit at the tables, monsieur.'

'I can't sit, in any comfort.'

'Not sit?'

'An old wound.' The left leg: gazing down at it. 'Knee won't bend. So if you don't mind . . .'

'Old soldier, eh?' She smiled at Rosie, and giving her her cordial, addressed her as mam'selle. Jake said, after he'd paid and she'd left them, 'You must be dying to take the weight off, Suzie.'

'Well. Since you mention it.' Pointing with her chin towards a sign that read *Toilette*. 'Might take a break in there.'

'Good idea.'

'You don't know *how* good.'

Watching her go. He was all right, having anointed some shrubbery flanking one of those *allées*, earlier. Sipping his tasteless beer, keeping himself to himself and ten minutes later watching her come back. 'All right?'

'You should try it. But nothing to the relief when you turned up!'

'They have to be either stupid or new to the job, don't they, setting up a checkpoint with nothing to stop people just ducking out of it? I was thinking, too, if there was anything in your notion of them being on the lookout for a pianist, why should they have picked on that particular train?'

'If an informer had got it slightly wrong?' Blinking at him. To any interested observer's eyes, this could have been an episode in a flirtation: the quality of her smile, and the way he was concentrating on her. 'See – first an intercepted signal – one that went or came through the pianist in Lyon –'

'Or Wiggy?'

'No. Discount that. Really, I think one has to.'

'All right. But –'

'Intercepted signal first, some unidentifiable informer then told to keep his or her ear to the ground – before long gets to think he/she's on to something?'

'Monique Déclan?'

'But he put me on the *early morning* train. If she featured in this at all she'd have known that – if she'd have given two hoots anyway – and hadn't been miles away, wherever it is they live. Léguevin? Any case, he told me he never spoke to her about anything except boreholes and farm machinery, so forth – might say he was really giving me the same warning that you did?'

'I'd say he was just telling you the plain, honest truth. There doesn't have to be any informer. Darned nuisance, is all.'

'Yes. Sorry. I'll learn, won't I. This is only rhubarb–rhubarb talk, anyway.' Smiling into his eyes again. 'It's a foul drink, this. Are you married, by the way?'

'I was, but we broke up.'

'I'm sorry.'

'Don't know why you should be. How about you? Well, no, surely – but you could be engaged?'

'I *was* married. Late lamented got himself shot down in flames – a year ago. Actually not lamented all that much, truth is we wouldn't have lasted.' She'd been watching the exit – *whispered* now, 'Our friend on the door is being relieved. No – better than that, believe it or not, Jean –'

'Opening up?'

'They *are*!'

'Settles *that*, then. But let's give it a few minutes now . . .'

Old Rosie had described the incident rather more sketchily than that, mostly in the taxi that had picked us up in the Rue Gambetta, but I was storing it in memory pretty well as I thought I'd write it, rough first draft to go on the laptop that evening. In fact maybe before bathing and changing and picking her up for dinner, since there'd be more later, as well as notes to be made on earlier stuff.

Time now five twenty-five. We'd be at l'Ambassade in just minutes.

'Quite some day, Rosie, your first one in the field. Even if you demolished two or three *galettes*. Must have been just about on your knees.'

'I might have been. Write it that way if you want. More to the point, though, I'm looking forward to a long soak in a hot tub right now!'

'And you're entitled. Problem is, having such a lot of ground to cover in rather a short time. I'm sorry.'

'My fault at least as much as yours.' She'd yawned.

76

'Heavens. Tub *and* snooze between now and seven-thirty!'

'Like to make it *eight*-thirty?'

'You know, that isn't a bad idea?'

'Eight-thirty, then. By which time I'll have today's cardinal points on disk. Winding that last scene up, incidentally – from the station you and Jake would have gone to the house on Place Marengo and met Berthe Devrèque?'

'Yes. Large blonde woman, was our Berthe. Quite pleasant. About forty-five, seemed rather keen on Jake, I thought. I was quite impressed with him myself, in the course of the afternoon he'd grown on one. I mean, as a nice guy, kindred spirit, one to take notice of and rely on – which to a beginner was – reassuring. It must have been on the way to Berthe's place, I think, that he said that while he didn't believe the business at the station could have had anything to do with any search for a replacement pianist – it was on the air waves they'd be looking for me, not on the ground – one couldn't be too careful, and keen as he was on getting back into regular contact with Baker Street, this Saturday night might be rushing it a bit; he didn't want to look back on events and think, *should* have bloody waited . . . So – best to lie low for a couple of nights, make my start on the Sunday – and as discussed earlier, from a fair distance out of town, best achieved by using Voreux and his van. As it happened he was seeing him next day, meeting at the Saturday market in Carcassonne, could thus set it up without any special prior contact. A rendezvous for let's say Sunday noon – but where . . . Well, maybe at Revel, which for me would mean a couple of hours' bike ride – south-east of town, on the D2. Or make it a bit later in the day – say three p.m. Berthe would have a road map. And tomorrow, Saturday, I could take it easy, have a look around the town maybe – with Berthe as guide, if she felt up to it. Voreux's van, though, was off-white with Marc's initials *MV* and *Poissonnier* on its sides in blue: 'Suzie, tell you what – at Revel, three p.m., you might have had a puncture, be sitting on the right-hand verge looking helpless?'

5

Saturday, late afternoon: Voreux slowed as he passed the church and entered the village of Villerouge-Ségure. It had taken him more than an hour through the lanes and broken country from Carcassonne, where he'd spent a couple of hours in Jean Samblat's company, and done good business in the market before that. He'd sold all the crabs he'd picked up the evening before at Canet-Plage, might have been heading back there in the hope of restocking except that (a) it would have been a long haul, (b) have left him facing a much longer one in the morning, and (c) he had plenty of jars of salted anchovies here in Villerouge, more than enough to justify his being on the road tomorrow.

The anchovies were hand-processed in Collioure by women who spent their whole lives at it. Margins weren't as good as with fresh crabs and lobsters, but much as one liked to show good profit this had never been a purely commercial enterprise and never would be, had to look as if he was busting his guts to make it so, was all. For tomorrow he'd put in a stack of empty fish-boxes as well as the crate of jars, and if he was stopped could say he'd *been* doing great business. Sundays usually weren't days for trading, more for cleaning out and preparation for the week ahead; but this trip might well extend itself into Monday – having picked up the new pianist, he was to transport her eastward or north-eastward as far as *she* insisted.

And feed her. He had a cooked chicken, bread and a bottle of white wine in the back, in a fish-box; Samblat had not only suggested this, but paid for it – in the market, black-market prices too. She'd have brought funds with her from London, of course, and presumably he was feeling flush. Seemed also to have a high regard for his new pianist: Marc had asked him whether he thought she knew her business, and he'd snapped almost angrily yes, she most certainly did – adding then with a smile, 'Despite being young and extremely attractive.'

'That a fact, Jean?'

'See for yourself, then you tell *me*!'

'Interesting. But you're saying she calls the shots?'

'As far as her piano-playing's concerned, yes. On this trip and others like it, it's for her to decide where you stop and for how long or where you drop her and pick her up again. She's an experienced pianist and has clear ideas on what risks she will or won't take; effectively you're her chauffeur and escort, enabling her to do the job she has to do.'

'*How* young is she?'

'Couple of years older than you, as it happens, but you'd never guess it. Might work in her favour – no Boche would see her as old enough to have the skills she does have.'

'Intriguing.'

'Well – you know the rules on that one. SOE's *and* mine. I'd imagine you'd be banging your head on a brick wall anyway, but – don't try, Marc. I'm serious now. If she felt harassed in that way –'

'Don't worry.' He'd shrugged. 'I've better uses for my head than banging it on walls.'

Although walls had a tendency to crumble, in his experience. One accepted Samblat's point of principle, at least when it concerned a fellow *réseau* member; his private reservation was only that – well, *that* – what one might call the crumble factor. Gabrielle for instance had told him a few days ago when at her insistence he'd taken off his glasses that he looked like an assassin, anyone would know at a glance he was trouble. She'd been joking, of course, or at least half-joking, had said it with that certain smile, implication being that 'trouble' could be fun to have around. She was – well, *really* special; so much so that initially he'd assumed she was out of his reach, only more recently wondered whether crumbling might not be on the cards.

Might have chanced it this evening, he thought. Made for the Vérisoins' place, maybe got lucky, *and* had a shorter trip to Revel in the morning.

Dangerous at weekends, though. Too late now, in any case.

Braking, then taking the corner to the right, out of the narrow village street into a steeper slot that was more like a drain than any kind of thoroughfare. Scabrous house-fronts in varying shades of grey, dun and greenish mould, stone and cracked plaster interspersed with sagging timber, patches of corrugated iron, here and there rusty iron balconies you wouldn't have dared set foot on, and the upper storeys leaning inward to leave only a jagged streak of sky up there. Marc bearing left where the slot levelled in the approach to the old wreck of a building some of which he rented – four rooms of which only one was rain-proof, *toilette* out back, large cellar-like ground floor that was cool enough for ice to last a day or two even in high summer.

Another asset was this space beside it which had been heaped with rubble but which he'd cleared to provide a parking space for the van.

Van's engine chugging powerfully into silence. *Sounded*

powerful, in fact had only about half the power it had had before on Samblat's insistence Alain Déclan had converted it from petrol to charcoal, the *réseau* being low in funds at that time, Marc's black-market petrol no longer affordable.

He'd opened his front door – a padlock and chain – and had left the van's doors open, there being fish-boxes and a large galvanised tank to bring in; had gone inside to check on how much ice remained in the old bath-tub. Not much: later he'd hose it out, and would need to get down to Perpignan for fresh supplies. Monday or Tuesday maybe . . .

Fit the partition before picking up this girl?

He'd made it out of fish-boxes; it fitted across the cargo-space so that any nosy gendarme peering in through the rear doors would think he was looking at a van full of fish, whereas there was room for two or at a pinch three passengers crouching between it and the cab. A girl on her own – with a blanket or two – would find it comfortable enough.

On the other hand, she could just as well keep him company in the cab. She'd have her own cover story, obviously, but if she was as attractive as Jean had said, gendarmes on a checkpoint would hardly bother to ask for one. Most likely a nod and a wink, and wave him through.

A thump from outside, and a shout of 'Hey, Voreux – you there?'

Knowing he was here, obviously. Old swine must have been lying in wait for him out there somewhere. For what purpose would no doubt emerge within the next few minutes – chit-chat first, then what he'd really come for. Hoping to cadge a fish supper, maybe. In which case, hard luck. Marc moved into his doorway, stood there looking out at *sergeant de ville* Mico Hoeigrand, who'd just leant or rather crashed his bike against the van. Thickset, greying, with a sallow complexion, thin moustache and even thinner hair: complaining as he picked his way over the uneven ground, 'My third call on you, is this. Where've you been all day?'

'Carcassonne. Market-day. As usual.' He'd removed his glasses, was demisting the lenses with the ball of a thumb. 'Why?'

'You're wanted in Narbonne, that's why!'

'Wanted?' It took a moment to understand. 'You don't mean wanted by *your* crowd?'

Hoeigrand nodding slowly – from only a couple of feet away, as if to block him from making a dash for it – which he could have done easily if there'd been any point in doing so. He was taller than Hoeigrand, as well as slimmer, harder, fitter. Well – *young*. His only disability in fact was his eyesight, while Hoeigrand's included a paunch and disproportionately short legs. Telling him in his croaky tones, in reply to a genuinely puzzled exclamation of 'But what for?': 'All I know is I'm to bring you in. And starting this late – well, if you need a wash, or somesuch –'

'I certainly do, and there's stuff needs to be unloaded from the van – work to do inside here, what's more. Who's sending for me anyway, who gave you such an order?' Shake of the head then – 'Doesn't matter, does it. I tell you what, though – ask 'em can I stop by next time I'm passing. Tuesday, say. They'll only want to see my papers are up to date – driving licence, road permits, rubbish of that kind . . .' A pause, and a new thought: 'Anyway *how*, bring me in?'

'In *that*.' The van. 'Dropping my bike off at Jonquières *en route*. We'll either come back together, or if they're holding you –'

'*Holding* me . . . And fifty kilometres in *my gazo* – who pays for that?'

'Forty-five kilometres at most. And how else? Look, it's just the way things are – slightly upside-down right at this moment. Argue the toss when we get there, lad – with *them*

– if they're in a mood to listen. Come on now, what's to be offloaded?'

No partition. Hoeigrand would just about wet himself if he saw that. Jean's girl would have to ride up front.

Through Talairan – after the stop at Hoeigrand's cottage at Jonquières – turning right on to the metalled road at Talairan, and then through the larger village of St-Laurent-de-la-Cabrarisse; having by that time clocked up twenty kilometres and knowing for a fact that the distance from La Cabrarisse to Narbonne was another thirty-four, total therefore fifty-four. He didn't bother to mention it. Hoeigrand, who as *sergeant de ville* was in fact an ordinary though senior gendarme responsible for law and order in a whole group of villages back there, was not outstandingly intelligent, tended to have his own rudimentary ideas and stick to them. Asking Marc at about this stage whether it was really true he had no clue as to why the Narbonne commissariat might want him.

'Absolutely. Unless as I said it's to check my papers. Otherwise I suppose I'm going to be accused of *something*. Denounced for farting in church, perhaps.'

'Be attending Mass tomorrow, will you?'

Almost as if he thought that *could* be it. More likely, just not thinking at all. Marc shrugged, slowing for the crossroads at Ste-Marie, and shortly afterwards trundling across the Ausson. Very little water in it, especially considering the time of year. If they were going to hold him overnight as Hoeigrand had suggested they might – and he might know more about this than he was letting on, going so far as to advise him to bring a razor and other necessities – well, God's sake, what about that girl? Because they wouldn't lock a man up in the evening only to let him go after breakfast next day; and tomorrow being Sunday – well, leave one for the whole weekend in the bloody lock-up, even? Wouldn't put it past

84

them. No way to let Samblat know, either: certainly couldn't telephone *him* from a gendarmerie *poste*, even if they let one near a telephone. Not Déclan either. One had those numbers in one's head for emergencies, Déclan's in particular not to be used for anything short of a real disaster scenario.

Like *We're blown, best run for it . . .*

Ring Gabi?

She'd do it for him all right – pick the girl up, or tell her what had happened – if she was in a position to, she'd do it. She'd done something rather similar for him before he'd even known her: in fact that was how he'd met her. But there again, weekends *were* dangerous, chances being that Charles-Henri would be around.

The new girl would have to look after herself, if the Narbonne police did hold him overnight. Obviously she'd cope – realise there'd been some cock-up and push on solo, do what she had to do.

No reason to assume they *would* hold one, though. But then no reason they should be having one brought in, either.

At least, no *trivial* reason.

Frightening thought, that. Denunciations weren't all that uncommon, in this day and age. Some, of course, could be demonstrated as false within just minutes – if they *were* false, the boys in blue or the DST only following them up in order to keep their own noses clean. But – well, touch wood. Grasping it, sweat on his palms on the jolting wheel; trying *not* to think *Gestapo, even*?

It wouldn't have to be anything of recent origin. A denunciation could date from one's activities at some much earlier stage.

But these were the outskirts of Narbonne, at last. He told Hoeigrand, startling him out of *his* long silence, 'You'll have to direct me, from here on.'

'Huh?' Had apparently been dozing. Blinking, staring round

. . . 'Yes. Course. Keep on as we are, over the canal – in a few minutes – then to the right. The Palais des Archevèques will be up ahead on your left, continue past it and – and I'll tell you when to turn again.' Shaking his grey head and yawning. 'I'd have thought with all your knocking around you'd know this town.'

'Not well, as it happens. Only – you know, passing through.'

Except for a safe-house on the Rue des Trois Moulins that he'd made use of maybe half a dozen times, in the course of his escape-line work. House belonging to an elderly couple who'd risked their lives time and time again to save those of complete strangers. Magnificent – and a constant surprise, how many of that kind there were. Hoeigrand said – blurting it out as if it had been in his mind to say it and he'd only now brought himself to the point of doing so – 'I suppose you realise why we've been called on to follow what's actually a most unorthodox procedure, bringing you here in your own transport?'

'I haven't. As it happens.'

'Well. Arrival of the Occupying Power?'

'What's that to do with it?'

'Everything. Sixes and sevens – transport in particular, they've commandeered most of it. And routine procedures countermanded – according to what one's heard, that is – and officers ordered to attend meetings here, there and every-where –'

'That the bridge ahead now?'

'Uh? Oh – yes . . .'

'What I want to know is why I've been sent for anyway, let alone how. Orders from some damn Boche, are you telling me?'

'No, I'm not. Simply don't know. But in your shoes I'd watch the language – uh?'

Shifting gear. 'Boches be here to meet us, d'you expect?'

No immediate reply – beyond a worried glance; but sweat on *his* snout and forehead, and the beginnings of denial. Embarrassment – the Judas factor, might call it? Marc raised his voice: 'There *will* be, huh?'

'I don't know. Honest to God, I—'

'No.' Nodding grimly. 'Dare say you wouldn't.'

In the front office at the *poste* he caught the scent of it at once. Confusion, insecurity. No Germans in sight or sound, and no mention of them – confirmation, he thought, of Boche machinations lying at the root of it. And even if there'd never been one in the place you could bet there soon would be. He saw it in the eyes of the *brigadier* – meaning the sergeant in charge of the *poste* – and in those of others, including of course Hoeigrand's. Decent men at heart, probably – at least, some of them would be – Pétainists now because they had to be if they wanted to keep their jobs, but not necessarily with their hearts in it. In fact there were gendarmes who sympathised with the Resistance, and some who actually worked for it. That might be comparatively rare, might not be the case at all with this bunch, but one definitely could sense what in Hoeigrand's case he'd thought of as the Judas factor.

Orders from Vichy being one thing, but from the Boche quite another? Especially when seemingly directed against one of their own people?

He thought cynically then, take 'em a while to get used to it, no doubt.

The *brigadier* was telling Hoeigrand, 'Give your wife a buzz if you want, tell her you'll be home for your Sunday lunch. One way or another we'll get you back there.' He looked at Marc: 'All I can say is the order came to us from Lyon.'

'Lyon.' Gesture of incomprehension. 'But from whom?'

'From the *préfecture*, monsieur.'

'Telling you to hold me on what charge?'

87

'No charge. You're being detained for questioning, that's all.' A shrug. 'Regrettably, there's only one type of accommodation I can offer you.'

A cell, measuring about four metres by two. At least he had it to himself. Planks with a palliasse on them and a single blanket, supper consisting of rabbit soup and bread. He asked the young gendarme who brought it, 'Can you tell me who'll be questioning me, and when?'

'Some Germans who were taking the night train from Marseille, was what I heard.'

'*Tonight*, then?'

'Uh-huh. Morning, I'm sure.'

'And Germans, plural, but what kind? Gestapo, for instance?'

'That I *don't* know. What would they have against you, d'you know that?'

'All I'm thinking is maybe they've got the wrong Voreux.'

'Well. Let's hope so.'

'That or some swine's got it in for me.'

'Denunciation, you mean.'

He shrugged. 'False accusation of some kind. Happens often enough, one's heard.'

'You haven't let some girl down recently, I suppose?'

'I *never* let girls down. Anyway why would it interest the Gestapo?'

They were more likely to be Abwehr than Gestapo, he thought. At least, if it had anything to do with the escape-line, since it had been Abwehr, Boche military intelligence on the trail of shot-down airmen, who'd discovered and somehow penetrated that. Touch wood, one might be better off with Abwehr than with Gestapo.

In the short term, anyway. Longer term, one was as likely to finish up in Belsen or Buchenwald either way.

Right from the start though, he reminded himself, we recognised this sort of outcome as a possibility, knew it was a chance we had to take. *Just pray to God they're on to me alone, not Denise as well.*

Can't be. Grasping the edge of a plank. *As long as she's kept her head down and her mouth shut – as she will have – won't be. Please God.*

That same young gendarme came later to collect the tin plate and soup bowl.

'All right, was it?'

'Not bad at all.'

'I'll say goodnight, then. Good luck tomorrow.'

'Thanks. Tell me something?'

'Uh?'

'I'm not charged with anything, you're just putting me up for the night, why lock the door?'

'Oh.' Jiggling the key in his palm. 'Sorry. Thing is, if you walked out, *we*'d be answerable.'

Answerable, he thought, to our *real* gaolers – gaolers, torturers and murderers: in the presence of whom tomorrow I'll have to pretend innocence, even indicate goodwill.

If there's any point in doing so, if they don't know it all already. All in the past tense, surely, nothing of what I'm doing now – except they'll want to *know* what I'm doing now – much more likely it's a continuance of their investigation of the escape-line, continuance which one might have antici-pated, only tried not to think about, the probability that in arresting and interrogating others they would almost certainly have become aware of my existence – though not, please God, identity. Not until *now*, that is – thanks to the cut-outs we had in place. Had in place *then*. And what they'll want to screw out of me . . . Well, (a) maybe whether any remnants of the line are still operating, (b) other identities – names –

in particular of course that of Denise. They'll know of her existence, just as they'll have known of mine, but the system of anonymity we built around her – *her* priority being to shelter the rest of us – was quite elaborate, with provision for her to sever all connections pretty well at the drop of a hat and fall back into a completely law-abiding, pedestrian style of life. So she's right out of it, and stays there; while the only names I might very reluctantly divulge, either tomorrow or any other time, might be ones they'll know already, people they'll have caught.

And that'll be that. Except that needing a motive other than family connection, my line will be that I ducked out of that business because it got so that there was nothing in it for me – as well, admittedly, as being extremely wearing on the nerves. Having been in it initially for the money, a fair amount of our traffic in those early stages being the kind that paid. Jews, of course, rich ones – a market to be exploited, in other words. But that – financial reward – went by the board quite early on, the vast majority of *colis* coming through didn't pay a *sou*, hadn't forked out higher up the line either – and one was running the same risks – or worse ones, things certainly weren't getting any easier.

That's the outline of it, then. Won't let me off the hook, but at least doesn't involve anyone else, or admit *political* motivation. And stage two – what I'm up to on this coast, *if* they're interested, as they *may* be, in which case I'd need to account for how I make my living – well, what Hoeigrand and his colleagues will surely tell them, may have done before I'm interviewed – the fish business, and maybe on the side a little smuggling, to make ends meet until the crabs and lobsters begin to pay their way. If these Boches know anything about me – as they must do – they'll know I'm by repute a chancer, not invariably on the straight and narrow – like anyone else lacking either connections or qualifications but needing to make a living of some kind, not too choosy about how I do it. Well, look – there are the mountains, Spain's on the other side of them, there's merchandise Spaniards will pay for – perfume from Grasse for instance – and other stuff that comes back . . .

'Tobacco, cigars and cigarettes is what you think of first, but – well, take saccharin, for instance. In case you didn't know, it's a sweetening agent, comes in little pills, thousands of 'em in a single pack. Five hundred times the sweetening power of sugar – which you can't get anyway, not more than a tablespoon a month on the bloody ration – and food factories needing this stuff in quantity *and* paying through the nose for it – oh, and a medical necessity too, for instance, for diabetics –'

'Hold it there, Voreux.' Slight smile, shake of the head. 'We really don't want to hear about diabetics.'

Abwehr Leutnant Hohler might by the look and sound of him have been a professor conducting a tutorial. In his late twenties, with thick, reddish-brown hair and blue eyes in a pale, intelligent face, his expression more of concern, even friendly interest, than enmity. He also spoke excellent French with very little German accent. A different creature altogether from the brutish interrogator Marc had visualised in half-waking, restless spasms all through the night – rehearsing, ingratiating himself or trying to, persuading, wheedling – or at appropriate stages, standing on one's dignity.

Wished he hadn't now. Wished he'd slept. He'd be coping better with this if he had.

Hohler, having checked that flow with a slightly raised hand, was watching him amusedly across the boxwood table. His sergeant – uniformed, name of Bemm or maybe Behm – booted legs apart and back to the grey-painted door, Walther 9-mm holstered on his belt – had actually chuckled. He'd come to the cell with the *brigadier* who'd been on the desk

91

last evening, and brought Marc along to this interview room, where the *brigadier* had left them.

Hohler said, fingering a slim notebook which lay on the table in front of him with a silver propelling pencil beside it – *looked* like real silver – 'Forget the diabetics, Voreux. Let's talk about your sister.'

He'd started. Actually winced, and the German of course had seen it.

'You do have a sister?'

He nodded. 'Yes.' Even that admission felt like treachery. But since they did know she existed . . .

'Yes.' The German had a note of it. 'Her name is Denise, and you and she are extremely close – am I right?'

Marc said, 'Well – brother and sister, you know. Yes, I suppose . . .'

'Quite unusually close. Didn't she more or less take your mother's place – bring you up?'

'Well.' A gesture. 'Our mother died giving birth to me, Denise was then nine years old.'

'And your father decamped with a Parisian *fille de joie*?'

'I barely knew him. He – I mean, I was no more than a toddler when –'

'He left you, and as I said, Denise virtually raised you, *did* effectively take your mother's place.'

'Being that much older, she – well, naturally –'

'It's hardly surprising therefore that the pair of you *are* extremely close. Far more so than in your average brother and sister relationship.'

'You're probably right – but since it's the only family relationship of which I've experience—'

'You'd give your life for her, wouldn't you?'

Staring at him . . . Then: 'I suppose there could be circumstances –'

'You bet there could.' That smile again – and as backup,

the sergeant's chuckle. 'I suppose you're frequently in touch with her?'

'No, as a matter of fact –'

'Why not?'

Gesture of surrender: hands spread, raised slightly above the table. A sigh, then nodding as if in acquiescence. 'I think you must know that for a period of – oh, best part of a year, at least – I worked for an escape-line. Getting people out of France. That's what this is all about, isn't it?'

'The escape-line which your sister set up and controlled – yes, we know about it, naturally. Also that when the line was penetrated and effectively broken up –'

'You have some reason to think *my sister* was involved in it?'

'Voreux, we *know* she set it up and ran it!'

'You're quite wrong. She never would have done anything of that kind. Whoever laid such information against her was lying. *I* took part in it, yes, but only – well, in the expectation of making money, especially from rich fugitives – and when I realised that effectively I'd been tricked into it, I backed out. It had *nothing* to do with my sister, in fact I'd hate her to know I'd been involved in such – such activities . . . Look – she's a married woman, also as it happens a qualified accountant, she has more than enough on her plate without – well, I can only assure you, lieutenant –'

'Her husband got away to England in 1940, and subsequently she set up her escape-line which naturally enough you joined. Having the same disposition and political attitudes, and defective eyesight having disbarred you from military service – then this chance of working with *her*?'

It seemed they didn't know he'd started as an agent of BCRA. Probably no way they would. If their informants, whoever they might be, had no knowledge of it – which they might well not have done . . . Looking up at him again.

'I can see how you might tie all that together and make entirely spurious sense of it. Simply because she and I *are* close. Happens not to be true, that's all, I'd guess at deliberate misinformation. The truth is that I was brought into the escape-line work by a man named Bertillon – Pièrre Bertillon, who'd been with me when I started as a sales representative – in photographic materials, as it happens. Bertillon in fact –'

'– is either in prison or dead. As I'm sure you'd know. Let's cut the cackle now, Voreux' – a glance at his watch – 'since neither I nor the sergeant have all day for this. The fact of the matter is that after my people smashed your sister's escape-line, you and she would naturally enough go your separate ways, severing all communications.'

'None of this is true. You've been misinformed, or –'

'*Almost all* communications. You'd still be able to contact her in any real emergency – to save her life or your own, for instance. So tell me where she is now? Address, telephone, current employer –'

'She *did* work for a group of restaurants.'

'Her home address?'

'I can't remember. I mean, it *is* some time since –'

'*Can't* remember?'

'No – I'm sorry, but –'

'Wouldn't know where to address a letter – if out of your deep affection for her you thought you could take that much of a risk?'

He'd swallowed: hesitated for about two seconds. 'I only –'

'Your determination to maintain the fiction of her innocence is actually quite pointless – more so than you realise. Which I must say makes you rather less intelligent than I'd thought you might be. But leave that, for the moment. We know, as I've said, all about the escape-line, her part in it as well as your own – and that your pretence of having been in it only to enrich yourself is nonsense. You joined it because you were joining *her*. I don't intend to waste time on any further discussion of this, so please don't reassert it: we'll switch to what really interests me and Sergeant Behm here and of course our colleagues elsewhere – the subject of what you're doing *now*, Voreux.'

'But I was telling you –'

'A load of garbage. Just tell me what all that is a cover for.'

Blinking at him. Internally, a rising sickness. Which would show as pallor, naturally olive skin fading to ivory. Rehearsals and the sleepless night certainly hadn't helped.

'Cover . . .'

'Let's see if I can jog your memory. Twice in recent times for instance you've visited Lyon and made contact with a woman – United States national, correspondent of the *New York Times* – who since then has taken to her heels. What was the purpose of those visits?'

'I'm trying to raise capital for my fish business. For premises, equipment and transport – which I need in order to get it realistically off the ground. In fact I did mention, earlier –'

'Part of that rubbish. You're wasting our time, Voreux. You were not visiting that American in order to raise money.'

Hohler's tone was less kindly than it had been. Marc blinking, waiting for what might prove to be the *coup de grâce*. The German flicking over a page of notes.

'Here we are. The code-name "Jake" mean anything to you?'

'Code-name?'

'In radio communications, code-names are used quite frequently. As of course you know. "Jake" is one that's been picked out of clandestine transmissions from this area, also at the times of your visits to Lyon.'

'I know nothing of any radio.'

'Also a code-*word* that's intrigued us. "Hardball". English, of course – as is the name "Jake". Proper names, I'm told, are more easily decrypted, at least in certain types of code.'

'None of this means anything to me at all.'

'Are you – or *were* you – acquainted with an individual by the name of Roger St Droix?'

'Not that I recall.'

'He was the operator of a clandestine radio. What the so-called "Resistance" and in particular the British "Special Operations Executive" call a "pianist". He was a member of SOE, incidentally.'

'I could take your word for it, but your previous assertions are so far from anything I ever *heard* of –'

'How about BCRA?'

'I beg your pardon?'

'Bureau Central des Renseignements et d'Action. A terrorist organisation operated by French traitors currently sheltering in London.'

'One had heard there are such people –'

'And *one had heard* –' mimicking him – 'that you were employed by them, made use of their facilities – communications in particular – in connection with your sister's escape-line, and are now almost certainly back in their employ.'

'I'm in my own employ. For some reason you won't believe me, but it's the simple truth!'

'Roger St Droix was the radio operator or "pianist" in this *réseau*. Regrettably, is no longer in a position to assist us. But you knew him, as well as others in the same conspiracy – and you *will* know the operator who'll take his place – or may already have done so.' A pause, and a quizzical look: 'No comment, uh?'

'As I said, it's –' hands spread, lips trembling – 'beyond my comprehension.'

'Would you like me to tell you where your sister is at this moment?'

'Where she –'

'You claim to have forgotten her address. And it's a fact she hasn't lived at that one for quite some while now.'

'Please – maybe I'm stupid –'

'I think you must be, but try to grasp this. We had to find your sister alternative accommodation. On the Paris outskirts – actually a prison, run by – well, I don't want to alarm you, but she's in the custody of the *Geheime Staatspolizei*. Despite which, I'm authorised to tell you, she's all right at the moment.' A shrug. '*More or less* all right, anyway. How it may go for her from now on – well, depends on you, Voreux. Gestapo being as they are. You either give them what they want of you, or you don't. For which there's invariably a heavy price. Depends on how much you *really* care for her – uh?'

6

Rosie told me, after I'd picked her up at l'Ambassade at eight-thirty and taken her by taxi to our usual restaurant, where we sipped martinis and chatted while studying the menu, that in accordance with Jake's instructions received on that Friday evening sixty years ago she was cycling south-eastward out of town by mid-forenoon on the Sunday – November 15th 1942 – and getting into Revel by not long after 2 p.m., i.e. an hour ahead of schedule. As far as she could recall the detail of it, this was; mentioning not for the first time that ever since we'd arranged this get-together she'd been racking her brains and memory, making notes, getting times and dates to fit and adjusting them when they didn't, generally finding it difficult enough but then out of the blue remembering quite small things – for instance, acquiring an old road map from a second-hand bookshop during her exploration of Toulouse the day before – new maps on security grounds being *verboten*; and that she'd been on her own in the morning, but had Berthe as her guide in the afternoon, having met for lunch in a café in the town centre of which she actually recalled the name. Adding thoughtfully, as much to herself as to me, 'Nice woman, Berthe. Oh, except she'd no sense of humour.' On the Sunday, anyway, approaching Revel on a mostly straight road lined with elms, having by this time come about fifty kilometres from Toulouse *centre* – started earlier than she'd really needed to, and really pushed it along, allowing for real punctures or other hold-ups and anxious not to keep the man waiting – but hoping by this time that he might be early too.

He wasn't, of course. Not *this* early, anyway. In fact if he'd any sense he'd arrive a bit late, so as to find the allegedly punctured cyclist already there, his excuse to pull in and help.

He did have a good head on his shoulders, according to Jake. Old for his years – in Jake's view – certainly *looked* older, hard-faced behind the thick-lensed glasses – toughened maybe by his parentless and poverty-stricken childhood. Mother dead in childbirth – Marc's – the father soon afterwards bolting with some other woman, leaving him and his sister to fend for themselves. The sister, nine years older than infant Marc, had naturally done most of the fending, and Marc idolised her.

'Only thing I might mention is he's said to be a bit of a Don Juan. And since you, Suzie, are as attractive as you are, my advice would be to let him know at an early stage that you're seriously committed elsewhere.'

'Invent a boyfriend, you mean.'

'I'd have thought you'd have dozens!'

'That intended as a compliment?'

'Observation, that's all. But why not make it a fiancé?'

'Well, why not. But in any case he must know SOE's rules. Even if his origins are BCRA, as I think you said.'

'He's aware of the rules, all right, but in the first place he's French – a Frenchman in France, which might make him feel contemptuous of what might seem to him a peculiarly British discipline. Another thing is that by the nature of the job, especially in the work-up to Hardball, you and he'll be spending a lot of time together.'

'Thanks for the warning anyway.'

It was still well short of three when she dismounted, pushed her bike across the right-hand verge and leant it against a tree. The transceiver wasn't in its case now; she'd disassembled it, dividing its component parts and battery between a hatbox in the panier and a small attaché case on the rear carrier, both items borrowed from Berthe Devrèque, who must have wondered what was going on but had wisely or politely refrained from asking questions. Just as on the Friday evening she'd tactfully left Rosie and Jake on their own for his extended briefing, centring round the encyphering of the stuff she'd be sending Baker Street.

It hadn't been practical, Jake had insisted, to do so without briefing her there and then on Hardball. She'd wanted to avoid this, or delay it, would have been happy to send the page of five-letter groups out without knowing what she was sending; after all, she wouldn't be decyphering Baker Street's responses until she was back in Toulouse, when he'd be joining her and could *then* explain it.

'Even decypher their stuff on your own, couldn't you?'

'No, Suzie, I could not. Simple reason that in the meantime *I* could be nobbled. We touched on this earlier, didn't we – that I have to leave you in a position to carry on?'

Gave her the shivers. Her first time out, at that: even in the most general way, the possibility of being left without his support and guidance let alone in handling or coordinating what was obviously a fairly major operation. Wouldn't amount to being in command, exactly – once the commando team was here its leader would effectively assume that role, at least, once he and they had been received, rested, fed and watered and steered to their target. But this *réseau* and its Organiser – he was the key to all of it, and if he happened to do a Wiggy – well, for *he*, read *she*. Recalling her exchanges with Alain Déclan, for instance, there'd be no question of *his* taking over: while Marc Voreux – French, aged only twenty-two and closer to BCRA than SOE – Baker Street wouldn't wear *that*.

No reason though, thank God, to anticipate Jake being 'nobbled'. No justification therefore for that flare of panic. If the worst did come to the worst – which it *could*, obviously – well, you'd cope, simply because you'd bloody have to. Scream for help to Baker Street maybe, but otherwise just get on with it.

And here and now, remove hatbox, rolled-up overcoat and attaché case from the bike – then take the front wheel off – for the look of things?

Seven minutes to three. Marc would surely be here by say five past, and having taken a wheel off there'd be the chore of fixing it back on again. And she wasn't exactly in the public eye: the only vehicle that had passed since she'd stopped had been a lorry loaded with wine barrels – and in sight now, a couple of hundred metres away, a horse and cart turning out of a side-road – other side, and turning the other way. So the hell with it – had stopped to eat one's lunchtime sandwiches, was all. Hadn't felt like doing so on the move, but was hungry enough now all right, even for jam sandwiches – Berthe's.

Plum jam. Not bad. Berthe was a calm, slow-moving, thoughtful woman. Or for 'slow-moving' perhaps read 'unhurried'. Contemplative, might be the word. She was probably a very good headmistress.

Made not a bad sandwich, either, considering there was no butter in them – butter being one of the more drastically rationed commodities.

She lit a cigarette. Two minutes past three now. Come on, Marc, your time is up . . .

Two cars passing – in the direction of Toulouse, and neither of them white vans. Driver of the first one seeing her and staring, slowing; second one coming up on him quite fast – horn blaring then as he trod on *his* brake, and the first one, startled, accelerating away. Her fault, she realised, turning her back on the road – drivers all too ready to stop and render assistance, if one so much as looked at them.

Have a look at the map instead – to be ready to account for oneself if called upon to do so by gendarmes or Boches. Which could happen, being *potentially* conspicuous on one's own here – thanks to bloody Marc . . . So – might be *en route* to visit one's former mother-in-law at – say Montpellier? Picking on that as a place of some size and at a good distance, and because coming from Toulouse a cyclist might well have taken this road rather than the busier one through Carcassonne.

Hang on, though. Light-coloured vehicle – coming in the direction of – well, as if from Toulouse, but could have come up from – here on the map, Castelnaudary – which *would* be how you'd get here from Carcassonne, or from anywhere east or south-east, the way *he*'d come. There were several places he used, Jake had told her, but from any of them that was surely . . .

Might be his van. Light-coloured, medium-small. Would have come up from Castelnaudary and turned right on to this road. Quarter of an hour late now, but –

No – damn it. Damn *him*. Not a van, but a pick-up truck – rumbling past her now. Time three twenty-two, and the thought suddenly: *What if he isn't coming?*

Go on without him, obviously. In fact leave here no later than 4 p.m., to put enough distance between oneself and Toulouse despite slower progress than one would have made in the van. Push on until about midnight or thereabouts – depending on progress, and how it looked. By then one really *would* be hungry. Had counted on Raoul – Marc – either having rations with him or knowing of a safe-house in which to rest and eat: whereas on one's own and in unfamiliar territory one would (a) go hungry, (b) sleep in a ditch. Or if it was too cold for that – well, out of the wind, and it was quite a thick old coat . . .

Imagining cycling on through that dark and empty hill country though, caught suddenly in a car's headlight in one of those narrow, twisting lanes. Imagining it at its worst, say a Boche car – Gestapo or Feldpolizei . . .

Half-three, for God's sake!

But – steady on . . .

A lorry and two cars, all *gazo,* and swerving out to overtake them at something like twice their speed a petrol-driven saloon – Citroen, the 15-hp front-wheel-drive variety allegedly favoured by Gestapo. An experienced field agent resting between deployments had told Rosie's class, 'See a Citroen Light Fifteen, eyes *down* . . .' Receding now, already a hundred or more metres away, but definitely the kind of vehicle she'd visualised, its headlights sweeping up from behind her on a country road in the small hours of the morning.

But suppose at dusk or thereabouts she found herself in the right kind of surroundings – remote, with good off-road cover and high ground – well, settle for that, get into cover, do the business, stay hidden all night and set off homeward at first light.

With an empty tummy and November night-time temperatures having guaranteed a sleepless night. But also having learnt some lessons – next time to bring one's own rations including a flask of pseudo coffee, never to take anyone else's reliability for granted, and maybe – but think about this – rethink one's strategy and stay closer to Toulouse.

Three-forty . . .

Jake had told her, 'We need the *parachutage* first in order to arm a Maquis group who're going to provide backup to the commando unit. Whose task – well, history first, Suzie. In the years leading up to this fracas a lot of Germans departed their native land. Preponderance of Jews of course, but others too, people who didn't like the Nazis or the way things were going, and consequently moved out – some of them to France, where naturally at that time they found refuge. Then – extraordinarily enough – in 1940 after France surrendered and the Vichy state was set up, Pétain's boys or very likely Laval had the poor devils arrested and interned – in a camp at a place called Gurs in the Pyrenees. Extremely unpleasant, by all accounts, concentration-camp conditions, high incidence of deaths from starvation, cold, and general ill-treatment. They've moved them now – the survivors, that is, quite recently brought them to a prison camp at Noé, no more than forty kilometres south of Toulouse, where Vichy's been holding Jews before entraining them for Germany and the gas chambers. And now the Boches have moved in on us here, it's virtually certain the former émigrés will get the same treatment.'

Rosie had begun, after a moment's hesitation, 'I'm not sure how to put this –'

'Without seeming to be nasty to good Germans?'

She'd nodded. Jake was a reader of minds, she'd noticed. Admitting, 'Tell the truth, I've never thought of there being good ones. Or now, that we'd be especially interested in them. Some special reason, must be?'

He'd nodded. 'I'll give you the gist of it – which *I* got, incidentally, from the Organiser of a *réseau* working in the Pau, Tarbes, Lourdes region. Gurs is something like thirty kilometres west of Pau. Baker Street instructed this guy to come and brief me, after the people I'm talking about were moved from his backyard to ours – which as it happened was at about the time we lost Wiggy. So – short answer to

104

your question – there's one individual in that lot who if the Germans got him back would go straight into the hands of the SD or Gestapo, and they'd beat a whole lot of stuff out of him which would lead to the immediate arrest and no doubt early demise of a number of other people, including several Wehrmacht generals, whom London would sooner were left free.'

'German *generals*? Now *in* Germany?'

'And other notables, all basically or potentially anti-Nazi. Background to *this* being that in the last months of peace this small but influential group were plotting to stop Hitler in his tracks, in particular stop him invading Poland, which they knew would lead to war. The generals apparently didn't want war because they didn't think they could win one. Churchill was in touch with some of them, incidentally. They included the chief of their General Staff – oh, and Admiral Wilhelm Canaris, chief of the military intelligence bureau, Abwehr. He still is, of course. Surprising, sure, but true. Their plan before the balloon went up was for an army *putsch*, Hitler to be arrested and put on trial; they failed to act – in time, anyway – but apparently they're still in touch with us.'

'How would they manage that?'

'I'd guess *we* manage it.'

'SOE in Germany?'

'Or SIS. Or – gifted individuals. Unknowns. With what in view, I couldn't say. Well – conceivably, assassination? But returning to what I was telling you about the others who'd got out of Germany in 1937–38, some of them mistakenly believing they'd be safe enough in France – well, one of them, a former ambassador by name of Schurmann, and his wife, both fairly long in the tooth – settled on the Riviera somewhere.' He'd tapped his forehead. 'Exercising memory now: these are the names that matter, in connection with Hardball. Schurmann's wife's family name had been von

Schleben. And in the summer of 1939 her nephew Colonel Ulrich von Schleben was on the staff of one of the more senior generals in the conspiracy. He was this one's leg-man, and being at the hub of it he knew all the conspirators who mattered. Then he was tipped off that he'd been informed on and the SD were about to arrest him, and wisely did a runner – turned up at the Schurmanns' villa and settled in with them, adopting the name Schurmann as his own, uncle and aunty presumably going along with it. Until in 1940 Frogs throw in the towel and resident anti-Nazi Germans are rounded up and packed off to Gurs – *Camp* Gurs, I think they call it – where the old Schurmanns died but Ulrich von Schleben has so far survived, and he's the man London want extracted.'

'Before he's shipped back and tortured into naming names.'

'Exactly.'

She'd touched his arm. 'May I risk sounding horrible again?'

'You're thinking it might be easier to kill him than extract him.' Jake had nodded. 'Perfectly sound thought too. I reacted similarly when the man from Pau was briefing me, and believe it or not he told me that the same thing had occurred to him, he'd proposed it to Baker Street and been told to pipe down, do as he was told.'

'So you don't have to stick *your* neck out.'

'Although one might expect the commandos' orders to cover all possible contingencies.' He shrugged. '*Their* business, of course, not ours.'

'Does anyone know anything about the set-up at Noé?'

'Well, as it happens –' He'd checked himself. 'Actually, Suzie, in the interests of not over-informing you –'

'Oh, you're right . . .'

In principle one preferred not to know, although by instinct, natural reaction to there being something *to* know, one had been sufficiently caught up in it to have asked. And logically, she'd thought since then, if one was to be in a position to keep things going if Jake came to grief – well, surely . . .

Although Jake being no fool, one might assume that any such knowledge – Noé prison-camp info, access to it – would somehow become available to one in those circumstances, i.e. if/when one needed it. She thought – 4 p.m. now, it was ticking over in her mind as she put her bike back on the road – Alain Déclan might know all about it? Living as he did just west of Toulouse, and Noé being to the south-west? Check it on the map, she thought, when one next stopped. Name of Déclan's village being – Léguevin. Not that geographical propinquity would exactly clinch what was no more than a hunch, but if the hypothesis was that someone other than Jake had to know about it, Déclan did seem the most likely choice. Also – new thought – any worthwhile intelligence would surely have been passed by Jake to London. Through 'Germaine' 's pianist in or near Lyon, maybe. That seemed likely, since Jake had only become responsible for Hardball at about the time of Wiggy's disappearance.

So the commando team would have the information, she herself wouldn't need to. Which would explain Jake's not having burdened her with it.

Pedalling east now, into the scattering of buildings that comprised Revel, she decided that at the crossroads she'd turn right, making for a village called Sorèze, from there north-east to one called Dourone, continuing in that direction for about twenty-five kilometres and bearing right to pass well south of Castres; and at some point thereafter stop and consult the map again, decide on an amended fictional destination, i.e. supposed place of residence of former ma-in-law.

It was ten past four when she turned right at the cross-roads. Riding with her eyes on the road, not looking at

107

passing traffic any more than she had to, and never at car or lorry drivers' faces. She was thinking again that despite her own earlier intentions and Jake's ideas on the subject these long-distance trips weren't worth the effort. And although Déclan would probably be more reliable than Marc, the snag with him, Jake had mentioned, was that his farm-machinery business tended to come first, making him less readily available at short notice.

So go it alone. Accept the risk. At least making shorter trips you'd waste less time.

Car horn behind her: a double toot. She edged over, closer to the verge. Cowpats all over both road and verge, around here. No cows or traffic or even a bicycle on the road ahead though, nothing to stop this bastard passing.

Two more toots: and he seemed to be holding his distance behind her. *One of those*, she thought, as finally whatever it was did begin to close up and pass – but overhauling her very slowly, well out in the road.

It was a van – dirty-white *gazo* with *MV Poissonnier* in blue lettering on its side, and came as a complete surprise, she'd effectively written Marc off by this time. But the man himself – dark-haired, long-faced individual in an overcoat with its collar turned up, no hat, spectacles that caught the light, was leaning across with a hand raised to her as he crawled by. She'd taken that much in before he speeded up and half a minute later pulled into a farm gateway forty or fifty metres ahead there.

No doubt who *he* was, but how he could be so sure that this was her or that at the crossroads she'd have turned right? Well, the general intention had been to head east, of course. She'd stopped pedalling, was freewheeling up to where he was now standing watching her approach: shabby old French army greatcoat open and his hands on his hips.

Cowpats everywhere around the gateway. Around *him*.

Some of them looked recent. This morning's, no doubt, after milking.

'Madame Treniard?'

She dismounted, being careful about where she put her feet, and he was opening the van's rear doors. Tallish, broad-shouldered, eyes small-looking behind the wire-framed glasses when he looked round at her. A gesture: 'I'll put the bike in, all right?'

Paris accent, and not from any of the smarter arrondisse-ments.

'What happened to you?'

'I'm sorry – very *very* sorry –'

'Three o'clock, heaven's sake!'

'I know. I'll explain. Truly am *desolated* to have let you down, but – first let's get on the move, please? D'you want these articles off the bike?'

Hatbox, coat and attaché case: she shook her head. 'Sooner leave it as it is.' Then: 'Oh, my coat, I'd better have.' For the rest of it, when they stopped and she parted company with him she'd be taking the bike as well as her gear with her, wasn't going to risk being left bloody stranded. Once bitten, twice shy. Even though in momentary close-up with him it did look like genuine contrition. Damn well *should* be too: although she guessed he might have had some kind of acci-dent. He pushed the bike up into the van, climbed in after it, settling it carefully and moving stuff – boxes, an aroma indicating that they contained or had contained fish – to wedge it in, one under the upturned front wheel for instance. Testing to ensure it stayed put: now restowing other stuff, and backing out.

He looked as if he might not have slept for a week. Close-cropped dark hair, dark complexion, and he hadn't shaved this morning. He'd slammed the rear doors and was locking them. There was still nothing else on the road then, but by the time she'd put her coat on and reached the passenger door there was a lorry coming up from a few hundred metres behind. Marc getting in but then just sitting with his eyes on the rear mirror, waiting for it to pass. He hadn't switched off the van's engine; maybe with a *gazo* one didn't, for short stops. Lorry passing now, Marc for some reason signalling with a thumbs-up gesture to its driver: then he had the van in gear and was edging out.

'I'll explain in a minute, but the first thing is if we're questioned what to say of ourselves. You were stopped at the roadside and I offered you a lift?'

'Why not the puncture story? While you were fixing it you asked me where I was going and it happened to be on your own route?'

'Which town or village would you have named? Might Mazamet do? That's just beyond Aussilon.' Shake of the head. 'No – I'm being stupid, somewhere much further . . . For instance there's a sizeable village, St-Pons-de-Thomières, which is near enough equidistant from Carcassonne, Narbonne and Béziers –'

'St-Pons would do. My story is I'm hoping to find my former aunt-in-law, and that could be where I'm almost sure she's living – or was when I last heard.'

'That's it, then. From here about the same distance – fifty kilometres, maybe a bit less. Still too near, maybe?'

'High ground?'

'Oh, high enough. And it's a road junction, from there we could turn north, north-east, east, south-east . . . South-east might be the best, and it's the road for Béziers, where incidentally I have customers.'

'Make Béziers our destination, then.' As with Montpellier, which she'd had in mind earlier, it was large enough for the old aunt to have inhabited at some earlier stage and left no abiding memories. She told him, 'If on that road there's some-

110

where that looks good for me to drop off, you could go on into Béziers and pick me up on your way back – at first light maybe.'

'Find you on the roadside with your famous puncture?'

'Why not – and in Béziers you might find us some food.'

'Difficult. Times of stores opening and one's need to be on the road as early as curfew permits. Besides, rationing's no help.' A shrug. 'I'm glad to say I have our supper on board in any case. Courtesy of Jean Samblat, a chicken and some wine, bread that'll be stale.'

'Well . . .' They were passing three boys on bicycles, who waved to them: she waved back, feeling better for knowing of Jake's provisions. 'Won't starve, anyway. How kind of him. That did have me a little worried.' She suggested almost humorously, 'Let's hear the excuses now?'

He nodded. 'Yes.' Gesture of helplessness. 'The cause, in a single word, was charcoal. A lack of it. The fuel a *gazo* runs on? Before, this van used petrol and it was much, much better. But – see, I make use of an old house in the village of Villerouge-Ségure – down towards Perpignan, a good locality for me. I keep there, always – naturally – a reserve of charcoal. But last night I'm back late and tired, have chores I must do so it's even later when I get to bed, well aware I've some hours of driving to make our rendezvous mid-afternoon. About a hundred and fifty kilometres, in fact, so an early start with maybe a stop in Carcassonne or Castelnaudary . . . Anyway, I woke later than I'd expected to, and on waking, before shaving or even getting myself some coffee, I've remembered the motor needs to be refuelled. I'd been too tired, last night, also it's easier in daylight. I went straight out to do it – why wash and *then* get dirty – and found the shed had been broken into, they'd smashed the padlock and helped themselves – all my charcoal gone, huh?

111

Sunday morning, and no merchant nearer than Tuchan, which is all of twelve kilometres!'

'No one in your village you could have borrowed some from?'

'Not any at Tuchan either, the guy's place was empty and locked up, and a neighbour tells me he's taken his wife and children to – oh, God knows, but now I have a twelve-kilometre ride back, and *then* what? Well, there's a farmer not so far from my village – other side of it, and this is another hour gone, mind you, that I'm back in Villerouge – well, happens this farmer owes me, a favour I did him, and if he'd let me borrow a sackful it would get me to a place called St-Martin-des-Puits where the gravedigger keeps it as a sideline. But the farmer is not there. His wife says sure he'd help me out, but that barn's locked and he has the key with him . . . There's more to this yet, does it bore you?'

'No. Go on.'

'Well, the wife says he'll be back in an hour, might there not be enough left over in my van's burner to bring it just this far, have it here when her husband returns. See, when you stop a *gazo* the stuff's still burning, you cut down the draught and so forth but after a while there's less than when you stopped. So – seemed to me perhaps worth trying, if it came off I might just about get to you by three.'

'It didn't come off.'

'You're right. Got halfway, and – on *foot* then back to the farm . . .'

'Quite a morning, you had.'

'I am truly, *truly* sorry . . .'

Slowing, for an old crone and a dog herding a dozen ewes. Rosie telling him, 'I'll forgive you, Marc.'

'Mean it?' Face lighting up, as he passed the huddle of sheep and put his foot down. 'Truly?'

'For the rotten day you've had.' Checking the time; and

to her own surprise quite liking him. 'All we've lost is an hour and a half. What will you do about your charcoal store?'

'Put a new lock on it, obviously. I'll see what else. Also talk to our *sergeant de ville* – that's the best solution, catch the swine.' Looking at her, his eyes examining her features. 'You're kind as well as very pretty. Call you Suzette, may I?'

'That's supposed to be my name. Although Jake calls me Suzie. He's a nice man, isn't he?'

'He's OK. Yeah. Good Organiser as well. You've been here just two days, am I right?'

A shrug. 'Feels longer, somehow.'

'Well, you've had a hard day too – long ride from Toulouse, then left in the lurch. Jake found you some place to live, I suppose?'

'As you say, he's a good Organiser.'

'A *planque* in Toulouse?'

She glanced at him. 'If you needed to get in touch, you'd do it through him, huh?'

'By the sound of it, I suppose I'd have to.' He smiled slightly, studying her as if she puzzled him. 'Perhaps I shouldn't have told you where *I* live.'

'I gather you have several addresses.'

'In a way, that's true. At any rate, places I can use. But one other personal question, Suzie?'

Shaved and spruced up a bit and without the pebble-glasses, she thought, he might be quite good-looking. A bit 'flash' maybe. Jake's 'bit of a Don Juan', she remembered. But hardly that: although he might see *himself* that way. She'd cocked an eyebrow: 'Well?'

'Are you by origin French, or English?'

'My father was French. In France I *feel* French. But technically I'm English.'

'Mother English, father deceased? You said *was* French.'

'Yes, exactly.'

113

'I would have guessed you were French entirely. There's no trace of any English accent.'

'Suzette Treniard *is* plain French, that's all that matters. What's this village now?'

'It's called Pont-Crozet.' Taking a sharp left turn into what became a short main street with a few closed shops and a donkey drooping sadly in the shafts of a milk-cart, but no human beings in sight. Main road swinging right now. Marc added, 'Next comes Sorèze, then St-Amancat. Do you expect to be making many trips of this kind?'

'Can't really tell, can one. See how it goes.'

'Depending on how frequently you have to talk to London, you mean.' She didn't answer, and he went on, 'There's a *parachutage* to finalise, of course – or two *parachutages*, I think Jake said at one point?'

'No idea. This trip I have a jumble of code to fire off, that's all.'

'Are you an experienced pianist?'

'Been at it a while. Why d'you ask?'

'I had the impression – something Jake said, it must have been – that this might be your first deployment.'

'Never mind – I'm a *very* experienced pianist.'

'Well, good. Tonight, as well as sending whatever Jake's given you, I imagine you'll have London's material to receive.'

'*If* they have any for me – of course.'

'A date and coordinates for the *parachutage*, for one thing, and the so-called *message personnel* that's to be listened for – that at least, but I'd guess that after so long there'd be some backlog.'

She looked at him with an eyebrow raised. 'You could be right, Marc.'

'Oh. You think I'm over-curious?'

'That "one other personal question" has stretched a bit, hasn't it?'

114

'Apologies. But how much you'll be sending and/or receiving must affect how long I should leave you to it, or expect to wait. Unless you really want to be on your own all night, as you proposed.'

'I do think piano-playing's best done solo. In this case on the Béziers road somewhere, and we can decide in advance on a pick-up point?'

'As you like, of course.'

Actually, she hardly knew why. Did have this inclination to work on her own, but that was about all she could say about it. Just as she'd always envisaged doing it, maybe, when in the field. Marc smiling: 'Don't you think you might wish you had a nice warm van to climb into, when you're through?'

'Might, but – I'll be all right.'

'Well, please make sure you are. You know your business and the dangers. I'd shoot myself if I lost you like Alain Déclan lost St Droix.'

'Surely that was no more Déclan's fault than it would be yours.'

'Perhaps not. But he *felt* as if it had been. So would I. Circumstances really quite similar. And from an entirely practical angle, now we do have our own pianist again – especially with so much pending, this *parachutage* or maybe two of them, and then what they're calling "Hardball"?'

'Hardball?'

'Jake not briefed you on that?'

'I never heard of it.'

'I'd thought he would have and you might let me in on it. It's a special operation of some kind, that's all I know. When we were without a pianist, see, Déclan and I took turns visiting Lyon, where an American agent was handling stuff Jake coded and decoded, he felt we didn't have to know what it was about. He's like that, you'll find. But as it happened I and "Germaine", the American woman, knew each other from before – *she*'d put me in touch with Jake, in fact – and she mentioned Operation Hardball to me on one of those visits. Then caught on that I'd never heard of it and clammed up tight. Hell, Suzie, when it's something unusual and exciting we've got ahead of us, one *is* curious! Aren't *you* now?'

'I suppose – mildly so. If it's still on. When was this – a couple of weeks ago, or more?'

A shrug, wag of the head. 'I suppose . . .'

'Might have been abandoned, then.'

'Might, might not.' Glancing at her irritably. A hand off the wheel then, pointing ahead: 'Here's Sorèze now . . .'

In the restaurant in Rue Bayard – the Colombier – Rosie said she'd realised that young Marc Voreux, while twenty-two years of age to her own twenty-four and actually *looking* nearer thirty, was still boyish in his outlook.

'The way he'd said that – "Something *exciting* coming . . ." Expecting me to feel the same and slightly miffed when I didn't. Made me feel like a grown-up with a schoolboy – although we were reasonably well *en rapport* by that time. *Isn't* this steak good!'

'It's terrific. How was your chicken that night?'

She laughed. 'Don't remember. Must have been all right, we ate about half of it, kept the rest for breakfast. Ditto wine. I'd agreed by then that if we found a good place where he could get the van well out of sight I'd just climb a hill or something. He could catch up on his sleep and in the morning we'd set off homeward at first light. It was the simplest way to do it, and we were chummy enough by then. Well, as I said . . .'

'Need a side-road, don't we . . .'

Not far short of dusk, they'd come through St-Pons-de-Thomières, swung south and after a few kilometres east again. Woods climbed steeply on the right, valley floor more extensive on the other side – with wooded hillside behind that too – but no way off the road and no cover if one *did* get off it. Marc having to watch his driving fairly closely meanwhile, as the road was fairly narrow and never anything like straight for long; he was easing up a bit, telling her, 'About twenty kilometres ahead there's a terrific canyon runs down to just above St-Chinian – much lower terrain, all vineyards – start of the coastal plain, in fact.'

'Last thing I want.'

'I know. I'm sorry, I should have forked left instead of right after St-Pons; to aim for Béziers was senseless. Place called Olargues, for instance, on that other road, has much higher – well, mountainous terrain to the north of it. All of thirty kilometres from here though, so if we turned back – be pitch dark damn soon –'

'See *there*, Marc?'

A road-widening operation, by the looks of it. Forest clearance, levelling for some building purpose. Trees had been felled and stacked here and there over an acre or half-acre of bare earth, rock-outcrops and flattened scrub, earth scarred and rutted, pitted where stumps had been dragged out: and beyond the area of devastation, what looked like an opening into the trees where the forest began to climb. Marc had braked and stopped: she jumped out, climbed a bare-earth slope.

No other traffic and no sound of any. This might be not only their one and only hope, but a darned good one. Turning to Marc as he reached her: 'If your van's springs could take it – see, through there? If I scout ahead of you –'

'Let's try it.'

Didn't want to put his headlights on, and with the light failing the sooner they could get in there, into the standing trees at the back of all this, the better. Into that opening, in fact. Not so good at all if he got stuck. She got out a white handkerchief for him to sight on, holding it up while scrambling over the churned-up ground with an eye out for hazards he mightn't otherwise see from inside – van lurching and crashing over terrain it certainly hadn't been built for. But thus far, holding together.

Rosie calling back, 'Easier there, Marc see, *that* side?' Directing him round to the right of a mound of earth beyond which a track *had* been started – a flattening process which then came to nothing as it approached the standing trees.

He'd stopped. Couldn't see much from inside now, she guessed, not unless he did switch on his lights. Dirty windscreen probably not helping much. Moving again though: with his head out of the lowered window: engine grinding, screaming, tyres slipping, she realised, not liking this at all.

Still moving, though . . . But stopped again. Rosie getting herself round to that side. 'Marc –'

'Yeah. Be fine, if I can turn her.'

'Well enough hidden to use the lights?'

'No. I'll back between those. *Those.* Direct me from behind, uh?'

'All right.'

The van was on a scary sideways slant at one stage, very nearly going over – might even have ended up leaning against a tree – but he stuck at it and came out of it all right, was finally pointing back the way they'd come and on a more or less even keel.

'Well *done*, Marc. I thought for a moment –'

'So did I.' He'd switched off. '*Nasty* moment. Well, several.' *Gazo* coughing itself into silence, Marc climbing out. 'Sheer luck – another five minutes, couldn't have done it. Well, with lights, maybe . . .' A hand on her arm then: 'Suzie, listen – if anyone did take interest in us here, tell 'em nothing, just act embarrassed – eh?'

★ ★ ★

The forested hillside took quite a bit of climbing in the dark. There was a glimmer of moon which had first appeared when they'd been eating supper and was visible now sporadically through fast-moving broken cloud, as well as the near-leafless tops of beeches, and that helped but never for long enough. She did have a torch with her, but was saving it for use on the ridge when she got up there. It was a very small torch which her Uncle Bertie Mathieson, her mother's brother, had given her; he was mad keen on night fishing for sea-trout, and the torch was small enough to hold in one's mouth while changing flies or disentangling casts – standing in waders in mid-river in the dark and conversing if at all in whispers. Rosie had done it a few times, and had realised that such a torch was exactly what one needed – especially when receiving, jotting down the coded groups as fast as they came in, while crouched over the set and needing both hands, sometimes even wishing one had a third.

OK – at last. This had to be the crest – ridge – more or less level ground that didn't start sloping up again. That had been the case once, and being somewhat exhausted she'd been tempted to settle for it, gamble on being *near enough* at the top; in fact hadn't been more than halfway, which she'd discovered by making herself struggle on, rather than waste the whole day's efforts on a signal that mightn't be strong enough for them to hear. 'Them' in practice meaning her specially allocated wireless operator to whom her call would go as a result of her having inserted her own night-time crystal in the set – doing so in the van at the same time as transferring the various components including battery to Berthe Devrèque's attaché case.

Setting it down on a bed of fallen leaves – and glad to – and extracting the coil of aerial wire – seventy feet of it – which she'd now rig up between trees. Torch in her mouth even for this, and markers – white bandage – on the first and last of them. If you lost track of the wire you really *would* have lost it – it was not only about as thin as a wire could be, but coloured black so it could be slung from a high window without much danger of it being spotted.

With the aerial strung out now, back to the set, check connections and plug in to the battery. Headphones on: no longer hearing the wind in the trees or the rustle of dead leaves around her. Torch in hand, and the page of cypher in a spring-clip in the lid of the attaché case. Switch on, with the transmitter/receiver switch to 'Send'. Little red pinpoint glowing. Torch in mouth: two fingers and a thumb settling comfortably around the key's Bakelite knob, and beginning to send A's – tap-*tap*, tap-*tap* . . . Knowing from her own experience how startled the operator in Sevenoaks would be, after long hours of listening-out with no certainty of anything *ever* coming through, heart really jumping at the first bleeps and the sight of the quivering needle, excitement simmering as she minutely adjusted her own set's megacycles to it and gave Rosie when she paused and switched from 'Send' to 'Receive' a code-group signifying *Receiving you strength* (whatever), *send your message, over* . . .

Done. She'd sent her stuff, had it acknowledged, then taken in the screed from Baker Street which would be likely to contain answers to some of the questions she'd put to them – date of the *parachutage*, for instance, and detail of Stage One of Hardball, i.e. likely date of arrival of the commandos and whether by paradrop or beach landing. Thinking about this, also that her own request for two spare transceivers to be included in this next drop might be answered when she started her listening-watch in Berthe's attic this next night. She'd told them she'd be listening-out on Mondays, Wednesdays and Fridays from 2300 to 0100 CET – Central European Time.

Headphones off: wind's rush and rattle in the trees. Traffic sound too, though: single vehicle, she guessed. Petrol engine, and from the direction of St-Pons. Close – and rather dawdling?

Passing down there now, she guessed, moving to recover the aerial wire. Slightly longer job than stringing it up, as it had to be wound evenly around its reel; unwinding it, the reel span, did the job for you. Moving from tree to tree now, winding. No moon at present, but didn't need the torch either, simply followed the wire, winding it. Hearing that engine sound fade, and thinking maybe it had picked up speed. Not that it could have anything to do with her and Marc or the transmission: couldn't possibly be, that sense of alarm had been only the way one's nerves reacted. The RHSA – *Reichssicherheitshauptamt*, the Nazis' central intelligence organisation – had a very elaborate radio-detection and direction-finding set-up in Paris; they'd get a bearing on you at long range pretty well as soon as you went on the air, but unless they had one or more of their detector vans actually standing by in the more or less immediate area they'd have no cross-bearing, therefore no fix, not even an approximate one.

They'd have all that on tape, of course. They had a whole battery of recorders, apparently, which were triggered by the first bleep of a transmission. What they couldn't do – touch wood – was break the cypher, especially the one-time-pad variety.

Could have had a van standing by, she supposed. If they'd felt they had reason to – for instance if they'd been desperate to catch any successor to old Wiggy suddenly giving tongue?

Last few feet of the wire. That vehicle had passed out of earshot – in the direction of St-Chinian, i.e. away St-Pons and Toulouse. It annoyed her that she was even thinking about it. If the Boches were on the qui vive to catch a new pianist's first efforts they'd concentrate on the centre, surely, not some remote area such as this.

Forget it. Bear it in mind this next night in the Place Marengo. They *might* have a detector van or two in Toulouse by now.

7

There wasn't a lot of sleep, the rest of that night. When she got down from the ridge Marc climbed out and opened a rear door, stowed the attaché case in there while she got in up front. The cabin was blue with smoke: seemed he'd been at it more or less continuously while she'd been up there. He'd heard that car of course and seen its lights; it had crept past, he'd thought it was going to stop, had been preparing a story that left her out of it: as far as she remembered, that he'd been making for Béziers where a customer whom he could name would have put him up if he'd got there earlier, but he'd been delayed somehow and realised that he'd be infringing curfew. He hadn't been at all happy with this, since it didn't explain the bicycle or the hatbox with girlie stuff in it, or why he'd gone to such lengths to get his van this far off the road.

'Why should whoever it was go to the lengths of finding you – let alone questioning or searching?'

'I don't know.' Pulling his door shut. 'But I'd dropped off, and – anyway, it *didn't* stop.' Getting his Gitanes out again. 'Smoke?'

'Well, why not.' Deserving one, she felt, after that climb. Coming down hadn't been much easier than getting up there had been. Then she'd had another thought – to take the transceiver apart again, redistribute its components as she'd had them before, so as to be ready for an early start. Marc had pointed out that she could just as well do this when there was a bit of daylight and he'd be refuelling; he had charcoal in a large sailcloth container in the back. Anyway she'd preferred to do it right away, for one thing to have the transceiver less easily recognisable as what it was – which she'd explained to him, then gone to do it, and was crouched in the cargo-space with the torch in her mouth again when she heard the car returning.

Heard *a* car anyway – approaching from the direction of St-Chinian and Béziers. Coming at a normal speed, she thought – and by the sound of it a petrol engine. No reason to think of it at that stage as *the* car, but still hurrying now, especially with dismantling the transceiver and getting its parts out of sight. Using the torch was OK even, with the van facing the road and a solid partition between her and its cab.

It was slowing, was either going to stop or creep past at walking pace again. One could assume now therefore that it *was* the same vehicle: listening to it and thinking of Marc and his state of nerves – need of nicotine no doubt increasing even further, when she realized that it *had* stopped.

He obviously had been in a state, during her absence. It had come as a surprise, disappointed her, rather. Although she thought the best answer to their situation as it looked right now was probably what he'd suggested a few hours ago – say nothing, act embarrassed, let whoever it was conclude that they had come here for immoral purposes. Even if it turned out to be police of some kind, let them think that.

Crouching, listening for movement, footsteps, voices. If voices, try to catch what *language* . . .

Thump of a car door slamming shut. Then its engine revving. First reaction – considerable relief: then more guardedly, could be they were settling in, getting *their* car off the road . . . But no: definitely were leaving. Stopped for a look – or for a pee, timing would have been about right for that . . .

Might have been some kind of patrol – gendarmerie, or worse. Having had some reason to be interested in this place on their way east, and now on the way back stopped for another look. For whatever reason – which was hard to guess at. Anyway she'd done her packing; she slid out, shut the rear doors carefully, and back in the cab, found Marc – believe it or not – lighting yet another cigarette. Asking her with his head low and the match cupped between his palms, its flare suddenly dazzling in those thick lenses, 'Want one?'

'No. Marc, I suppose that was the same car as before. It must have been, mustn't it? Any case all that matters is—' Checking as her left hand encountered cold metal – on the seat: 'What have we here, then?'

Pistol – in fact the distinctive shape of a Luger. Although they were no longer standard issue to the German military there were a lot of them about. He'd taken it, transferred it to a pocket of his greatcoat.

'Going into action, were we?'

'I'd pushed it down between the seat and the backrest. What you were saying – must've been the same car – yes. Although what they were doing –'

'Stopped for a pee, was my guess.'

'Could be right, at that. But this gun – no, I wasn't going to use it, only (a) have it where I could get at it if I needed it, (b) where it wouldn't be found on me if I happened to be searched.'

'Expecting the worst, then. Although how they could have had anything to do with us –'

'Not *expecting*, no. For that very reason. Only if one does have a gun –'

'I don't. By choice. I was given the option – and trained in their use of course, but – by and large, sooner not.'

'Could be wise. On the other hand, circumstances could arise when you'd wish you'd had one.'

'Well – with your escape-line, you've had more experience in the field than I have, but as you just said, if one did happen to be searched –'

'I know. It's debatable.'

'Have you ever actually used yours?'

'No – as it happens . . .'

'Mightn't be around now if you had. After all, it's the enemy that has the fire-power, isn't it – when it comes down to it?'

'Yeah. Well . . .'

Silence then: five, ten minutes, during which time he got rid of his cigarette and almost immediately lit another.

'Oh – I'm sorry, should've –'

'Thanks, but I wouldn't have wanted one. Any case I have my own.'

'I smoke too much, I know.'

She hadn't noticed that he did, until that car's appearance, but she let it go. Thinking about the return to Toulouse and seeing Jake, decyphering whatever Baker Street had sent them, and this now being Monday, listening-out from 11 p.m. to 1 a.m. in Berthe's attic. With any luck they'd come through soon after eleven so she could shut down then and get some sleep.

She broke this silence, with 'In the morning you might take me a few kilometres beyond Revel, save my poor legs.'

'Take you to your door, if you like.'

'No need for that – thanks all the same. Will you be going back to where they stole the charcoal?'

'See to that and a few other things, then on down to the coast for fish.'

'Near Perpignan somewhere?'

'Beach-launched boats all along that stretch, yes. But I could easily take you all the way into town, Suzie – it'd get you there sooner to get on with your decoding.'

'Don't worry about that.'

'What about the poor legs you mentioned?'

'Not about them either. They'll have had a good rest by then.'

'You don't want me to know where you're living.'

'That's true, I don't. But you see, it's the same reciprocally, *I* don't want to know anything I don't need to.'

'On Jake's advice, is that?'

'No. Entirely my own philosophy. Or – self-doubt, call it.'

'It's very much Jake's line. I don't even know where *he* hangs out – or what his cover is. Businessman of some sort, that's all. Not that I give a damn . . . How d'you mean, self-doubt?'

'Well – the thought of Gestapo-type interrogation. Torture. How I'd face up to it. Whether I *could*. Especially the principle of holding out for forty-eight hours. And my point – personal, nothing to do with Jake – is that what one doesn't know one can't betray.'

'Betray.' If he'd been looking at her he'd turned awa;, she'd seen or sensed the movement as a reflex – the shift of his cigarette, and that hand moving to the wheel. Repeating the word – in French, the language they were using – '*Trahir*.' A sigh then; she followed up with 'Forty-eight hours is what our people *expect*, you know. Not just hope for, regard as – well, the very least.'

'Think about such things much, do you?'

'Don't *you*?'

'I've always tried not to. If it happens it happens, better to think of ways of ensuring it doesn't.'

'Well — I dare say that makes a lot of sense. If one could do it. Thanks, I'll try. Might be a very good tip . . . I'll come clean with you, Marc, the self-doubt's because I'm new to this, it's something I never *had* to think about before, and — well, suddenly there it is.'

'Despite being such an experienced pianist?'

'Radio operator. In England. Other end of the line, like the one I was talking with tonight.'

'Ah, well.' A last drag at the glowing stub, then opening the window, no doubt pinching it out before dropping it. Window up again. 'As to the other thing — interrogation, torture — SOE issue you with suicide pills, don't they?'

'Yes. Don't BCRA?'

'No. Didn't when I started. Could you get me one?'

'I don't know how. I could ask, but — why don't you ask Jean?'

'Working with SOE as I am, I'd have thought they'd —'

'Maybe they would, too. Ask Jean, he's the boss.'

'But you're my partner —'

'I doubt we'll be making many of these trips together, frankly. It was Jake's idea, but I think it's better to move around quite independently.'

'And the piano-playing?'

'Keep it in cycling distance, that's all.'

'Any particular reason?'

'Save time, mainly — a few hours instead of a day and a half. Probably more secure too, in some ways. Another thing is I've asked London for spare radios that I could set up in different locations.'

'So as not to have one with you on the bike.'

'Exactly. Except when moving them to new places.'

'Are you expecting them in this next *parachutage*?'

'That's what I've asked for.'

'The dropping-ground near Montbrun-Bocage, that's to be.'

'Are you asking me or telling me?'

'Telling you – if you didn't already know.'

'Where *is* Montbrun-Bocage?'

'About – oh, a hundred kilometres due south of Toulouse. But this one was set up some little while ago, then postponed. It's a couple of kilometres from Montbrun, a field we've used before. Déclan mentioned it the other day – it's in his territory, you might say, not likely they'll need my help.'

'I thought he went pretty well all over.'

'He does. But last time they made use of it for a Maquis band not far from Carcassonne, which was a very long haul and I helped with it.'

'So where's the Maquis who'll be getting this next lot?'

'I don't know. Somewhere closer to it, I imagine.'

'Well, well . . . Marc, I'm going to open this window, just for a minute.'

'All right.'

'Clear the air a bit. Might try to sleep then.'

Rosie told me in our restaurant, 'Must have managed a few hours, I suppose. I do remember that dawn, the sky silvering over the Cevennes and wine for breakfast, then Marc tipping charcoal into his van's burner and me getting my stuff back on the bike. Well, to be accurate, don't recall actually doing it, but I know I did – to have it ready for when we stopped somewhere short of Toulouse where I'd take off. But he'd talked in his sleep. I think that's the memory that sticks – the rest sort of clings around it. He said – more like shouted, as I remember it – "Oh, Denise, Denise, what*ever* the *salauds* want –" and a moment later, "Christ almighty, if one could even *trust* the pigs!"'

She'd just murmured this. Just as well – the place was full, it might have attracted embarrassing attention. She added, still *sotto voce*, 'Waking then, he actually moaned – loud, despairing. I didn't react, pretended I was still flat out, didn't mention it during the drive back either, but it stayed with me. OK, just nightmare, but a high degree of reality about it – frightening just to *hear*, for some reason. Partly because it seemed rather starkly to contradict what he'd said about not thinking of – well, what that had sounded like.' She smothered a yawn. 'We ought to be getting along quite soon – d'you think?'

I considered that, and came up with 'How about a kümmel, for the road?'

'Oh, *isn't* that a beaut of an idea!'

It had been her favourite liqueur, apparently, and so long since she'd had any that she'd almost forgotten its existence. Suggesting ungratefully though, after I'd sent for some, 'Just to keep me gassing, eh?'

'Not a bit of it. Prolonging the enjoyment of your company, Rosie. And the night's still *fairly* young.'

'Even if we *aren't*. Well, who cares.' A smile, shake of the head. 'But I really *must* cut a corner or two from here on. Tomorrow being our last full day. Mind you, with no functions I need to attend, we can spend the whole day at it.' A flutter of eyelashes: 'As the actress said to the bishop . . .'

Jake enquired, limping after her from Berthe's front door to the sitting-room, 'Did *you* get any lunch?'

Because she'd asked him if he'd like tea – this was mid-afternoon – and he'd said no, he'd come straight from a rather long, late lunch with Mahossier, Jorisse clients, which was why he was later than he'd meant to be. She'd told him

130

before this that she'd done the deciphering, encountering no problems, had it upstairs, would get it; answering the lunch question now though: 'Onion soup and cheese in a café on my way into town. Marc dropped me at a place called Labastide-Beauvoir, which gave me about twenty kilometres to pedal, and he turned down towards – well, Castelnaudary eventually, *en route* to whatever that village of his is called.'

'Villerouge-Ségure. Did you get on with him all right?'

'Oh, yes. A bit jumpy though, isn't he?'

'Marc, jumpy?'

She told him briefly about the spooky car, Marc's subsequent chain-smoking, and the Luger, adding that they'd concluded the car – or patrol – could hardly have had anything to do with them.

'Right. How could it . . . Unless – oh, if you'd passed it in one of the villages and they'd recognised the van, thought they'd see what he was up to. Pretty girl with him they hadn't seen before? The local gendarmes all know him: to them he's a *gars* – bit of a lad.' Jake nodded. 'That could have been it. If they'd tailed along keeping well back, maybe got as far as Béziers then realised they'd lost you, thought your clearing was the sort of place he'd make use of?'

'For what?'

'Well – guess.'

'That was going to be our act if we needed one. *His* idea, I may say. But if that had been it – tailing us, lost us, coming back – gone to that much effort, they'd have searched around and found us, surely.'

'Van was so well hidden, accepted they'd drawn a blank, gave up? But – Suzie, Baker Street's latest?'

'I'll get it.' From upstairs where she had it all – one-time pads, the transceiver itself and its separately-wrapped crystals

131

– under loose floorboards in the attic. Telling Jake over her shoulder as she left, '*Parachutage* Thursday – day after tomorrow.'

'Crikey, *that* soon?'

She came back down with the single page torn from her notebook; skimming through it, he muttered the salient points aloud . . . 'Thursday November 19th, ETA on coordinates as arranged, 2300/2330. Containers 8, of which 5 for Printemps, 3 for Charpentier, marked respectively P and C, recognition signal likewise PC.' He shrugged: 'At least taking care of both in one drop. It'll be a Lancaster, of course – round trip's about a thousand miles.'

'Those are Maquis code-names, are they?'

'Just for this operation – the drop and then Hardball, in which they'll both be taking part. "Printemps" being the maquis de St-Girons, leader by name of Emile Fernier, and "Charpentier" the bunch at Montgazin. Actually St-Sulpice-sur-Lèze, *near* Montgazin, which is only spitting distance from the target. Leader's Michel Loubert, ex Foreign Legion. Hang on though.' Eyes down again . . . 'BBC message to be "Véronique dances like an angel". And Hardball Stage One provisionally between 28th and 30th, confirmation by the 27th, Le Barcarès or St-Pierre, team of 5 plus 3 BCRA agents for on-routing to Marseille.' A shrug: 'Feluccas still at work, then.'

'But no time for the training programme you had hopes for.'

'No. But there *are* experienced men among them. Loubert for instance exceptionally so. They'll be all right.' He'd crossed his fingers. 'And finally – oh, here I detect the cheering tones of Buck!'

The last item, which he was attributing to Maurice Buckmaster, head of 'F' Section SOE, read: 'For info of you all, churchbells are ringing throughout Britain today Sunday in celebration of victory by Eighth Army at El Alamein. Lovely sound, wish you could hear it.' Jake handed her back the signal. 'Old Buck's a charmer, isn't he. D'you know much about Maquis in general, Suzie?'

'Only that they live in the woods and kill Germans when they get the chance.'

'Well, I'll give you a run-down on it later. Immediate priority is to get hold of Déclan. He'll have his work cut out now – visiting those two, also the farmer whose land the drop's to be on. He's a good man and we've used his place before.'

'At Montbrun-Bocage?'

'How on earth –'

'Marc mentioned it. Déclan told him – that he, Marc, wasn't likely to be concerned in it, as he *was* apparently on some previous occasion.'

'Well.' Thinking about it for a moment. 'Yes, he was. And since he knew you'd have to know about it –'

'No harm done.'

'Although Déclan would have done better to keep his trap shut. Anyway, I must call him. You should know about this too. A tobacconist he's in daily contact with, I call and ask whether he has any of his own rather special tobacco-mix in stock, Déclan gets the message and we foregather. I'll give you details of that procedure too.'

Wry smile. 'In case I ever need it.'

'Exactly, Suzie.'

'Will you make the call from here?'

'Heavens, no. Public box. Station'll be the handiest. Be back in twenty or thirty minutes, OK?'

Old Rosie said, having refused a second tot of kümmel, 'In some areas memory doesn't fail, it's non-existent. So it's odd how one does recall a lot of names. People, villages, whatever.

Couldn't be because one memorised them sixty years ago – d'you think?'

'Extraordinary, but how else? Locked in there. Wouldn't last five minutes in *my* memory.' Which was why I'd been jotting them down in my notebook – St-Girons, Montgazin, St-Sulpice. Names of Maquis leaders didn't matter, for the fiction I'd invent some, but the villages had to make sense – distances between them, and so forth. Rosie was saying as I put the notebook away, 'I'd guess you'll want to jump a couple of days now. I mean with the story – jump to the 19th and me on my bike heading for a rendezvous with Alain Déclan?'

'To attend the *parachutage*?'

'Well, yes. Oh, haven't mentioned this yet, but listening-out that night – aerial wire dangling from the attic window and the set plugged into the mains – actually into a light-socket, so I was working in the dark again –'

She'd paused while I glanced at the bill and gave the man a credit card; then went on, 'Sevenoaks came through within minutes of my setting up shop, notifying me when translated into plain language that my spare sets and batteries had been ordered for inclusion in Thursday's drop, in a container of their own marked L for Lucy. And you're right, this meant I'd have to get there myself, since Déclan would have his hands full ensuring that each Maquis got the goodies it was entitled to, with no poaching, and that whatever transport had been organised was loaded accordingly, and nothing left behind, so forth. Well, you can bet that any of 'em'd pinch my transceivers, given half a chance. Wouldn't know how to use 'em but that'd make no odds, they were after anything they could get. Can't use it, find a market for it. Most of the bands lived to some extent from pilfering, even robbing the odd bank. Not on their own doorsteps, tended to go foraging elsewhere. They had supporters – suppliers – priests, local farmers and others who contributed either goods or cash – church collections, local whip-rounds, and here and there some baron organising behind the scenes. All set, are we?'

We were. Had only to get into our coats and find a taxi, which might best be done on the boulevard. Heading that way along Rue Bayard with her arm hooked into mine, Rosie rattled on about the Maquis, how since the German invasion of what had been unoccupied France their numbers had been swollen by new people, in some cases even whole families. Hardcore members were escapers and evaders, Jews on the run from *rafles* – round-ups – and young men avoiding compulsory labour service – STO – which had been set up that summer by Laval. Those were known as *réfractaires*. Some of the bands were in fact becoming over-large, the ideal strength for active Resistance purposes being no more than fifteen men, under leaders who ranked militarily as lieutenants. In that shape, in times of emergency – army sweeps, for instance, for which the Boches tended to use their imported Cossacks, oddly enough – they could shift camp swiftly, usually to another forest hideout ten or more kilometres away. Whereas cluttered-up with what might best be called camp-followers –

'Not so good. But –' I gently disengaged my arm from hers, needing it to wave with – 'we're in luck, Rosie, here's a taxi.'

8

She'd crossed the Garonne by way of the St-Pierre bridge and at the first intersection thereafter got herself on to the road for Tournefeuille and Plaisance-du-Touch, which was as far as she'd be going by bicycle. As long as Déclan came up to scratch and no one had pinched *his* charcoal. Meeting her there wasn't going to be much of an effort for him anyway, Plaisance-du-Touch being only about six kilometres from Leguevin where he and his wife lived. Destination then the dropping-ground on François Legrand's farm near Montbrun-Bocage, which if she'd been making the trip on her own would have meant four or five hours of pedalling.

Grey day, cold, wind from the north with low cloud and intervals of drizzle. She wondered how it would be for the Lancaster tonight, on its thousand-mile round-trip from Tempsford. A low ceiling wouldn't exactly help with navigation, which obviously had to be pinpoint accurate while also flying high enough to avoid detection from the ground, then ground defences and Luftwaffe night-fighters. Fingers crossed: and they might as well stay crossed all day, you'd get no answer until 7 p.m. when the BBC would either come up with a reference to Véronique's dancing or they wouldn't. A mention at seven would be the signal to stand by, and a repetition at nine would clinch it – Lanc on its way. Alternatively, if no mention of Véronique – Lanc not coming, drop postponed. To be laid on again presumably when conditions allowed. Which would mean a lot of hanging around, listening-out and so forth, might also lead to the postponement of Hardball. In which event you'd be facing two new uncertainties – one, in the interval Herr Ulrich von Schleben might have been shipped east, and two, the feluccas might have gone out of business. They were expecting to be still on the go at the end of the month – 28th/30th – but that might contain an element of wishful thinking, they couldn't *know* they would be. As Jake had said last night, you had Germans on this coast now, and Germans tended to throw their weight about. He was instructing Marc to make discreet enquiries among his fishermen friends for news or rumours of new lookout posts or Boche takeovers of existing ones, or of offshore patrols by naval vessels, army posts on the dunes, whatever.

Longish uphill stretch here. Leaning into it, legs pumping hard. There'd soon be a right fork for Tournefeuille, and from there about six kilometres to Plaisance. She guessed that if Marc came up with news of that kind, Jake would have her pass it double-quick to Baker Street and from there it would go to whoever organised felucca operations out of Gib. And if the coast did become unusable, the commandos would have to be parachuted in. She'd asked Jake why did he imagine they were being sent in by sea, wouldn't it be simpler and quicker to have them dropped in – maybe closer to their target, at that – and his guess had been that the three BCRA agents accompanying them could have been lined up for delivery by felucca, a beach-landing would have been laid on for them anyway – if that suited their purposes and/or destinations – so why not make use of it for the commando team as well? Especially if he was correct in his belief that the Special Duties Squadron still didn't have many Lancasters permanently allocated to it. A drop at this range couldn't be made by anything but a Lanc, so – from the planners' point of view, economy of *those* efforts, it would make sense.

She definitely liked Jake. Liked his quiet, effective but totally un-bossy manner.

Right fork coming up ahead; the going was easier now, in fact slightly downhill. But as passing traffic cleared away ahead of her, most of it continuing on the road she was on now, she caught sight of a black gendarmerie van parked just around that wide corner on the right-hand side: and – Christ – what *might* be a Citroen Light 15 beyond it. Gendarmes – three of them, in rain capes – were pulling a red-and-white striped pole out from the van's rear – presumably to set up a checkpoint – but meanwhile allowing a lorry to pass, swinging out around them, one of the three waving it on; and a civilian – raincoat, pork pie hat – had got out of the car. Tubby-looking, middle-aged, standing with his hands in the coat's pockets, pale clean-shaven face screwed-up against the rain. The car was a Peugeot, not a Citroen. Proving nothing, she'd simply noted this, thinking at the same time *French, not German* – reason unspecifiable, just her instant, off-the-cuff impression – anyway he'd retired into the van's shelter. Rosie covering these last few metres more slowly, with her arm out to the right, no other traffic close to her at this moment and none of this lot taking the least notice of her. Despite which, glad she hadn't brought her transceiver with her on this trip, only Berthe's hatbox wrapped in a shiny kitchen tablecloth and containing personal items such as a change of undies, pullover, spare pair of shoes, towel and tooth-brush – all of French origin, naturally. The gendarmes had noticed her and were waiting for her to pass now – two of them with the pole and the third with trestles to support it. It was the other lane they were going to block, traffic coming *this* way. The three of them pausing as she turned out around them and their van – smallish, nondescript female *cycliste* in a damp overcoat with its collar up round her ears, headscarf covering the rest; who'd even think of stopping *her*?

Three, three and a half kilometres beyond Tournefeuille, Plaisance-du-Touch was the usual miscellany of businesses and dwellings huddled around a market square, one side of which was occupied by a church that dwarfed its surround-ings. She had to pass it and turn left down a side-street, then take another left and the garage would be on her right – as it was, an iron-roofed open-fronted barn and a petrol pump with a notice on it saying 'Out of Order', three *gazos* one of which she recognised as Déclan's pick-up, and Déclan himself exactly as she'd last seen him – unshaven and wearing that same peaked cap – raising a hand to her as if in salute. He had a tin mug of coffee or somesuch in the other.

Not bad. It was still ten or twelve minutes before the agreed time of rendezvous. And the rain had stopped – for the moment, anyway.

'Bonjour.'

'Mam'selle . . .'

She told him, nodding down at the bike, 'Front wheel seems to have a wobble, and I've a long, long way to go. If you could possibly –'

'Wouldn't be popular if I did. I'm a customer, like your-self.' Jerk of the head on the short, thick neck. 'Here's the man you want.' Turning to a spindly, grey-headed garagist who was approaching with a mug in *his* hand too. 'Wheel-wobble on the front, Georges. Fix that easy enough, won't you?'

'Not if there's much wrong, I won't. Not today, with this lot, and –' a nod towards the barn, none the less taking the bike from her and up-ending it, giving that wheel a spin. Glancing at her with his eyebrows raised, then doing the same again. 'No wobble I can see.'

'Let's have a squint?'

Georges holding the bike with that wheel off the ground while Déclan examined it. Telling Rosie then, 'He's right. Sound as a bell, Miss.'

'Well, I'd have sworn –'

'Saying you'd some way to go? Where, exactly?'

She grimaced. 'Believe it or not, Tarbes.'

'*Zut, alors* . . . Hundred and fifty kilometres, thereabouts.' Looking at Georges. 'Give *anyone* a bloody wobble.'

Georges sucked at his enamel mug. 'Whyn't you take her, then?'

'To bloody *Tarbes*?'

'Of course not.' She was embarrassed. 'No question of –'

'I could take you as far as – what's the place called – oh, Boulogne-sur-Geste, know where that is?'

'No, but –'

'Be halfway for you, near enough. It's where I turn off from what'd be your route.' A glance at Georges, who advised her, 'Grab it, if I was you.' A gesture towards Déclan. 'He's all right, don't worry. Grab it, mam'selle.'

'I can hardly believe this. D'you really mean it?'

'Glad to have the company. Name's Déclan, Alain Déclan – from Léguevin up the road there. See, room enough for your bike in there – and that box in the cab with you, d'you think?'

★   ★   ★

She asked him when they were back up in the square and tuning west, 'Is there such a place as Boulogne-sur-Geste?'

'Sure, there is — on the way to Tarbes, what's more. Consequently we won't be going anywhere near it. I'll be turning south at St-Foy-de-Peyrolières. Not long after St-Lys. Before that we pass through Fonsorbes, where my wife works in the hospital. Suzie, if we ran into a checkpoint or what have you, what's your story?'

'Visiting or say seeking out an old aunt of my late husband's. Maybe in Foix?'

'You said before, a village in the Cevennes.'

'So I did. Good memory, Alain. Fact is, old Tante Ursule's — well, whichever way I'm going, that's where she might be, or I *think* was when I last heard. I keep thinking this or that place-name rings a bell, but —'

'I'd be intending to drop you off somewhere *en route* to Foix, then.'

She nodded. 'Up to you where, since I don't know the area.'

'When you find this aunt, you might move in with her, I dare say.'

'Well, if she liked the idea. She might. Must be a fair age by now.'

'Which is why you're not in a hurry to find other work, meanwhile.'

'Believable, would you say?'

'*I'd* believe it. This is Fonsorbes coming up now.'

'Should I duck down in case your wife spots me?'

'Won't be passing the hospital, don't worry.'

'Give you a hard time, would she?'

'I'd just lie my head off. Not for the first time either.'

'D'you mean you make a habit of picking up girls?'

'I'm not that daft, Suzie. I'm talking about — well, must've told you, what I live on is installing and fixing up borehole pumps and suchlike, I don't have any other interests and it's important Monique never gets to think I might have.'

'Yes, I understood that.'

'Like what I've been doing the last couple of days for instance.'

'D'you think there *will* be a drop tonight?'

'The weather, you mean.'

Looking out and up at it. 'Although it's better than it was first thing. Do Lancaster drops often get called off?'

'Has been known. Hospital's up there to the right, by the way. Care for a smoke?'

'Well, why not. Use mine, though, it's easier.'

'If you insist. I was going to ask, is your transceiver in that box?'

'Uh-huh.' She struck a match, lit two cigarettes and passed one to him. 'No. But as you know, they're dropping spare sets to me tonight, and I have my crystals with me, so –'

'But no drop, no set.'

'That's one reason I'm hoping it won't be cancelled.'

'Yeah. I understand that. Same as old Wiggy – he had a spare or two. But if they do postpone, must be a threat to Hardball too, eh?'

'D'you know all about Hardball?'

'As much as I need to, here and now. I did some research Jean wanted, then set up a meeting old Michel Loubert was at. Know who he is?'

'Leader of the St-Sulpice Maquis, formerly a *légionnaire*?'

'*Have* done your homework, Suzie. Yeah, he's important to us. Knows his onions, and – see, where that band's located, between Montgazin and St-Sulpice, well, his band couldn't be better placed. He was a sergeant-major in the Legion, saw a lot of service, got his head screwed on, hates Vichy as much as he does the Boche.'

'You said *old* Michel Loubert.'

'Well – maybe not much older than me. Been through it though, by all accounts.'

'He'll be at the drop tonight, will he?'

'At Legrand's farm tonight, sure. Him with two or three others. Emile Fernier's lot – the St-Girons band – is a different kettle of fish, they won't leave home until they hear the first *message personnel*. I've hired a truck for them and their five containers – half a dozen maquisards I'd guess, but they won't start without word of Véronique.'

'Loubert will, though?'

'Has to. Coming on their bikes, so they need to start early. If there's a broadcast at seven they won't hear it, just come *hoping*. Oh, and *we* take 'em home – after the drop or non-drop, as the case may be.'

'You and I do?'

'Yup. In this contrivance, in the back under the tarpaulin. Three containers, three or four of them and their bikes.'

'Four containers in all, then.'

'Ah – yeah. But we might leave yours for Legrand to bury. Maquisards usually bury them – have 'em out of sight's the main thing, and often as not use for storage of weaponry, so forth.'

'We'll have three anyway. Something like twenty kilometres, is it, Montbrun to Montgazin?'

'Bit more than that. But nothing to worry about – I mean, small country lanes, dark night, miles from anywhere anyone ever heard of?'

'I'll take your word for it.'

A glance at her, leaking smoke. 'You can, Suzie. You can.' Frowning at her lingering uncertainty. 'You can *believe* me, damn it!'

'We wouldn't be doing it if you weren't sure, would we?'

143

'Wouldn't be *saying* it if I wasn't. Get along all right with Voreux, did you?'

'Well enough. Yes, fine.'

'Didn't try to sweep you off your feet, then?'

'Not that I noticed.'

A chuckle. 'He wouldn't like to hear *that*.'

'Seemed a perfectly nice young man to me.'

'Well, I'm glad. Jean and I pull his leg a bit much, I dare say.'

'Jean's terrific, isn't he?'

'Knows what he's about, for sure. And he thinks well of you, so – yeah, he's sound, all right . . . Listen, Suzie – I got bread and sausage we can have when we want it – might as well get past St-Foy first, eh? – then when we're over the main road, the 64, I'll be visiting a farm – alibi, reason to've been in the area, see, checking his pump's OK. Might put you under the tarp while I'm there, best have 'em think I'm on my own – OK?'

'Alibi's essential, is it?'

'Desirable, I'd call it. Fact is there's half a dozen farms I could drop in on, any of 'em I'd have had good reason to. And nothing *else* I'm there for.'

'Have you ever actually needed that kind of alibi?'

'No, but always made sure I *would* have. And with this drop tonight, see –'

'Although you say "no worries"?'

'Well, it's the truth. Even though I'll admit now we got the Boches here –'

'Could change.'

'Could, yeah.' Winding the window down to flick his cigarette stub away. 'But hardly this quick, and they couldn't ever watch all the little lanes, not even one in ten of 'em. Well – you'll see . . . But listen, I got you a present in the back there – battery for your radio.'

'For the transceiver – a spare?'

'Was Wiggy's. Always got me to charge 'em for him, I had this one when –'

'Alain, that really is a present and a half! Will you recharge others when they need it?'

'Sure. No problem . . .'

They ate the bread and sausage and drank a flask-full of pseudo coffee after the turn-off at St-Foy-de-Peyrolières, half an hour south of which at a village called Rieumes he pointed at a left fork and told her, 'That way'd take us to Noé.'

Noé where the Hardball target was situated.

He'd added, 'Which I'm steering clear of since I wouldn't want it thought I might've been sussing the place out.'

'If it took us to Noé, it'd also pass somewhere near Montgazin or Sulpice, where your friend Loubert hangs out?'

He glanced at her and nodded. 'Bravo, mam'selle. But you're thinking why not pick 'em up and take 'em along, save 'em the bike ride later?'

'Obviously you've reason not to, but –'

'They'll get 'emselves down there each on his own, not a whole bunch together. I wouldn't want a truckload of 'em in broad daylight, what's more, wouldn't care to be seen picking 'em up in that region neither.' Passing her his crumpled pack of Gauloises. 'We'll cross over the 64 about thirty kilometres south of Noé. Another hour south from here, near enough.' He waited, then took the lighted Gauloi from her. 'Thanks. But you got the geography pretty well in mind – eh?'

'Bits of it – sort of.'

'There's a bit of an old map under this seat, if you want.'

Twenty kilometres south from there, they were crossing the River Touch, last seen when starting out from Plaisance, and soon after passing through a hamlet unmarked on the map but identified by Déclan as Labastide-Clermont. After which he bore right – with the same object in mind, he explained: to cross the main Toulouse–Tarbes road at a good distance from Noé.

Villages followed at varying intervals: after Marignac-Casclaus, another that was unmarked and which he didn't name but knew well enough to tell her that they had only a dozen kilometres to cover before crossing the 64.

'*Then* how far?' Eyes on the map. 'Forty?'

A shrug. 'Forty, forty-five.'

'So with this other call to make, it'll be dark before we're there.'

'Won't stop at Cazalet's any longer than I have to. Like you to see Legrand's place in daylight.'

'Like a sight of the dropping field, certainly.'

The Pyrenees loomed distantly ahead, a broad spread and depth of foothills as a foreground to that massive, jagged barrier under a mix of clear sky and grey-black cloud. A lot more cloud than clear sky admittedly, but she thought the cloud was higher than it had been this morning, and since the turn south at St-Foy there'd been no rain. Please God the Lanc *would* come.

Crossed fingers. What sort of weather they might have further north was something else entirely.

'Coming up ahead now, Suzie –' Rosie jerking out of some dream, and Déclan's thick forefinger stabbing at the smeared windscreen – 'that's Lafitte-Vigordane, and the main road's just beyond.'

He'd been letting her sleep for some while, she realised – catching up on sleep missed through having listened-out last night – and updating herself on the map now, noting that not long after leaving the main road behind them they'd be crossing the Garonne – near a village called – couldn't make out its name . . . This was a small-scale as well as much used map, with smudges and even blank areas near what had been folds . . . Anyway, back to *this* village, Lafitte-Whatsit, Déclan whistling softly between his teeth as he drove slowly through into the centre and on round, then ignoring a left fork which she'd have thought would have been their way out, but evidently wasn't. Narrower here now, and after a hundred or two hundred metres the start of a long bend. Following that round into the straight – which she guessed would lead finally to a crossing of the main road.

Studying their route again, whereabouts of the Garonne bridge two or three kilometres further on . . .

'Oh hell, what's –'

Braking: Rosie focusing on it too: a motorbike parked broadside across the road a couple of hundred metres ahead. They'd come round the bend and there it was after a straightish couple of hundred metres – less than that now, he'd eased up on the brakes, muttering something about going through with this, other crossings'd be blocked as well, you could bet on it . . . Braking harder, and stopping ten metres short of them – a booted and helmeted Boche soldier straddling the bike and a tall uniformed gendarme near him in the middle of the road – hand up with its palm towards them. Déclan growling like a ventriloquist, lips hardly moving, 'Take it easy now, nowt to do with us, is this.' Winding his window down, staring out at the gendarme as he reached them. Tall man with a big nose: might make a good stand-in for de Gaulle, she thought.

'Some problem, captain?'

'You're not from anywhere around here.'

'That's the truth, but I'd not call it a problem. I'm from Léguevin. What's this about, then?'

'Military convoy in transit is what. Léguevin, eh. Heading where?'

She could see the big greenish army trucks passing, hear each of them as it hammered past the end of this approach-road – *thump thump thump*, travelling quite fast and almost nose to tail. Déclan had shouted back, 'Farm near Carrière, fellow name of Cazalet –'

'And what's your business with Leon Cazalet?'

'I put a new pump on his well for him, come to check on it as I'm bound to. Why, though –'

'And you, Miss?'

'Making for Foix to visit a relative, and this gentleman very kindly –'

Whumph, whumph, whumph . . .

'Whole Boche army on the move, is it?'

'You'd think so, wouldn't you. Takes twenty minutes to get by.' Jerk of the head towards the trooper on the bike. 'So *he* says. When it's gone he overtakes, blocks another crossing up ahead – must be fifty more like him, eh?'

'Up to twenty minutes' wait then.' Déclan shrugging, telling Rosie, 'Might as well light up.' His Gauloises again on offer, but she didn't want one. A pony-trap had pulled up behind them, the gendarme straightening from the window and now sauntering back to talk to the women in it, friends of his, no doubt. Déclan said, 'Might time this – number of trucks per minute, then multiply by twenty?'

'Already doing that.' She added, 'If your chum comes back, ask him if he knows where they're going.'

Even fragments of intelligence could add up and have their uses. The motorbike for instance had a yellow plate on it with what looked like XXI in white on a black triangle. *Might* enable some War Office boffin to identify the unit.

Thanks to that hold-up and then the stop at the farm near Carrière it was more than half-dark when they got to

Legrand's at Montbrun-Bocage, turning in around a low stone farmhouse that was right on the lane and continuing across a yard to park between barns where it was even darker.

'Wait here a mo', Suzie?'

'All right, but –'

'Shan't be long.'

'Please don't be.'

She needed a pee. Old Rosie had remembered this of all things, although detail of the rest of it was at best vague; but she must have had her pee, because she remembered meeting Madame Legrand, being with her in the house at that early stage, which otherwise she would not have been: and Déclan fretting because he wanted to show her the dropping-ground while there was still *some* light. There was a chance of a half-moon later, if by some miracle the cloud should thin or partially break up, but you'd have been mad to count on it or even really hope. At this stage it must have been about 6 p.m. she guessed. Or say five-thirty, when she was inside the house for those few minutes. She remembered Madame Legrand as large and her husband as rather small, grey-headed, she thought quite a bit older than his wife. There were children around, although they were kept out of her sight – or she was kept out of theirs – and she was in the house only as long as she needed to be. One of the barns was where the *parachutage* party would congregate and pass the waiting hours; this was primarily for the children's sake, the principle being that they shouldn't know what was going on, shouldn't be endangered with such knowledge.

For everyone's sake, in fact. You could hardly blame children if they chattered.

'They'll be told it's the vet who's come. Something of that kind. Or me, maybe, seeing to the bloody borehole pump.

149

You'd be the vet's or engineer's daughter, as like as not.' Rosie and Déclan back in the pick-up, making slow progress uphill over a rocky track, making for the higher part of the farm where the drop was to be. She'd have been keen to see it perhaps especially because this would be her first *parachutage* ever – if it came off at all – and in any case she was to take a leading part in it, having agreed with Déclan that she'd flash the recognition signal to the incoming aircraft, using a white torch from the apex of the dropping-zone, southern end of it, flashing the initial letters of the two Maquis bands' specially allocated code-names.

As she'd learnt in her SOE training, a *parachutage* field should ideally be level, minimally about seventy-five metres wide and a hundred long – and high, so as not to be over-looked from any nearby ground that might be higher. It should also be bordered by forestry as cover for the recep-tion party and their vehicles. In fact this field of Legrand's was about 300 metres long, which was fine, but more like fifty than seventy-five in width, had a stand of conifers on its western side but was open on the other to a scrubby, rock-strewn down-slope – scrubby enough with gorse, bram-bles and assorted saplings to stop any containers that might fall that far out of line. Containers being six feet long and heavy, torpedo-shaped, and dropped on cotton parachutes, which were less reliable than the nylon ones used for human loads.

'I'll be at this end, out in the middle, uh?'

'Right. Me and Legrand opposite each other this side and that about halfway along, two others ditto on the start-line. Loubert and Fernier probably. The rest stay put until I blow my whistle – when the plane's gone over, that is, and I'm sure there's no more to come. Otherwise could be dangerous – damn great loads crashing down, you need to watch it, Suzie.'

'And you've a torch I can use. Mine's only a titchy one I use sometimes when I'm transmitting.'

'What we *need* is a moon.' Looking up at what was still hundred-per-cent cloud-cover. 'Fat hope. Although by eleven or half-past – well, say our prayers. But while there's a few spare minutes, I'll just refuel.'

Rosie's scant memories of the hours of waiting were colour-washed by a brazier's glow and a storm-lantern's yellowish light, scented by the smell of both and centred on an old box-shaped wireless with a fretsawn front panel and unsafe-looking cables connecting it to the battery of a Ford tractor. There was also a crowd of mostly bearded faces – a whole barn-full of them, was her visual recollection, and since in fact there were no more than about a dozen men including Déclan and Legrand one might assume the barn wasn't all that spacious. A detail was that the trestle table on which the lantern and the wireless stood was jammed right up against the tractor; she'd concluded that this would be so the wires would reach, eliminating any need to remove battery from tractor, Legrand's motivation being less laziness than caution – in emergency such as a raid by gendarmerie or Boches the set-up could be instantly dismantled.

There was evidently a recognition of that danger. Hence the posting of guards outside.

She thought Loubert must have been there with Legrand when she and Déclan returned from their inspection of the dropping-zone and refuelling. He'd have left Montgazin early, in that case, well ahead of his fellow maquisards who arrived one by one during the next hours. Déclan had told him about the Wehrmacht convoy on route 64 that afternoon, and he'd said yes, there'd been movements of that kind all day, he'd seen some of it, and yes, he would contact Déclan when he had responses to enquiries he'd initiated.

He was a big man, actually quite fat, which had surprised, even rather disappointed her – there'd been no fat men as far as she remembered in the pages of *Beau Geste*. Although he did have what looked like a bayonet scar on one side of his face.

The maquisards from St-Girons, about six of them including their leader Emile Fernier, must have arrived in their lorry, the *gazo* hired by Déclan at SOE's expense, at about six-forty or forty-five, were certainly there by the time Legrand switched on the wireless, fiddling with its knobs until he got the BBC's French service and set himself to cutting down the static. This must have been ten minutes or so before the first lot of *messages personnels* were due and please God would include mention of Véronique the dancer. Would or would not: it really mattered quite enormously, for the obvious reasons including the effect of any postponement on Hardball, and for Déclan on his own account since from the Maquis point of view he'd set all this up and involved them in it. He'd mentioned this to Rosie earlier in the day as his own particular concern, the effect of postponement or cancellation on his standing with the Maquis in general and long-term, and she could see the anxiety in him now. He was in desultory conversation with Loubert and Fernier – a scrawny, dark-complexioned man with one wild eye – close to the brazier, all three of them smoking and with their eyes on Legrand who'd just turned the shrieks and crackling down to practically nothing and was crouched with his ear against the fretwork. Déclan moving to join him, with a wink at Rosie; Loubert also then lumbering over – into range of the sound presumably, but also into her field of view, blocking her sight of Legrand, of his expression if it changed . . .

Still a minute to go, probably. Or half a minute. He was making as sure as possible of being tuned-in, in particular not missing those few words that mattered, had only to turn up the volume when the moment came. Even then, nothing was guaranteed, with all that interference, some of which was most likely Boche jamming. *Seconds* to go, and one of the two maquisards they'd had outside on guard was in the doorway asking had they heard yet – Fernier snapping at him to shut his face, get back out there, Christ's sake, and Legrand had turned the sound up to a Frenchman telling them from London through continuing, maddening howls and crackles, 'Now here are some personal messages. Marcel and Marianne are to marry in the spring. Marcel and Marianne are to marry in the spring. The strength of a chain is the strength of its weakest link. The strength of a chain is the strength of its weakest link. Jeanette sends her love to all the family. Jeanette sends –'

Rosie thinking miserably, *The drop's off, damn it. Might have known. Oh, have known all day . . .*

'Véronique –'

'Hah!' Loubert had thrown up his arms. 'Ca va!' There were a lot of such body movements – exclamations, whistles, and the man in London had said it again, 'like an angel'. Véronique was tops all right, and not just for her dancing. Rosie crying with the relief of it, Déclan surprising himself and her by hugging her, Legrand meanwhile switching off the wireless then hushing them with a reminder that confirmation at nine o'clock was still essential, boys . . .

'Long enough wait, Rosie – seven to nine, then I suppose nine to eleven or thereabouts?'

Shrug of her pleasantly rounded shoulders. 'I got special treatment, though. After the nine o'clock confirmation I was let into the house. Through the front door, would you believe it? By Legrand, obviouly with his wife's sanction. Not exactly *tout confort* as the hoteliers put it, but warmer than the barn and a lot quieter and I slept – on a hard chair at the kitchen table, kitchen was probably the only warm room in the house. I'm sure Madame was happier for me to sleep alone in her kitchen than in a barn with a dozen men, or however many there were, all snoring and God knows what else. The Legrand children would have been upstairs in bed, of course, and there wouldn't have been a spare bed, no more than there'd have been a comfy chair or sofa. Madame gave me some coffee and a piece of cake, then excused herself, and I must have gone out for the count, woke with a start and maybe a stiff neck when Legrand came to tell me it was – I don't know, some time before eleven. Déclan had left his truck up there in the trees, we'd walked back to the barn – six-thirty, whenever that was – and I remember wishing he hadn't. At least I *think* I remember that – longish plod in pitch darkness, using our torches as little as possible. There was no moon, that's for sure. A lot of this – when I say I remember it's mostly how it *must* have been, how I've thought it out in the course of deciding what's worth telling and what I simply *don't* remember. To get it as near right as possible's the great thing, after all. Especially as you'll be applying your novelist's licence to it, I imagine.'

'Well – where that seems justifiable.'

'I'll be seeing the script before it goes to your publisher, won't I, we agreed on that, didn't we?'

'We did indeed, Rosie.'

'That's all right, then. And as for the *parachutage* that night – well, you know the routine, you described a couple in the earlier books – in *Into the Fire* for instance –'

'Where your Mauritian colleague gets killed and the Gestapo gets you. And in *In at the Kill* – with the Maquis group run by that man we met in your pub.'

She'd nodded. 'So you know the form. Us lot waiting in

the dark, straining our ears for the first sound of the Lancaster's four engines, me at *pointe* ready to flash the recognition signal, morse letters PC, and four others with red lamps – hurricane lamps with red cloth over them – marking the flight-path left and right, and – oh, the rest of 'em spread around listening and watching out for – you know, trouble, such as did happen that night outside Rouen, you got that about right, one of my *nastier* recollections . . . *This* night though' – her hand closed on my wrist – 'God, the sheer *thrill* of it, that I really *do* remember. Catching that first whisper of distant sound that built through a hum into a roar, knowing that after all the doubt and waiting here it *was*, deafening great black shadow hurtling at us, me and my winking torch, smack over the top of us at five hundred feet with containers spewing out –'

'You're writing the story for me, Rosie!'

'Oh, the *most* exciting thing. Far more so than the repeat message we'd had at nine. One heard only the last of the containers thudding into the ground because of being deafened by the blessed Lanc pounding over – blessed's the word for it too, those *marvellous* guys who'd come six or seven hundred miles and now had the same distance back – well, one felt so darned *grateful,* you know? Sound falling away though, Déclan's whistle like a ref's blowing time, and the rush of maquisards – in fact all of us –'

'Rushing to locate your goodies.'

'Yeah, and finding all of them except mine. Five for the St-Girons band marked P and three for Loubert's marked C. *None* marked as promised L for my code-name Lucy. First thoughts were OK, so it was out there in the dark someplace, the 'chute might have failed and it could more or less have buried itself in the soft ground – or rolled away some distance down that incline. But – hadn't, simply wasn't *there*. The whole crowd of us finally combed the area in line-abreast with torches, but — no go, nothing. The Maquis had their Stens and ammo and whatever else, but I did *not* have my spare transceivers. Sort of thing one *does* remember.'

9

'Can't hang around, Suzie. Sorry.'

'No. I mean, sure.' They were back at the truck, Loubert's men preparing to embark. 'Thanks for the efforts anyway – and for yours, Monsieur Loubert.'

'Regrettably, mam'selle, for nothing.'

It was past midnight, and they should have been on their way by now. The St-Girons team had loaded their five containers and rumbled off down the track some while ago, but Déclan had proposed one more quick search, since Rosie did have serious need of the transceivers, and one more try might strike lucky. Loubert had reluctantly agreed to accept the delay – which *had* been kind of him and possibly, Rosie thought, unwise. The Lanc having woken the entire populace including gendarmerie and doubtless a fair number of Boches, the sooner one could get away with the night's spoils the better. The main purpose of the operation had after all been achieved. Legrand would search every square metre of this high ground at first light, and if he found the missing container would transfer its contents to some secure hiding-place before burying it and contacting Déclan.

'Thanks for all of this, François.'

'If you don't hear from me it's no go, stay away.'

Because there'd be patrols out in the morning if not before, and probably descents on farms here and there, especially to those whose occupants' loyalties might be in doubt. Which might well apply to Legrand: except he'd done this before and was no fool, wouldn't advertise his politics. He'd be up most of the rest of the night, she guessed, clearing out the barn, maybe running his tractor up here to obliterate other tyre-tracks.

Knowing it wasn't just *his* life that would be at stake, but his whole family's. You had to hand it to them, Rosie thought. You really did.

Loubert's three men were in under the tarp, already complaining about the cramped conditions, the big man himself crawling in behind them. There wouldn't be all that much room, with five bicycles and three containers as well as Déclan's tool-chest and fuel locker – full width of the truck and a metre deep. Now Loubert himself, about the size of a fourth container. Déclan slamming the tailgate up and fastening it, then joining Rosie in the cab.

'OK?'

She shrugged. '*Main* object achieved.'

'They cocked up in England on your gear, is my guess. Missed the bus.'

'In which case it'll be an age before I get them. And considering I had it set up before I left –'

'Yeah. You said. Hold tight . . .'

Down to the yard and across it, turning right into the lane and soon afterwards right again into one so narrow that if you met another vehicle one of you'd have to get off into a gateway or the ditch. Driving slowly and with only side-lights that wouldn't be visible to oncomers at more than a few metres' range, muttering to Rosie, 'Won't break any records, but we'll get there, eh?'

'I'm sure we will, Alain.'

'Without passing even a house let alone through villages – at *this* stage. Over the 628 by and by, then one *large* village – Carla-Bayle – and on to the 919 at Le Fossat.'

'You've lost me already.'

'The 919 takes us north to St-Sulpice-sur-Lèze.'

'Ah. Where we drop our friends.'

'Not exactly. Nearer Montgazin, sort of between them. We'll turn off in fact at Lézat-sur-Lèze. Farmyard near there, we offload the containers, the lads take to their bikes and come back with a donkey-cart after dark tomorrow. Well, today, now. Important thing for us is getting shot of 'em before dawn. And listen, once we're on the 919 we've come from Foix and we're headed for Toulouse – OK?'

'On the road in these early hours, curfew notwithstanding?'

'Safe enough because I'm known. One job takes half the night, I'm held up – need to get to the next where I should've been already – and only using – well, mostly *very* minor roads, and places where I'm welcome, none of 'em's going to let me down.'

'But with the Boches here now, Alain –'

'Yeah. There's that. But then again, this isn't happening every week, not every *month*. More like once in a blue moon, eh?'

'You're not known to the Boches though, are you? And how d'you explain me?'

'Well – gendarmerie'd explain me to them, and when a man has a girl with him, Suzie, especially a very attractive one –'

She snorted. 'Marc's notion too, that was, and frankly –'

'I know, I know – it's nothing I'd go for, only the assumption *they*'d make. You start in about looking for your ex's old aunt in Foix, and they're letting you think they're taking it seriously – while I'm naturally embarrassed –'

'In a nutshell I'm a tart on the road with a man infringing curfew, uh?'

'Suzie, the *simple* answer is we don't get stopped. Fact is, I never have been. Like I was saying—'

'What's *that*?'

Winding her window down fast. He'd heard it too, was doing the same on his side, foot off the gas, listening to machine-guns' distant chatter. Machine-pistols, she thought – as heard in night training exercises at and around Arisaig in the west of Scotland. Schmeissers' fast high-pitched shortish bursts – and grenades now – two, three explosions then more Schmeisser-scream. Déclan concurring with her terse analysis of it while stopping the truck with her side flattening the thorn hedgerow, a lot of it right in the window. He'd told her 'Stay put', had kicked the door open on his side and was clambering out: conversing out there with Loubert – sounds of action meanwhile thinning and petering out. Loubert and Déclan agreeing that it must have been five or six kilometres away south-westward, where Fernier's lot *would* have been on their way south to St-Girons; and Déclan now urging him to open one container and have his men arm themselves with Stens and a couple of magazines apiece. Now – and quick, so he could get going. No, not for himself and Suzie, in the cab they were too open to inspection. Loubert was having his lads get on with it: Rosie wondering how much sense it made – that brief action having been at some distance, and not obviously suggesting any threat to *this* party in the maze of lanes. One guessed at a Boche patrol having been sent out after a general alert caused by the Lanc, the patrol striking lucky by running slap into the St-Girons crew who might have been taking it too easy, *not* with Déclan's caution. Rather than getting Stens out, better surely to crack on, put more distance behind them? She could hear the maquisards clattering around in the rear of the truck – and Déclan's voice outside asking, 'All set, then?'

Loubert's answer was inaudible but must have been affirmative. Half a minute later Déclan was climbing back into the cab.

'All right?'

'*I* am, but –'

'Poor sods.' He wasn't wasting any *more* time, had the truck in reverse, backing out of the hedgerow. She'd been on the point of asking about the Stens – was there reason to think there might be some threat *here* or where they were heading – but instead deciding to keep quiet; it was done with, they were on their way, very little time had been lost, and he'd been in the business a lot longer than she had, what was more had been a soldier before that, even – as had Loubert, for heaven's sake . . .

Back in the middle now, lurching along at about twenty kph. Glancing her way for a second: 'No panic, Suzie. Having Stens handy is only a precaution. We know one patrol's out – or road-block, whatever – and there could be others – over a wide area maybe and could spread wider after that fracas. Patrols and/or road-blocks. Our Lanc having stirred things up, they've straffed that one lot and they'd guess there might be more, right? *So*, I'm going to skirt around Carla-Bayle, and give Le Fossat a miss too, but I've got to get on that 919 at *some* fairly early stage so as not to have this crowd on board in bloody daylight.'

She was glad she'd held her peace. Acknowledged, 'You know your business, Alain.'

'Hope so. But so did Fernier – according to Loubert.'

'Fernier *did*, you say.'

'Well. Some of 'em might've got away. Not all though, and odds-on not the leader. Maybe none. Boches'll be well off for Stens and nine-millimetre, sod 'em. Schmeisser and

161

Sten magazines are interchangeable, too. Pity Fernier didn't have his boys break out a few Stens. If he had, odds are we'd have heard 'em.'

'I suppose . . . Where are we now?'

'We've passed what they call the Bourrets. Little hamlet coming up, I'll take us through it on tippy-toes. Don't want 'em saying *Oui, Mein Herr, salauds passed about one-twenty heading east* or even *Sure, know that old camionette anywhere – bugger fixes pumps an' that.*'

'Would they?'

'Maybe not. Not even ones that aren't my friends. Sooner not be involved either way. Neighbours who *are* friends might hear about it and take it out on 'em.'

'Would you say you're a natural optimist, Alain?'

'Certainly not. Realist, more like – knowing what I *have* been able to get away with. Might *sound* like over-confidence, but . . . Oh, here, now. Forget what they call this place, but –' Slowing: and almost unbelievably, a faint miasma of moon penetrating cloud. The rectangle of a house black against it, farm sheds and a cottage materialising beyond that. Even sidelights off now: but slowing further for the corner. A single-storey building which she thought might have been a blacksmith's, and a cottage close to it on the other side. Turning left, into a fair width of country lane as distinct from narrow unmade track: another *chaumière* on the right. Dog barking – and another joining in – but that was behind them now.

Picking up a little speed . . .

'Next thing you know, we'll be coming to the 628. Which they might keep an eye on.'

'Think so?'

'If they've got their heads screwed on. Anyway when they're organised, which maybe they aren't yet. You'd watch the main cross-country roads because you can't watch all these little ones. Way we're doing it now, sticking to little winding lanes – fine, but we still have to cross some main roads, even use some. The 919 for instance, when we get that far. This 628 now, you could think of it as open ground the game's got to cross before it can – hell, get to its water-hole, whatever . . . Hey, see *that*?'

'Yes. *On* the 628, was it?'

'Sooner than I'd reckoned. But you see . . .'

A light – or lights, a shifting blur of them – had glowed briefly, passing from left to right a hundred or so metres ahead. Déclan braking again. Whatever it was it was travelling comparatively fast, forty or fifty kph she guessed. And lights bright enough to show up from this distance. Whatever the distance was – or had been. She'd got her window down again, but there was nothing to hear, although engine-sound *would* have been drawing away on this side. Passed now anyway, gone. Unless it had seen them and stopped. Couldn't have, though. The truck down to no more than ten or twelve kph, Déclan still coping without lights: she'd been slow winding the window down, and the truck itself was rattly enough to smother other more distant sound.

Déclan muttering, 'Wouldn't usually expect much traffic on it, this time of night.'

'Forces of law and order then, d'you think?'

'Could've been. Headlights an'all, not curfew-breakers' style.'

'What I thought too. Near miss, eh?'

'Another minute – if we'd met him at the corner –'

'Or if he'd spotted us *en passant*. Which since we're showing no lights . . .'

A grunt. Throttled right down, more or less free-wheeling. Muttering, '*Dead* lucky. In the midst of life, might say . . . There's a bit of a village at this crossing, I'd forgotten. Called Campagne-sur-whatever the river's name is.'

163

Hardly needing to brake, to stop there at the crossing. Buildings looming on the other side, all silent as the grave and no glimmer showing. Into gear therefore and edging forward, watching carefully both ways before chugging on over and through this minuscule habitation. Mightn't be more than a dozen inhabitants, she guessed, tucked up in their beds, not hearing anything except each others' snores. Would definitely not have heard the gunfire, fifteen kilometres away at least, but like the rest of the countryside might well have been woken by the Lanc, and stayed awake, *might* hear them creeping by? Might be better to drive normally, rather the way they were doing?

Perhaps not. This time of night, *any* traffic would probably be suspect. And the peasantry most likely inclined to mind their own business. *Watch the wall, my darling, while the Gentlemen go by!* Who wrote that? Masefield? *Five and twenty ponies, Trotting through the dark – Brandy for the Parson, 'Baccy for the Clerk; Laces for a lady, letters for a spy* . . . Not Masefield – Kipling, must have been. She asked Déclan, 'Are you religiously inclined, Alain?'

'Me?' Straight, narrow lane now, that handful of buildings already lost astern; but still dead slow, keeping the speed down. 'Why?' She quoted him – 'In the midst of life we are in death?'

'Religious, is that? Comes to mind. More like – well, observation, how it *is*, I mean . . . Suzie, listen – three kilometres from here we'll turn left – Carla-Bayle would be straight on, bearing left'll take us clear. Junction of four or five lanes, sort of place *might* be gendarmes posted. And from where we turn, roughly ten kilometres'll bring us around the back of Le Fossat, put us on the 919 somewhere north of that. An hour, say, taking it careful like we're doing now. Sense?'

'More than I'd make.'

'But listen. Kilometre or two north and east from where we'll join the 919 there's a village called St-Ybars – biggish church, priest called Father Duhourceau. If I fouled up some way so you found yourself on your tod, could do worse than knock him up. House behind the church – ask him for shelter and to send word to Jean Samblat. If you're stuck, that is.'

'Father Duhourceau, in St-Ybars. You're not likely to foul up though, are you?'

'I mean not just tonight, *any* old time.'

Rough diamond, she thought, my foot.

After the left turn he'd mentioned she'd dozed, woke feeling ashamed of herself about five kilometres further on, at another left turn in a hamlet which he said was called Pigailh and had to spell to her. They were in a narrow little high-banked lane then, but only for a kilometre or so, where a turn to the right brought them on to a less confining track.

'Glad to be out of that ditch.'

'Beats me how you do it, Alain.'

'We're spitting distance from the 919 here. And we've bypassed Le Fossat. Reckon I'll get on the 919 at a place called Ste-Suzanne – give us about 15 kilometres to Lézat-sur-Lèze. Remember what happens at Lézat?'

'We get *off* the main road.'

'*That* we do. Turn off it and heave sighs of relief.'

'If it's like that, is it worth getting on it in the first place?'

'If we didn't we'd lose an hour or more, and we can't afford it. A lot more little lanes, through an area I'm not familiar with. See it on the map, you'd realise – wouldn't bother getting a torch out, but –'

'I've enormous faith in your navigation.'

'Happens we been dodging through country I know well

enough. Elsewhere I could get us lost easy as pie, you'd lose *all* your faith. May be a dicey fifteen kilometres on the 919, but things being as they are it's our best bet.'

'Fingers crossed, then.'

'You're a great girl, Suzie. Have you thought how you'll make out without the transceivers?'

'Well – standard routine, and taking a lot of care. Out of town to send and *chez moi* to receive. Means lugging the set around with me, which – well, can't be helped, can it.'

'The out-of-town trips, you'd travel with me or Marc, depending which of us is –'

'I think I'll do it mainly solo, thanks all the same. Limits the range, but arguably more secure. You have your own work anyway, especially with Hardball coming up – *if* it still is. By more secure I mean – well, that van of Marc's a bit conspicuous, isn't it? Whereas just another female on a bike –'

'About four hundred of 'em to the square mile – in daylight. But at night, and wanting to cover a lot of ground –'

'A lot of pedalling. And sleeping in ditches sometimes. Not so bad in summer, but – anyway, *can* be done. Incidentally I'll have to go on the air tonight, for starters.'

Friday, this was now. One of her listening-out nights, but no reason she shouldn't also transmit. Maybe from not very far out of town, on this occasion. See Jake, compose a report to Baker Street and encypher it, get some rest if possible, and a meal – count on Berthe for that – and be somewhere or other listening-out by eleven. Take in whatever Sevenoaks might have for her, and strum out her report on the *parachutage*, mixture of good news and bad.

More bad than good: sum total of the good being that three containers of Stens and whatever else Loubert had asked for were safely in his hands.

166

Were *now*, anyway. Touch wood, still would be by Lézat-sur-Lèze – and beyond. She asked Déclan, 'Think Hardball'd be at risk through the loss of those containers and Fernier's team?'

'Can't tell until we know the score, but I doubt it. I guess the personnel'd be easy enough replaceable. I'll have that on *my* plate, you bet. But Loubert's got what he needed and I reckon he could put a few more in the field if St-Girons can't. Jean'll want me to do a recce down that way, for sure. Be more grist to *your* mill then – at least if there's doubts.'

'Up to Baker Street to confirm it or call it off, you mean.'

'If there was any question of calling it off, yeah.'

'A recce of the band at St-Girons – whatever's left of it?'

'Not actually at St-Girons. They shifted not long ago. There'll be plenty left of it, main question's who'll take over from Fernier if he's had it. Mind you, if it doesn't look good, there's alternatives.'

'You mean other bands.'

'Right.'

'And *en route* to St-Girons or wherever, will you call in at Legrand's?'

'Not unless I hear he's got your stuff.'

'That *was* what I was wondering. But you're really on the go, aren't you? I mean on top of the job you're supposed to make your living at?'

'Yeah, well. Happens they sort of complement each other. Suzie, we're going to need lights again any minute now.'

'I was thinking we might.'

'Cloud must've thickened. What you were saying, though – what's time-consuming is the hours on the road and working on machinery. Calling in on Maquis hideouts here and there's usually just minutes, half an hour maybe – get the local gossip, hear what they want from us – cash, mostly. Well, *always*, but

167

sometimes paradrops, so forth. Tell you one thing, Suzie, having you along to chat with's really nice. Any time you want, girl, only too glad.'

'Except if I wasn't with you you'd have Loubert up front here, wouldn't you?'

'Never. Michel's known – and not hard to recognise, eh?'

'To the gendarmerie, you mean?'

'On the wanted list for sure. Wouldn't care to be seen hobnobbing, neither – so no, I *wouldn't* put him on display. Light's not getting any better, darn it. Get round this corner though, *then* –'

'Must have cat's eyes . . .'

'Raw carrot's supposed to help. But after this it's a straight – oh, kilometre, say, to our road.'

'Do we go through Ste-Suzanne?'

'No, don't go into it, it's off on the east side of the road, turning left we put our backs to it.' He'd switched on his sidelights, their small radiance enough to light up the verge and hedgerow on her side. 'Trouble with using lights is it's not easy to turn 'em off again.'

'Doesn't the glow from your burner show up about as much as sidelights do anyway?'

'Not in a forward direction, no.'

'Will you use headlights on the main road?'

'Have to, I'd guess. Look less like what we are, what's more.'

'Sorry for all the questions, but one more – do we pass through other villages before St-Lézat?'

'None I can think of. No, there's none that's right on the road.'

'Good . . . Smoke, Alain?'

'Now *that's* an idea. Here, use mine?'

'No, it's OK.' Crouching right down, hearing him say it would be roughly four kilometres to the St-Ybars turn-off,

168

but the village itself was well clear of the road. They'd've built the road to bypass it, he guessed. Rosie reflecting that (a) she'd only have a couple of cigarettes left after this, (b) she'd never been scared of a road before. Not in fact that it was the road that scared one, only what might be on it. But the hell, only fifteen kilometres of it – twenty, twenty-five minutes say? Then home and dry, more or less. Eyes half shut at the flare of the match: then back up.

'Here you are.'

'Thanks. I was thinking – good news for you, won't be as much as fifteen kilometres, more like twelve.'

'Better and better. Almost at it, are we?'

'I reckon.' A nod, in semi-profile against the faint, close radiance from that sidelight. Exhaling smoke. 'But another thought I had – if they were putting a block on it they'd do it at Lacroix Falgarde – where the road from Auterive and Pamiers joins. Two main roads, one block – eh?'

'If they had reason to think we'd be making for Toulouse –'

'Not *we*, Suzie, they don't know we exist. Coming up to it now though. Nice empty thoroughfare, you'll see.'

'The smoke was a good idea, wasn't it?'

'Certainly was.' Easing down: sidelights still burning. 'Certainly was.' Darkness fairly total out there, but he was braking, had to be seeing *something*. Hadn't had the flare of that match under his nose, of course, to spoil his night vision.

Stopping. Rosie keeping her hand cupped around the cigarette, to hide even that small pinpoint glow. Sidelights putting a just-visible gleam on paved roadway around the forefront: otherwise only dark night in both directions. A lurch as he edged the truck forward, shifting gear, and the hand with the cigarette in it reaching to switch on headlights – which were *not* all that bright. Accelerating slantwise across the road, the fag now in his mouth brightening as he inhaled.

169

'Here we are then, Suzie.'

'And we have the place to ourselves. Must say I'm glad I'm not under that tarpaulin.'

'I'm glad you're not, too.'

'Not only the discomfort, but not knowing where the heck one is.'

'Michel Loubert's own choice. They could have done it on their bikes, and I'd have delivered the containers to that yard.'

'He'd have wanted to stay with them, I imagine.'

'And I'd have needed help with the unloading. That or waited there half the night. Thing is, one doesn't bring more people into it than one has to. The fewer in the know, the safer.'

'Which is why we had so few maquisards at the drop, I dare say. How many'll be needed for Hardball?'

'I honestly couldn't tell you, Suzie.'

She laughed. '*Bet* you couldn't.'

'A lot'll be up to the guys who'll be at the sharp end – our visitors, uh?'

'Ah. Right . . . What are we doing now – forty, forty-five?'

'Forty-four. Might coax her up to fifty on the flat.'

'Fifteen minutes, say.'

'About that – and a couple gone already.'

'If we *were* stopped – OK, we won't be, but if we *were* –'

'I've been servicing pumps at a couple of farms they could check on if they wanted, I'm on my way home to Léguevin, taking a chance on sneaking by as far as curfew's concerned because I should've been home hours ago and there's a job I *must* get to tomorrow – and I'm giving you a lift back from Foix – oh, my God –'

'*Christ!*'

Lights ahead: a whole lit-up section, abrupt entry to

perdition: to her mind, *finish*. They'd come round this shallow left-hand bend, and – floodlights, road-block, vehicles and – Christ, four or five hundred metres ahead, no more . . .

'Hold tight.' He'd switched his lights off. Road straight as a ruler here, he had those others to sight on, was heading straight at them – at fifty or thereabouts, to Rosie's expanding horror, foot hard down – aiming to ram, crash through them, end up smashed and burning? He'd yelled again, 'Hang on!' But dragging the wheel hard right then, the truck juddering and on the tilt as well as turn, stink of burning rubber and actually travelling sideways – level again, back on four wheels for the moment – Déclan having wrenched the wheel back *into* the skid, Rosie just hanging on in her seat as far as she was able, 'as instructed' was her way of putting it, hearing a thunder of destruction from the rear, visualising containers crushing bodies, bicycles . . .

'No such thing.' Telling me this, old Rosie had been wide-eyed, shaking her head and sounding at that stage more Australian than French or Anglo-French. 'Believe me – he had the truck back under control *some* bloody how, heading east now mind instead of north, we'd been sort of rocking to a halt right out of that spinning skid but he had her steady then and picking up speed, headlights on – such as they were, didn't make *all* that difference – then off again after a couple of seconds as if he'd seen all he needed. I hadn't seen any turn-off, but here we were on it, a side-road leading to the place with the funny name where Father Whatsit'd help out if called upon to do so, eh? St-Ybars, right. It was a fair-sized turning and country road with another right turn, a lane, about a hundred metres up, and Alain swung into that without taking his foot off the gas, after which – me having suppressed a shriek – I *hope*

171

suppressed it – we were heading south, almost but not quite parallel to the 919 – and the gendarmes or Boches, one car or more, I've no idea – never saw 'em, but Alain thought there'd have been at least two – most likely roared on into St-Ybars and I suppose right on through it. I remember as much as I do – or think I do, if you know what I mean – because it truly was a heck of a near squeak. Alain explained it to me afterwards on the map and bloody *years* later I told Ben about it.'

'How about the maquisards, bicycles etc?'

'There'd have been injuries all right – things like bruises and twisted knees, and some damage to the bikes no doubt. Not to mine, maybe because it had been put in there by Alain and better secured, or one or two of the others weighting it down maybe. Any case Alain would've fixed it. Ditto the others', if they couldn't themselves – at the farm where we stopped to offload the containers and where Alain and I spent the rest of the night seeing out the curfew hours.'

'So you got to Lézat-sur-Lèze all right.'

'Oh, sure, but not on the 919. Alain found us a wiggly, narrow lane to the east of it, northward out of St-Ybars, wove its way right up to Lézat. I thought he might've known of it, wondered why he hadn't opted for it in the first place. Set on using the faster road, I suppose. Well, no one's perfect, and by and large he'd been bloody marvellous, no doubt of that. We groped our way through St-Ybars – without lights, knowing we could've run into trouble any moment – if those others had given up and been coming back, for instance. So – yes, St-Lézat, then via back ways to the farm, and – so much for that, huh?'

10

The doorbell penetrated her dream like a dentist's drill, in the moment of waking could almost have been one. She'd gone to sleep on the couch in Berthe's *salon* and had been dreaming, she realised, about the man she'd thought of at that time as 'the Australian', never expected to see again and who had no business in her sleeping *or* waking mind. Although the dream hadn't been in the least unpleasant. In point of fact –

No. Forget it. Wide awake now, crossing the room barefooted to the bay window to see who this was, checking the time *en route* – it was getting towards half-three – and hoping it might be Jake.

Which it was. On the lower step, having turned his back on the house, looking back along the pavement and around Place Marengo generally; by the time she'd got to the front door and opened it he was on the upper step again and facing her, half-smiling.

'Suzie.' Leather jacket, cream shirt, narrow tie. 'Woke you, did I?'

'I *had* dropped off.' Giving him room to edge in past her, then shutting the door and relocking it. 'Berthe's going to be late, she left a note that after school she's having to preside over some meeting. Last night's drop didn't have my spare sets in it, Jake. Jean, I mean. And what's more –'

'The St-Girons band were ambushed. I know. I've been talking with Déclan.' Turning to look at her again: an up-and-down look, and the smile returning. 'My word, Suzie, without shoes on, you're – five foot, even?'

'Five-four.' Back in the sitting-room, recovering her shoes, which with their articulated wooden soles – French wartime manufacture, all leather being requisitioned by the Boche – gave her an extra inch. Of course there'd been plenty of time for Jake and Alain to have got together; she hadn't foreseen it, but Alain had dropped her at Plaisance-du-Touch at about eleven, would have made contact with Jake by whatever means he had of doing that by say noon, and got into town probably by bus. While she'd had an early snack at the café she'd used similarly on Monday, before coming on here. Three-thirty now. She told him, 'I've drafted a report on last night. If you'd check over it I'll encypher it and get it off tonight. It's my night to receive, but –'

'Transmitting from where?'

'Yes, that's rather the question. I'll go by bike, of course. I thought maybe head for Revel, since I know that road. When I was meeting Marc on Sunday it took me about three hours – in daylight, admittedly – but I don't think I need go that far. There were farm buildings and suchlike set back from the road here and there, and some of it looked suitably derelict, so I might allow three hours to include selecting some reasonably good spot?'

'Curfew at eleven, you know.'

'Yes, well –'

'Smoke?'

It was an almost full pack of Disques Bleus he was proffering. She nodded. 'I'd love one. Getting a bit low, myself. Alain and I –'

'You had an anxious time, I gather.'

She'd taken a cigarette. 'Had its moments. One in partic-ular. I must say, he was marvellous.' Inclining to the match: 'Thanks, Jake.' Straightening: 'Really was. Steady as a rock. As you'd know, of course.' Inhaling, then letting it all go: 'Ah, heaven . . .'

'I gather he enjoyed your company too. He's going down to St-Girons first thing tomorrow, by the way – which should mean another transmission maybe Sunday night.'

'Is whatever happened there likely to affect Hardball?'

Shake of the greying head. 'I'd say the only thing might do that would be if Von Whatshisname was shipped off to Germany before they got here. No – might have to bring others into it, or borrow weaponry.'

'Would we have news of it, if the man was shipped away?'

'Yes. At least, I'd expect to. But Suzie, this transmission tonight – well, for *one* thing, if you were on the way to Revel and allowing three hours, and you'll want to be listening-out by eleven – I'd think it's likely they *will* have stuff for us – you'd hardly be through before say eleven-thirty, and with curfew starting at eleven –'

'I get there before dark if possible, find a place and hole-up, do my stuff and stay there until first light.' She checked the time again: three thirty-five. 'I'd start as soon as possible, in fact. Do the encyphering now – if you'd OK the script – take in some bread and cheese or something – I've brought Berthe eggs and parsnips from the farm we were at last night, incidentally. But I'll wrap up warmly – and find some place that's sheltered –'

'Timing's not the only snag with your planning, Suzie. Sorry, but – that whole stretch is flat and relatively low-lying, isn't it? Not a single hill – that I recall – no man-made eminences either. I'd say it's about the most unpromising terrain you could have picked on.'

Staring at him: knowing he was right.

'Should have thought a bit longer, shouldn't I!'

'Frankly, I'm surprised you didn't.'

She held his gaze: nodded, surprised at *herself*. 'Specially as I've been rethinking the whole thing, as it happens. Since not getting the spare sets – but before that, occurred to me on Sunday when I was with Marc – fact is I'd sooner do it on my own. Ride out in daylight, hole-up, and come back in daylight – is what it'd amount to. Right now of course – short notice, and what you just said . . . Look, shall I send from here, just this once?'

'*No*, Suzie. On no account. Not from this house, ever. Absolutely no question of it.'

'All right. I only thought – if it absolutely *had* to go out tonight . . . But if it doesn't – if we could leave it twenty-four hours say, and tomorrow I'd settle on a good location that's suitable and reachable? A daylight reconnaissance first, in whichever direction you'd propose?'

'There's one *possibility* – now *I* come to think of it. Taking a hell of a chance, mind you . . .'

'Uh?'

'Talking about tonight still, not tomorrow. Since it *is* actually rather urgent. It'd be what you call reachable, all right – half an hour or three-quarters maybe, on your bike . . . Do we have a map of the town centre here?'

'Town *centre* . . .'

'Almost. Other side of the river, at least, but still –'

'Berthe has one, I'll get it. Meanwhile, since we may be a bit pushed, here's the draft for you to approve.'

A nod. 'OK.' His hand on it on the table, though, not looking at it, looking hard at *her*. 'I'm by no means sure of this, Suzie.'

'I'll get the map anyway.'

When she came back with it, he'd skimmed over the draft of her report to Baker Street; she'd written it in pencil on an unused page in a school exercise book which also contained some history student's notes on General Pétain's brilliant defence of Verdun in '16.

'Nice idea, this. A snooper'd read no further, would he? Re. the missing transceivers though, I wouldn't be surprised if there was a message on the way explaining some balls-up or other. But not a chance they'd lay on a special drop.'

'I suppose not.'

'Unless the St-Girons weaponry's to be replaced, of course. And *that*'s not likely, one reason being there isn't time. Well – barely . . . Anyway – show you this now.' She'd opened the map on the table and he leant over it. 'Pont St-Michel – you'd find your way there, all right. So – over it, on to the *rond-point* and off to the right here – Allée What d'you call it – about a kilometre to this intersection, then left here and right *here*, and – bob's your uncle.' Tapping it with a middle finger. 'Old gaol, site of; originally a fortress, so it has a tower. Won't have for long, they're in the process of knocking the whole lot down, site's earmarked for some new hospital. It did have railings all around it but they've already torn those out, and most of this end's gone – including most of an ancient perimeter wall – this side, facing you as you approach from either of these streets.'

'And is the tower accessible?'

He'd nodded. 'And externally more or less intact. Stone staircase inside and a way in about here. Crumbly, probably dangerous – must have been part of the old fort. Whereas the cell-block built inside the old keep – *this* end – may have been put up only about a hundred years ago. I don't know, offhand, anyway that's already flattened. As a firm we're only concerned with the approach roads, not the building itself.'

'That's how you know about it?'

'It's there in plain view, open to all eyes. Jacques Jorisse as it happens *was* talking about it the other day – not that he's working on it yet, won't be until contractors have cleared the site, and they only started a week ago. He'd paid the place a visit thinking he'd like to see the view from the top while it's still there, but at close quarters decided not to risk it. Which makes me slightly hesitant, I must say – apparently they've plastered it with *affiches* warning people to keep out. I doubt they'd have a nightwatchman on it – knowing *them*.'

'Looks good for our purposes, Jake.' Checking the time again, thinking, since there's no alternative in any case. 'I'd get there in daylight, have a snoop round and –'

'Yes. Close look before the light goes, and – the way I'd play it if it was *me* sticking my neck out – as I wish it could be – well, move in when the light's gone or half gone.' Looking at her again: '*If* you wanted to do this – bearing in mind you'd be running all the pianist's normal risks plus unsafe structure, and right in town, for heaven's sake!'

'Do we know whether the RHSA have detector vans here yet?'

'Don't *know*, but I'd guess they would have. One's heard there are *Funkabwehr* around, and they're the boys who specialise in it, aren't they? I'd guess they'd have been here about as long as you have, Suzie.'

'Just have to pray they're not too quick off the mark.'

He'd shrugged. 'Pray if you like – I'd say just be *bloody* careful.' He paused, looking at her: then shook his head, slapped his palm down on the map. 'Suzie, let's rethink, give it twenty-four hours. Tomorrow night, as you suggested –

reconnaissance by day, etc. We *could* – and it might obviate the need for a second transmission when Déclan's reported.'

'But he's not likely to be back before Sunday, Baker Street does need to know we only got three out of eight containers – *and* that there should've been nine – and with Hardball Stage One as little as a week from now, if there *did* have to be another drop – not all that much time, is there? Jake, I'll manage this all right. Leave here at five, I'm into the place by – what, six-thirty? Do my stuff and be back here seven-thirty, say – beating curfew hollow *and* listening-out by eleven. OK, a once-only, wouldn't try it a second time – well, obviously not, but –'

He'd sighed, lifting his hands. 'All right.'

'Good. *Good.*'

'But go very, *very* cautiously.'

'You bet I will.'

'And out like a scalded cat soon as you're done.'

'Like *two* scalded cats.' She nodded. 'Promise. Absolutely.'

'I'll be here biting my nails until you're back.'

'Oh, I'll fairly *scoot* back, Jake!'

He wouldn't be there when she started her listening-out though, would need to be back in his own flat before curfew. So they'd get together tomorrow, Saturday. Café des Beaux Arts about one o'clock. Berthe had agreed to meet him there at that time, so come with her?

She'd smiled: wondering *Jake and Berthe?* and he'd seen the question in her eyes, frowned slightly, told her, 'I'll need to visit here quite often, to see *you*, and to justify that I want her to be seen with me in public now and then. The odd meal or *promenade*, so forth.'

'Then mightn't I be somewhat *de trop* at lunch with you?'

'Not at all. If the question were ever to be asked how come you're living in this house, an answer might be that

179

you're more or less her *protégée*, she's hoping to get you fixed up with a job in some nursery school. She knows which, I don't – no reason I should, is there? But that's how I know you, Suzie – through *her*. It's not the sort of cover one would invent or offer readily to an enquirer – more like background that might emerge if a questioner persisted – and it wouldn't conflict with the rest of your act – your late husband's aunt, all that.'

'I like it. Has a *natural* feel to it.'

'I was going to talk to you about it, should have before this. But incidentally, best not say anything that might suggest I've ulterior motives in seeking Berthe's company. She's no fool, she's probably as aware of it as I am, only I wouldn't rub it in, you know? The stuff about nursery school is something she and I concocted rather vaguely before you arrived – best *keep* it vague, don't you agree? Only a *hope*, on the other hand we wouldn't contradict each other about it if the subject happened to come up.'

'You're thinking of interrogations and matching stories.'

'In such circumstances – yes, might come in handy?'

'You're lucky to have found Berthe, aren't you?'

'I am. *And* to have had *you* dumped on me.' Patting her hand. 'You're a gift from the gods, Suzie. Truly are. Which is why – well, please be more careful this evening than you've ever been? However sound our cover stories, it's being caught in – you know, situations –'

'Wiggy-type.'

A grimace, small shake of the head. 'Get this screed into cypher now, shall we?'

By five-fifteen she'd crossed the Canal du Midi and was pedalling up the Allée Jean Jaurès. Grey sky, cold north wind, light already fading a little. Jaurès, she recalled from her readings of history, had founded the French socialist

180

party and edited *L'Humanité*, and had been assassinated for his pains. In – oh, 1914. Three-quarters of a kilometre, roughly, on this stretch, then left into Boulevard Lazare and another kilometre south into the Allée Verdier, where not much more than a week ago she'd walked in those gardens with total stranger James Kinnear alias Jean Samblat. It seemed much more than a week: and although she hadn't spent more than a few hours of it in his company, she thought of him now not only as her *Chef de Réseau* but also as a close friend.

Really *very* close, as *she* saw it. Couldn't have said exactly why or when she'd become aware of it, he'd simply grown on one.

He'd been down to Carcassonne on Tuesday, he'd told her, to confer with Marc on the subject of the beaches at St-Pierre, Canet-Plage and Barcarès, and felucca operations, whether their continuance might or might not be possible, and he'd found to his surprise that Rosie hadn't been far wrong when she'd described Marc as being in a state of nerves – or on edge, however she'd described it – and after some gentle probing had elicited from him that he'd lost his girlfriend.

'Didn't know he had one.' Her own voice in retrospect, thinking back on their exchanges in Berthe's kitchen, where she'd been slicing cheese to melt over beans on toast; she'd considered poaching an egg to put on top but had resisted the temptation. She'd brought half a dozen from last night's farm but they were fairly precious objects and like every-thing else strictly rationed. She'd surrendered her own forged ration cards to Berthe, of course, but when eating on her own still felt as if she was guzzling someone else's food.

Jake had limited himself to a cup of so-called coffee – he'd eat when he got back to his own place later – but at her urging had accepted one of the farm eggs, wrapping it carefully and putting it in his briefcase, which otherwise held nothing other than Mahossier, Jorisse paperwork. Anything more vital went inside his shirt or undervest, he'd told her.

Left into the boulevard. Traffic not very heavy at this stage, but likely soon to be thickening with homebound workers.

On the subject of Marc Voreux having lost his girlfriend, she'd added, 'Didn't know he had any special one, I mean.'

'Very special, that one. Must be about ten years older than him, has two small children and a husband who's something of a VIP. I've never set eyes on her but according to Marc she's ravishingly beautiful as well as strongly anti-German and anti-Vichy, while the husband's a dyed-in-the-wool Pétainist and something of a stuffed shirt.'

'Doesn't sound like an ideal match, exactly. When you say she's Marc's girlfriend, d'you mean they're lovers?'

'I don't know. If Marc had his way, I'm sure they would be. But the husband's a well-heeled lawyer, offices in two or three different places – Narbonne, Perpignan and I think Montpellier – and on top of that he's the local *Chef des Compagnons de France*, Pétain's version of the Hitler Youth, sort of, although I'm told it's more like the Boy Scouts. He's its local chieftain anyway, takes the salute at march-pasts, all that.'

'And his wife's done a bunk.'

'Disappeared, Marc said. He went to the house – big old place, Manoir de l'Aude – as he does periodically when he's got lobsters, and – no Gabrielle.'

'Gabrielle . . .'

'He calls her Gabi.'

'Is the fish business how he got to know her?'

'No. If he'd been only a hawker I doubt she'd have had

182

anything to do with him. It'd be the cook dealing with him anyway. In fact it was in connection with the escape-line I told you about. Two of his "parcels" were in need of help, and she provided it. I think the lobsters were probably his excuse for continuing to visit her after that. And hers maybe for – well, receiving him, as one might put it.'

'Unless she just likes lobsters?'

Jake had liked that.

Due north and south, the Allée Verdier ran, southbound and northbound routes divided by a strip of trees, shrubs and grass. Half a kilometre of this and then the Grand Rond, from which one would fork right towards Pont St-Michel. Approaching five-thirty – and the quick glance at her watch overtaken by the scream of a motorbike coming up fast behind her. Thundering by now – and a second one, accounting for that volume of sound. Riders in helmets, boots, greenish-khaki greatcoats: noise fading ahead where they'd swung into the Grand Rond – then away to the right, the engine scream picking up initially, then swiftly dying.

Rosie muttering as she pedalled, *Bastards*. This is *France*! Lost your way or something?

She'd asked Jake while eating her beans an hour ago whether Marc knew that the Hardball commando team was more likely to be arriving by felucca than by *parachutage*, and the answer had been no, he hadn't told him, the only action required of him at this stage being to nose around among his fishermen friends and others to pick up any whispers about new coastal-defence measures the Boches might be introducing.

Jake had said, 'There's no certainty they'll come in by sea. As I said, Suzie, time's really very short. The likely dates of 28th/30th only give us a week now – and they said confirmation by 27th, right? Well, before that they'd have to be flown out to Gib – where, all right, there'd be a felucca vict-ualled and standing by to shove off as soon as they arrived – as long as RN reconnaissance gave the go-ahead – but depending on wind and weather they wouldn't make it from Gib in less than three days – uh? D'you see – for a landing on the 28th they'd need to be at sea by the 25th at the latest. So London's deadline for decision's has to be – what, 22nd?'

'Two days' time.'

'Right. Consequently, if Marc came up with bad news from the beaches, we'd need to get it to Baker Street virtu-ally in minutes – uh?'

'Wish to God they'd sent the spare transceivers.'

She'd have had one in place – some *good* place – so all she'd need do was ride out to it. Move it before the *next* transmission, sure, but there it'd be, and with two sets to deploy you'd alternate between them. They'd be in widely separated areas and you'd shift each of them to a different location every time.

Very different from *this* – transceiver and battery awkwardly heavy in the bike's panier, under an assortment of clothes for laundering.

Jake had said, 'What it comes down to is that as far as we're concerned, time's likely to be very short when we do get a decision. And if it's not to be a beach landing, obvi-ously a *parachutage*. Preferably nowhere near last night's.'

'Where they dropped *me* might be best – vicinity of Cahors?'

He'd agreed: 'As good as anywhere.'

Scraping up the last of her cheesy beans . . . 'It would have been the Lancaster's racket alerting a patrol, I suppose. The St-Girons thing, I mean.'

'As like as not. Or just bad luck. Well, that anyway.'

'Not a leak – remotely possible?'

'A leak by whom? How and when?'

'I only wondered when we nearly ran into that other road-block. But who – well, you know better than I do, but with two Maquis bands involved and having to know in advance where and when – wouldn't have to be any of those actually taking part, would it? I mean, others who stayed home would have *known* about it?'

'Surely. But we need them, we have to trust them. If there's a rotten apple in this or that barrel, up to the bands' leaders, isn't it?'

'You mean nothing we could do about it.' She'd been at the sink, washing the plate she'd used. 'We're in their hands.'

'Any case, Suzie, what the maquisards would have known in advance – from Déclan – would be date, time and dropping-zone. If the Boches had had that much passed to them, don't you think they'd have had the farm surrounded, all of you in the bag?'

He was right, of course. By now one would have been either dead or in a Gestapo cell, certainly not indulging in that enjoyable as well as useful *tête-à-tête* with him – or now crossing this long bridge over the grey, wind-streaked Garonne. With German army trucks coming the other way: personnel-carriers, troops on bench seats with slung rifles, heads in helmets swivelling to stare at her as the things growled past. Because she happened to be female, no other reason: despite her shapelessness in the thick coat and headscarf.

Well. Staring at everyone and every *thing*, probably. Slum rats and country bumpkins. Gone now anyway, forget them. Too much in one's head already, when one needed to be right on the ball. Would have maybe half an hour to kill before the light went, she thought. Enough light between now and then to check out not only the ruin or as much as was left of it but also its surroundings, so as to have a return route in mind. There were a lot of cyclists around now as well as *gazos* of all shapes and sizes, but by the time she was on her way back it would probably have thinned out quite a bit – less good, making one more conspicuous especially when riding as it were against the tide. Although there'd be some, surely, coming *into* town. Pedalling round the elevated *rond-point* now and slanting away free-wheeling on the down-gradient into Charles de Fitte, which was an avenue running ruler-straight northwestward to the Pont des Catalans. Might conceivably take that route home: but maybe not, maybe wiser to stay off any major thoroughfare by then. Allowing for the possibility of the bastards having taken bearings on the source of transmissions and being on their way by the time she started back: their receivers having fallen silent, they'd know she'd be on the move, if they'd any gumption would have their eyes open for solitaries coming from that direction.

Use minor roads then, on this side of the river. Use the Pont St-Michel again but approach its *rond-point* from the south, having detoured west and south to confuse the issue and evade them – 'them' being the *Funkabwehr* radio-detection goons of the RHSA or *Reichssicherheitshauptamt*, Himmler's security executive.

And bugger *him*. Better still, hang him. One of these days, please God?

Pedalling at about twelve or fifteen kph with that attractive thought in mind: not hurrying, just pushing along like any other homegoing worker at Friday closing-time, eight minutes to the big intersection – crossing a very large *place* which she remembered from the map to be in fact two *places*, one right and one left. Busy with traffic, and pedestrians crowding over at crossings controlled by gendarmes, but by luck she was making it without stopping – *had* made it. So only about a minute now to where she'd be turning off. Left now – and a slight wobble caused by the transceiver's weight directly above the front wheel, when one lost that much speed. She was almost on her own here, most of the crowd having either turned off in those twin *places*, or stayed on Charles de Fitte. And the *right* turn coming up now – with the map in mind, Jake's finger descending and his 'bob's your uncle!' Tower with a jagged top at the back of an area littered with blocks of stone and pinkish brick, a widespread mess of earth and rubble where they'd ripped out what must have been fairly colossal iron railings, and inside brought down some sections of a wall which from as much as one could see of its foundations must have been about four metres thick.

Like a partially cleared, extensive bomb-site. But stop at that corner. Wheel-wobble – stop to fix it. Rash of 'Keep Out' signs clearly visible, white rectangles in the fading light. A male cyclist called out angrily, swerving outward as she swerved *in* and braked and a black-and-white van which had overtaken her half a minute ago had turned down to the right there. Check on it in a minute. Meanwhile, no problem seeing where she might best get in there, a curving path through the litter of demolition and maybe continuing to the tower. Internal stone staircase, allegedly: and better be. How the hell else . . . In that way, then the same way out, presumably. Why not – as long as no one saw one getting *in*. Unless some better alternative revealed itself when one was in there. OK, long enough, wheel fixed, let's say: so try it out – walking the bike back the way she'd come, for a different perspective – from which as it happened she could see the way in – *a* way in – to the tower itself, an aperture that had been an archway. So now circle the whole site, checking for other entrances or exits – *and* see where that van went, because it had sounded as if it had been stopping, not far down there. No particular reason to be wary of it, no way it could have anything to do with her or her business here, only seemed

187

sensible to check. Jake adding, in her imagination, 'Idiotic *not* to, Suzie. Check *every* bloody thing . . .'

Circling left-handed. Quite a few cyclists, and pedestrians – but all going somewhere – home, presumably, and preoccupied in doing so, no reason even to glance at others. The ten- or fifteen-metre-high perimeter wall towered dramatically around this end, immense against the darkening sky. Surely would take *some* knocking down. Weeks of it, she guessed. There were no 'Danger, Keep Out' signs on this part – simple reason, no way anyone could have got in. She could see the tower's crumbly-looking summit again now, in consequence of being further back from the wall after rounding that end of it.

Nothing to be seen or discovered on this flank anyway. No reason not to get on with it, get inside. Find the inner stairs – that was the really crucial thing – but first a hiding-place for the bike. And before that – *now* – check what had happened to the black-and-white van. Slowing, as she completed the circuit, to get a view down that side-street, she could see the glow of the *gazo* burner – van parked on the right, not far down from the corner. Narrow road, wide van – any other vehicle wanting to come through would have a job getting past it. Might assume therefore it wouldn't be left there very long. And it had been turned, was facing up this way. Well, never mind, someone *else's* business. Foot down on the kerb, just past that corner, and two cyclists coming this way – both women, both highly voluble. Screeching goodbyes now as one of them wheeled across the road and into the street where the van was. Rosie had turned to see where the other had gone, but she'd vanished, and neither of them had even glanced her way.

So, OK. No one giving a damn: and it was dark enough, too. Wait too long, be *too* dark. She didn't want to use her torch until she absolutely had to, and that would be inside the tower. Hang on, though – big, low-slung motor coming – *gazo*-powered but something like a Daimler-Benz. Switching its lights on at this moment: huge great headlights, tiny lights. Somehow incongruous anyway, a car of such distinction with a funnel on it. She watched it pass, then pushed her bike across the road into the deepening shadows of the wall and tower.

Wasn't a lot of choice about where to leave the bike, one place being about as good as any other, and she settled for semi-hiding it on its side between a waist-high heap of stone and a buttress of the tower itself. Hidden at least in the sense that it wouldn't be visible from the road. On her feet again, having taken the transceiver out of the panier and stuffed the dirty clothes back in. Anyone did stumble on it – well they *would*, but – oh, patrolling gendarme, maybe, if there were such things . . . *Could* probably have lugged it with her right into the tower – did consider that for a moment, but it would take some doing – also take *time*, especially when one had finished and didn't have any to spare.

Leave it. Wasting time already.

She had Uncle Bertie's torch in a coat pocket, easily accessible when she needed it – inside, of course, not out here, and with luck not until she was ready to transmit. Up *there*, somewhere. As long as there *was* a staircase, and it was negotiable – which might be the snag, it might well not be. This far everything straightforward enough despite Jake's trepidation and – now, on the brink so to speak, a sense of one's own damn cheek . . .

At the breach with its arched top she was peering into blackness and a scent of rot, a mess of soft rotten timber no doubt hundreds of years old, knowing it as timber by its feel and that smell, guessing some of it would be the remnants of ancient doors – and maybe collapsed floors and/or galleries

189

from above. Picking her way over it, into it – stone as well as timber – and quite suddenly making – she *thought* – OK, use the torch – what *was* the bottom of a stone staircase and its upward curve.

It looked climbable – at *this* level.

Climbing. Torch back in the right-hand coat pocket, to prevent herself from using it. Getting used to the steps' height and depths. Five – six – seven . . . At one stage hearing whoops and laughter, male voices, from somewhere outside. Passing on bikes she guessed, students at the start of the weekend, getting out of it or *to* it, whatever it might be – anyway had passed, were gone, leaving her with the silence and the smell, the only sounds being those she was making – including her own whispers, mutters. Stone dust and grit all over these steps, which so far seemed sound enough: telling herself that such an immensely solid weight of stone surely *had* to be. Despite Jacques Jorisse, who as an engineer would know about unsafe structures, having decided *not* to trust it? She was keeping to the right, arm and shoulder against the curve of wall, brushing each step with the sole of her shoe before putting weight on it. Transceiver case in her left hand close against her body, the other one maintaining contact with the wall.

Get all the way up if possible. Having got this far, it would be silly not to. Not quite as silly as I'd have been in making for Revel, but –

Explosive rush of wings around her head – flock of birds all breaking out in panic. Intruder also scared – frozen for a moment before telling herself *Only pigeons* . . . Starting again, taking longer, slower breaths to slow her heartbeat, and her foot encountering loose rubble on this next step. Could shift it, all right, but there was more of it than there'd been anywhere lower down, and amongst it were some quite large pieces.

190

Kneeling, clearing it by hand. Pausing to transfer the transceiver case to her right side, between her hip and the wall. Both hands free now to get rid of rubble that landed what sounded like a heck of a long way down.

Might have come from the tower's partially disintegrated top?

On her feet again, transceiver back in her left hand, moving on to the cleared next step. Right hand checking the wall above her head, finding deep scores in the stone – thinking of *this* as the source of fallen rubble – but then – one step higher – fingers encountering a very large timber beam projecting from the wall at right angles to it. Cross-section at least a foot square, surely had supported a floor at this level. Must have been others lower down, of which she'd not come across such evidence but which in the past century or centuries would have rotted and collapsed. And if her weight dislodged *this* one or its stone housing – on or around which she guessed those pigeons might have been roosting and which might be the only cross-beam still in place – the size of a man-of-war's timbers and weighing God knew how much . . .

Wouldn't help Hardball much if it went and she went with it.

Shifting down one step, then another. On her knees again, and the case against the wall while she worked at *completely* clearing both steps of rubble – so as to have enough uncluttered, fairly level surface, room for the set and elbow-room for herself. Transceiver case then flat on the lower step, against the wall with its back against the rise to the higher one. Opening it – not needing torchlight yet – feeling for the reel of aerial wire. Check this end of it plugged in: OK, let the rest go, unreeling itself into the abyss close on her left. Check the battery connection, touch the *Off / On* switch and *thrill* to the little red bulb's glow.

191

Torch in mouth now. Delving in an inside pocket for the folded page of cypher, unfolding it and fixing it in the clip in the case's lid.

Now, torch on. Transmitter switch to 'Send'. Headphones on. The crystal for night transmissions was already in the set, she'd fitted it before starting out. Tips of right-hand fore-finger, middle finger and thumb settling *comme d'habitude* around the key's Bakelite knob: and here goes – no matter *who*'s bloody listening.

Calling, calling. Switch back to 'Receive', and giving them a jiffy, but no response yet. Over to 'Send' and call again. Then to 'Receive' and – oh, Christ's sake –

Receiving, though. Glory be. Rosie alias Suzette code-name Lucy sending the stuff rippling out – confirmation of paradrop Jake 7 having been received but 5 of its 8 containers lost in subsequent ambush of Printemps team, of which further detail probably tomorrow night, but the promised spare transceivers not received, still urgently required. Closing down now, shifting location for 2300 listening-out. *Out*.

Switch to 'Off'. Retrieve aerial wire – a very much slower process than letting it run out had been. Just seconds for that, then on the air for less than three minutes including the call-up process, and now about five minutes winding the damn wire in. A potentially useful thought while doing so – pianists might carry spare aerial wires: could have simply left this one then, saving those minutes. The thought overtaken by a vision of Boches in headphones in one or more detector vans – two if they'd been on the ball and out for cross-bearings, the way they'd have you actually pinpointed. But please God *not*: please God keep them fiddling around in expectation of more to come.

Done. Wire rewound and in its slot in the case, case shut. Swivelling carefully to face down into the tower, hefting the case right-handed, left hand for guidance on the wall and with the torch in it for minimal illumination when necessary, an occasional flash downward at her feet and the next few steps. *Not* looking into the void on her right: had never had a head for heights. Traffic sound growing as she neared the bottom – but only a *distant* hum, above all no crescendo backed by blaring horns and/or screeching tyres. At least, none of that *yet*.

Ground floor – amongst the litter of fallen stone and rotted timber and a stronger amalgam of smells than there'd been higher up. Pocketing the torch: even blind, you'd have found the gap in the wall, by the inflow of rain-chilled north wind: also a greying in the blackness, recognisable shape of the breach. And when *in* it, an aura of light from the streets and the traffic on them, sound also amplified.

Find the bike: and no problem, she was there, propping it against the wall and manoeuvring the transceiver case into the panier, then rearranging the musty-smelling laundry around and over it.

The van started up at that moment. The sound froze her – and she stayed frozen, lowering the bike and watching for the van's emergence from the side-street. As now . . . Lights scything weakly across this area as it swung out, lights that might conceivably have reflected on the bike's shiny handlebars but in fact posed no such hazard. She was crouching then, hearing bicycles – the whirr of their tyres, by the sound of it three or four of them. The van had stopped: at the corner, obviously, but – on the move again now, turning away – the way from which it had come, forty or forty-five minutes ago.

For the moment, nothing else. Oh, voices . . . But the hell, move out.

No more pauses either. No matter what, keep going. None of their business, ignore them. The one and only imperative now being to get clear. Out through the area of detritus, into the road and over it – no reason to give a damn for any other passer-by, once in the public road – there were people here and there, but none of them had any more interest in her than she had in them, the only menace was or *might* be *Funkabwehr* in a van or vans. They *were* still very much a danger because one was still in the crucial area and carrying the transceiver, which if discovered would mean – well, the end of everything.

Cover some distance, though, you'd cease to be of interest.

Getting there, Jake, getting there. In the alley where the van had been. Nearly seven. Freewheeling to the bottom of it and turning right: not racing, but not dawdling either. Visualising the map and telling herself that at the next corner she'd go left, should then be heading south; hold on that way about a kilometre, then another left should bring one to the river.

Old Rosie had told me, over a table in the Café des Beaux Arts, 'I was feeling cock-a-hoop, all right. You can say *that* without fear of contradiction.'

'I can imagine, Rosie.'

'Thought I'd licked it. Imagining the despatch rider being halfway from Sevenoaks to Baker Street with my signal for decoding by the night staff. Nearer the reality, however, they'd have had a draft of it in plain language on the Duty Officer's desk before I'd got *anywhere*. Must have taken me at least half an hour getting down to the river and then up to Pont St-Michel, and – well, that was fine – no hue and cry, no nothing, how pleased Jake was going to be, I'd have been thinking. But there was a surprising amount of traffic on the bridge and by the time I was halfway over, it was only moving at a crawl – the cause of which was a checkpoint they'd set up at this town-centre end.'

'Oh, crikey.'

'More like oh Jesus Christ Almighty. Me with my little old transceiver and no way to go except right ahead where the bridge joins Allée Feuga, where they had a barrier across it. Gendarmes with vans, also Boches with Schmeissers and a couple of Light Fifteens. All slow-moving as hell – must have been the best part of another hour before it came to my turn. Can't swear to that, it's not the sort of detail one does remember after sixty years, but the rest of it – especially how it *felt* – well, I did contemplate throwing the transceiver off the bridge. No one could have stopped me, and I had all that time to think about it. It could have saved my life – but what for? I mean, without that piece of equipment, what was I? And what about Hardball, how'd I have told Jake?'

Slow shaking of the head as she stubbed out her cigarette, her eyes showing how vividly she *did* remember it.

'Just no way out, you see . . .'

A *gazo*-powered Renault that had been inching along in front of her for the past hour had been examined and waved on around the end of the barrier, and one of two uniformed gendarmes who'd been searching it and questioned its driver had gestured to her to approach him. Watching from the side were three or four Boche soldiers, one an NCO with a Schmeisser and the others riflemen.

Rosie scared, uncertain, looking from face to face as she wheeled her bike up closer. Encountering another one who'd crossed over from the other side where he'd been watching the other traffic-stream filing westward. Trench coat and soft hat, obviously Gestapo. That stream wasn't being checked, only slowed by the constriction.

'Where from?'

The shorter of the two gendarmes had shouted the question at her. She told him, waving back the way she'd come

– westward, then adjusting that to south-westward – 'From the hospital at Fonsorbes, monsieur.'

'Hospital *where*?'

'Fonsorbes – Sacré-Coeur.' Déclan's wife's place of work. 'See, my mother's –'

'What's this?'

The pannier full of dirty clothes. She told him, '*Blanchissage* – my mother's. She's ill, not capable, but they won't –'

The taller one reached across his colleague to lift a chemise – an old one of Berthe's – fastidiously between finger and thumb before allowing it to fall back. It was a joke of sorts: he'd winked at the other one. Rosie stuttering, close to tears, 'I'm taking it home to wash for her. At the hospital they would not permit –'

The German in the trilby cut in with 'You're wasting everyone's time, including mine. Let the child go.'

Child gazing at him – damp-eyed, trembly. Looking back at the gendarmes uncertainly: 'Messieurs?'

'Get along, then.'

Around the end of the barrier – a pole resting on oil drums which also had storm-lanterns on them – before mounting. Passing between the vans and a Citroen Light 15 that would be the German's. Feeling the stares of Boche soldiery as she mounted, and thanking God for the impatient one. Gestapist, of all unlikely saviours. The gendarmes on their own would have made her empty the panier, bet your boots they would. In fact, hadn't even got around to asking for her papers, which was usually the very first thing. Not that they wouldn't have passed muster, it was the transceiver that would have put her in a cattle-truck for Ravensbrück. Thank *God* for that Boche with his impatience or intolerance. More than ready for home now, one way and another, and putting all she had into it – up Allée Jules Guesde to the Grand Rond to start with, thence into the northbound Allée Verdier. On the home run, believe it or not, might almost call it one's home ground – from Boulevard Lazare Carnot into Jean Jaurès, Place Marengo only a kilometre ahead then, just over the canal.

11

Old Rosie smiled. 'You bet he was glad to see me. So was I to see him. He kissed me, for Pete's sake!'

'In defiance of SOE regulations?'

She touched her cheek. 'Kissed me *here*. Or this side, I don't remember. Well I mean, *would* one. Also hugged though, hugged each other. But if I have to go into this much detail we aren't going to get through the rest of it by tonight, are we?'

This was at breakfast in the Brasserie des Aviateurs. I'd not bothered having mine at the Mermoz; I'd worked into the small hours on my laptop, had the outlines of her story so far on the hard disk and backup, and we'd met here an hour earlier than we had the day before. I'd asked her whether their guest of honour was still expected to clock in on the Sunday morning, and she'd said yes, there was to be a Memorial Mass at St-Sernin's in the morning; he might or might not be there in time for that but definitely would be for the lunch. She'd booked me in for it as well – in the hotel's banqueting hall, opening with apéritifs at noon.

'OK?'

'Yes, of course, thank you very much –'

'Despite – I didn't mention this before – it'll mean having to listen to me again, since I'm down as a secondary guest speaker?'

'You are?'

'I offered – after the reunion's president had rather hinted – me being SOE's only representative – sort of tribute to the hero, old comradeship and so forth, although at higher levels it barely existed . . . Grim prospect, but –'

'Very good idea, I think. I'll look forward to it immensely, Rosie. Have you worked out what you'll tell them?'

She shrugged. 'Near enough. There's another speaker too, sort of backing me up. You met her, actually – in here, day or so ago –'

'Rosie – I was thinking, on my way here – sorry, abrupt change of subject – thinking that even with the whole of today, if there's as much to come as I anticipate we'll surely need the rest of Sunday – and listen, rather than risk spoiling the ship for a ha'p'orth of tar, which it *might* come to, how about staying over to Monday, make sure of it?'

'You mean change our flights.'

'Yes. If it cost anything – well, *would*, extending hotel bookings –'

'Don't worry about that. In for a penny . . . See how we're doing, and decide at lunchtime, shall we? I'd have to make a call or two, that's all – and you'd ring your wife, of course –'

'This evening, yes. *If* we're going to. This was to have been her last day in Ireland, she might extend that too. Decide at lunchtime, then, and meanwhile let's push it along a bit? Not blaming *you* in the least, I tend to pump you for detail I dare say I don't need – up to me to put flesh on the bones when I'm back *chez moi*, isn't it?'

'Meaning you'll be dreaming half of it up in any case. Here's coffee, at last.'

'Thing is, when we're home and I need some elaboration I've only to pick up the phone – eh?'

'We'll set hours for it.' She thanked the waitress, and began pouring coffee. Croissants and fruit would be coming, but she'd told the girl she'd have two dead or crazy customers on her hands if we didn't get coffee instantly. She added now, 'I won't be there every day – but you won't have all that many queries either, I hope.'

'I'll try not to, but –'

'See how it goes.'

'Absolutely. And to kick off with – if you're ready for this – what about your developing relationship with Jake?'

'If you think that's important.'

'Well – yes, I certainly do!'

'All right, then. In a nutshell – let's say I felt warmly towards him, and he felt *protective* of me. Coffee's not bad this morning, uh? He – well, because I was quite a bit younger than him – and I *looked* even younger than I was. And from time to time one did have to take quite serious risks, as often as not at his behest – that after all being part of his job as Chef de Réseau –'

'And you'd have responded to the protective attitude.'

'In how I *felt*, sure. Maybe would have more overtly, in other circumstances. Dare say we both would. We liked each other, were attracted to each other, and – all right, if things had turned out differently, might very well have come to something. You're wondering about Ben, aren't you, but – see, the plain fact is he doesn't feature in this. I'd had that little fling with him – which certainly was *not* any part of what you might call my repertoire –'

'You didn't expect to see him again.'

'I'd taken steps to ensure I didn't. Left no trail – you

200

know all that. Anyway – got the picture, me and Jake?'

'I think so. Enough to work on. Maybe when we approach the end –'

'Where do we go now?'

'That night at eleven, listening-out?'

Headphones on and ears peeled by two minutes past eleven, getting nothing but atmospherics and thinking *Come on, come on, let's get cracking, get it over?* They knew damn well this was a listening-out night, she'd even mentioned it in her transmission from the tower – in case having got her on the air at that earlier hour the Sevenoaks operator might have tried to cut a corner and get whatever she had for 'Lucy' off her chest; if she *had* tried to she'd have heard from Baker Street by now the reason she'd failed to connect – Baker Street having deciphered the tower signal and either redrafted whatever they'd meant to send or just added a follow-up.

Maybe told Sevenoaks to hold on, await new copy on its way down to them. Taking their bloody time about it, for some reason, perhaps having no option but to wait – Buck or one of his deputies to be consulted, for instance, unavailable for an hour or two. Shouldn't happen, but occasionally did, unavoidably. Listen-out time as established by Rosie's own message last Sunday night was 2300 to 0100; she could call it a night when she'd taken in whatever they might have for her, otherwise was stuck here for the full two hours.

After a longish day following a night that hadn't been exactly restful. She did have Benzedrine tablets in her room, but hadn't thought of them earlier and couldn't leave this now. Probably as well, in any case: they were fine if you knew it was going to be hours and hours, otherwise – well, just bloody well stay awake, was all, even if it took a bit of doing. Jake had urged her to be ready to respond to the first peep of the call when it came, and to be equally quick with her *Message received, out* when they signed off. He'd been into his nail-biting mode on account of having used the tower, almost certainly alerting the *Funkabwehr* to there being a pianist at work right here in town; they'd know there had to be messages inward as well as out, and that just a short burst of acknowledgement was as much as they could expect from the recipient, so they'd be sharpish on it, desperate not to miss any scrap of a clue to her locality. In fact to have picked up her earlier transmission they'd have been ranging the frequencies – and would now know which to be listening-out on in further attempts at eavesdropping; if they'd missed out on it, might get a helping hand from the RHSA radio-intercept centre in Paris, which was powerfully equipped, listened twenty-four hours a day and 365 days a year, supposedly retrieving and recording every syllable that *wasn't* lost to jamming or atmospherics. The recordings would then of course be worked on by code-breakers, who might or might not get lucky. They were alleged to find BCRA codes easier to break than the SOE ones. One didn't know very much about that operation – beyond the fact that it was to be feared.

Or respected, say. As were those bloody vans. One level down from which were goons on foot, in civvies, radio sets bulging like eight-month pregnancies under their topcoats, ear-plugs concealed by turned-up collars and turned-down hat-brims. If the vans got cross-bearings on Place Marengo for instance, and then you saw one of those types shuffling round – well, Benzedrine might come in handy if you were in a position to make a run for it, otherwise might think seriously about getting the cyanide capsule out of the elastic of one's knickers.

Never had seen one of those wired-up goons of course, only been told about them, but she thought she'd know one when she did. Anyway if you were at your set you couldn't also be watching the street. But then again wouldn't be transmitting either, not at any rate from this city. In warning her about minimising the receiving/acknowledging procedures, Jake had seemed to be wondering whether even *that* might not be reviewed. He hadn't got any distance with it, it had cropped up in a last-minute soliloquy when he'd been on the point of leaving, but if he was thinking of doing away with the listening-out routine from *chez soi*, presumably one would be expected to get out of town for that as well.

Not, she thought, while she had only the one set. Draw the line at *that* prospect. Cycling out of town minimally three nights a week with a transceiver on your bike, you'd inevitably wind up done for — meaning dead, like Wiggy. You could hope to get away with it now and again — like last night, for instance — but —

Sevenoaks calling.

She was on to it like a hawk, answering with a single blip — *Send your message: over* . . . It came in fast, wasn't very long and mercifully was all they had for her tonight. Lucy therefore signing-off instantly before switching off, unplugging from the mains then winding in the black wire. Time, eleven thirty-seven. Could have been a lot worse: so decypher this stuff before hitting the sack. And let no one ever say a pianist didn't earn her crust. With all the bits and pieces packed away and the case shut and locked and stowed away under the floorboards, she crept down to her room — tiptoeing because Berthe had turned in soon after Jake had left — and settled down with her school exercise book and one-time pad in the hope of making sense of this.

It came out as —

Transceivers which regrettably were not included in Jake 7 drop will be delivered by Hardball team on Canet-Plage night 29th November subject confirmation on 27th and 28th. Notification of adverse developments at your end should be sent urgently by day or night right up to 29th. Hardball team of 5 to be deployed as planned, Jake making whatever adjustments may be necessary following the Printemps losses. BCRA trio will require separate transportation to safe-house and on-routing to Marseille.

Made perfect sense, she thought, reading it over. Jake would cope all right, of course he would. And she'd have her transceivers, even though she'd need to be on that beach to receive them. And might find herself distinctly busy around the 27th–29th.

Head down now, and sweet dreams please, not nightmares. Just as well she hadn't taken Benzedrine . . .

Saturday morning, then – a fairly late one, after a good night's sleep with no 'three a.m. sweats', breakfast with Berthe and then a few routine chores. She'd memorised the salient points in Baker Street's spiel, had them in her head for Jake when they met him at the Café des Beaux Arts at one o'clock. Jake kissed them both, making rather more of a fuss of Berthe than of Rosie, and Berthe then tactfully withdrew: 'Telephone call that I'd forgotten, *must* make. I'll have whatever you're having.'

In other words whatever the café was offering this Saturday, which turned out to be bean soup followed if so desired by sliced sausage and onion. The place was quite full, there were a number of Germans in uniform and one pair in civilian clothes who had girls with them. Jake commented, '*Les occupants* quick enough to make 'emselves at home, eh?'

'The girls look happy, I must say.'

'Bound to. Invasions are always good for business. What came in, Suzie?'

She'd nodded, told him in a tone she might have used if he'd asked her what she'd been up to lately – confidential, but mildly entertaining – 'Twenty-ninth, Canet-Plage, subject to confirmation on the 27th *and* 28th. Any problems we have they want to hear of at once, up to the last minute. Hardball plans unchanged but it's up to you to make any quote adjustments unquote necessitated by the Printemps débâcle. *And*, the commandos will have my transceivers with them, and the three BCRA are to be conducted to a safe-house and on-routed to Marseille.' A smile. 'That's the lot.'

A nod and an easy smile: lunchtime gossip this, not war talk. 'We'll go over it later, Suzie.'

'Berthe has a hair appointment at two.'

'So she has. I'd forgotten that. And here she is . . .'

'Apologies, Jean.' Jake halfway to his feet, Berthe shaking her head as Rosie began to move, and murmuring, 'So nice to see you, and sweet of you to ask us. Isn't it cold, though!'

'The tramontane.' Pyrenean north wind, inducer of foul moods known as *le cafard*. 'Anyway soup should warm us. You're looking awfully well, Berthe.'

His hand resting on hers for a moment: Rosie thinking she'd turned a little pink. Well, she had. Smiling, baring a lot of teeth, telling him she'd never felt better. It might be that a sparse diet was actually beneficial. Incidentally, *wasn't* it thoughtful of Suzette to have brought the eggs and parsnips? Parsnip soup was one of her favourites, especially when combined with carrots; she'd be attending to that this evening. And so forth, with her eyes most of the time on Jake, and keeping the chatter going, while a German artillery major eating on his own was having difficulty keeping his eyes off her. Rosie recalling being told by an experienced SOE girl that on her first deployment, joining a *réseau* in Paris, on her first day there her Organiser had taken her to lunch at one of the premier restaurants in order to accustom her to the proximity of Krauts. He'd advised, 'When they're all around you, try thinking of yourself as a collaborator.'

205

She remarked when the major had left, 'Made a hit there, Berthe.'

'Oh, nonsense!'

Jake commented, 'Even Boches *can* show good taste.' He added, 'As well as bloody cheek.'

After lunch they walked her to the hairdresser's, Rosie having expressed interest in seeing where it was and getting something done about her awful mop some time – if it wasn't too exorbitant. Leaving Berthe there, strolling on down Rue Romiquières, Jake said, 'Awful mop, my foot. Make for the river, shall we?'

Through Rue Romiquières into Pargaminières, by which time she'd taken his arm. No one would have guessed at their being enemies of the State: just *promeneurs*, like many others, while Jake in fact asked her to go over the contents of last night's message again, and agreed she'd better be with the Canet-Plage reception party to take charge of her transceivers.

'Any apology for not sending them in the drop?'

'A hint of one – went so far as to use the word "regrettably".'

'I'd imagine *they* were somehow let down. Anyway you can be pretty sure they'll make certain of it this time.'

'Unless the felucca or its boat came to grief.'

'Sink us all, that, wouldn't it. Suzie, I'd better give you an outline of Stage One – so you can at least think for yourself if something comes in and I'm not around. From my own immediate angle of course – "adjustments" if any – I need Déclan's report on the St-Girons situation – late tomorrow, maybe – and Marc's on the coastal side of it. I'll be seeing him tomorrow too. Anyway – Fernier's band, whether or not he's still with it, is actually holed-up a dozen or more miles south-west of St-Girons now, and once we've got the commandos ashore that's where Déclan will leave them and where they'll stay while their CO, in care of Déclan,

206

confers with an individual who's familiar with the inside of the Noé prison camp. You asked about this, I remember – but the fact of his existence is as much as you need know. Déclan recruited him and there's a pecuniary inducement, of course. So – they'll be settling detail, timings of this and that – Michel Loubert'll be in on it too. Day or two or even three. Basically, the plan involves maquisards covering the perimeters of the action and the line of withdrawal – lines plural actually – and the commandos penetrating and touch wood scoring.'

'Withdrawing with their German, you mean.'

'Germans, plural. At which stage we – Countryman – will come into it again, but – leave that for the moment, better limit ourselves to Stage One – the commandos' transfer to St-Girons and then moving up to Montgazin. That was to have been covered by Fernier's bunch; if they're out of it, too bad – but wouldn't be catastrophic, they'll be replaced, that's all. Déclan'll be seeing Loubert as well as Fernier or Fernier's deputy – today, I mean – and if it's left them short-handed or with other problems they'll come up with a solution. Which I'll go along with, unless it can be improved on, obviously. All right that far, Suzie?'

'With maquisards forming a perimeter around Noé and covering more than one withdrawal route, you're going to need plenty, aren't you?'

A nod. 'May need reinforcing from elsewhere, as I said. Have all to volunteer, what's more, may not be any picnic and there's no point disguising that. There are also major rivalries between different Maquis groups, which doesn't help.'

'Is the lost weaponry no problem?'

'Same answer, really. For the time being beg, borrow or steal – and in the longer term another *parachutage*.'

'Their task – the maquisards' – being to hold off intervention and/or pursuit, presumably.'

'That's about it. As you say, in some strength. The snag isn't so much numbers *per se* as numbers with adequate military training – a problem we were aware of before, now somewhat exacerbated, and very little time to do anything much about it. Suzie, how d'you feel – carry on down to the river, or turn back up here?'

'Up here', she saw, meant up the Rue Valade. She shrugged. 'Don't mind. If you're pressed for time –'

'Quick look at the river from Place St-Pierre, *then* back?'

'Fine.'

'Next thing, then – night of the 29th. Just off the cuff, subject to further thought, discussion and so forth ... Déclan's got his work cut out, he's really the prime mover and he'll be at it for – well, maybe a week, starting by getting our visitors away inland as smartly as it can be done. Incidentally, Baker Street's confirmation on those two nights probably means that on the 27th they'll confirm it's on for the 29th, and on the 28th give us a time and location for the actual landing. Felucca skipper being close enough by then to give at least an approximation of his landfall. He tells them, they tell us – and one item in your next transmission, Suzie, must be that he should put them ashore as soon after dark as possible – to give Déclan time to have them under cover before daylight on the 30th.'

'Right. But confirmation coming in on the 28th – a Saturday, not a routine listening-out night – they'd stick to the 2300–0100, I suppose ...'

'You're the authority on that. But yes, surely. Anyway – it's a long haul for Déclan – on the 117, through Quillan and Foix. Precipitous here and there – you know, deep gorges and hairpin bends. But not a *bad* road, and if the landing's gone smoothly the opposition won't have been alerted as it was by your Lanc.'

'Something to be said for beach landings.'

'Well – touch wood. But this brings us to the three BCRA agents, which is an obvious job for young Marc, especially with his own BCRA background. He can take 'em in his van to one of the *planques* he used in his escape-line work, put 'em on a train in the morning – I'd guess from Narbonne. Won't tell him yet – don't want him briefing his safe-house friends days before it's necessary. And last but far from least, Suzie, I think I'll bring *you* along in a Mahossier, Jorisse *gazo*. Wouldn't normally take one that distance out of town, I'd use the train, but I'll find reason for it. One advantage being that we might return here by way of places from which you could (a) let Baker Street know the ball's rolling – and/or whatever else – and (b) maybe stash one or both transceivers in locations you'd find handy.'

'Beginning to sound like genius.'

'Maybe has its merits. We'll work on it. But now here's another stroke of genius for you.' Waiting for traffic, before crossing into Place St-Pierre, he had a hand on her arm as if he thought she needed to be restrained. She didn't mind that: but postponed his change of subject by asking whether she shouldn't have *some* notion of what was to follow Stage One.

'The break-in and/or break-out, obviously, and while that's happening we're on the sidelines, but then what? I'm not asking for detail, but –'

'No. All right . . . Déclan's in the driving seat, and he'll be in touch with me, or if anything should have happened to me, with you. But our main concern – after they've got him out – the ball we'll have our eye on will be the number-one German – uh?'

'Ulrich von Schleben, alias Schurmann.'

'*Very* good, Suzie. And you might as well know Baker Street's code-name for him is Gustave. He's our concern, the others aren't.'

'Poor them.'

'Not necessarily. For us anyway it hangs on whether von Schleben's alive and in Déclan's and Loubert's hands. He'll be in touch – Déclan will – and there you are. I'm a little hesitant in going further – you made rather a point of not wanting to know more than you need.'

She'd nodded. 'Only I wouldn't want to find myself out on a limb without any of the answers, if you happened not to be around to provide them. And the closer we get to the action –'

'Absolutely right – but if I wasn't around, you'd get all you'd need from Déclan. He'd need *you* as much as you'd need him – and as you have confidence in each other – there you are, no problem.'

'Touch wood. But yes, sure, Jake.'

'You really should call me Jean.'

'I know. Sorry.'

'River's looking gloomy, isn't it.'

'It's the weather, not the river. Like the lochs in Scotland – dour as hell on a day like this, then the sky turns blue and they take your breath away . . . I interrupted, about Hardball, you were starting on something else?'

He nodded, checking the time. 'Start heading back, d'you think?'

'OK.' She took his arm again: exchange of smiles in so doing. A pair of gendarmes passing, eyes flickering over her then Jake, returning to her: then gone. Jake squeezing her arm inside his: 'See those envious looks? Asking each other now "How's *that* for cradle-snatching?"'

'Oh, nonsense!'

'Green with blooming envy . . . Suzie, here it is. Your next listening-out night is Monday. I'd sooner you didn't do it from Berthe's, at any rate in this next week. As it happens, I'll almost certainly have stuff for you to send, but in any case, even listening-out, we've alerted them to a pianist tinkling away right here in town, and for the time being let's not remind them.'

'So I'm on my bike again?'

'Marc's van. After last night's performance, the safer we play it the better, and that means well out in the sticks. He'll be here tomorrow, returning coastward Monday, I'll have him pick you up on his way out of town – you plus bike and transceiver – midday? How about at the café where you and I met?'

'Outside it, maybe. That's Rue Tivoli, isn't it . . . Look, close by there – Rue Sabatier, runs between the Grand Rond and the canal. There's a stretch of greenery, more natural place to be dawdling around – if it rains and he's late I can be sheltering under a tree, for instance.'

'All right. Rue Sabatier under the trees, twelve noon. Then as to where he takes you, how about somewhere north of St-Pons-de-Thomières – climbs steeply there, little place called Brassac for instance –'

'I'll check on the map. St-Pons I remember though, last Sunday, we held straight on, the route to Béziers, which was a mistake of course –'

'Say *that* again. Our young friend's mind must have been wandering. Best in fact to turn north before that junction – straight up into country that's actually mountainous – not *straight* by any means, but –'

'He can drop me and push on, and I'll bike back on Tuesday. What about the stuff you want sent?'

'I'll bring it to Berthe's, Monday morning. I'll have had Déclan's report as well as Marc's by then. That's about all there'll be, as far as one can see at this moment. And I think it's about all I need plague you with. Got over the shock of last night's road-block, I hope, slept all right?'

'Like an old dog.'

211

'Some little old dog.' He'd laughed. 'Sevenoaks didn't keep you waiting too long?'

'Long enough that I was getting a *little* frantic.'

'Tomorrow, enjoy your day of rest. Two full nights and the day between. If I were you I'd take it *very* easy.'

'I will. Wash my smalls and oil the bike . . . Will you be seeing Déclan when he's back, or just – communicating?'

'Seeing – probably Sunday evening. Why?'

'I'd like to get a battery to him for charging. He's presented me with one that was Wiggy's, I'll switch to that now. Mine still has life in it, but after a couple more trips including this one with Marc –'

'I'll collect it from you on Monday, give it to him either Wednesday or Thursday. Wednesday probably for Déclan and see Marc Thursday. Tomorrow week you'll have your spares with their own batteries in any case, and –'

He'd jerked her to a halt. 'Look out.'

A car coming very fast out of the road that joined this one from the right: coming *very* fast although it was a *gazo*, and taking the corner – this way, into Rue Valade and towards the river – on two screaming tyres – a Renault, dark-coloured, with that high sweep of mudguards – all out of nowhere so fast she didn't see the pursuing Citroen until it was taking the same corner and the Renault out of control had cannoned off the corner and gone over on its side, crumpled metal instead of rubber doing the screaming now, also showering sparks. She'd heard shots and a man had either jumped or been flung into the road, was running – doubled, baboon-like – for the church steps, the Citroen skidding to a halt, two men out of it with pistols in their hands and the runner had been hit, gone sprawling on his face, the man who'd shot him – soft hat, trench coat, no prizes for any guesswork *there* – blundering after him, pistol in one hand and with the other waving shocked bystanders out of his way, snarling at

212

them in that ugly language while his partner dragged another body out of the smashed and smoking Renault, which if it had been petrol-powered would surely have been in flames. This second victim was just a boy, and was alive she thought, although the one leaving a trail of blood on the damp roadway as his assassin dragged him to the Citroen probably was not. They were slinging both of them inside, booting a trailing leg in so the door would shut. Bystanders including Jake with an arm round Rosie watching motionless and speechless as the car reversed to the corner, turned, drove off – through Place Anatole France then right into Rue des Lois.

Women were giving tongue now. And an old man hobbling on two sticks called in a high tone, 'Heroes of the Resistance!' Jake nodded to him: 'If they're lucky, *grandpère*, dead ones.'

Rosie said, 'Gave one thought, that incident. How I happened to recall it as clearly as I do – or think I do. Really quite early in one's field career, you know, to have seen that man shot down, his blood on the road and the people just snarled at, waved aside – as if the swine considered themselves justified, in the right, even *entitled* to be made way for while they did it. And all of us just *standing* aside, watching. Me included. My reaction – I can still feel it – mixture of astonishment and pure hate. That such creatures shared the earth with us, even presented themselves as part of the human race. I know I tried to express this to Jake when we were on our way again, and his comment was simply "Why we're here, isn't it. What it's about. At least, far as *I'm* concerned." *That* simple – dare say because he'd been at it long enough that it didn't have the impact it had on me, but on top of that – occurred to me then, still does after sixty years – surprise that one's feelings did *not* include any great sense of – well, personal insecurity. *Fright*. One was seething, loathing, but for some reason *not* quaking.'

213

'I know pretty well what you mean.'

'I'm sure you do. You got that feeling across more than once in the other books. For *me* you did.'

'Remarkable how clearly it's stuck in your memory, for all that. You had quite a few much nastier experiences in the next few years, didn't you. The Gestapo in Rouen, for instance – and in Paris, Rue des Saussaies? And what about the market-place in – oh, St-Valéry-sur-Vanne?'

She'd nodded. 'Happened to be the first time I'd seen cold-blooded murder, I suppose. And – out for a stroll, out of the blue that savagery, and just minutes later there we still were – strolling on.'

After a bit of a pause, I switched the subject – as we'd agreed I might without offending her. 'Rosie – while I think of it – is there anything special to record about your sortie in Marc's van that Monday? You'd have had a quiet Sunday, Jake would have visited you on the Monday morning, and at noon or thereabouts you'd have met Marc in Rue Sabatier?'

'As arranged. Yes. Must have. Rue Sabatier . . . Why, yes – when he told me about Gabrielle Vérisoin. In fact I'd have asked him about her.'

'Has the girl you lost turned up yet, Marc?'

A glance at her, and no immediate answer. She shrugged: 'Don't want to seem nosy, if it's – you know, private and personal. But you mentioned it to Jake –'

'Who told you, evidently.'

'I'd asked how you were, he said you were in the dumps, and losing the girl as a reason for it. Good enough reason too, if –'

'Yes.' Blinking through thick lenses at the road ahead. 'I think it's likely she's been arrested. In which case –'

'By whom, arrested?'

A shrug. 'Gestapo. Abwehr. Not all that much difference,

214

is there. What for, I don't know either. But why else would she simply vanish, without a prior word to anyone, not even to her children's nursemaid? None of the servants have any idea – why, even her husband doesn't!'

'D'you mean – you've been in touch with him?'

'As it happens, I've arranged to meet him.' Shifting gear, turning on to the 622, the stretch of it leading to Revel. 'Never set eyes on him before, and he'd apparently never heard of me, although he agreed to see me – which in a way surprised me. What do you know about either of them?'

'Only what you must have told Jake. She helped you somehow with customers of your escape-line, and she's a raving beauty – and Jake – Jean – referred to her as your girlfriend. Whether or not that means –'

'Hang on.' Manoeuvring around a cartload of logs. 'I'll tell you –'

'– also she's Gaullist, but her husband's Pétainist and *Chef des Compagnons de France*?'

'A bigwig, yes. Offices all over the place, knows all the other high-ups and Vichy swine.'

'Despite which she helped you with escapers?'

'People change, is her answer to that. And war changes everything. On the face of it in any case she's a happily or say *successfully* married woman – who still has her own you might say *private* life. How she explained it to me, that is, or in so many words. *His* concern as she explained it is first and foremost to hold on to what he's got. In his view Germany's bound to win the war, how would it help for him to throw everything away?'

'What's happening with the children, d'you know?'

'They have a nanny, and attend nursery school. The time I told Jean about, Gabi was in fact in Lézignan-Corbières to pick them up from school that afternoon, lunching by herself in a *restaurant avec chambres* of which I myself had made use occasionally. In fact it's — was, effectively — a safe-house, although not much used I thought by anyone but me. Anyway, at that time there was a couple my sister had sent down — Jewish, a surgeon and his wife, arriving that morning on the bus from — oh, Montpellier, most likely — they'd have arrived before noon if the bus had been on time, and I'd have collected them that evening, moved them on to Perpignan. Whereas all that had arrived was an individual who must have been DST, accompanied by gendarmes who remained in their van outside while this one ordered lunch for himself and said he'd like to look around the place. If the food was as good as he'd heard he might bring his wife for a weekend, some time. Bullshit like that — which they had to pretend to believe, and the *patronne*'s daughter showed him round — bedrooms, even the attic rooms and cellar, he insisted. Gabi meanwhile had had her lunch — knowing her, probably no more than a salad — and while the man was still upstairs the *patronne*, who'd become a friend of mine in recent months but must have known *her* for years, whispered to her could she possibly do her the huge favour of going by the bus stop in the square, with an eye out for a pair of strangers, the man actually a surgeon, Jewish, they'd probably have some baggage but not more than they could carry — well, Gabi checked the flow — yes, of course she would. Behind her the DST person had entered, *patronne* turning to give him a smile and indicate a table, murmuring "*Un petit moment, monsieur*" and to Gabi then: "Enchanting to have seen you again, madame. I trust *Monsieur le Chef des Compagnons* is in good health?" Gabi replying affirmatively, adding in not much more than a breath, "I'll do what I can."'

Through Revel, the crossroads where ten days earlier on her bike she'd taken pot-luck on which way to go, the van picking up speed now on that same route, for Sorèze and eventually St-Pons-de-Thomières. Marc continuing, 'By luck, she was in the square only minutes after the bus had pulled in and disgorged some passengers, including a couple recognisable as my *colis*. Those who'd got out had already more or less dispersed, while these two strangers had made a show of knowing exactly where they were going, and actually started, she told me afterwards, in precisely the wrong direction. Anyway she took them home with her and installed them in the chauffeur's cottage, which happened to be empty – still is, they have no chauffeur – and which with her permission I've made use of a couple of times since then. But I called at the manor that evening – back door of course, offering lobsters, and she'd been on the lookout for me, came to the door herself – dressed for the evening as she would be, in such a house, that style of living – but obviously expecting me or someone of my sort, anticipating a servant answering the bell and scaring me off, or worse still her husband taking an interest –'

He'd checked himself: adding, 'No, actually he wouldn't . . .'

'She must have had some connection with the Resistance?'

'I don't know. Only that she was there answering my ring at the back door, which by the look of her – she looked absolutely stunning – she might never have done in her life before – and the cook, huge woman, close behind her, probably scandalised by such conduct. Anyway she – *Madame* as she was to me then – bought the lobsters I had with me, directed me to the cottage, said "Come by again", then smiled and added "With lobsters, any time", then in a murmur, "Best not at weekends."'

'Ho-hum.'

'Well – quite.' Thumb on the van's horn as he swerved to avoid some children. Resuming then: 'I took her up on it, naturally. Not daring to believe in – well, *that* aspect of it, but anyway what it came down to was I could use the cottage if I ever needed to, but if I ran into her husband I'd be on my own, she'd only recognise me as the *poissonnier*, would never have given me any such invitation.'

'Would she have had much to tell the Gestapo about you?'

'About *me*? Why would she? Even if –'

'Your escape-line, she knew about. And to have reacted so swiftly and positively must have – I mean, can't have been exactly new to that kind of thing – d'you think? What about your involvement since then with *us*?'

Glance of surprise, sharp tone: 'What d'you think I am – a halfwit?'

'Well – she might surely have suspected –'

'For all she knows, the escape-line's still in operation.'

'But even knowing that much about you, Marc – under Gestapo pressure –'

'*If* she's in their hands, it's on account of her own activities. Poor darling. What good would it do her to bring me into it – involving herself in that as well?'

Made sense, she realised. In her shoes, one would hardly be inclined to admit complicity in anything they didn't already know about. Marc, reckless or slapdash as he might be, did more or less have his head screwed on. Except – in her own view – in this intention of contacting Gabrielle's husband. Not, admittedly, that one knew anything much about the man. Nothing, really, beyond an impression that each of them minded his/her business. Marc would presumably have a much greater insight into the couple's relationship – as well as his own with Gabi – and it might well justify that intention. Of which he was sure enough to make no secret: which otherwise he might have. One tended to think of him as a boy, she recognised, even as something of a tearaway – the Don Juan element referred to earlier by Jake, for instance, making it not improbable that he'd at least have had aspirations of that kind in regard to Gabi – one had also to bear in mind that his had never been a *trivial* occupation.

Any more than hers was. From the moment she'd landed in France, as an agent of SOE she'd effectively been under sentence of death. As had the surgeon and his wife: Jews caught on the move, even out of the *Zone Occupée* into what had been the *non-occupée*, knew it before they started. And the *patronne* of that restaurant – as well as her daughter and anyone else in her employ.

And anyone who'd helped them along the way. For every single escaper, an awful lot of heads on the block.

'What happened to the owner of the *restaurant avec chambres*, Marc?'

'Nothing, as far as I know. It's no longer usable as a safe-house, of course: even though they've no proof it ever was. DST must have had a tip-off, that's all. Thanks to Gabi, as long as the woman keeps her nose clean from now on, she may be OK. Imagine, though – those two would simply have walked into the bastards' waiting arms: and the *patronne* and her family would be either dead or in Ravensbrück.' He changed the subject: 'Sending London my report on the beaches tonight, eh?'

'Amongst other stuff. Not such a lot from you, was there?'

'Not so much yet. But – early days, huh?'

He'd reported that certain lookout posts had been taken over by Boches, and that an armed launch or patrol boat had based itself in Port Vendres. It had two heavy machine-guns on it, and small depth-charges on its stern. The rest of his information was of general rather than specifically coast-defence interest: Perpignan full of Boche troops, Gestapo setting themselves up in a luxurious villa just outside the town, governor and army commander establishing themselves in the castle. The governor – named – was reputedly a drunken sadist.

Marc said, pushing a pack of Gitanes in her direction, 'So the feluccas are still operating.'

'Are they?'

A smile, of sorts, lift of the eyebrows. 'Why else am I required to do all this research?'

'Surely because the future of felucca operations is uncertain and they don't want them running into trouble as they might be, with our *occupants* on this coast now. That's what I'm given to understand.'

'You don't think it might be something to do with Hardball?'

'Don't *think* so.' She shrugged. 'There's a lot I don't get told, though. Some of what I *do* know is only because I have to code it or decode it. I've discussed this several times with Jake. Jean, I mean. He's inclined to be secretive, as we all know, but that happens to suit me and he knows it. Those beaches, though, all north of Perpignan – I'd have thought somewhere nearer the Spanish border'd be easier from the feluccas' point of view?'

'Uh-huh. Not from ours either. There *are* landing places further south – including some smugglers are said to use. But that's something else. For the felucca operations – well, for one thing we have a low coastline up this way – whereas down there you're into the foothills and it's mountainous, cliffs precipitous. See, a felucca sending a boat in needs to come fairly close in itself, but it can't show itself offshore in daylight, so it starts inshore after dusk – and where you have that high coastline – I'm talking about visibility range from shore – they'd need to start from a long way out. Uh? Then again, these are fine, long beaches. Shingle ridges that hide the actual shoreline from coast roads – and a wide landing area for the boat to steer for – which in foul weather –'

'I can imagine.'

'Also from our point of view, access. Whereas nearer the border you have the *Zone Interdite* – entry banned, patrols who shoot at anything that moves. Even before the Boches moved in –'

'OK.' Expelling smoke. 'I get the picture.'

'Ask *me* a question, see, you get an answer.'

'That's a little unfair, Marc.'

'Is it?' Drawing on his cigarette, and looking at her.

'A test of it – were you and Gabi lovers?'

Hard look, then. Expulsion of breath and Gitane fumes, shake of the head as he turned away. Meaning, she wondered, *mind your own business*, or *no, we weren't*? And another question – which she would *not* put to him – might be whether apart from any physical relationship, he might actually be *in love* with her, really deeply so, therefore not thinking straight?

Telling him, crushing out the stub of her cigarette, 'It's nothing to me, Marc. Entirely your own affair. Only I do wonder whether it mightn't be wiser to steer clear of the husband. If Gestapo *is* involved, Christ's sake, best to keep your distance?'

12

Rosie told me, touching her ruby brooch, 'Never was sure about Voreux's relationship with Gabrielle. He neither confirmed nor denied it, just wouldn't discuss it. I've been racking my brains to sort it out, but if I ever did have it making sense I'm darned if I do now.'

She'd told me she wasn't sure whether Marc ever did keep the appointment he'd made with Vérisoin. She *thought* he'd told Jake a day or two later that he'd decided not to go through with it: and Jake was told at some point by his business partner Jacques Jorisse that according to gossip circulating at his golf club Charles-Henri Vérisoin had been arrested and his offices were being searched. Jake himself being up to his eyes in Hardball detail by then, especially in Déclan's end of it, really not having time to spend on side-issues of this kind.

'In any case, nothing he could have done about it.'

'Absolutely not, but –'

'You see – some of my thinking at that stage was that if he was madly in love with his Gabi – which he might have been, wasn't the sort of guy who'd bare his soul – to me or perhaps even less to Jake –'

'I'm sure not. No. Could be part of the answer. But sticking to our narrative line, Rosie – if we may – you got your message out that night, I suppose? Jake's summary of his and Déclan's situation reports? Marc dropped you and drove on, you came back here on the Tuesday on your long-suffering *bicyclette*?'

We'd finished our breakfast some time ago. I had the contents of that last chapter in my head and a few notes to support it, despite there having been a highly frustrating hiatus in the form of the couple from Rennes, the man I'd called Guy Lannuzel in *Return to the Field*, and another pair with them. They'd all drifted off, at last, still talking nineteen to the dozen, and Rosie had dealt with the waitress – the redhead again – while musing on whether Voreux and his Gabi had or had not been lovers, which didn't seem to me to be of great significance – at this stage, anyway. She did tend to get stuck from time to time on some such issue, worrying at it like a little old terrier until called off. Had left it now, in any case: telling me, 'Wasn't the damn *bicyclette* that suffered . . . But yes, must have. I remember spending one night in a damp bean-stack, it could have been that one. I'd have had food and a flask of coffee with me too – learnt my lesson that first time, saved only by Jake's chicken and the wine. And I'd have waited for daylight before starting the long slog back. Seventy bloody miles or so – if you'll excuse my French – but I must have been back at Berthe's late after-noon or early evening, because Jake was there and Berthe wasn't. I remember this because it was a relief to tell him about Marc's intention of calling on Gabrielle's husband, which had been worrying me.'

'Worry *him*?'

'Yes. Simple and obvious truth being that any situation in which one might find oneself brushing up against *La Geste*, as *résistants* called the Gestapo, was to be avoided. Our golden

223

rule was not *ever* to stick our necks out. Very *last* thing. Which oddly enough was why Jake had decided against moving out of his apartment in that square although Gestapo had set themselves up in a hotel barely spitting-distance away from him; if he'd moved, *might* have drawn attention to himself. And if Gabrielle was in the bastards' clutches, Marc should have stuck to minding his own business. Anyway, Jake was meeting him in Carcassonne next day or the one after, there was nothing he could do about it any sooner, he'd either find out then what had transpired or try to talk him out of it. The fear was that Vérisoin might be provoked into putting the Gestapo on to him: on the other hand Marc wasn't actually an imbecile, would surely make his approach in some acceptable manner.'

'And Vérisoin'd hardly be hobnobbing with Gestapists, in those circumstances.'

'You're right, of course. And as Marc would have reasoned, before making his appointment.'

'Presenting himself would you guess as the fishmonger or as Gabrielle's admirer?'

'Perhaps to start with, fishmonger. With an eye to his business and apparent loss of a valued customer. Touch of admiration for *Madame* thrown in, maybe. Valued customer for whom he'd developed a respect. Respect rather than admiration – or respect tinged with admiration, say. Really a very French thing, isn't it – they being so much more class-conscious than we are. *En passant* he'd acknowledge his own presumption in claiming any degree of friendship even, with one so very much his social superior. That'd be essential, wouldn't it – perhaps doubly so with a man like Vérisoin.' She'd flipped a hand, in her characteristic manner. 'Roughly on those lines.'

'As a smart lawyer he'd be concerned to rumble Marc's real motive, wouldn't he? Which is not entirely clear to *me*, I may say.'

In my imagination I saw Jake thoughtfully stubbing out a cigarette, probably not *quite* understanding it himself. Marc so crazy about the woman that his thinking might not be entirely rational? A concept that had occurred to Rosie earlier, one remembered. And at an earlier stage he *had* given Jake the impression of being – what did they call it then – *smitten*? Although what he might have hoped to get out of the woman's husband . . .

Shrugging it off, anyway, with a repetition of 'If I'm in time, I'll try to talk him out of it.' And then, 'You must be whacked, Rosie.'

'The old pins *are* feeling it a bit.'

Chef de Réseau's eyes on them: 'Some "old pins", if I may say so.'

'But speaking of being whacked – my next listening-out night being tomorrow, Wednesday – if you're still against my doing it from here –'

A nod. 'So happens I've hit on another location you could get to and from easily enough by bike. Nothing like as far as last night's, but a reasonable distance – northeast from here, high, fair-sized patch of forest – I'd say as good as anywhere we'd find, in these parts.'

'Show me?'

How these sessions tended to go: Rosie recalling or semi-recalling events and conversations, and me visualising and expanding on them. Fictionalising, you might call it, but essentially putting bare facts or fragments of fact into a shape that more or less made sense – with snatches of dialogue insinuating themselves more or less of their own accord.

Prompting her now with 'So you'd have had to cycle to this new place on the Wednesday, and again – somewhere – on the Friday *and* Saturday – 27th and 28th, as per London's message after you'd reported on the *parachutage*?'

'In theory yes, but I was thinking I might dig my heels

225

in when it came to the Saturday. To come pedalling back into town Sunday morning, *and* get down to the coast with Jake that same day – and that night on the *plage* or thereabouts probably no sleep at all . . .' Pausing, gazing past my shoulder into the grey, wet street: 'Rain's stopped, might as well get along, d'you think? Actually I do rather need –'

'Snap.'

'Well. Great minds . . . In fact Jake was right to play it as safe as it could be played. Especially remembering how determined I'd been not to take risks I didn't have to – "do a Wiggy", all that stuff – and the degree of risk we'd already taken, using that tower.' On her feet now, adding 'And as to the listening-out excursions, if he was taking me down there in his office car, I could sleep then, couldn't I, several hours of kip.' That sudden smile of hers: when she'd been twenty-four, it must have been quite devastating. 'Meet in the foyer in ten minutes, shall we?'

Waiting for her in the Ambassade's foyer, thinking it over and making a few more notes – the ten minutes becoming fifteen or twenty – I realised the Wednesday or Thursday might have been too late for Jake to have advised Marc against keeping his appointment with Vérisoin; I could see that at about the time Jake and Rosie were discussing it, on that Tuesday, he'd more likely have been parking his van in the yard of the ice factory and walking through into Perpignan's business centre to Rue Mirabeau where the lawyer had his office. *Head* office – which Marc would no doubt have seen often enough from the outside, *Charles-Henri Vérisoin, Avocat* – etc. – in gilt lettering on the curtained glass, and trying to visualise the man of that name as Gabi had once described him – 'Brain like a razor, *looks* more of a donkey. No – be fair to him, say a horse. He's not a *small* man. Actually he's quite sweet – and *very* kind, but –'

A sigh: with her eyes lingering on Marc's lean, rather swarthy face. So *strong*, Denise had often said: 'A brother to rely on through thick and thin – eh, Marc?' While Gabi had called it an assassin's face – and meant that as a compliment!

Should have made a move then – when *she*, he thought, had been in a mood not to resist. In retrospect, one saw it: at the time, may have missed an opportunity. Equally though, should *not* have risked involving her with Denise. Not that there was any certainty or evidence it was that that had brought in the Abwehr here or *La Geste* up there: the notion had hit him during the interview in Narbonne, returned and tormented him since Gabi's disappearance.

His fault they'd got her . . .

Number 114. *Charles-Henri Vérisoin*. Heavy oak door with a brass bell-push on it. Slight constriction in the gut as he put his thumb on it and a moment later heard a key turn in the lock. Surprised – slightly – that it should have been locked in the first place.

'Bonjour, monsieur . . .'

A clerk – young, dark-haired, pale, nervy-looking.

'My name's Voreux. I have an appointment with Monsieur Vérisoin. I'm a few minutes early, but –'

'Come in.'

'Thank you.' Removing his broad-brimmed rain-hat as he stepped inside and the clerk pushed the door shut, lock snapping down. There was a stout, older man at one desk, two others unoccupied, at that end of the room. All quiet, not at all the busy office he'd imagined.

Strain in the older one's face, and something peculiar in this other's.

'A moment, please.'

Clerk moving towards one of two inner doors. Hadn't invited him to sit down, although there were several chairs at a round table with some newspapers and a large glass ashtray

227

on it; so presumably he wasn't to be kept waiting. The clerk had gone through, and Marc heard, 'Monsieur . . .'

'Here already?'

Not quite real French. Not far off it, but –

'Show him in.'

The same slight harshness, foreignness. And a growl in another voice – both recognisable suddenly, and this second one – Abwehr sergeant, name of Behm – in civvies this time – appearing now behind the clerk – who'd given Marc a helpless, 'not *our* fault' look . . .

Jerk of the sergeant's head: 'Viens.'

No Charles-Henri Vérisoin: only Abwehr lieutenant Hohler: in a light-grey suit, green silk tie. He'd been in civvies last time, of course: but he'd had a haircut, looked less like a young university lecturer, more like a young soldier slightly dandified. Marc pretty well stunned, fighting for self-control in this situation he was simply going to have to cope with – surprise being natural enough therefore OK, shock or panic definitely not to be evinced. The *leutnant* was seated at a large, roll-top desk that had to be Vérisoin's, and he'd nodded towards a narrow, walnut chair facing it from a distance of two or three metres, obviously placed there for Marc's use. And a litter of stuff – drawers that had been pulled out of the desk, their contents and those of cupboards strewn around, a search in progress which he'd interrupted. The sergeant had shut the door and was standing – presumably – somewhere behind him. Back against the door, maybe, as he had last time.

In case their prisoner made a bolt for it?

Would have, given half a chance you'd get away.

'Sit, Voreux.'

'All right.'

On the desk, a silver-framed portrait of Gabrielle. Her

film-star looks, mass of dark hair, décolletage, eyes dreamy with her own awareness of the general effect.

'Tell me what's your business with Charles-Henri Vérisoin.'

'Well – I'd made an appointment –'

'We know that, it's in the diary, I'm asking you what for.'

'Well –'

'Come on – what for?'

'To discuss the – the apparent disappearance of his wife.'

'Some reason to think he'd want to discuss it with you?'

'No. I was surprised when he agreed to see me, but –'

'This would have been your first meeting with him, would it?'

'Yes – as it happens –'

'Never met him at his house, either?'

'Never anywhere. But I know his wife –' movement of the head towards her portrait – 'who's vanished, and –'

'What has been the nature of your relationship with Madame Vérisoin?'

'Well, she's been a customer – for lobsters primarily –'

Hohler looked boyish when he laughed. The sergeant had chuckled too, somewhere behind there. Marc lifted his hands: 'I've no idea why I should be questioned like this, what I'm supposed to have done or how what I said then amuses you.'

'Lobsters *primarily*, eh?'

Shrugging slightly. 'See, people of their kind, who have a taste for such things and can afford them – lobsters, crabs, oysters, scallops, langoustine and other special items – turbot for instance – which in present circumstances tend not to come their way because the regular merchants rail such luxuries away to Paris –'

'Quite a looker, isn't she?'

Leaning back in his chair, feasting blue eyes on Gabi. 'The other photo he had there is of himself shaking hands with

229

General Pétain. I've turned that one on its face, but she – no one in his right mind would turn *her* down – uh?'

Marc looking from her portrait back to Hohler. There'd been a snort of amusement from the sergeant. He said evenly, 'She's an extremely nice woman, as well as beautiful.'

'I'll take your word for that. As to the turbot – last time we met you tried to bore us silly on the subject of saccharin. Let's not do the same with fish now. You came to see Vérisoin because until very recently you've had his lovely wife whispering sweet somethings in your ear and now suddenly you haven't, you're consequently sort of headless, purposeless? And assuming she'd have had it all from *him* – wouldn't *that* explain your anxiety to see him?'

'I find you difficult to understand, lieutenant. Vérisoin as far as I know had little interest in anything except the conduct of his legal businesses. To him I'd have been nothing more than the door-to-door salesman from whom she – or more often her cook – bought certain items – if indeed she'd have bothered to tell him even that much!'

'So back to my question, why come to him now?'

'Because he might know where she is. If for instance she'd just gone away for a few days –'

'Funny sort of husband who'd pander to an itinerant lobster salesman's curiosity. In fact you didn't answer my question as to the precise nature of your relationship with her. Customer for lobsters – that might have served as justification for your frequent visits – just as making an appointment in office hours, ostensibly perhaps to obtain legal advice on some aspect of your wretched business, but actually as cover for seeking fresh instructions directly from the boss?'

'The boss . . .'

'Or "le patron", as he's known in certain quarters.'

A frown: puzzlement, more than any serious interest. 'What quarters would those be?'

'She's his wife, after all. Running you on his behalf – *their* affair, although you may have thought of it as hers –'

'*Running* me?'

'You may have enjoyed a more personal relationship with her, of course – for which *I'd* hardly blame you –'

'If I undersand correctly what you're implying –'

'It doesn't matter anyway. What does – whether or not this is news to you, Voreux – Charles-Henri Vérisoin has for some period of time been the main organiser of financial support for so-called Resistance groups throughout Haut-Garonne, l'Aude and Pyrénées Orientales.'

'I don't believe it . . .'

'It's not what you believe or don't, Voreux, that's of importance to us.'

'But he's *Chef des Compagnons de France*!'

'A man can pin on a pair of wings, doesn't make him cherubim or seraphim – isn't that what they say?'

'But she –'

He'd checked himself.

He *had* come to suspect, from things she'd let drop from time to time, that the Vérisoins had not been as far apart in their political views as she'd initially given him to understand. It might be nearer the truth, he'd begun to think, to say that Charles-Henri had simply not wanted to be personally involved or have his status as *Chef des Compagnons* compromised. This feeling had in fact considerably reduced the perceived risk in contacting him.

'Yes? But she *what*?'

'I'm simply – bemused . . .'

'What did you know of *her* activities?'

Determined shake of the head. 'I sold fish to her – or to the cook on her authority. They were regular customers who knew what was what and paid on the nail. Now in her absence the cook maintains she has no such authority – isn't

231

it natural enough I'd turn to her husband?' He did look as well as sound astonished. 'You've *amazed* me, lieutenant –'

'We're talking about *her* activities now. For instance, not to have to go too far back, wasn't there a Jewish couple – at the tail end of your sister's escape-line operation – *she*'d sent them on their way – not by any means the first, I'm sure, she may well have sent dozens –'

'No – I *swear* –'

'You were to take care of this pair – as you've done often enough, but this was only a few weeks ago. Madame Vérisoin intervened personally at what might otherwise have been an awkward moment for you. We know of this incidentally from – a third party, let's call him. But thanks to *her* –' a nod at Gabi's portrait – 'you got them away.' Hohler looked down his nose at him. 'You might well look shocked, she's holding very little back. I think what broke the dam was her realising we knew about her husband.' A glance in the direction of the sergeant. 'We're better informed than he is, Behm!'

'Seems so . . .'

'And with both of them now off the map, Voreux, how will you get your instructions from now on?'

'Instructions?'

'Of course – you're nothing but a *poissonnier* – I'd forgotten. Despite which, you told us of an imminent *parachutage*, location and date unknown to you, but – well, there *was* one, somewhere or other, and it was the first for months. So even on those slender grounds, giving you the benefit of the doubt –'

'I'd only heard a rumour.'

'Where from? *Who* from?'

'I don't remember. It was so vague – even *then* –'

'From Madame, perhaps?'

Gazing at the portrait again: then back to Marc: 'What can you tell me now about Operation Hardball?'

232

'I still don't know there's any such thing. The only mention of it – I told you – the American woman in Lyon – which was some time ago –'

'The one source we can bank on – since this is one of the subjects on which Madame is proving obdurate – although that may change soon enough – the one *certain* source is your new pianist. Any lead on him or her?'

'You said *my* pianist, but if there's any such person –'

'There is, and he's at work all right. I'd have expected him to have made contact with you by now. With the Vérisoins both out of circulation – of which he may not yet be aware – certainly not in Charles-Henri's case. Obviously he's in touch with London – has been several times, I'm told – but here on the ground you're all he or she's got – isn't that the case?'

'I've no idea at all. I'm completely at a loss—'

'How would you expect him or her to contact you, when he or she does?'

'The question's unanswerable. As far as I know there's no such person – and even if there was –'

'There is a pianist at work and he or she must know about Hardball, must also know how to contact you, *will* do so once he/she learns that both the Vérisoins are behind bars.'

'If I might say this –' shifting on his chair: and sweating now . . . 'I'd say if Hardball still exists. Very likely did – must have – but with your arrival it might *well* have been called off?'

'So we need your pianist. Who beyond any doubt at all *will* contact you. Unless there are others he'd contact – connections you've not as yet revealed to us?'

'If by "connections" you mean acquaintances –'

'You were more than an *acquaintance* of Madame Vérisoin. Close enough to have persuaded her to act as *poste restante* in efforts to contact your sister?'

Frowning: as if recalling. No point whatsoever *denying*. How they'd got on to both him and Gabi. Through Gabi, then her husband too? *That* much damage from the one living person Denise had thought she could utterly rely on?

Hohler broke the new silence with 'Let's think about your sister, then. Should I remind you of her predicament?'

'No.' Looking down at his clasped hands. 'No . . .'

'You see – well, here's the worst of it. A form of reminder that's been suggested is for them to send you one of her fingers – perhaps with a ring on it that you'd recognise.' Small shake of the head, expression of disdain. 'I have to say, this is not how the Abwehr operates, but your sister is not physically or technically our prisoner – the suggestion comes from those who have her in their custody, and they as you know are the Geheime Staatspolizei. Who you must also know, Voreux, aren't *nice*. For instance, the individual to whom I spoke actually suggested that if a finger didn't do the trick they'd follow up with the rest of that hand. Then the other – whole. Which would come to you through *me*. Believe me, they're more than capable of it. The aim behind it is of course to secure your active cooperation – at this stage, details of Hardball and/or information leading to the arrest of the pianist.'

There was a pause before he added, 'In exchange, you might say they'd allow your sister to retain her hands, or whatever other body parts might come into it if you failed to comply.'

'It's unbelievable.'

'Believe it, all the same. And then consider this. Having discussed it with my superiors, I'm authorised to propose an entirely different course for us to follow. For your full and active cooperation, we'd offer you your own continued freedom, and the very early release of your sister. When you've delivered the goods and it's all wound up – well, there'd have to be a time-limit, a deadline, obviously – *think* of it, Voreux – continued freedom and conceivably further employment with us – in Abwehr undercover operations, I mean. Maybe for your sister too, if she was open to it – and fit enough, of course . . .'

'Are you so sure you'd be able to get her away from – those –'

'My superiors at a much higher level would have that competence.'

Staring at him. Having been told they'd sometimes offer this kind of deal, money and so forth, get whatever they wanted then send you to be killed.

Time, though. Gaining *time*. Then if the feluccas *were* still coming . . .

He'd sworn to Denise that he'd never leave France without her – if she could get to him, be *got* to him . . . Feluccas weren't the only way out, by any means.

It was *La Geste* who'd got her, but if high-level Abwehr influence could be brought to bear, and meanwhile –

Play for time. Nothing to gain any *other* way.

13

On the Wednesday by mid-morning, 25th this was, she was on her bike pedalling out of Toulouse north-eastward, out through St-Jean on the road for Sulpice. Not St-Sulpice-sur-Lèze near Montgazin where Loubert hung out – and Jake would be today, with Déclan – but plain St-Sulpice which was on the road for Gaillac and beyond that Albi where old Wiggy had come to grief. Albi had caught her eye on Berthe's map when Jake had been pointing out the highish, wooded area he'd been suggesting she might use tonight and maybe again on Friday – on which she'd decide for herself later, not being all that keen on gracing the same district twice in a row. In this instance it was only think-able because there was a lot of forestry out that way, so that Friday's choice of location could be a long way from tonight's.

Wouldn't be going anywhere near Albi anyway. Not that there was any logic in running scared of a place just because it had seen the end of one's predecessor. Could have happened anywhere, if they'd been on to him somehow, as one might guess they had. He might have used *that* area once too often;

or told someone he trusted that was where he'd be. Someone helping with the research he'd expected to be doing in Albi that next morning, maybe.

Some girl, perhaps. None of the others seemed to know much about his private life.

Anyway, Jake's forefinger-tip following this road – *this* one – yesterday on Berthe's map had forked left at St-Sulpice – thirty kilometres out of Toulouse – and continued effectively due north from there, through Salvagnac, Puycelci . . .

'Seventy-five, eighty kilometres – a hundred even, by the time you've found a spot that suits you – *nothing* to the "old pins", eh?'

'As long as I don't have to do it again on Thursday, making it *four* days running.'

'Not likely, Suzie.'

'But possible?'

Point being that after Jake's consultations with Déclan, Loubert and whoever else, he might have stuff to be sent out tomorrow. Info for instance for the commando team and / or felucca skippers which it would still be possible to get to them at Gib preferably but otherwise at sea. And Marc's, especially any update on the beach situation when Jake saw him tomorrow. That might have to go out on Friday – in daylight even, if it was really urgent. Tonight she had nothing to transmit, and the same *might* apply tomorrow, but she'd still have to be listening-out on Friday and Saturday – Hardball confirmation on 27th *and* 28th, they'd said.

Surprising, when one came to think of it, that when SOE had recruited her – graciously permitted her to enrol as a field agent, having turned her down with a paternal pat on the head a couple of days earlier – the one question they hadn't thought of asking was whether she had strong legs. Which one bloody well did need, on this job. Pedalling pretty well full-tilt with them now, overtaking most other cyclists, all the horse-drawn traffic of course and even some of the slower gazos. Should make it easily enough into the forested area by early evening – unless she was held up somewhere or other – but wanted as much time as possible for prospecting around before the light went; and by Sulpice she'd have covered only about a third of the distance. This part of it was pretty well all flat, too, which later on it wouldn't be, so make the most of it. Fairly flying – even at risk of making oneself conspicuous – bat out of hell being the phrase one might have used, but *looking* perhaps more like a speeding hedgehog – in her shabby overcoat and head-scarf, tatty old suitcase lashed on the carrier with frayed string and a bundle of what you might call iron rations – including soup in a thermos – in the panier. She had the dismantled transceiver and its battery in the suitcase, packed in among various articles of clothing including a sweater which as it was warmer than it had been recently she didn't need – but would tonight – the overcoat being more than enough, especially after about a dozen kilometres of this. Headscarf if anything *too* warm, but effective as concealment – and overall effect being that no one in his right mind would look at you more than once.

Except maybe to wonder where the fire was . . .

So ease off a bit. But bear in mind that there were thousands of women and girls on bicycles, all over France, most of them fairly shabby. Reminding oneself that one *was* only one of thousands did help – not only on the bike, but in pretty well any situation. When you didn't *feel* like anything out of the ordinary, you didn't look it.

The only thing one really did have to worry about – at checkpoints for instance, if you ran into any – was the transceiver.

If a searcher happened to recognise any of its component

parts. The transmitter key for instance just on its own would be a dead give-away, to anyone but the village idiot.

Name of that village where the priest, Father Christophe, might know the present whereabouts of one's late husband's Aunt Ursule?

St-Antonin Noble Val was the village. Bit of a mouthful. Berthe happened to know that priest. He would *not* remember Aunt Ursule, since no such person had ever walked this earth, but if she had and had lived within a dozen kilometres of that village he surely would have. In point of fact no one was going to ask him, it was only something Suzette Treniard could go on about if she needed to identify herself and explain what she was doing so far from home. Home being Toulouse – having recently moved there from Paris – all that stuff, including down with the filthy British – and having hopes of a job as a trainee teacher in a nursery school. She had the school's name now and that of its headmistress. Berthe had said yesterday, 'She does know of you and your ambitions, but there's not much chance of a vacancy in anything like the near future, I'm sorry to say.' Rosie had shrugged that off with 'Just being cautious, isn't she. I'm an optimist, I'm counting on it.'

Old Rosie told me, in the Café des Beaux Arts – we'd had a leisurely stroll around the town, but it had begun drizzling again – 'I never actually had to trot out all that stuff. Had it ready, must have rehearsed it to myself a hundred times, but I simply wasn't ever asked for it. Actually not all *that* surprising – as I was saying, one tended to feel vulnerable, but looking at it from a gendarme's or say *Funkabwehr*'s angle – well, city's full of people, crowded roads, pavements and cafés, unless someone does something staggeringly stupid why pick on *her*? If one can just look and sound like one's part of it all –'

239

'Dressed like Charlie's aunt on a bicycle licking along at fifty or sixty kph –'

She smiled. '*Slight* exaggeration.'

'Let's get back to that. Except that if nothing untoward did happen – you were speeding towards St-Sulpice –'

'One thing potentially untoward did happen. About – I suppose halfway between here and St-Sulpice I found I was bashing along through an edge of woodland. Rising ground on my left, and thickish woodland. *Now*, it's probably all red-brick bungalows, factories, *supermarchés* – there's a multi-lane highway of course, wherever you go you find those, don't you –'

'But you'd have been on something like a *route nationale* through open countryside – well, forest – what was "untoward" about it?'

'I think I'd have to look that word up in a dictionary. How about "not so good"?'

'Near enough. Dictionary'd more likely give you "unlucky" or "unfortunate".'

'Both of those. Although as it turned out – well, thing was, I'd been worrying about having to bike myself into a frazzle maybe three or four days in a row, and here was this high ground and good cover only about a fifth of the distance out of town that I'd settled on for that night's perform-ance. This being Wednesday – which I'd continue with as planned, the next night I might have "off" – free, depending on developments and his nibs – while on the Friday and Saturday I'd no option, had to be listening-out no matter what.'

'As you were saying.'

'I'm summing it up for you, damn it, making sure you –'

'Sorry, but –'

'I thought I might save this much handier location for use on the Saturday. Would have just about had it, by then, and an easy one for a change would be just the job – as one used to say. Especially with Sunday being H-day for Hardball, so forth.'

'OK. So carried on as planned, found a good place for listening-out that night –'

'Yes. And same Thursday. I mean Friday. Thursday, had the luxury of staying home, Berthe and I made ourselves a good supper and then had an early night. Bliss, it must have been. Friday then was a regular listening-out night but I had to transmit as well, Marc having told Jake that there were now *two* patrol boats based in Port Vendres and dumps of barbed wire at intervals of a few hundred metres all along the beaches. Truck-loads of it were being brought up every day apparently. Obviously Baker Street and the Hardball team had to be tipped off, but Jake wasn't as worried as he might have been; for one thing, he said, commandos on a job like this would be equipped with wire-cutters – and so could we be, Déclan could see to that – and for another, with only two days to go and the wire not actually strung up, needing some kind of posts, probably metal things that'd be half-buried in the shingle, we had the Boches you might say pipped at the post as far as Sunday night was concerned. But – this incidentally must have been the first I'd heard of it – there was to be a pick-up by felucca a few days later, and of course by that time they *might* have the whole coastline wired off – and then they'd be likely to patrol it as well, he thought. *Not* so bright an outlook. Dear old Jake, though – no panic stations, ever, worked a thing like that out and then stuck with it – for the Sunday night, that was it, no loss of sleep or resolution – inform Baker Street, natch, mentioning the likelihood of there being wire all over the beaches by early next week, but otherwise – no sweat.'

'So on the Friday –'

'Hang on. While I think of it. Another thing Marc had told Jake was he'd thought it over and decided not to keep his appointment with Gabrielle's husband. Which removed *that* slight anxiety.'

'Did Jake ask him why he'd ever contemplated such a thing?'

'Yes, he did, but . . . Hang on, see if I can get it straight. Yes. First of all he had reason to believe that Vérisoin wasn't as pro-Vichy as Gabi had made out. That had been her way of disassociating him from whatever *she* might get up to. Shielding him, you might say, socially and politically. So, he thought there was a good enough chance he'd be in sympathy at any rate to some degree with his own nefarious activities – the escape-line and so forth – and he was worried for his sister, because he'd told Gabi about her and was losing sleep over it – whether under Gestapo ministrations Gabi might drop *her* in it.' A shrug. 'If that adds up.'

'Can't really see what Vérisoin could have done about it. But Marc must have had something in mind. Or – your thought this, wasn't it, and distinctly possible – if he was really gone on Gabi, floundering? The fact he'd dropped the idea rather suggests – confusion, doesn't it . . . Anyway, Rosie – same bike-ride on the Friday, listening-out *and* telling Baker Street about the wire?'

'Yes. I settled for a spot maybe thirty or forty kilometres from Wednesday's, and still felt edgy about it. Same general area, they *might* have had a van patrolling on the off-chance of a repetition. But I sent my stuff out and took in Baker Street's, which when I'd got back and with Jake's help deciphered it turned out to be confirmation that the landing was to be on Canet-Plage, approx two hours after nautical twilight – which Jake interpreted as meaning about nine-thirty – and any amendment to this to be radio'd the next night.'

'Saturday. Lucky you.'

'Nothing new in it – I mean that I had to listen-out 27th *and* 28th. But that screed wound up with another of old Buck's morale-builders, like the one when he'd told us the church-bells had been ringing for Alamein. This was the French fleet having scuttled itself in harbour at Toulon. It was to be reported on the BBC's French-language news bulletin in the morning – so listen-out, boys and girls! They *had*, of course – listened-out – at least Berthe had. It was about midday by the time I was with them, the bulletin had come over at seven, so they told *me* about it.'

'I'd forgotten all about that. They scuttled the ships we hadn't accounted for at Mers-el-Kebir, didn't they?'

'Oran, yes. Where my alleged husband Paul got *his*. But it was a dramatic event, all right. Brought on, obviously, by the Boches having invaded the south. They'd have seen that fleet as up for grabs – including a modern battleship and a couple of battle-cruisers. Balance of naval power would have been affected very seriously, and now it wouldn't. French captains had stayed on their bridges, gone down with *tricolores* flying, oil installations and ammunition stores in the naval dockyard had been blown up – you know, you could really take your hat off to the old Frog *marin*. And with the BBC report there'd been a stirring oration from de Gaulle. Berthe had wept, she told me – half the people in the streets had been in tears apparently. Jake had been there with her awaiting my return of course, to get whatever I'd have had from Baker Street – which in fact was only what we'd expected, nothing new or startling. Well – on the face of it I'd have been setting off again pretty soon – to be on the air again by listening-out time, take in the "any adjustment" as promised – pretty shattering prospect really, almost perpetual bloody motion – but in fact I had time for a substantial meal, as I'd prearranged with Berthe – having been on sandwiches, soup and water for the past twenty-four hours – and I was reckoning on a couple of hours' kip too, asked Berthe to be sure of waking me – don't know what time, but early afternoon – and Jake expressed surprise – how would I get there before dark, find a good location, etcetera? He was actually quite embarrassed, asking me this, adding something like "I know it's just about asking the impossible, don't know how you do it, damn sure *I* couldn't –" and I explained I wasn't going anything like as far as he imagined, only about twenty kilometres. Having found this much nearer patch of forest covering uplands of sorts, which since I'd now used the more distant region twice running would actually be less dangerous – also being so much less of a marathon might even leave me still capable of staggering around under my own power next day – so on, so forth. And that was OK; we agreed we'd meet back there in Place Marengo next day about mid-forenoon or earlier, and that was that.' She checked the time, and asked me, 'What would you say to a small cognac?'

'Well.' Blinking at her . . . 'I think I might say to it, "*Why* do you have to be so small?"'

Would have been a bit much if she'd had to go all the way back to St-Sulpice and minimally another thirty kilometres north from there. But with this much easier trip in view, and having taken in sustenance as well as a couple of hours' sleep, she felt pretty well on top of it again. Out through St-Jean, Castelmaurou, and now Garidec: this was the 988, and before long she'd be turning off it into a track of which she'd taken mental / visual note that morning. Checking on the map at Berthe's since then she'd seen there was a place called Buzet up there, with vineyards around it, and higher, wooded ridges sheltering these lower, vine-bearing slopes from prevailing westerlies, Atlantic winds further cooled by the Pyrenean snows.

More traffic than there'd been last evening. Both ways, into and out of town. Saturday, of course. Still quite early evening, but the light already less good than it might have been. There was a place called Montastruc-la-Conseillère coming up next, then a hamlet the map didn't show, and then – up into the woods.

Actually had cut it a *little* fine.

Jake was really splendid, she thought. In all sorts of ways. Well – just generally, the cat's whiskers. Berthe certainly was nuts about him – had almost given up trying to disguise the fact. Which one could see at times embarrassed him a little – as it would, since the last thing he'd want would be to embarrass *her* in any way.

Mind on the job now though – pedalling into Montastruc – into and out of, and really not far to go now – and a grey Citroen Light 15, *traction avant* as they called it, overtaking actually on the corner, crowding her, and the front-seat passenger – soft hat and moon face was as much as she saw of *him*, but he was subjecting her to a close inspection as the thing swept by. *Bastard*. Rosie with her head down and legs pumping, not letting up at all, might almost have been trying to stay with it. As if she didn't know poison when she saw it.

Gone now – same way she'd be going.

Jake had murmured when saying goodbye – inside the house of course – 'Good luck, Suzie. Remember now, ultra-caution.'

'Betcha life, boss.'

'I mean it, though. Couldn't do without you. Have I said that before, or is it just so darned obvious I didn't need to?'

He'd better watch it too, she thought. *And* be lucky. If they both exercised caution and had luck – well, who could tell, might *really* make something of it. Fingers crossed, on jolting handlebars; dreams *could* come true, *had* been known to. Not that it had to be mere dream, depended surely on how hard you worked at it. If you got the chance to work on *anything*. That you might call the 'luck' element – after which it would be up to you – if he felt similarly inclined, of course. She was around that corner now and into the straight where the forest sloped down to straddle it; then in a few minutes, having passed that little group of farm buildings and cottages – could see their chimneys now, and the road ahead was clear, that car having hurtled on – no problem *there*, thank God. Better step on it though: didn't want to be in sight of other traffic when she turned up into the trees, and with the light going quite fast now couldn't afford to hang around.

The dirt track left the road with branches each way, one to the right into vineyard and one left into the edge of forest. This one led back westward, roughly parallel to the road, before it curved right and began to climb – not all that steeply to start with, but enough of a gradient, over earth and loose stones, that she found it easier to get off and push. From the road when passing that morning it had looked easier than this. Still – making progress: one's chief concern was the light, wanting if possible to get up there – wherever – and rig the aerial wire without having to use Uncle Bertie's torch. Next thing then was that after about a quarter of an hour the track having passed over a ridge continued *downward*, facing her with the decision whether to stay with it, down into the dip – its depth in this failing light unassessable – before climbing the *next* ridge, or striking off through the trees along this one.

Didn't need to be any higher, she decided. And it would be *really* dark before she'd have got back up to this level. So leave the track, follow the ridge eastward, install oneself somewhere on the wood's eastern fringe, where when the sun rose you'd have a view down to the road on that side.

Leave the bike somewhere near the track here?

No. Hump it along. *Imagine*, if one came back for it at first light and it wasn't there. Scruffy-looking female with tired eyes and a battered suitcase, begging for a lift – having been *where* all night, for God's sake, doing *what*? OK, against that, how many potential bicycle thieves were likely to be prowling around in woodland miles from anywhere on a late November night?

Answer, mentally shrugging, not so many. But still – *ultra-caution, Suzie* . . .

Humping it along. Staying on this contour this way and that through leaflesss trees. It was less the awkwardness of the bike itself than the transceiver's weight on its rear end. Would have to use the torch, she realised, to all intents and purposes it was already dark, and there'd be no moon. The monthly dark period only began tomorrow, but cloud-cover would take care of that in any case. Somewhat blundering progress – actually quite awkward, one way and another. So take it easy now? Had been expending a lot of effort, but mainly to beat the darkness, and you'd lost out on that, as far as *time* was concerned, the listening-out period began only at eleven, and it couldn't be much after eight yet.

So stop and rest. Give it until nine, say. Get the torch out first, to check the time, *then* flop out.

Actually, nine-fifteen. It didn't look all that much darker. Hefting the loaded bike again and plodding on. Simple enough strategy – get to the eastern side of this stretch of forest, see how it looked down there, if there was *anything* to see, then retire into the trees' cover, set up shop and await the magic hour. About another half-hour's slog now, she guessed, and then – hour, hour and a half maybe.

Might have made more sense to have left the bike back there near the track. As it was, she was going to have to lug this bloody encumbrance all the way back there at first light . . .

Jake had mentioned the moonless period starting tomorrow night. It must have been basic to the planning, timetable of events, the felucca's arrival offshore and its boat's approach, and the pick-up operation three nights later. Moonless periods lasting three or four days – which would impose its own time-limit on the Noé operation. But if there happened to be a change in the weather and a clear night sky, no matter. Only a little radiance from stars, she supposed. On the other hand, if the commandos couldn't do it in the three days or four it might still be OK, with continuing cloud-cover. Moonless plus overcast would be the ideal – what Jake had called a belt-and-braces situation.

She'd asked Jake whether the felucca on its second visit would be picking up *the* German, von Schleben, and he'd cocked an eyebrow: '*Really* want to know?'

'Not all that desperately, I suppose.'

'Well, then.'

'The other party goes over the mountains, does it?'

Because something he'd said recently had indicated that von Schleben and his Boche companions would be taking different exit routes. Which might be the safest or surest – sea or mountains – well, since he hadn't been in a mood for answering questions – and incidentally there was *now* the likelihood of beaches being wired and patrolled . . . All he'd said *then* had been 'Aren't so many alternatives, Suzie, are there?'

Both lots over the mountains, maybe. German troops busy patrolling beaches that would now be unusable. They'd also be patrolling the *Zone Interdite*, of course – would be doing that already – as Marc had said, shooting at anything that moved.

Slight greying of the dark ahead of her, the trees' vertical

248

stripes blacker than they had been, against that background. And a detectable down-gradient now. Then from the straggly fringe of this strip of forest she was looking down over the regularly patterned expanse of vineyard: making out in the far corner close to the road a single-storey shack – or *chai* – stone-built and she thought most likely white-washed, accounting for its visibility. No lights, she guessed it wasn't lived in. So of no concern. Access to it though would be by way of the track on which she'd turned in from the road – if one had turned right instead of left – and where beyond a black line of hedgerow vehicles were still passing this way and that – mostly *gazos* by the sound of them.

OK. Orientation complete. Wondering whether at daybreak she might go straight down through the trees from here, rather than the longer route she'd come by. Maybe: but think of that when there was light to see by – how good or difficult the going might be directly downhill. For now, back into cover, assemble transceiver and rig up the aerial wire, remove overcoat, pull on sweater then coat too and wrap up in it. Sit then, drink some so-called coffee, maybe snooze.

What seemed to have woken her was a car door slamming – at some distance, but loud enough in the quiet of the night – and in the moment of waking, awareness of an engine having just been switched off. Petrol engine. To know this she knew she must actually have heard it, been listening to it maybe in half-sleep.

Stopped now, anyway. But – a car driven in from the road and stopped somewhere down there?

Unlikely, surely. Just stopped *in* the road, she guessed. Checking the time, which was ten thirty-two. Less than half an hour to listen-out time. It gave her a jolt – hadn't reckoned on sleeping deeply or for so long. Three-quarters of an hour, roughly. Sliding the torch back into her coat pocket as she got up, pushing herself off from the tree she'd been using as a backrest, moving quietly to see what, if anything, might be visible down there. Expecting – brain more or less in gear by this time – a car stopped on the roadside, its driver most likely out of it for a leak.

Wrong. No car, and not in the road – a van, close to that single-storey shack and with its lights on, lighting itself up – reflection of its headlights on the whitewashed wall: light also visible inside it, the rectangle of one rear door standing open. Had only in that moment been opened, was blacked-out now for a moment by an emerging human form, yellowish-glowing rectangle now visible again.

And a voice – male, and German-sounding. Answered by another one – a man passing through the headlight beams between van and shack. In sight again briefly before – no, still there. The van's driver maybe, who'd got out and slammed that door – joining his friend who was peeing against the shack's wall.

Yes – wasn't *their* shack, must belong to the vineyard – French, therefore OK for a Boche to pee on. Both of them at it now – and both in uniform, light glinting on their caps' peaks and insignia.

One of them had climbed back inside. *Funkabwehr*, she guessed – security police. And if she was right on *that*, it was a radio-detection van. *Here*, of all places . . . Thinking about it, though, not all that far from where she'd been on the air yesterday and Wednesday. Might be more than one of them on the job, at that, around the area generally. Not such a wild coincidence therefore. Second one lighting a cigarette: flare of match or lighter, then a pause while he looked around before joining his colleague in the van. Almost as if they knew about the 2300 deadline – which they *might*, come to think of it. Ridiculous – right here, almost in spitting distance: something rather more bothersome than 'ridiculous' though, seeing as she was going to have to answer Sevenoaks very shortly with *Receiving you strength X, send your message* – and the German listener down there, if he was on the ball and correct frequency . . .

Well. Might *not* be tuned-in in time. But in any case one did *have* to take in whatever was being sent. Hardball postponed, for instance, or the landing at some place other than Canet-Plage. Lives might hang on it.

But if there was a second van at work and they managed to get cross-bearings . . .

Might beat the bastards to it?

Time now 2254. Six minutes, if Sevenoaks came through on time. Might not, hadn't always, even quite recently had not. She was backing into the trees: actually edging backwards as if she was only a few feet away from them rather than a few hundred metres. Then after a moment's near-panic – having picked the wrong tree then finding the right one and the set and flopping down beside it, muttering to herself – headscarf back out of the way, head*phones* over her ears and the Send / Receive switch to 'Receive' . . . Time by torchlight 2257. Three minutes. Telling herself she needn't give the Sevenoaks girl the strength of her transmission, just *Send your message* and let her get on with it: then not acknowledge, either, trust the girl to cotton-on and those sods down there to be still swapping dirty jokes or making tea, whatever.

Minute to go, maybe. Battery switch to 'On'. Little red light, and a *mélange* of sounds in the headphones. Volume up just a little, whooshing noise mounting to a howl. Down a fraction: and fiddling with the tuner: interference still there but lower-pitched. Further *tiny* adjustment . . .

Sevenoaks calling!

Bless her. Bang on time. Picked the right night for punctuality, precious! Series of A's going on longer than it need have, but –

A one-second pause, and *Over*.

Torch on and pad in place, pencil poised. Fingers of left hand inviting the girl to send her message – *Over* . . . A group of four letters had encompassed that, a ripple of dots and dashes that had taken about *half* a second. And getting it now – what she'd come all this way for – ten or twelve seconds' worth was all it came to, before the familiar AR for *Message ends, out* . . .

Which one should have acknowledged with the single letter K – but she could do without it, and the bloody *Funkabwehr* most certainly could. Instead, battery switch to 'Off', and –

Nothing. Except pack up, be ready to leg it if she had to. Praying meanwhile that between her and the Sevenoaks kid they'd had it over and done with before those sods had even got round to switching on.

14

Baker Street's message had been simply a go-ahead — no changes contemplated to Hardball Stage One. Jake had been happy with that — last-minute changes not being easy to cope with, with the communications problems — only initially puzzled by the absence of reaction to Rosie's Friday-night report of imminent wiring of the beaches. Anyway, he and Rosie had unscrambled the message in her first few minutes in the house — Sunday, this was, lunchtime, in point of fact *late* lunchtime; she'd got back two hours later than expected and he'd been in a state of some anxiety. The nail-biting mode. But on account of *her* safety or lack of it: nothing to criticise in *that*. Relaxing now, in any case — she'd given him an outline of the night's small crisis, which had led to her taking a much longer, roundabout route back into town. Explaining, 'You see, it struck me as not impossible they'd have picked up my Friday transmission — after all, I'd used roughly that same location on Wednesday — give or take about fifty kilometres this way or that — and this time if they'd decided to make a job of it they might well have had more than one van out, to get cross-bearings on me. If they'd got on to me *at all* – you got it, uh? What I'd seen – impression I'd had – was these two not being in any hurry or at all *purposeful* when they'd climbed back into their van, might only have been getting out of the cold night air. So perhaps I'd be ahead of them – if I was really quick – and obviously I was darn lucky the other end was, too, and had only that short message.'

'Some luck maybe, but ninety-per-cent smart reaction, Suzie.'

'Came off, anyway. At the time of course no way of knowing it had or hadn't – would or wouldn't. Slightly unnerving . . . If *they*'d been quick off the mark – another van already at it, even – next thing might have been a few truckloads of troops arriving to beat the forest, flush me out.'

She laughed: it *had* been unnerving. Added, 'That was what I was watching and listening for, most of the night. Didn't seem wise to move. Principle of *not* being on the roads between dusk and dawn.'

'They'd have set up road-blocks too, wouldn't they, spread a net.'

'I guessed they might have. Hence the detour and holding you up. Sorry, Jake.' She smiled at him: he *had* been in a bit of a state. She went on, 'I set off as soon as I saw my Boches departing. Heard the van start up, then saw its lights come on. Daybreak, this was. They went out of sight to the right, didn't reappear on the road, so had to be making for Toulouse. I galloped down through the trees, got out on to the road, off it on the other side at the first intersection, then through bloody miles of little lanes southward until I hit the 112. Came back on that – traffic building up by then, no problem.'

'*Quite* some detour.'

'Extra forty kilometres, roughly.' She shrugged. 'Not much

option, though, wouldn't have been a good time to get arrested, would it?'

'Certainly would not. No – you couldn't have done better.' A glance over his shoulder: all clear – door open but Berthe still busy in her kitchen, you could hear her. *And* smell rabbit stew. Some kind of vegetables, she was preparing now. Jake said quietly, 'You really are quite a girl, one way and another. Exhausted, are you?'

'Somewhat. But peckish, mostly. And doesn't that smell good?'

'Does indeed. Sleep in the car, eh?'

'*Had* crossed my mind. Is it somewhere close?'

'At the station. Not wanting to draw attention unnecessarily to these premises. It's a *gazo* Buick, not in its first youth, but your bike'll go in the back all right. You could have come off a train – bike and all – and I'm there to meet you –'

'I'd have a suitcase, wouldn't I – transceiver in it?'

'Suitcase, yes, transceiver, no. Don't need it on this stage, safer without it, and touch wood they're bringing you your spares. Déclan has that battery for charging, by the way.'

'Thanks. Not that I'm in any hurry for that. But I'm Berthe's protégée, the would-be nursery-school trainee, am I?'

'Might as well be. I'm giving you a lift to Perpignan, where you think your late husband's aunt might have settled. Happen to be going there myself to take a look at the projected bypass, in particular where a bridge has to be replaced. Not strictly my business, only I do know my bridges and I'm doing it at the request of my colleague Jacques Jorisse, who feels they may be running into problems they may be running into problems they don't comprehend. Hence my doing it on a Sunday – back here early Monday, pressure of my own work and so forth.'

'Sounds real enough. Does Jorisse have any idea what it's about?'

'None at all. Oh, in his heart of hearts, he does, in the most general way. He knows my name's not Samblat, for instance, and that I'm here for purposes other than – you know, practising our mutual trade.'

'Isn't he ever curious about the rest of it?'

'If he is, he's never shown it. And he's already done more than his share just taking me on and more or less giving me my head. But talking of names, Suzie – since we're going to be in each other's pockets for a while, with others as often as not in earshot – call me Jean, the name that's on my papers?'

'Of course – Jean. Sorry. As of now – promise . . . But what do we do about the barbed wire and next week's pick-up?'

'Well.' He shrugged. 'Nothing – for the moment. Up to Marc of course to give us a yell when there's any move – once he's got his BCRA friends away, that's all we'll want from him. Then if or when the work starts, you'll have to get back on the old piano, pronto. That's the answer, of course, they're waiting to hear more from us – disinclined to send the felucca away empty-handed if they don't have to. Might be an idea to have a signal ready coded up. And I'll have a word with the commandos' CO tonight. Touch wood . . . Berthe – don't mean to say you're going to feed us now?'

Old Rosie had told me, 'There was a funny little incident at the station that I remember. Gare Matabiau – Jake had parked the Jorisse car there. Big old thing – blue-black and sort of bulbous as I remember it – how those old limos used to look? Very roomy – our cases went on the floor in the back, and my bike the whole width of the rear seat – boot of course being reserved for charcoal. Well – Jake had parked

256

it with its front against the pavement along this side of the station building – cars all along it – and there was a gendarme watching us from the shelter of a doorway right in front of us It was raining, incidentally. Anyway – young gendarme in *kepi* and cloak, and as I see him now – well, as it happens he was watching *me*, mostly. People milling around, other cars coming and going, and this cove just – anyway, Jake outside the car, shoving the bike in, me inside at the *other* side, pulling and sort of keeping it straight, you know. Then – we're out, rear doors shut, getting in up front on our respective sides – and blow me down, gendarme still goofing at me – me naturally and properly ignoring him, but Jake at that stage losing his rag – one hand on top of the open driver's-side door, challenging him with 'Ça va, huh?'

Imagining, visualising it . . . Gendarme staring at *him* now – calm, maybe slightly poe-faced, but after a few seconds giving him a nod, calling back 'Va bien, merci.' Gallic shrug then, and 'Va *assez* bien, alors' before looking back at me, and Jake – inside by this time, pulling the door shut, saying loudly and sarcastically, in English, 'That's good. I'm *so* glad.' He was fumbling a bit, getting the car into reverse, Rosie at that moment looking up and seeing a trio of uniformed Germans emerging from that doorway and gazing around as if they'd expected to be met – or didn't like being rained on, were pulling back out of it – Jake catching sight of them too and exclaiming, 'Bloody Luftwaffe . . .' Those three meanwhile crowding around our gendarme, wanting information of some kind but addressing him she guessed either in German or incomprehensible French – gendarme open-mouthed, eyebrows hooped, hands up as if in self-defence . . . Then they were going back inside and he'd caught *her* eye again – eloquently this time, expression and gesture asking 'What price *that* bunch, then?'

She was laughing. Jake had the car round, ready to go. She said, 'Not exactly pro-Boche that one.'

Car into gear, and revving a little. He wasn't used to it yet. Glancing at her: 'Pro *you*, though.' A nod, and another glance, accusatory: 'Come to think of it, not unlike that pair the other day.'

'Oh, *Jake* . . .'

'Jean.'

'Damn it, sorry . . .'

'First Luftwaffe I've seen here. No doubt taking over the airfield. Might inconvenience us a little. Felucca operations, for instance.'

Out of the station and over the canal, then left, heading south. It was a comfortable, softly-sprung old car, but its windscreen wipers squeaked atrociously. He pointed ahead: 'The 113, we want. Castelnaudary, Carcassonne, Narbonne, then down-coast. Couple of hundred kilometres, bit more. Want to catch up on some kip, Suzie, go ahead, I'll keep quiet. Sorry about the wipers.'

When she woke it was dark and they were in or near Narbonne, switching from the 113 to the road down-coast for Perpignan and the Spanish border. She'd slept for about four hours, wipers or no wipers; it hadn't rained all the time apparently, although it had started again now, which was probably what had woken her.

Jake – Jean – told her, 'Something like sixty kilometres to go. An hour, say. Why not go back to sleep?'

'No, I'm OK. Give you a spell, if you like.'

'Thanks, but all the same –'

'If you're sure. Safer, at that. But Jean, if we were stopped and questioned, where would I be expecting to spend the night?'

'Might say you were leaving it to me. And I might have

said I was hoping we might get into l'Hôtel du Centre. That's in Perpignan – best not to mention Canet-Plage. I might also have said I'd take you to dine at the Valencia – swanky place, expensive, very good grub.'

'Idea being to seduce me, or something?'

'Whoever was asking the questions might guess at something of that sort. But in fact, we're expected at l'Hôtel du Tennis – at Canet-Plage. Ropy old dump right on the sea, proprietress Madame Quétin. She and Marc Voreux are particularly good friends.'

'What sort of age?'

'Oh, forty, forty-five? Marc used the place quite a bit in his escape-line work. And she has nieces who work for her. It's a natural rendezvous for the local fishermen as well as weekenders and so forth.' He'd jerked the wheel over, avoiding a *camionette* showing no lights and hugging the middle of the road. 'Idiot . . .'

'They'll have room for us all, will they?'

'Only you and I'll need rooms, and I've booked them. Déclan will want to be off with his lot the minute they land, and Marc with his three won't hang around. He won't be expecting you or Déclan, incidentally. I only briefed him when I saw him on – oh, Thursday – and he doesn't know about the Hardball element.'

'Commandos arriving, you mean.'

'Doesn't affect him, does it. As it happens, there's something else he may not know about as yet. Remember he'd made an appointment to see the girl's husband – Vérisoin?'

'And then decided to drop it.'

'Could be just as well he did. Jacques told me this – Gestapo have arrested Vérisoin, it seems. Vanished just like his wife did, and they've been turning his three offices *and* the house inside-out, apparently. Supposition is they got enough out of *her* to haul him in too.'

Pausing: shifting gear for a sharpish bend in the narrow road . . .

'Despite his connections, *Chef des Compagnons*, etcetera. Jacques says he's actually quite a decent fellow. They belong to the same club; he doesn't claim to know him all that well, but –'

'Gabrielle's really been through it, then.'

'One would imagine so.' A shrug in the dark beside her. '*Would* have been, wouldn't she.'

'What'll be happening with the children, I wonder . . . But Marc *had* made an appointment. He told me so – on Monday. And if it was in an appointment book in one of the offices they've been searching –'

'Quite likely to have been just verbal – don't you think? Subject of Gabrielle, private and extremely personal?'

'Well. Maybe. Poor, *poor* Gabrielle . . . Otherwise I suppose he might tell them he was seeking professional advice on some legal matter – lobster business?'

'I'll tip him off, anyway.'

It took more than an hour, became especially slow-going on minor roads around the back of Perpignan and the last few kilometres out to Canet-Plage, some of it on unpaved roads. Continuing rain and the car's weak lights didn't help. It was getting on for eight-thirty when Jake told her, 'Believe it or not, we're here.'

Tall old building, and a scattering of shingle on the road itself. Turning off it on to an asphalted, weedy area – might once have been a tennis court? she wondered – with a few vehicles parked randomly here and there. Then she was upright, nodding through wet glass and rain-streaked darkness to a light-coloured shape close to a porch with a glow of light inside it. 'Our *poissonnier*, Jean?'

'Looks like it.' In first gear, scrunching up and stopping

beside it: Rosie meanwhile looking for Déclan's truck and not finding it. Jake had added, 'To him, this is a home from home, he may have been here all day.'

'On account of the nieces?'

'They certainly wouldn't *spoil* it for him, but the main thing is it's used by fishermen.' He'd stopped, switched off, checking the time before he cut the lights. 'Half-eight. An hour to go if they're on time. Which in this they may well not be. Hope to God they are, though. Suzie, we'll risk leaving your bike where it is, OK?'

'OK. *You* must be whacked now.'

'Moderately. But look, I'll bring the bags, you run for it – side-door where the light is, right?'

The rain was less heavy than she'd expected – and not all *that* much wind, although the sea was noisy. The door opened to a sharp pull, and she was in a lobby with a wet floor, narrow flight of stairs leading up to her right, a reception counter of sorts and in the wall facing her, swing doors with brass handles. Smell of cooking-oil and damp, and on the walls several heads of horned animals. She was holding the door for Jake who was blundering in behind her with the cases, but behind *him* Marc Voreux, looking wet and dirty in his old French army coat, shouting 'Jean, hello!'

Jake had dumped the cases and clanged a brass bell – ship's bell – that hung over the counter. 'Heck *you* sprung from, Marc?' The answer being that he'd been out there refuelling his van, then inside it squaring things off to have it tidy before his passengers arrived, had seen what looked like a hearse drive in and waited to see who or what it was.

'And lo and behold, Suzette!'

'Hello, Marc.'

'I didn't expect to see you here.'

'I didn't either, until pretty well the last minute.'

'Jean and his little surprises, huh?'

Forced laughter, she thought: actually not much liking the surprise.

Jake was greeting a gaunt, dark woman who had to be the proprietress. Nearer fifty than forty, Rosie thought – explaining to Marc that there'd be a message to send tomorrow, also she had radio equipment arriving in the boat with his BCRA people, and she'd needed to be here to make sure of getting it. Then, Madame Quétin – Jake introducing them to each other and Madame taking one of Rosie's hands in both of hers, murmuring, 'Ah, charmante, charmante, how *lovely* for you, Jean . . .'

Old Rosie looked thoughtfully at her empty brandy glass.

'Might, I suppose. But *let*'s make them small ones this time?'

'OK.' A friendly waiter had his eye on us already, smiled as he came over. I told him, 'Singles.' Rosie continuing, 'Damn cheek, of course, but if that was what the woman wanted to think – well, who cared. The alternative being some tale about a missing aunt-in-law, hardly relevant to the circumstances. Bloody Marc though making the same assumption was something else – pretending to be surprised – helping with the baggage – that we were using two rooms. We were in the room they were giving me – he'd dumped my case on the bed, I'd cut up rough and he was apologising – in a flippant sort of way, only joking, etc. – when Jake appeared, asking was the room OK and telling Marc he wanted a word with him.

'We don't have a lot of time. Lanterns need to be set – do that while we're talking – and Alain will be here any minute –'

'Him too?'

262

'Yes.' Telling me then, 'Suzie – dining-room's on the ground floor through those double doors and to your left. Madame Quétin recommends the fish pie, and the sooner we get at it the better. Give me and Marc ten minutes?'

In the Café des Beaux Arts, I touched her glass with mine. 'Santé, Rosie. Good fish pie, was it?'

'I dare say. We weren't too fussy in those days. Just hungry. But we were in a good place for fish, after all. Anyway – as far as pushing this story along is concerned – we were at supper when Déclan turned up – which made for a pleasant reunion from my point of view, but Marc seemed rather subdued – had done since his talk with Jake and still was; while telling Déclan how good it was to see him again, he was – well, preoccupied. Jake would have told him about Charles-Henri being arrested, the chance of a note of his appointment with him being found – and virtual certainty that Gabrielle had been given a hard time. And that if she'd let her husband down – as it seemed she might have, poor creature – would also have divulged anything she might have had on *him* – if they'd had any reason to ask about him, of course. All of which *would* be – to say the least, depressing. But Gabi anyway, the hell she'd have been through: one might assume, the Gestapo's foul and terrifying utmost, best *not* dwelt on. Also, Jake would have told him about the commandos arriving and Déclan looking after them, obviously all of this to do with Hardball and he, Marc, being kept out on the sidelines. I thought I knew him well enough to guess that none of this would exactly thrill him. All right, Jake would surely have pointed out to him that he hadn't needed to know – just as Déclan for instance would be surprised to see *him* there, hadn't known anything about BCRA arrivals – or even that I'd be there – so what was *his* beef?

'Well – Gabi Vérisoin, you'd hardly have expected him to be *happy*. Unlike Déclan, whom I'd really come to admire, first in the course of our *parachutage* outing and more recently in respect of the Hardball complications he'd been handling – Déclan as always imperturbable, in his own way somewhat Jake-like, was shovelling the fish pie down at an enormous rate – having brought his truck at least as far as Jake and I had come, and having yet to refuel it and whatever else might need doing to it before setting off with the commandos in not much more than about half an hour now – *if* they were on time. A big "if", that, a heck of a lot riding on it. Well – obviously – the distance Alain had to cover before daylight as the most obvious concern, but by no means *only* a matter of time and distance; there was also the very real chance of running into road-blocks or mobile patrols – chances increasing in direct proportion to distance covered – uh?' She spread her small hands: 'I knew, I'd *been* there!'

'And one stroke of that kind of luck liable to blow the whole thing.' I sipped cognac. 'One way and another, Rosie, this was a particularly chancy operation, wasn't it?'

'Yes. It was.' Twiddling her glass. 'My first, though, so one took it all more or less for granted – you know, simply what was expected of one, what the job was *about*. That and knowing that Déclan was *extremely* competent. While Jake – well, he was aware that orders for Hardball had emanated virtually from God – orders to SOE to set it up, that is – anyway from something like War Cabinet level. He'd had that from the *Chef de Réseau* in the Pau region who'd had the brief originally and transferred it to us – Countryman – on Baker Street's orders when von Schleben and company were moved from Gurs to Noé.'

'And for all anyone could have foretold might well have been moved on to Germany by this time. Taking *that* chance too.'

'I gathered – either from Jake or in London half a lifetime later – due to Berlin's own comparative disinterest. It was mainly Jews who were being railed east from Noé, and even with them one gathers the Boches seemed less interested in taking them in than Vichy was in shipping them out. Laval and that shit Bousquet being the prime movers in that area, and they'd probably little or no idea of any particular importance attaching to a handful of anti-Nazis – *former* anti-Nazis, even.'

'You're saying that until they actually had them back and interrogated them –'

'Even identified them, looked into their histories – von Schleben's anyway –'

'London – SIS maybe – was a jump ahead of *La Geste* or the Abwehr, in fact.'

'Might guess so. And were pressing us to bloody well get on with it. Which you and I should be doing now, don't you think?'

'You're dead right, Rosie. Sorry. Back to Canet-Plage?'

Jake had suggested to her that she'd get as good a view from an upstairs window as she would from the beach itself, with the advantage of staying dry; he and the other two had to be down there, of course, and he'd make sure of getting hold of the transceivers for her.

'Thanks, Jean, very kind, but I'd sooner be down there with you. Any case, Alain says the rain's nothing now.'

'Just as you like. Slight chance of running into trouble, mind – Boche or gendarmerie patrol, whatever –'

'In which case who *isn't* in trouble?'

There wasn't time to go on about it. Déclan had gone to move his truck to some place behind the hotel – oh, *the cabine*, holiday shack they had the use of. He'd refuelled, incidentally, on arrival, before joining them in the hotel for supper etc. – and she'd seen both Jake and Marc checking their handguns – Marc's Luger, and Jake with a Lama – Spanish-made 9-millimetre similar to a Colt .45 – which did rather emphasise the possibility of trouble, in which being unarmed she of course would be something of a liability to them – anyway, Déclan returned at that moment at a trot, muttering, 'Sorry, Jean – let's go?' Telling *her* as they started out – Jake going ahead with Marc, talking to him about the pick-up in a few nights' time, wire etc. permitting – Déclan warning her, 'Could be a long wait, Suzie.'

'Hope not, for your sake.'

Meaning the drive he had ahead of him, his need to get on the road double-quick. He had about a hundred and fifty kilometres to cover, to some place near Foix, Jake had mentioned. Taking her arm as they crossed the road – in wet wind, not rain, a lightish but cold south-westerly and the sound of a million tons of shingle shifting around at the water's edge, she guessed a couple of hundred metres away at least and unlikely to be in sight until they'd crossed at least one ridge piled up by the tide. The shape of the beach varied tremendously, Déclan told her, shouting down at her; a shift of wind and a hard blow for a day or two would change the whole scene.

'But see there now?'

Holding her arm to turn her, halfway up a slope, turning to look back at the roofline of l'Hôtel du Tennis – at two yellowish lights, attic windows each with what she guessed might be a storm-lantern in it. She remembered Jake saying something about setting lanterns.

'Leading-mark for the launch to come in on. There's three windows in that roof-space though, if all three was lit it'd mean clear off, stay away. Never had that happen yet – thanks be.'

'But they do patrol the beach?'

'Came near running into some of 'em once – not here, at Barcarès – but you hear 'em coming, crunch crunch crunch, drop flat an' let 'em crunch on by. Gendarmes, those were. Now we're looking out for Boches – account of these dumps of wire?'

'Yes – next week, they think – *maybe*, but –'

They were on the last or highest ridge, closing up behind the other two and crouching, looking down on a broad, white flood of surf and the heave of dark, jumbled sea beyond it. White foreground unbroken, uninterrupted. Remembering Marc's reports of patrol boats based at Port Vendres, thirty kilometres down-coast there, southward: but then again, those lights in the hotel's attics weren't the only ones visible, there was a confusion of them here and there at different heights and in varying combinations. The felucca's boat's coxswain or officer would no doubt be familiar with that pair – or others elsewhere, such as Barcarès for instance – which was to the north of this place . . .

'To the left there!'

Sighting by Jake, who had binoculars. Déclan shifting to see which way they were pointing: Rosie with a sense of surprise as well as excitement, as if at some miracle achieved. Jake again: 'Felucca's boat all right, I *think*. But – hang on . . .'

In case it might be one of the craft out of Port Vendres, she guessed. Would hardly come close enough inshore to be visible in that obscurity, though. Jake was leaning back, passing the glasses to Déclan – who'd been a seaman of sorts at one time, she remembered. Engineer on a cross-Channel ferry-steamer? Jake pointing, shouting: '*There*. See it easily now –'

So could Rosie. 'Yes!' Blossom of white in the darkness, and whiteness streaming: Déclan exclaiming, 'Our bird, all right. Ship's launch – wheel aft, cabin amidships – yeah,

267

them's ours!' He added, giving Jake back the glasses, 'Banging around like buggery, sick as dogs I bet.'

Eight men to get ashore now, plus whatever gear. Rosie's, anyway. Marc offering, to her surprise, 'I'll get your stuff, you stay dry. What is it, spare transceivers?'

'Yes – thank you – two. You know what they look like.'

Got over his sulks, she thought. Good for him. The boat was entering the surf-white area, its shape clearly visible – even to Marc with *his* eyes, she guessed. It wouldn't, she thought, come much further in. These three were on their way down already and she was following them: they'd wade out presumably, help with the disembarkation, steadying the boat in the shallows there – where it now looked fairly huge, bigger than she'd expected, its flared bow seemingly towering over them as they reached it and closed in around it. A lot of shouting – French, otherwise indistinguishable over the general racket – and suddenly a dark flood of men over its forepart – not just the three there in the water now, but an expanding group of which they were the nucleus thickening in this direction, elongating itself shorewards and finally becoming a stream of individuals lurching this way in twos and threes through the surge of foam – and out there beyond them, the boat backing away stern-first.

She herself was in up to her knees, she realised. Backing out of it: calling to the front-runners, 'Bienvenus, messieurs!' As if she belonged here, had any *right* to welcome them to their own damn country. But she *had*, damn it – *was* French, certainly felt it at this moment – a truly *exciting* moment, that sense of the near-miraculous still with her – all of this to be happening exactly as planned, and near enough perfect timing.

Thanks largely to a bunch of crazy Poles out there, of course.

'Take this one, Suzette?' Marc with her transceivers. 'I'll bring the other. Both dry, you'll be glad to hear.' She'd got it, thanked him. Commandos hunched under enormous packs plodding up out of the wash of sea, dressed as far as she could make out like fishermen. One of them in close-up suddenly, gleam of white teeth in a dark, unshaven face, wool hat down to the level of his eyes: a growl of 'Salut, mam'selle'; then Jake on her other side telling her, 'Warmer in than out, would you believe it?'

'I did believe it. Had cold feet and then some. But could dry them and other items during the night, of course, and the commandos would have dry gear in their packs. There was this *cabine* behind the hotel – actually several, but this one owned by the hotel – by Madame Quétin – and used as summer accommodation for staff, I think – a timber shack, was all – and Jake had arranged to have it for the commandos' use – it was where Déclan had parked his truck, and they didn't have to go into the hotel itself – to change into dry gear, you see. They had a whole night's journey ahead of them, no doubt could have endured it if they'd had to, but they did need to be reasonably fit at the end of it and four of them were going to be under the tarpaulin in the back of the truck, the way Loubert and his maquisards had travelled. You wouldn't want to do that soaking wet, would you.'

'What about Marc's group?'

'They didn't get to change. He was only taking them to this safe-house near Narbonne, they could stick it that long – something like fifty kilometres I suppose – and change when they got there. Even luxuriate in nice hot tubs while the commandos were still crouched under Déclan's tarp. They weren't actually of very great concern to us – Marc was to deliver them to this place, boarding-house, whatever it was, and put them on a train in the morning. He had a load of fish in his van to confuse the issue if he happened to be stopped – but that never worried him much, you know, gendarmes all knowing him as they did.'

'The BCRA agents would have been in ordinary street clothes, I suppose.'

'Yes. Overcoats and soft hats. Wettish, of course, *otherwise* just ordinary-looking. I scrounged some fish from Marc to take back to Berthe, I remember, put it in the Jorisse car and told Jake she'd love him for it. He said, "She loves me already. Don't want to overdo it", but then added when I'd commented on that ironic tone, Berthe being so valuable to us – and wholehearted, *decent*, I thought genuinely affectionate in her attitude to *him* – "I agree, Rosie, she's a splendid woman and a tremendous asset to the *réseau*." He could be a touch ruthless at times, you know. I suppose in fact he had to be – a necessary attribute for the job. But then again –'

'Rosie –'

'Yes, all right. Well – Marc took off, with those three. Jake's instructions to him were that when he'd seen them on their way he was to hang around and concentrate on the beaches, the wire and all that, and get in touch promptly if and when there was reason to. Jake would be in touch with *him* when there was a decision about the felucca pick-up. He'd told him there'd be a pick-up, if beaches remained usable and there were no other felucca-type problems, i.e. bad news either from him or Baker Street.'

I cut in with a question I'd meant to ask earlier, had she seen any dumps of wire herself, and she said she wasn't sure. Might have, had an image of them in her mind but might only have visualised them, she and Jake having had the likely obstruction of the beaches very much in mind.

'And on that subject – beach pick-up or no pick-up –

Marc had asked him what the alternative would be, and the obvious answer was to get the "parcel" and its escorts over the mountains into Spain. Much, much easier over a beach into a boat, of course, beach being usable and felucca still around, but the Pyrenean crossing was a much-used route in which Marc in his escape-line rôle had been something of a specialist. Jake hadn't told him anything about the "parcel" whom the commandos would be bringing out, only that there'd be one and that this in fact constituted the whole "object of the exercise", to use the military terminology then prevalent. In fact in this brief exposition, conducted in shouts on their way down the beach ahead of me and Déclan, he'd been stalling Marc. Marc's idea of a route out over the mountains would have been at this eastern end of the range, virtually where it abutted the coast. Whereas following the action at Noé there'd be a choice of other routes, one of which had already been selected for use by commandos escorting two of three anti-Nazi Germans they'd have got out of Noé. The third, von Schleben, was to be brought down to this coast in Déclan's truck with the commando CO, Commandant Marteneau, to a beach pick-up all of their own.'

'Marc would have had no idea of any of that.'

'None. Jake's guiding principle – what you don't need to know, best *not* to.'

'That wasn't a bad scheme though, was it – I mean, wouldn't have been, but with the bonus now that if a beach pick-up wasn't on, it'd be simple enough to send them all out over that mountain route?'

'Precisely. Which was why Jake hadn't been thrown, exactly, by the prospect of barbed wire and / or patrols, when Marc had come up with it. Alternative route already there, laid on for the others. Guides, Maquis rearguard, the lot – you'd simply switch those two to it. What you'd be losing of course would be the rather neat device of one group withdrawing in the obvious direction while a smaller one dodged off *this* way.'

You could see the dodge working, too. Boches with their eyes on Noé from where there's been an escape, and the obvious line of disengagement directly south or south-west into the mountains: and there *is* a move in that direction, with maquis acting as rearguard to it. Why guess at there being a smaller party sneaking out as it were on the blind side?

Old Rosie adding, 'Jake discussed the possible change of plan with Déclan and Commandant Marteneau in the *cabine* while they were changing. I *think* Marteneau already knew the beach might not be usable. If they could use it they would, but there had to be a deadline for the decision – Tuesday or Wednesday, say. I don't remember exactly, but we can work that out. For *me*, though, what it came down to was I'd have to be listening-out on Monday, Tuesday and Wednesday, maybe even Thursday – Friday too if there were any serious complications – and everything of course dependent on a successful outcome at Noé. This meant I'd have to do at least some of it from Place Marengo. Not necessarily fatal, by any means, Jake had rightly been ultra-cautious after the transmission from the tower, but a single blip even three nights running wasn't necessarily going to bring the swine hotfoot to Berthe's door.'

'If you had to transmit – if Jake got beach news from Marc for instance –'

'Get out to one of my pre-stashed transceivers by bike. Thing was, I'd likely be on my own – Jake wanting to be in close touch with Déclan pretty well up to the last minute. I might warn you, incidentally, I don't know a heck of a lot about that end of it.'

'So we'll stick to *your* end. Which is what primarily

concerns us anyway. Tell me though, Rosie – did you happen to see some rather delicious-looking soles going past a minute or two ago?'

'Well, by sheer coincidence –'

'Place is looking up. Think a couple of those and a bottle of Sancerre might hit the spot?'

'You know darn well it would!'

15

Voreux asked his front-seat passenger – unlikely-looking character, BCRA field-name Gérone – 'See this? Here, my side?' On the left as they drove north on the narrow road which in some recent southerly gale had become strewn with beach, shingle which from time to time crashed and rattled under the body of the van. Gérone asking him somewhat disinterestedly what he was supposed to have seen and was now somewhere astern: Marc told him, 'Barbed wire, great stack of it, similar dump every half-kilometre. In a matter of days they'll have it set up and the beaches won't be usable. I've warned my colleagues but they're still reckoning on a pick-up by felucca – probably not the one you came in, I imagine –'

'Why not?'

'Well – suppose the pick-up's in a week or ten days' time. I mean, they've just landed, got to have time to draw breath and suss the job out, so forth?'

'You could be right. No idea. Certainly the Pole wouldn't want to hang around out there more than a day or two. He's jumpy even now. How long has the wire been there?'

'A few days. Needs posts, I'm told – iron supports to hold it. Local fishermen, men I deal with, say otherwise the force of the waves and shifting shingle –'

'May not have it in place all that soon, then.'

'The Boche doesn't usually leave things half done for long, does he? In fact when I first saw it I thought they'd got wind of *you* being on the way. Incidentally, d'you know who or what the soldier-boys'll be bringing out – or where from?'

Wincing in reaction to a crashing of stones under the sump, and edging over to the wrong side of the narrow road, that lot having been flung up out of the declivity on the right. A cracked sump would *not* be convenient here and now. He'd eased his foot off the accelerator slightly: glancing then at his passenger's rather large grey head – only a shadow now, but earlier he'd seen him and the others in the light, knew him to be tallish, scrawny, middle-aged with a sharp nose and an Adam's apple – hardly a type one would have expected to come wading ashore in the middle of the night.

'What did you ask me then?'

'Only wondered if you'd any idea what those guys are here for.'

'Don't *you* know?'

'My brief was simply to meet you and your friends. But I'd have thought that after several days on a felucca with them –'

'They weren't talking to us about it, and we weren't asking. Being sick, most of the time, as it happens. But if your own colleagues keep it to themselves, presumably that's how it's supposed to be.'

'My *Chef de Réseau* is cagey in the extreme. Fair enough – has his reasons, I dare say. But it's not every night one gets half-drowned without knowing what for, uh?'

'At least you're young, and in dry trousers. I'm *still* frozen

– and where it matters. Bit much for a man not exactly in his first youth, eh?'

Marc had changed out of his wet things in the hotel. He'd left trousers, socks and shoes ready to shift into and had done it in about two and a half minutes while his passengers had been installing themselves in the van; had then found time to embrace Madame Quétin and ask her to tell the nieces he'd call by soon, had been disappointed they weren't around. Sunday, of course, just hadn't thought . . . In fact making efforts to sound casual, relaxed, which he certainly had not been feeling. And dashing out then, he'd found this old turd in the cab instead of in the back behind the fish-box partition with the others. He'd intended putting all three of them in there, but this one had stated flatly that he preferred to see where he was going – implication being that what he preferred, he got – and the others, names Basan and Lallande, had been in favour of it since it gave them more space for themselves, would make it possible for them to get out of their own wet gear *en route*.

Rosie had been there to wave Marc goodbye. She and Jake had seen Déclan and the commandos on their way, Jake had then gone into the hotel for a word with Madame Quétin about accommodating some of them – a meal for half a dozen men, say – in the early hours of Friday, and she'd heard Marc's slight altercation with the grey-haired BCRA agent. She herself staying out of it – Marc's van, Marc's business, at any rate not hers, and the BCRA man anyway taking no notice of her at all. She'd gone round to Marc's side though, tapped on the window and when he slid it down wished him good luck. He'd acknowledged this, wiping the window with his sleeve, asked her, 'When do we meet next, d'you suppose?'

'No idea.' A smile. 'But I'll look forward to it.'

'According to the dictates of our lord and master, of course.

276

Who's as busy as ever not letting the left hand know what the right hand doeth – huh?'

'Happens to suit me very well – as I've mentioned a few times. Anyway here he is.'

Jake joining them at that moment, asking, 'Front-seat passenger, Marc?'

A shrug. 'He insists, that's all.'

'You don't think you should do the insisting?'

'Sooner just get going – get as far as I can before curfew.' Jerk of a thumb towards the rear: 'All shut up inside now, and –'

'All right, Marc. Good luck.'

Old Rosie told *me*, when I was pouring the Sancerre, 'Went *something* like that. Jake was never one for laying down the law – unless he absolutely had to. Anyway Marc drove off, and how the trip went from there on until he got to his so-called safe-house – I got to know much, much later what transpired *then* –'

'You say *so-called* safe-house?'

'Yes.' Touching the stem of her wine-glass. 'Turned out to be more of what we used to call a *souricière*. Remember those?'

Souricière meaning mouse-trap. More realistically, might say 'agent-trap'. She'd come close to one or two in her later deployments, but luckily for her managed to stay out of them.

I toasted her: 'Blessings, Rosie.'

'And to you.' Then: 'Oh, yummy . . .'

Marc shifted gear again, suggested to Gérone, 'You could get into dry pants anyway, couldn't you?'

'I'll bear it. I have rather long legs – as you may have noticed. Also one's clothes may dry on one, to some extent.'

Might have been a schoolmaster, with that authoritative,

confident way of speaking, Marc thought. Forking left off the coast road, at last.

'An end to the damn shingle, anyway. I was getting scared for the sump, I can tell you.'

'Yes, occurred to me too. Heading for Saises-le-Château now, huh?'

'You know the district?'

'I should say I do. Why, when I was a boy I used to paddle in the *étangs* down here. Caught a fish in a straw hat once.' A bark of laughter and a scooping motion in the dark. 'I mean like *so*! Not a fish *in* a hat.' More chuckles: Marc with other things on his mind, less easily amused. Gérone then adding, 'As it happens I'm from Narbonne, to which metropolis you're so kindly taking us.'

'The others aren't from around here, though.'

'No. Basan's a Parisian – as you are, uh? – and the little fellow, Lallande – ill-mannered brute – is from Marseille. Is this safe-house you're taking us to actually in Narbonne?'

'Outside it – north-west, halfway to – oh, the Fresquet direction. A farmhouse I've used a good few times. I was running this end of an escape-line – *au fond* a BCRA operation, which is what I was, you see, technically still *am*.'

'Voreux – forgive the interruption, but don't give me your life story, and in return I'll spare you mine. But – right out there . . . No, I'd sooner be in the town, I think. I have friends whom I'd like to see and who'd put me up, not a doubt of it. Put *us* up, if the others want. Basan anyway.'

'My instructions are to take you there and run you in to the station in the morning. Staying there myself, of course. I've set it all up – with André and Candice Anslan, who'll have a meal prepared and –'

'Thank them for me, and leave it at that. From my friends' house in Narbonne I can *walk* to the station in the morning. If the others are with me we don't have to go on the same

278

train even, we're free elements, you might say . . . Yes, that's it, what I *will* do. On your way through the town I'll drop off, and if Basan – well, either or both, I suppose –'

Marc sighed. 'If you insist. Some way to go yet, though. When we're there – OK, if you still want to . . . Whatever you feel's best for you, of course, but –'

'You can take it as read, that's what I'm going to do. Meanwhile, though, what's the form if we're stopped along the way here?'

'Checkpoint, or –'

'Whatever.'

'Odds are we won't be. I never have been, on this route. Although – see, with you here in front, as I was saying – every gendarme for miles around knows *me*, but a passenger –'

'How about the Boches, *they* know you?'

He frowned, sighed, glancing at Gérone before answering. 'As it happens, I haven't seen a Boche patrol on any of these minor roads yet. All right, we've only had 'em with us – what, three weeks, I suppose they've barely got themselves organised yet. But what I'm saying – I did try to persuade you we'd be better off with the three of you inside.'

'Curfew starts at eleven, right?'

'Yes. So it'll be in force before we're in Narbonne. But you see, there are risks one *has* to take – otherwise – hell, one does have to move around –'

'But not teach one's grandfather to suck eggs, young man.' A chuckle, and a pat on the shoulder. 'It's not behind the ears that I'm still wet, eh?'

'I wasn't meaning to –'

'I'm sure you weren't. How old are you, Voreux?'

'Twenty-three next month.'

'Saints alive. I'd guessed twenty-five, twenty-six. Twenty-*two*, for God's sake. Anyway – pull off the road somewhere along here, and I'll join them in there. Then in Narbonne – you'll be taking the Capestang road out, will you?'

'No. Back-streets, then a small country road, don't offhand know if it has a number.'

'So let me off in the back-streets somewhere.'

'*Sure* that's what you want?'

'A man's usually better off on his own two feet, Voreux. That's always been my philosophy and experience.'

And he'd be wise to stick to it. Thinking this a few minutes later, getting the van off the verge, back into the roadway. Soggy wet verge and muddy, unkempt road, but rain still holding off. No traffic had passed while they'd been stopped. He'd let Gérone into the cargo-space, replaced the partition and left them to it – leaving the other two less comfortable than they had been, having to crowd up to make room for the new arrival with his long legs and snooty manner.

Sticking to that philosophy of his might well save his bacon. Contrary to one's own interests, but – there you were. One wasn't greatly taken with him, could understand Lallande's dislike of him. That authoritative manner, air of superiority. Lallande almost for sure would *not* get off in Narbonne. Please God, wouldn't – simple reason he'd be glad to see the back of Gérone. Was certainly no smoothie. Short-arsed, hard-faced, like oneself dragged up the hard way – that was the impression one had of him. And a comic vision of Gérone coming up out of the sea soaked to the waist, Lallande beside him more like to the armpits. And with that bouncy walk – ape-like . . . Marc smiling to himself – the wheel juddering in his palms on the road's pot-holed surface, muddy water flying – thinking of Gérone's assumption of some kind of social background while also mentioning that as a child he'd paddled in the *étangs* – even caught fish – or *a* fish – using a straw hat as a scoop – at a time when the local sewage systems — well, as he'd also mentioned, didn't bear thinking about. And there was your answer, of course — *poor kid, now self-made man*. Lawyer maybe, having somehow got started as an office-boy. Something like that. Come to think of it, if that guess was a good one, coming from this district he might even have known — or known *of* — Charles-Henri Vérisoin.

On whom Gabi had evidently spilt the beans.

One had assumed she might have anyway. Knowing there wasn't anything they might *not* have done to her. For that matter, have done — have *been doing* — to Denise.

In connection with whom — well, what actually mattered here was (a) that Gérone would *not* be trying all that hard to persuade the other two to join him, (b) that even if Basan chose to, fifty to one Lallande would not.

Lallande's rotten luck. Shame. Would much rather have been putting Gérone in it.

Narbonne, at last. Between Bages and Les Hauts-de-Narbonne he'd thought there might be a tail on him — headlights that more or less stuck there, some vehicle keeping its distance — but he'd been wrong. There'd have been no reason for it anyway — unless either Hohler had decided not to trust him, or it wasn't connected in any way with the rest of this business. In which case it could have turned out to be a bloody nuisance and hard to deal with. And how *would* anyone have been following . . . Well — the van being instantly identifiable, to those who knew it: and some officious gendarme . . . Curfew in force too by that time. He'd thought about diverting right around the periphery of the town — might have if he hadn't made that arrangement with Gérone — and while considering this, the suspected tail had vanished.

On into town and over the canal, therefore, then bearing left. Asking himself yet another question now — why on earth he should oblige Gérone, why not keep going directly to the Anslans' farm, deliver the full cargo?

Hard left again . . .

Truck – petrol-powered, no chimney – turning into the road a hundred metres ahead. He'd doused his lights, in the hope it might *not* have seen him. The van's light-coloured paintwork wasn't ideal for this: and that truck *could* have held gendarmerie.

If not, other curfew-breakers.

If he'd locked the van's rear doors after putting Gérone in there – which he hadn't done because if you were stopped, if you could wave a hand towards the load and tell them, 'Fish for the first train to Toulouse – take a look if you want' – well, they might glance inside, see the wall of boxes and a few loose ones on the floor – and catch the smell – whereas otherwise the check would most likely be more thorough. Anyway if he *had* locked the doors, maybe would have risked pushing on to the farm, but as it was Gérone could break out at any time he wanted and thought the van was moving slowly enough; by the time they were pulling into the farm most likely *would* have been ready to burst out, which could have complicated matters.

With luck, both Lallande and Basan might be staying with the van. Two out of three then. Could also describe Gérone well enough – beanpole, large grey head, one suitcase, sure to turn up for a Marseille train some time during the day.

Warehouse district, this. Concrete and deep shadows, high wire fences. Slowing, to reduce the *gazo* clatter. No glimmer of light anywhere, no movement, not even a stray cat.

So turn left here – and if all clear . . .

Cul-de-sac. But the hell with it – pull in and stop, then *quick* –

Gérone sure enough met him at the van's rear end. One door open, Gérone emerging bent double, Basan close behind him. Marc face to face then with Gérone, asking him, 'All right?'

'Best not prolong this stop. Lallande's staying with you, by the way.' In the roadway, peering round. 'Where on earth –'

'Back-streets as you wanted. Industrial quarter.' Basan had passed a suitcase to Gérone and was pulling out his own, hadn't uttered a single word. Gérone asking Marc, 'Want to set up that partition thing?'

'I don't need help. Better get along, uh?'

'Goodbye, then. Thanks for the ride.'

'For nothing.' A pause, then 'Good luck.' They'd started away. Gérone, leading, wouldn't have heard that. Or for that matter know just how much luck he was going to need. Inside, working on the partition, Marc asked into the darkness, 'All right, Lallande?'

'Far as it goes, all right.' A growl like a dog's. 'How much longer?'

'Forty, forty-five minutes. When we get there, sit tight, keep quiet until I come and let you out. I'll be checking around first.'

He'd got the wall up. Two of the boxes in the top layer could be pulled out so you could put your hand through and engage latches at each side. He called, 'OK, we're off.' Out then – this time locking the rear door, eyes probing the wet dead-end, and in memory hearing Denise telling him more than a year ago when he'd been joining her on the escape-line, 'There's no limit to what you can get away with, Marc. Put your mind to it and keep your nerve, next thing you're *doing* it.'

In which spirit one might say one was here now, doing this. Words he'd never forgotten, bless her, and which over the past year or so had more than once served to stiffen his resolve.

After Jean had told him on Thursday that three BCRA

agents were to be landed on Sunday night and he was to take them to one of his safe-houses, after two sleepless nights and fretful days he'd got through to Hohler at the peculiar telephone number he'd given him, asked him whether the deal they'd discussed had yet been approved by his Abwehr chiefs in Paris. It hadn't, Hohler had said, but he expected an answer at any time now. Marc had jumped in quickly then, guessing from the German's tone that he was about to hang up on him, asked him whether it might help if he delivered three recently-arrived BCRA agents to them. To *him*. After giving it a moment's thought, Hohler had said yes, it would – as a token of good faith, in no way altering the deal as they'd tentatively agreed it.

A T-junction, then sharp left. The next turn would be to the right, where he'd be joining a lane that paralleled a disused railway-line.

He'd settled on the Anslans' place because of its being out on this side of Narbonne, nowhere near the sea or where one might stop if coming from any place along the coast. Not wanting to raise any thoughts of beach landings: just as he'd been inclined to avoid Boche interference on Canet-Plage this evening. Having known Jean would be there, for one thing, and for various reasons not keen to drop him in it at this stage.

Actually, just about anything could have happened. For one thing, they'd have had a fire-fight on their hands: might have lost it, or if they'd been there in sufficient strength might have snuffed out Hardball. Where'd Hohler's deal have been then?

Next question – in effect on similar lines – what if the Abwehr said 'no' to letting him have Denise?

He thought they'd be stupid not to. What they wanted, they wanted *quick*, and he was their quickest route to it.

Even if they had a high-level dispute with the Gestapo over it: which could be what had been holding things up. Right now as a guarantee of one's own compliance they'd be getting Lallande – the 'token' – and of course they'd have *him*, Marc Voreux. In regard to whom – well, if *La Geste* had their way – their *customary* way of obtaining information from prisoners – all right, they'd tear one apart and *eventually* get Jean, Alain and Suzette, but by giving him Denise they'd get them a lot sooner. Point being that Hardball was *now* or at any rate very soon and they needed to move against it right away. It had been in the air for weeks, now. Virtually Hohler's first question, arising apparently from some partly broken cypher passed through the American woman in Lyon. Hardball, Jake, and the replacement pianist had been the three specific interests he'd named, and that still applied except that one couldn't go on hiding behind the Vérisoins, who effectively had been a blind, a conclusion Hohler himself had jumped to. Now, when / if the deal *was* agreed, one was going to have to come up with something solid – they wouldn't just *give* him Denise, he was going to have to *earn* her.

Then move like greased lightning: facing the fact that having got what they were after they'd almost surely re-arrest her, and him as well. So given as much as a single day, even . . .

Face that, be ready for it, settle the mind to it. Settling meanwhile for Hohler's suggestion of the two of you working for *him*. Too bad about the others. A matter of facing reality, was all. Suppose one made contact with Jean – customary exchange of telephone calls through cut-outs to arrange a rendezvous which on this occasion Abwehr or Gestapo would keep. Could be set up, for sure. But how long might it take them, once they'd got him?

Too long, he guessed. Same probably with Déclan. And in Déclan's case although one could direct them to his house at Léguevin, odds were they'd only get his wretched wife, who wouldn't be able to tell them anything no matter *what* they did to her – which wouldn't stop them doing it.

Left only Suzette.

The hamlet with no name now: if it had one, he'd forgotten it. Only a few cottages, and no lights showing, nothing on the move except himself, this trundling van – and he was through it now, around a small lake then into a long curve of lane, a tunnel with trees' branches meeting overhead. Stone wall now on the right: trees behind it and a faint lightening in the sky above them.

Entrance here now. Shifting up a gear before turning into the cobbled yard. The house was at the back of it, stone-built and two-storeyed – with a yellowish light glowing over the front door, to which three or four steps led up between iron hand-rails. He stopped a few metres from them.

The yard was empty. Hohler and company's car or cars, van or whatever, would be round the side, he guessed, where the cobbles led around that end of the house to a stable-yard, cattle-pen and outbuildings. André Anslan was well-to-do, raised horses more or less as a hobby, and had allowed his house to be used as a *planque* only because he disliked Pétain and Vichy and of course detested the Boches.

Where might he and Candice be *now*?

Marc said, close to the van's side, 'Hold on now', and walked towards the house. Feeling slightly ill. In his mind, a paraphrase of those words of Denise's – *Next thing you know, you're killing people.*

What else – have them kill *her*?

Up the steps quietly, reaching to the brass horse's-head knocker. Finding it difficult actually to raise his hand to it – as if hand and wrist had become somehow weighted. But there was already movement . . .

'Finally, Voreux.' Hohler, in the abruptly-opened doorway:

286

now stepping out. Behm emerging from behind – beside him – and a third one. Uniformed – boots, belts, insignia, swastikas etcetera, and Hohler the only one bare-headed. 'Took you long enough, didn't it?'

'Well –'

'That thing locked?'

'Yes. Also there's a partition, hooks at the top –'

'Keys.' Behm's hand out, palm up. Marc put his van's keys on the thick hand, swivelling aside as the sergeant pushed past him – followed by the other one, also a sergeant – Feldwebel, whatever – Walther pistol in his fist. Boots loud on the cobbles – Behm working at the nearside rear door, Hohler motioning to Marc to stand clear, racking a round into his own pistol. Marc began, 'There's only *one* –'

'Huh?'

'Lallande, unhook the partition!'

'*One?*'

Sound like a scream of rage from Lallande. A fight in progress, van rocking on its springs, a yell in German from one of them and the sound of a heavy blow. Lallande ejecting then, crashing off one of the doors, sprawling face-down on the cobbles, Behm calling to Hohler what might have been German for 'Only one, not three!' Lallande half up, on his knees and one arm, the other hanging loose at a peculiar angle, the third Boche taking a step towards him and swinging a boot savagely into his ribs. A shout from Hohler: 'That's enough, Derzinger!' Adding, 'For the moment.' Turning on Marc then: 'Where are the other two?'

'You'll get them all right, I –'

He'd checked. Eyes on Lallande, who was glaring at *him*. On his back – face contorted, eyes – astonished, blazing, murderous. Marc finding his voice again – or a version of it – telling Hohler quietly, his back to the man on the ground now, 'Let them off in Narbonne – had to, or I'd have lost all

287

three. You can pick them up at the station in the morning, I'll give you descriptions. They'll be taking a train or maybe trains to Marseille.'

'Are you absolutely certain?'

Hohler's eyes hard and bright on his. Marc hearing what sounded like Lallande being dragged away – drag of his heels on the cobbles, and a moan. Behm's voice raised then, calling in German to the other one. He told Hohler, 'Yes, quite certain. Important, is it?'

'I told my people there'd be three agents and they'll be wanting to hear about them. Wouldn't be too good for you – even for me –'

'You mean in terms of our deal?'

'That's agreed – she'll be brought down to Castres tomorrow or the day after.'

'The prison, you mean –'

'Would you have expected the Grand Hotel?'

16

They'd made an early start from l'Hôtel du Tennis, and stopped at an impressively massive, empty, fort-like château on a wooded summit east or south-east of Quillan, to send a short message away to Baker Street. Jake had known about this château – she guessed he might have made use of it in company with Wiggy at some time; he'd given her the text of the message over breakfast in the hotel and they'd encyphered it an hour and a half later in the Buick, smoking Gitanes and looking down through pines and a lingering early mist into that fantastic gorge. It was a very steep approach-road and by the time they'd got up there she'd been scared the car might have been about to cough its lungs out.

The message was to tell Baker Street that having discussed it with the commandos' CO Jake's expectation for the Hardball pick-up was 0400 CET Saturday 5th December, subject to Canet-Plage remaining wire-free, which they should assume unless they were notified to the contrary, and that Lucy would be listening-out every night this week from 2300 to 2359. She'd commented after tapping out the coded groups and getting an acknowledgement from Sevenoaks, 'Cutting the listen-out period to one hour's a good wheeze, Jake.'

'I thought so too. Better be on our way though, when you're ready.'

'Of course . . .'

So peaceful up here you could forget you were handling equipment that was about as safe as dynamite, if you were caught with it. Anyway she wasn't delaying anything – had already wound the aerial-wire back on to its reel, slid in now with the case open on her lap, pulled the door shut and began fitting the bits and pieces into their slots. Reminding herself that she had her daytime crystals in the set now – best take them out right away. Since one was going to cache this set somewhere along the way home and didn't have spare crystals for use in the others: to have left these *in situ* would have been a really thoroughgoing cock-up. Jake had the Buick rolling, by this time.

'Wouldn't want to get caught up here – with only one way in or out. Otherwise not a bad spot, eh? For a summer picnic, say? Suzie – subject of listening-out time etcetera – yes, puts 'em on *their* toes, rather, and should get you earlier to bed. Which, as there's bound to be some transmitting to do as well – further news of wire on Canet-Plage, not to mention possible developments at the Noé end –'

'And if you're going to be out of reach –'

'Only twenty-four hours or so. Some time tomorrow until I'd guess Wednesday evening.' Thinking about it . . . 'Suzie, we'll work something out. Might give Marc a cut-out telephone number, for direct contact when there's anything that can't wait?'

'Would you want me going on the air to Baker Street without prior reference to you?'

'If it's straightforward – info they'd need double-quick for passing to the felucca, for instance – yes, surely. And if you did have to, Suzie, might make it from somewhere west or north-west of town. Vicinity of Cussecs, say – there are patches of forestry out that way. And two birds with one stone, leave the set somewhere around there when you've done it?'

'Cussecs. I'll look it up. But yes, fine – one on our way back today, and that one. No more toing and froing with sets on board – except just that once. Any thoughts on where we might dump today's? Not *too* far out of town, for choice?'

Rubbing his blunt jaw, thinking about it. 'Not easy to think of anywhere really handy. As we know – terrain being as it is. Unless – well, woodland to the north of Castelnaudary that might do – bit far out, mind . . .'

'Sixty kilometres?

'Christ. Yes, I suppose . . .'

'I could manage it. Out one day, back the next. Not for ever, but in this somewhat crucial period, and time a bit short –'

'As a temporary thing then, let's check it out. And I'll deliver the other set to you at Berthe's in the morning. You'll be listening-out tonight, I'll drop by earlyish for any results from that, and bring you the set then. So when you take to your bike later on today –'

'How far's the Cussecs place?'

'Twelve, fifteen kilometres?'

'That's *much* more like it!'

'Just a matter of finding some – what, shed, hole in the ground – needs to be waterproof, I suppose –'

'I'll find somewhere, don't worry.' Nodding to herself. 'Cussecs. OK. When I need to transmit, that's where I'll go.'

'Fine.' A glance at her, and a smile. Then he'd checked the road was clear and was turning into it. She asked him, 'You'll be with Déclan and his gang or gangs, will you?'

291

'I'll be seeing him, certainly. Train tomorrow a.m. to Pamirs is the first stage – and return some time Wednesday. Mahossier, Jorisse business, of course.'

I'd made a few notes on the laptop, back in my room in the Mermoz, of various things she'd recalled or semi-recalled during that session in the Beaux Arts. Jake's having told her for instance that Déclan and the commandos would have been spending that day holed-up in some Maquis hideout near Foix, and that the attack on the camp at Noé was to take place on the Wednesday night / Thursday morning. Actually Jake had amended this from 'attack on' to 'infiltration of', and this was a lot more than she'd have expected him to have let her know about that end of it. She'd have made her guesses, of course – Noé being something like 60 kilometres from Foix, for instance, the commandos would probably have made another move in the interim. And doubtless he as ringmaster so to speak would be conferring with Marteneau, Loubert and maybe the Noé insider as well as with Déclan. She was vague about it anyway – hadn't needed to know, therefore hadn't *wanted* to, and had no more to say about it now – left it to me to work out for myself I dare say. So over the black coffee with which we were finishing what had been a most enjoyable lunch, I suggested, 'How about siestas now? A taxi to l'Ambassade – couple of hours' rest, resume at teatime?'

She nodded happily. 'Then we could go right through to supper – take a stroll perhaps – and there's a tea-and-buns place we might stop at. Might be as well to keep clear of the Brasserie des Aviateurs at this stage. Our guest of honour being due here in the morning, as you know – *allegedly* in the morning but it's rumoured might clock in tonight. I've a suspicion some of his former associates may be hanging around in that hope – and one tends to get trapped, you know?'

'So, OK. Siesta now, then a walkabout and your tea place – then see how we feel. Might prop up a bar somewhere – the Grand Hôtel de l'Opéra, for instance?'

'And dine at our home from home?'

'Saturday, the Colombier's shut. Les Jardins de l'Opéra, on the other hand – supposedly the best in town – go for bust, shall we?' I'd signalled for the bill. Asking her, 'Concluding that last bit though, your trip back with Jake, did you find a hiding-place for the transceiver in woods near Castelnaudary?'

'Must have.' She nodded. 'And never saw that set again, come to think of it. So much effort getting the damn thing, and just that one message was all it ever sent. Same with the other one – took it out in the Cussecs direction the next evening – Tuesday, would have been – put it through its paces and then cached it. I remember that one well enough. It's odd – a lot of the time recollection's nil or at best hazy, then suddenly it goes vivid. At this stage maybe because it was what you might call the beginning of the end – all of it about to hit the fan, so one's thought back to it more often?'

She was in the house on Place Marengo by late afternoon that Monday, and the fish she'd brought from l'Hôtel du Tennis was not, she guessed, quite as recently out of the sea as Madame Quétin had asserted, so after she'd cleaned herself up a bit she found potatoes in the larder and made a pie of it. Homecoming surprise for Berthe a couple of hours later: she was delighted with it, went so far as to produce a bottle of white wine that had been a present from some pupil's parents.

'Jean should be here to have supper with us!'

'Yes, he should. But he had to clock in at Mahossier, Jorisse – and he was *very* tired.'

'I envy you your little trip with him. He's *such* a nice man. Don't you think?'

'Certainly do. He's very fond of you too.'

'Does he talk about me, then?'

'Well – you know, from time to time . . .'

'Saying what for instance?'

'How attractive you are, and amusing – and extraordinarily kind to us –'

'Is he likely to be calling in in the next day or two?'

'In the morning.' Rosie pointed upwards. 'I'll be doing my stuff tonight and he'll drop by for any messages.'

'Early, or –'

'Yes. He has a train to catch. Jorisse business again – a day and a night, I think, I don't know where.'

'I might wait to say hello. By the way, I suppose you heard the news from Stalingrad?'

'Haven't heard *any* –'

'They're all talking about it. Well – whispering, more like. Russians have got the Nazis well and truly on the ropes. General von Paulus's Sixth Army virtually destroyed – surrounded, something like eighty thousand of them killed or taken prisoner –'

'Magnificent!'

'Yes, it is. I personally have no time for communists, but those Russians must be really something.'

Berthe would have been in bed and probably asleep before Rosie had her set tuned in, a few minutes before eleven. Set plugged into the overhead light socket, torch in mouth in the attic's darkness – blanket covering the window, of course – headphones on, pad and pencil handy. Thinking she might use the set's battery next time, rather than the mains, not only for the convenience of it but because it was a way they caught you – if one had been transmitting, which of course tonight one was not, but still had to respond to any call.

Sevenoaks began its chatter at a minute past eleven, and within seconds she'd given them the go-ahead – *Receiving you strength 4* – which in fact improved when the message began stuttering in, Rosie jotting the groups down – not all that many of them, before the AR for *Message ends*, when she switched instantly from 'Receive' to 'Send' and gave them a K.

Done. Switched off . . . Visualising *Funkabwehr* listening now to nothing but atmospherics. They'd have the Sevenoaks message on tape in Paris, and might or might not have picked up Rosie's own two blurts on their direction-finders here too. Please God, would not have had the time, luck or skill to get a bearing on her, let alone a fix. Couldn't guarantee they hadn't – once again, simply a risk one had to take, couldn't spend *every* night in ditches . . . On her feet now, removing the plug from the overhead light fixture. The trick they'd been known to play with the mains supply when they had a pianist at work in an urban area was to cut off the power to one section after another while listening-in: when the transmission was cut off in full flow they knew which part of the town to target, with their vans and / or men on foot in the streets, all that.

Bed now. Decypher this lot in the morning. Prayers now, and bed.

She'd thought Jake might have been there by about seven, and had been ready for him at that time, but in fact he didn't show up until after nine. She'd been getting a bit worried, and Berthe had long departed to catch her bus.

He'd brought the other transceiver with him, as he'd said he would. Taking it from him in the front hall, she asked, 'Missed your train?'

He kissed her cheek. 'The early one, yes. Must *not* miss the next. Gives me about an hour. Everything all right?'

She'd nodded. 'Would you like coffee or –'

'No, thanks. Thing is, I've had Marc on the blower. He'd been trying to get through to me since some time yesterday, made his connection a couple of hours ago, and – you know, it can take a little while, the call back, and –'

'Your cut-out system.'

A nod. 'Did Baker Street have anything for us?'

'Had *this*.'

Her decrypt of it. They'd acknowledged the message she'd sent giving the pick-up as 0400 Saturday subject to the beach being still wire-free, and were warning that it might become necessary to cancel in the event of the felucca skipper crying off, for whatever reasons he might have.

Jake read it twice. 'Might, might not. Doesn't help much, does it.'

'What's Marc got to say?'

'That the Canet-Plage and Barcarès beach-launch fishermen have been told those beaches won't be available to them after Sunday, they're advised to make arrangements to shift to Port Vendres or Collioure. They're desperate about it – well, you can imagine!'

'At least OK until Sunday.'

'On the face of it. Bit of a close thing though, isn't it. Anyway we'd better let Baker Street and the mad Pole know. I've told Marc to keep his ear to the ground – and as we were saying yesterday, Suzie, since I'm going to be out of town—'

'He may want to contact *me*.'

'Easier in fact the other way about. I told him I'd give you *his* cut-out number. It's a bar in Perpignan. Here – this number. Call from a public phone, ask for Raoul, say you're Lucy and give them a pay-phone number to call you back at – at say two, three or four p.m., whatever suits you. Make your calls to him at midday today and tomorrow, using different call-boxes each day. Got it?'

'The onus being on him then to call back at whatever time I say.'

'Which I can tell you he doesn't much like. But as I said, at such short notice it's the easiest way to do it.'

'And tonight I'll go out to this Cussecs place or the woods around it, and tell Baker Street present indications are beach-wiring starts Sunday.'

'Unless you get any variation on that from Marc at noon.'

'Any reason to think there may be?'

'Well, who knows – but so far it's only what he'd *heard*. He was urgently seeking confirmation, but guessed we'd want to get it to Baker Street sooner rather than later anyway.' A shrug. 'As of course we must. But Suzie, listen – Marc doesn't know we're scheduling the pick-up for Saturday, for all he knows it mightn't be until some time next week. Which would make his news fairly vital, you see.'

'The need to know . . .'

'He *still* doesn't need to. Doesn't matter now, but Sunday night he was setting off with those BCRA characters who've damn-all to do with us but might on the other hand be thick with him, and I'd sooner did *not* know our business. Incidentally, he put them on their train, all right.'

'I'll keep off the subject of pick-up dates. Canet-Plage not looking too promising though, huh?'

'Because of this stuff of Marc's?' A shrug. 'I don't think it should worry us. 0400 Saturday's comfortably this side of Sunday, after all. Baker Street and the felucca's problems are another thing entirely, sure . . . But by and large, getting off a beach is a lot quicker and easier than climbing mountains – *if* the felucca's going to be here – and – hang on – another point is that after a couple of years in prison camps our Gustave may not be in exactly prime condition.'

'That *is* a thought . . .'

'On the other hand – *new* thought – the felucca skipper might decide to pull out of it later in the time-scale than we'd find easy to cope with. Or the beach-wiring might start say on Friday – if their posts and stuff arrived, for instance, or troops were suddenly available – so we'd have to rethink at dangerously short notice. Well, what did seem the obvious answer was to send him and the commandant with the rest of them, but now I'm not so sure. See – the main party's going straight from Noé into the mountains – initially in the hired lorry that's bringing them up to Noé – while Déclan brings Gustave and Marteneau down to a Maquis bolt-hole near Lavelanet. They get there around dawn on Thursday, lie low until dark on Friday – that's all set up and actually looks rather good. Earlier on Friday, for instance, Déclan's supposedly working on some borehole pump in the Lavelanet area – actual fact he can be catching up on sleep in his truck but it'd still explain his presence in the area if he should need to. And by that time the other lot'll be into the mountains, Maquis covering their withdrawal or at least hampering pursuit – if there is any, *if* the alarm's been raised, which with luck and good management it may not have been. One way and another, in fact, it's not bad: and on balance, if we can't have our beach pick-up I'd sooner send those two over the mountains on what one might call Marc's route – from Banyuls and through the *Zone Interdite*.'

'Have Marc set that up?'

'Maybe. Although he'd have to get there in the first place, he's not essential to it, and thanks to him we know of a café-bar in Banyuls he told me he'd used for most of his evaders – including the pair Gabrielle Vérisoin helped with. I think that was when he told me about it. The bar's proprietor's a Basque by name of – well, the bar's called the Etoile – I'm pretty sure –'

'Shall I ask him?'

Blinking at her. Fingering a pack of Gitanes: looking at them then and changing his mind, pushing them back in his pocket. 'Yes. Please. Then if we do have to switch –'

'I'll ask him when he calls me back this afternoon.'

'And then – listen, call me at Pamirs, so I can brief Alain and Marteneau. Marteneau does have to agree to any change, of course, he *is* the military commander. And if – no, no . . . Talking faster than I'm thinking . . . But listen – telephone directory – Berthe must have one here, I'm sure. L'Hôtel France in Pamirs. Ask for me – my own name, Samblat, you're Madame Samblat – give me the bar owner's name, and confirmation it is the Etoile. This Basque's a fixer – middle-man for the local *passeurs* – smugglers, smuggle people as well as other things.'

'Fascinating. But crikey – talk about "need to know"!'

'Well, you *do* need to!'

'Do *now*, sure. Don't I, just . . .'

Hands on her shoulders suddenly, and smiling down at her. 'I may have said this before, Suzie, but you really are quite a girl.'

'Oh. Well . . . But – what time will you be at that hotel for me to ring you?'

'Say between five and five-thirty? Then back again later, but you'll be on your bike by then . . . Suzie, plain fact is I'm nuts about you. D'you mind?' Laughing then – as if *at* her. Or at *them* maybe, this situation. A hug then – quick, tight bear-hug – and disengaging but still face to face. She said quietly, 'I rather go for you too – since you mention it. Might also mention though, Berthe really is a fervent admirer. A mere twenty-four-hours' absence seemingly making the heart grow fonder? She was hoping you'd be here before she took off this morning, but –'

'Oh, *Christ.*' He'd let go of her. 'That damn train . . .'

★　★　★

She was at the Matabiau station at noon, picked one of the half-dozen public phones at random, made a note of its number, asked for that number in Perpignan and put her money in. A male voice answered, and having established that Raoul wasn't there but would be later she left a message asking him to call Lucy at this Toulouse number at about 2 p.m.

Home for a snack then, and with time to kill she worked out the signal she'd send Baker Street tonight.

Your message received and understood. Present indications are that beaches should be accessible until the end of this week, but in case of need an alternative exit route for Gustave and escort is being prepared. Decision on this should please be made either by us or by felucca through you latest pm Thursday.

Which would be cutting it about as fine as one dared. Thursday being when Déclan would have von Schleben and Marteneau at the place near Lavelanet, Jake presumably having some way of communicating with him there.

She encyphered it, then put her feet up and thought about Jake for a while before setting out for the station and that call-box. To ensure the line stayed open she shut herself in the box and put the receiver to her ear while holding its bracket down and reciting snatches of verse into the speaker until the ringing started.

'Yes?'

'Lucy?'

'Yes, Raoul. I called on Jake's instructions –'

'It's nice to hear from you.'

'Thanks for calling back. Can you confirm what you told Jake this morning?'

'I think we can take it as certain, although I haven't been able to speak with the ones I need to. I'll have seen some of them by this time tomorrow, though. Will Jake be back by then?'

'Doubt it. I'll call you again at noon. But listen —'

'Why don't I call *you* when I've got the answer?'

'Because this is the way Jake wanted me to do it, and I don't know where I'll be at noon, or where I'll want you to call me back. There's a name Jake wants from you, though —'

'When will he be back?'

'I don't know. What he wants from you is the name of some café-bar in Banyuls you told him about — might be l'Etoile, he thought — and the name of the man who runs it. A Basque?'

'What's this for? Alternative to Canet-Plage — consequent on the news I gave him?'

'Your guess is as good as mine. Give me the answers for him, please?'

'The man who runs the Etoile calls himself Gérard. It's at the back of l'Hôtel des Pyrénées.'

'Right. Thank you.'

'When will you be seeing him, to pass this on? Might be better if I saw him myself — I could tell him plenty about Gérard, and the brother, and —'

'I'll call you tomorrow noon, Raoul.'

'Couldn't we meet, instead?'

'Let's do that soon, but I must run now. 'Bye.'

She hung up. L'Etoile, Gérard, back of l'Hôtel des Pyrénées . . . A couple of hours' snooze now maybe before calling Jake at Pamirs. Borrow Berthe's alarm clock . . .

The Hôtel France's number, the operator told her, was engaged. Five-twenty now. The boxes were in constant use at this time of day, and a large man in a fur coat and Homburg, who'd been glaring at her, took her place as she backed out of this one. She'd dwelt a brief pause before getting the operator back and asking her to try again – and finding it still busy – and he'd been looking daggers at her: having what he wanted now, he raised his hat and showed his teeth, muttered 'Mam'selle . . .' Half-smoked cigar back in his mouth then; he'd *have* to be a collaborator, she thought. Staying where she was therefore, guessing he'd have a clear purpose in mind, might therefore be quick – an instruction, a demand, and finish, bang the thing back on its hook . . . She'd guessed right, and after only about a minute was back in there, getting a different operator and this time thank God connecting, pushing the coins in.

'Hôtel France, how may I help you?'

'I think my husband, Monsieur Jean Samblat, may be waiting for this call?'

'He is indeed, madame. One little moment?'

A buzz, and clickings. Then: 'Lucy, that you?'

'You did catch your train, then.'

'*Chérie* – this line's not too good –'

She raised her voice: 'You had the name of that place right, and the man's name is Gérard. Our friend had no other news, won't be seeing those concerned until tomorrow.'

'So there we are. Sweet of you to have called. See you tomorrow.'

'Good. Take care.'

'Oh, you too. Goodnight, *chérie.*'

Old Rosie again now: smiling like a girl, in the course of our stroll later that Saturday afternoon . . . 'Calling me *chérie* – and *meaning* it – acting as my husband, of course, for the benefit of listeners-in – telephones were never safe, you realise, we were advised not to use them unless it was really necessary, a lot of the operators were said to be informers – but the *chérie* bit was more than that, sort of a reference to that earlier exchange – you know?'

302

'You'd fallen for him. You did touch on this earlier, I know, but –'

'We'd fallen for each other. You're thinking about Ben again, aren't you?'

'Well – to an extent –'

'I didn't *know* Ben at that stage. I was *getting to know* Jake. What had happened between me and Ben all that time ago had nothing to do with this. He was – like something out of a byegone dream I'd sooner have forgotten, I neither expected nor wanted ever to set eyes on him again – he'd *gone*, d'you understand me?'

'Yes, of course, Rosie. As you felt *then*. OK. Anyway, you'd made that phone call – to Pamirs –'

'I know *that* tone too. You're saying leave that, let's get on with the stuff that matters!'

'Well – we do need to get on with it – having only this evening and whatever's left of tomorrow after your lunchtime shindig – but obviously your relationship with Jake does matter – enormously. I thought you'd said as much as you were going to on the subject, that's all. In fact in that area I dare say I have a sort of preconception – prejudice, if you like – having written as much as I have about you and Ben, consequently seeing Ben as the man who *really* mattered in your life?'

She didn't comment, and I partially changed the subject. 'He'll be coming into it soon, will he?'

'*Quite* soon.' She'd nodded, but was pointing across the road at a patisserie – I guessed the 'tea and buns place' she'd had in mind. 'OK?'

'Cross at the lights, shall we?'

'What you were saying then . . . You're quite right, Ben was the man who as things turned out came to matter gigantically in my life. No argument, you know all that. But it only came about because of how things went with Jake. I'm not for a split second implying anything like Jake versus Ben, Jake comes out on top or Ben does – that'd be quite unreal. Leave it at that now, shall we?' She took my arm as we crossed the road. 'I'd like Lapsang Suchong and a chocolate éclair, please.'

After the call to Jake at Pamirs she went back to Berthe's, disassembled the new transceiver into its component parts and packed them and the battery into a jumble of spare clothing in the bike's panier, under an old macintosh. The transceiver's leather case, which was to all intents and purposes waterproof, went on to the bike's carrier with a thermos of coffee, sandwiches and her spare sweater to pad it out. Her thinking behind this being that a jumble of old clothes shouldn't attract much attention but the neat little transceiver case *might*. To any Gestapist or Abwehr officer who knew his onions, *would* – so one could only count on not running into any such creature . . . In which hope, having got herself dressed up – warm trousers, sweater, coat and headscarf – she set off shortly after dusk, and within a couple of hours was on a tree-covered hillside a few kilometres west of Cussecs. She made her transmission at eleven, the Sevenoaks operator acknowledged and then told her they'd nothing for her, so she didn't have to stay up, had several hours' broken sleep in the shelter of a fallen elm whose enormous upturned roots in an overhang of impacted soil would she thought serve as a hiding-place for the set. She fixed this at first light – the set by then assembled and in its case, of course – building it into a contrivance of sticks and other debris not unlike a ground-level squirrel's dray, before setting off for home.

Wednesday now. The Noé 'infiltration' would be taking place tonight and in the small hours of Thursday: by this time tomorrow, therefore – for better or for worse . . . Pedalling out of the forested area – and not through but past Cussecs

304

– she was visualising a successful outcome: Alain Déclan hunched over the wheel of his old truck, with the German and Commandant Marteneau under the tarp in rear, plugging southward towards Lavelanet, and the others in their hired lorry escaping into the foothills of that towering snowbound range. *Please God*, escaping, all of them. It would be a while before one knew for sure, she guessed, maybe several days.

It was past eight when she got back, and Berthe had already left for work. There was an ambulance parked on the other side of Marengo – white with a green cross on its side, and just sitting there, no activity around it. Traffic had been heavy on the way into town, at any rate the last hour of it, and she was looking forward to shedding the gear she'd biked and slept in, immersing or at least sluicing herself in water that with any luck might still be warm. After that – well, tea and toast, for want of anything more like a *proper* breakfast.

Washed and dressed, she went downstairs – first to her bike in the rear hallway, to clear out the panier – thermos to be rinsed out along with the breakfast things – might well need it again tonight, thermos *and* bike. Having the commitment to listening-out, of course, but odds-on that Jake would have stuff for Baker Street as well. For instance he'd have discussed the alternative exit-route via Banyuls with Marteneau and Déclan.

Kettle filled, hot-plate switched on. Tea . . .

Berthe had left her a note – a few scribbled lines on the bottom of their shopping-list.

An ambulance has been in the square all night and still is, is now quiet but when I went over to see what it was doing there were squeals and whistles audible which sounded like some kind of wireless activity. Most sincerely hope nothing to do with us?

This kettle was always slow in coming to the boil. She left it with the hotplate glowing red and ran upstairs – because from the ground floor one's view across this end of the square was interrupted by a stone memorial in the centre.

Ambulance no longer there.

Having spent the night listening-out for *her*? Would have heard her, too. But Berthe wandering over there out of curiosity, and sharp enough, considering her ignorance of pretty well everything that was going on, to have caught on to the likely truth of what it was about. She'd have been curious in the first place because ambulances didn't usually spend nights parked and doing nothing in town squares.

Thank God one had not been on listening-out watch here last night. But they'd have had some *reason* for picketing this quarter?

Kettle boiling. Toaster already plugged in. Wake up now – make the tea and slice bread. Tear off that lower part of the shopping-list and burn it.

Get rid of the set?

Dismantle it, toss it in the canal piece by piece, like someone feeding ducks?

Not yet, anyway. Have it *ready* for ditching. Jake would be back at any rate before dark, please God sooner, and this didn't *have* to mean curtains, shutting up shop. That in fact was practically inconceivable. *Unacceptable.* They were showing interest in this quarter of the town, not this house. Anyway not *yet* this one. And one did have the spare sets stashed away, thank heavens. Jake would certainly want her to be listening-out tonight – if not transmitting. One could hardly have picked a worse time to be even *considering* shutting down.

Even remembering being warned in the course of training: 'A show of interest often precedes a break-in. Never wise to stick around unless there's some absolute imperative . . .'

Might say there *was*?

Fumbling bread-slices into toaster. Accepting that on the night before last the *Funkabwehr* might have been either remarkably quick in their reactions or just plain lucky. Alerted by her response to the Sevenoaks call-up, then staying on-beam and the right megacycles to catch the blip of acknowledgement minutes later?

Ten to one, they'd only have got a single bearing – and with only about a second in which to adjust for direction, so no great accuracy. This square, the station area, a few acres of streets around, maybe – *any* house in that sort of area . . . But could have been other 'ambulances' around, not just that one. Jake would insist, obviously, no more listening-out from here: and that in coming or going on the bike one should be a lot more cautious than of late. *Nothing* from now on that risked drawing attention to this house.

Digging her toast out of the smoking toaster with the prongs of a fork; toast somewhat blackened, in need of a scrape. Hands betrayingly shaky while doing so, and heart-beat a little fast. Remembering her first days here, determination to take no risks, call her own shots. Even laying down the law to Jake about it – telling him *she'd* never 'do a Wiggy', all that stuff. Now of course one knew better what one was up against, the risks one *had* to accept if one was going to do the job at all.

Jam, but no butter. Most of the butter was being taken for the occupying forces or railed off to Germany, the ration was ridiculously small. Time now – nine-twenty. Had to be at the station at noon, to call Marc; in the interim might try to sleep, in preparation for a second night in the open, but doubted she'd be able to.

She'd done some housework, also attended to her bike – tightening nuts, oiling, and adjusting the chain, seeing to the tyres. She'd also checked that the transceiver was as well hidden amongst the attic junk as it could be, ditto smaller items – one-time pads and crystals.

Cyanide capsule secure in its very much more personal location.

Out of the south-east corner of Place Marengo – forty or so metres from where the ambulance had been parked – and to her right along the boulevard. Quite a lot of traffic on it: through that fluctuating racket, the regular clacking of her wooden-soled shoes on damp paving. A light drizzle was falling but it was warmer than it had been and she was wearing a raincoat which Berthe had said she could use whenever she wanted; it was loose on her, and too long, but that at least served to keep her legs dry.

Gare Matabiau. Several Boche army trucks were parked in the forecourt, other transport double-parked for want of space, gendarmes making an issue of it here and there. She went on in, picked a phone-box she hadn't used before, made a note of its number as the one he should call, used another one to call the bar in Perpignan and leave the message as before – *Raoul please to call Lucy at 2 p.m.* It was a woman who took the message this time.

She bought some cigarettes – Caporals, which was all the man had – at the corner-shop Jake had used on the day she'd first met him, her first day here, when they'd subsequently found themselves stuck in the station bar for a while and begun to get to know each other. But Caporals were OK as far as she was concerned; oddly enough, she hadn't been smoking much in recent days.

Was odd, when you came to think of it. From the way she felt now, might well change.

Better get some lunch anyway. Early for it, but having come this far, and not keen either on going back to the house or eating in the station bar, on the other hand remembering Berthe having told her of a café-restaurant on Place

Belfort, only six or seven hundred metres from here and not bad, not the kind of place you'd usually see Boches either, she decided to try it. She took her time getting there, smoked one cigarette over a small cognac before ordering her meal – soup, and some kind of pâté with bread – and another afterwards over a liquid they called coffee. It *wasn't* bad, there were no Boches, and it had taken about an hour, i.e. half the time she had to kill. The rain had stopped and she thought vaguely of taking a look at Place Victor Hugo, where Jake had his apartment and the Gestapo had taken over an hotel – l'Ours Blanc, the White Bear. That square was no great distance. On the other hand it would roughly double the distance she'd have to walk back, exercise was about the last thing she needed, and who'd want to see Gestapo head-quarters when they didn't bloody well have to?

She set off back – via the top end of Rue Bayard and that bridge over the canal – which brought her virtually into the station forecourt.

Still about forty minutes early. Find a bench maybe, take the weight off. Didn't want anything from the bar, and couldn't have sat for long without ordering something. Out again therefore: back into the main hall and past the line of phone-boxes. A couple of them were in use: she reckoned on following the same procedure as she had yesterday, estab-lishing occupancy of that one a few minutes before zero-hour.

Benches in railway stations really didn't attract one much. Wandering on, therefore. Thinking about the ambulance, that its camouflage actually made it very noticeable. Once you knew what it actually was, of course, which one did thanks only to Berthe's God-given curiosity. Without that, it was distinctly possible one *would* have been listening-out from the house tonight.

Curtains then, all right. Leading to – all that business. In the course of it, discovering basic truths about oneself, not least one's capacity to endure excruciating pain.

As an alternative to revisiting the Cussecs area though, take this set out to Buzet? Less dangerous than transmitting on two nights running from the same location, probably. That had been a near squeak a few nights ago, but the *Funkabwehr* didn't have to know she'd even been there, and there was a lot of forest, with more than one approach to it.

Discuss it with *him*.

She'd come to another exit, which she recognised as the one from which that young gendarme had stood watching her – and infuriating Jake – a few days ago when they'd been setting off for Canet-Plage. Smiling at the mental picture she had of him, in his cloak and *kepi*, confronting the Luftwaffe people with that air of slightly amused contempt.

Drizzling again. And only – twenty minutes to two, still. When you were in a tearing hurry, time flew, when you wanted it to fly –

To her left, opposite but this side of a more central entrance, a grey Citroen Light 15 had just swept in, was rocking to a halt with its front tyres against the kerb, where – unusually – there were several vacant parking spaces. She'd edged back under this doorway's arch – instinctive reaction, but doing it with a degree of stagecraft, glancing up as if being dripped on and for *that* reason withdrawing into shelter.

Driver getting out. Standard kit for *La Geste* – trench coat and soft hat. From the rear seat also on this side, that one's virtual twin except for having a fatter, whiter face, emerging simultaneously and pausing with a hand on the open rear door, waiting for some other person to slide over and climb out.

Marc.

Marc.

Rosie frozen. Trying to tell herself she had to be deluded: some flare of lunacy stemming from her jumpy, fraught imagination. It was him for sure, though – in that shabby old army greatcoat, rain-hat, pebble glasses glistening, already wet from the drizzle. And in no way the Gestapists' prisoner: addressing them by the look of it quite affably, even excitedly, waving a hand in the direction of the telephones – direction of other things too, but this was plainly telephone business. Where in about fifteen or twenty minutes she would have been, to receive his call. Or if she'd arrived nearer the appointed hour – in a hurry maybe and in any case unsuspecting, blind to any such possibility, *dementia* such as this . . .

Although she could see instantly how he or they might have pulled it off. Not having given it a thought until this second, but it was there in a flash. Shock galvanising the intelligence? *Should* have given it some bloody thought, *not* have used only station telephone numbers, both for calling and for him to call back on. This time after she'd called at noon, someone waiting for it in that bar in Perpignan would have called him – or them – in l'Ours Blanc, even.

They'd gone inside – doubtless to check which box then merge into the shifting throng, Marc eventually nudging them with a whispered 'There. That's her coming now . . .'

Nightmare in watery greyish daylight. Marc a traitor, a *vendu* – and the *réseau* blown. Not only the appalling, visible fact of it, sense of absolute enormity, but what it left you with – faced *her* with here and now – Jake on his way back from Pamirs, Déclan and company on the brink of action. Not even Déclan could have much chance of making it out, away – Marc knowing about Canet-Plage, l'Hôtel du Tennis *and* l'Etoile in Banyuls. Which – Christ – blew *everything*. He even knew where Déclan lived. Those three having gone

311

inside she'd moved instantly, was by this time halfway across the forecourt – stunned, never having wanted anything as badly as in that moment she wanted Jake.

17

Jake said – eventually – 'We can thank God the bastard didn't know anything about Hardball. Nothing about Noé or Gustave – *anything* that matters.'

'So it'll go ahead.'

'Damn sure it will. Incidentally, there's been a change of exit plan – and that's something else to be glad of, now. Marteneau was dead against going via Banyuls. The fact a beach pick-up can't be relied on decided him against being separated from his team at all – he'd never liked it, only went along with it because it did seem to give the extraction of Gustave a better chance, and he disliked even *that* because the corollary was his men getting the short end of the stick. Not necessarily true, but how he felt – his decision, and with things as they've gone now thank God for it.'

'Whole team with their Boches straight from Noé into the mountains.'

He'd touched wood. 'Have to warn Déclan. Through our tobacconist chum. Not a hope of getting it to him before the action, but –'

'*My* fault, Jake.'

'No.' Firm shake of the head. 'I should have been more explicit about cut-out calls – *and* have taken a more realistic view of Marc.'

'He doesn't know where you've been living?'

'No. Or working. Only that I'm some kind of city slicker. Matter of fact he's never made any serious attempt at finding out – despite wanting to know everything that's going on. Getting damn few answers, incidentally – I've never thought of him as all that security-conscious. By nature a bit of a chatterer, I've thought and didn't know the bloody half of it . . . Christ, Suzie, what a hell of a thing for you!'

'Incredible. *Staggering*. Had *me* staggering, pretty well.'

'Not surprised, not in the least. Action now anyway, postmortems if any much, much later. So – we'll leave after dark. After Berthe gets home. I'm going to my flat now – phone my tobacconist on the way there – for Déclan – and collect a big wad of francs – luckily there's a lot left of the cash you brought. Apart from anything else we'll need plenty for the *passeurs* – they don't risk their necks for nothing. Then –'

'Banyuls and trans-Pyrenees?'

'No option, is there. A beach pick-up'd be lovely but we couldn't count on it, couldn't wait anyway, just one day'd be too long – and Marc, damn him to hell –'

'Hear, hear.'

'Well. Be back soon as I can – with car, may leave it at the station – or *Gare Routière* maybe. This square could be under surveillance at any rate after sunset – the ambulance business, which incidentally may link to Marc – but meanwhile you pack *a* bag – all the warm kit you can get into it –'

'Will you manage all right over the mountains?'

Meaning his limp, his knee, and getting a hard look. 'Yes, Suzie, I assure you –'

'Transceiver?'

'We'll take it with us, yes. Might use it to put Baker Street in the picture – on our way. Or might use the one we dumped on Monday, drop this one in the Garonne. Let's think about that.'

'Food?'

'I'll bring what I've got, and recompense Berthe for whatever she can spare.'

'Isn't much in the house at all.'

'We'll just have to cope, Suzie. Forage along the way.' Holding her. 'You all right now?'

'Better, anyway. Thanks to you. I'm sorry . . .'

The sight of him on the doorstep half an hour ago had reduced her to tears. She'd told him most of it with his arms around her and her wet face close to his. But she *was* OK now.

'About Banyuls, Jake –'

'It'll be a race, won't it. He – they – don't know you saw him at the station, won't know we're legging it, and he *did* know I'd be out of town a while. I'd say we may have a twenty-four-hour start on him. I won't fool you though – we'll make it, damn sure we will, but at the best of times that coastal railway's *bloody* dangerous.'

'Better run, Jake.'

'I better had.' He kissed her. 'You're marvellous.'

'What made you say the ambulance ploy could have links to Marc?'

'He's in with the Gestapo – they'd surely know whatever results the detector-vans were getting, and on top of that there's telephonic activity around Gare Matabiau.'

He was back before Berthe got home, old Rosie told me, and they'd had some cyphering to do. He'd parked the Mahossier, Jorisse Buick at the bus station – in case there might be any kind of lookout for them at Gare Matabiau.

'I'd had another fit of the shakes while he'd been gone. I *was* young, you know, and still new to it. Especially to the feel of being hunted. Had my case packed, anyway, and the transceiver down from the attic, day and night crystals in an inside pocket, one-time pad . . . Once I had *him* back – ready to go, might say.'

She'd also had her little cyanide capsule in its usual stowage – a small pocket inside the elastic of her knickers. However brutal the circumstances of arrest and imprisonment might be, a visit to a lavatory would surely be permitted, and a minute, *half* a minute, was all she'd need.

('I'd actually practised it – gone through the motions. Would you *believe* it?' 'Believe anything of you, Rosie . . .')

Jake had called his tobacconist and instead of following the usual procedure – enquiring whether he had some particular mixture of pipe tobacco in stock, which would have led to Déclan contacting him in some way, setting up a rendezvous, he'd asked the man whether as a great favour he'd pass a message personally and secretly to their mutual friend. He'd said he would, *bien sûr*, and the message Jake gave him was *Raoul is vendu, they are hunting us, s.q.p.* – those letters standing for *sauve qui peut*. The tobacconist had begun to commiserate, he'd cut in with 'Adieu, my friend', and rung off.

He'd also called Jacques Jorisse. The firm's Buick would be found to have disappeared, as would their Associate, Jean Samblat. Gone off his head, run off with some girl, or both. There were commissions due to him that he wouldn't be claiming, might be set against the value of the car? Jacques – thanks for everything . . .

Rosie told me, in a taxi on our way to Number 1 Place Capitole, Les Jardins de l'Opéra, restaurant of the Grand Hôtel de l'Opéra, 'Berthe took it hard, poor dear. Jake was as kind to her as he could be, and gave her sound, practical advice. She *would* be sad – troubled – for Suzette Treniard, whom she'd befriended and tried to get into a trainee nursery-school teacher's job. Suzette, she might recall, had moved down here from Paris, had lost her husband in the British assault on the fleet at Mers-el-Kebir, had been hoping to locate an old aunt of her husband's, meanwhile had had some money from the sale of an apartment in the Paris area but no secure future beyond that unless she could find this aunt who she was hoping might need *her*, being fairly ancient. The nursery-school idea – Berthe's own – had been a possible solution, but now despite her efforts the wretched girl had just left without a word – no goodbye, no thanks. The only likely explanation is there was a man who used to visit and take her out for meals – middle-aged, lame, much too old for her, but – well, on a couple of occasions she was away for a day or two, taking an overnight bag with her, so – perhaps least said the better.

Rosie told me, 'It got to be embarrassing. Berthe said something like "To be frank with you, it's not so much *her* departure that breaks my heart", and he was – you know, trying to comfort her – while the best *I* could manage was to tell her I'd serviced the bike that morning.'

Then at the restaurant, or rather in its bar, we were on vodka martinis, which Rosie agreed with me have a lot going for them – hedging this with 'Although I suppose we'd better take it a *little* easy, make sure of covering ground I need to before bedtime ... Old Ben, I can tell you, used to make a real beaut of a vodka Marty, as he called them. His *usual* tipple was Scotch, mind you – had been gin in his naval days, then –'

'Here's to you, Rosie.'

'Good luck.' She was wearing her silver trousers and grey silk shirt this evening, ruby brooch and ear studs of course, and looked marvellous. Tasting the martini: 'H'm. Not *bad*. Best go *very* easy on them though, d'you think?'

'Will the ground we're covering include Ben and the Brisbane yacht club?'

'Middle Harbour Yacht Club. Brisbane's number one – Australia's, even . . . Well, no, I'd say that's best kept for the morning. Yes, definitely. Tonight in fact I don't need to rush it. Least, I think I don't. Perpignan, Banyuls, that awful journey – apart from its awfulness there's not all that much detail worth your while, I'll give you a *general* picture – all right?'

'If you think that's the best way – and I'd have latitude –'

'You'd take it, anyway. What one remembers mostly is just strain – about thirty-six hours of it. Wasn't over then either, not by a long chalk . . . But – *general* picture then – Jake like a rock, with a steadying effect on me – which believe me I needed – both of us tense as banjo strings but in the presence of others – or each other, come to that – doing our best to seem nonchalant – and / or in love, which was mostly *his* idea. Although I admit I did have it in mind – between whiles, in a subdued sort of way. Didn't feel – *safe*, you know? *Ghastly* bloody train – me from time to time dropping off out of sheer fatigue, waking minutes later with all of it thumping back into mind like as bad a dream as you ever had – realising in approx one point five seconds Christ, no dream, just how it bloody *is*, what we're *into*.'

'You get that much across all right, Rosie.'

'And then you see, Jake getting killed.'

'Oh, *Rosie* –'

'Telling about it's almost worse. In the train and then foot-slogging through the *Zone Interdite*, knowing damn-all o' what was coming – OK, one never does, obviously, but I mean, thinking back to it like this, one *does* know what's coming, one's seeing the pair of us like through the wrong end of binoculars, but with the focus very much on *him* because it's there, coming up just ahead . . .

Letting that tail off; looking quizzically into my eyes, wondering was I still with her. Small shrug, and touching her glass. 'Anyway – give you the prosaic start of it.'

It was dark when they left the house, after checking from upstairs windows that no watchers were visible in the square. Jake had left the Buick at the bus station, and there it was, attracting no special interest, just one in a line of other *gazos*, charcoal glowing in their burners. He'd been carrying the transceiver, was pushing it under his driver's seat while she dumped her suitcase in the back with his; she asked him wouldn't it be better to have it on her side and accessible – so if they were going to drop it in the Garonne he'd only need to stop on the bridge for a few seconds – or even just slow down.

'We'll hang on to it, Suzie. Getting to the other one would mean a diversion. Use this and ditch it later – anywhere.' They'd composed the message and encyphered it while awaiting Berthe's return. Pulling his door shut, switching on sidelights, starting up – which was always a bit of a challenge – adding as it fired, 'Might send from the ruin we used on Monday, d'you think?'

'Well – yes . . . Near Quillan, wasn't it? Turning down through Limoux, Quillan, Perpignan.'

'But not – as I'll explain – directly to the station. We'll have time in hand, and with a bit of an effort – anyway, still make the first train out . . . *Have* you got all your papers with you?'

'Except no *Ausweis.*'

Travel permit. Which until the recent occupation one hadn't needed, and could still get by without, although there'd been warnings in newspapers and on posters. Jake did have the equivalent, good enough touch wood still to satisfy gendarmerie. On Mahossier, Jorisse business, he explained, under the Vichy system they'd had blank forms they could fill in themselves and authenticate with the office stamp, and he'd kept some handy for emergencies.

'But I've got to break this to you, Suzie. You won't like it, but I'm – the phrase is, "taking advantage" of you. Taking you on a jaunt of a kind that – well, say I *shouldn't* have conned you into coming with me. I apologise, but it's so much the *obvious* thing – in terms of – you know, for nine people out of ten disbelief's suspended?'

On Boulevard de Bonrepos, rattling south through light-streaked darkness. She asked him, 'Where to, this jaunt?'

'Depends where we are when we're asked. In the long run, what about Collioure? Pretty little place – and Banyuls's just that much closer to the mountains and the border, more likely to arouse suspicions. Collioure'd maybe only raise eyebrows, if you see what I mean. The Brighton syndrome, even? *Do* you mind, Suzie?'

'I suppose if it'll save our bacon – it's not exactly a *new* idea –'

'Well, bless you!'

'Get tickets from Perpignan to Collioure, do we?'

'I think so. And the early train, allegedly so crowded the guards can't get through to check papers or whatever else. But dumping this car now, I'm thinking of Canet-en-Roussillon – not far inland of the beach, a hike of ten or twelve kilometres back to the station – face that, could you?'

'If you can.'

Thinking of his lameness. But hell, if he was going to

make it over the Pyrenees . . . You saw the limp, remembered a description of the accident, didn't actually know the extent of the problem the horse had left him with but thinking *He'll probably manage whatever he sets his mind to*. He was explaining, 'Thing is, whoever had abandoned it there *might* have been picked up from the beach?'

'Oh, that *is* an idea!'

'If they were to find it soon enough but not *too* soon. For all Marc knows, could even have been the Hardball exit. Wouldn't *that* rile 'em, just . . . I'm heading for the 113 now, incidentally. And just getting our act together, Suzie, if we were stopped around this stage I'd give Carcassonne as our destination. Hôtel la Barbacane – on the old city ramparts, *grande luxe* – sort of place one *might* . . .' Glancing at her in the half-dark: 'You could act as if I hadn't sprung it on you yet – you might have wondered, but –'

'Actually I wouldn't. Not as a way *you'd* behave.'

'I'm glad – but I'm saying if it was for real –'

'It's not – so leave it, please?'

'If we *were* stopped – with luck we *won't* be – if we were though, in the next hour say, we'd be on course to make Carcassonne well before curfew, our papers are in order, and as yet touch wood we *aren't* actually being hunted – what I'm saying is that at this stage we shouldn't have much to worry about.'

'Let's hope.'

Change of subject, a minute later: 'I suppose you realise Marc's incurred the death penalty.'

'SOE's sentence, you mean.'

'Yes – delegated to you and me. Shoot him on sight. Given the opportunity, it's our bounden duty and would be my pleasure.'

'So once he knows we know, he'll be twice as keen to kill *us*.'

'I doubt he'd be half-hearted about it even now. Giving you to the Gestapo wouldn't have been aimed at *prolonging* your life, would it. I wonder what turned him. They'd have got on to him through the Vérisoins, most likely: then he either plays ball or gets the chop. Often as not they offer money too . . . I'm turning right here, over the canal, then left on to the *route nationale*.'

'Are you carrying your Lama?'

'You bet.' His handgun. Close resemblance to a Colt .45 but Spanish-made, 9-millimetre so easy to get ammo for. Heavy, clumsy-looking thing, although in firearms training on the field agent's course she'd done surprisingly well with one, considering its weight and her small hands. Jake said, about the pistol, 'Touch wood, won't need to use it. The great thing for you and me is to slip through unseen, unheard.'

'Just possible, I suppose. Hope to God Déclan gets your message before it's too damn late.'

'I'll try to get through to him again – if that's remotely possible. The mountain's about all he can go for, and he may have had some route in mind. What a hole to be in, though. Can't take his poor wife, can't tell her anything – if he's lucky, just bloody vanish. We've discussed that, on occasion, possible cost of what's otherwise been the perfect cover . . . But Marteneau and his boys will be just about ready to go, you realise. Jump-off point's an old barn on the edge of Noé. Please God, at least we'll have pulled *that* off.'

'*Damn* Marc, for poor old Alain.'

'The most difficult thing to guard against is the knife in the back. Suzie, we've a long haul ahead of us, why don't you take a nap?'

'Doubt if I could – and since *you* obviously can't –'

'I wasn't up all night.'

'Nor was I, as it happens. But all right — if I *can* drop off . . .'

Trundling on. Jake silent, giving her a chance to sleep.

She woke when they were to the east of Quillan, having got past it by way of a country lane that avoided going through the town, cut the corner and eventually got them on to the 117 too far east for the ruined château; he had to turn back for a few kilometres to reach it, and was making that turn when she woke. Curfew was in force by then, had been when he'd been similarly detouring around Limoux, and he was using the car's lights as sparingly as possible. Any other traffic one encountered was as likely as not to mean trouble; he told her he'd turned off the 623 once when there'd been full headlights approaching from a then fairly distant curve of road before they vanished temporarily into a dip, and he'd spotted a farm entrance he could get into, switching the Buick's lights off and sitting tight, Rosie muttering to herself in her sleep, until the thing had gone blazing past — petrol engine and travelling fast, more than likely Boche.

Had to use lights getting up to the château, on that steep and narrow approach road snaking up through trees; then on the dangerously open summit, lights off and Rosie out — stringing out her aerial wire and then getting down to work between the car and a crumbling stone wall where she could safely use the little fishing torch — battery incidentally getting low. Last use of it in any case, last transmission — telling Baker Street that Raoul had been turned and Jake and Lucy were on the run making for the eastern Pyrenees. Raoul not having been apprised of Hardball's purpose, location or other operational detail, it was taking place as planned at the time of this transmission, and on completion all involved would be withdrawing by way of

Col de – whatever that mountain pass was called. No beach pick-up therefore required, and no further communication possible after this message. Warning of the betrayal had been passed through an intermediary to Batsman, but his movements henceforth were not predictable although a further attempt to contact him would be made.

She'd signed off with a coded 'Adieu'.

'Quite some news for Buck and his boys and girls to digest over Thursday breakfast.'

'And the last news they could hope for for some while.' Rosie added, 'I should mention, though, there was a way out for Déclan that Jake remembered having discussed with him – to contact the *réseau* Organiser in the Lourdes-Pau district, the man who'd passed Hardball to him. There was a safe-house between Pau and Tarbes, and some cleric – an abbot, might have been – who was Resistance-connected and was in touch with mountain guides in that area. Jake had forgotten about this, in our lightning evacuation of Toulouse, but he thought Déclan would probably have kept it in mind – and if he *could* get in touch with him again – the tobacconist, I suppose – he'd suggest it. By then of course if he'd had the first message he might already have taken off. That would have been the smart thing, not even to go home.'

'Monsieur, madame –'

Head waiter. We'd ordered our meal some time before telling him no rush but when you like . . . In fact I was relieved; we'd risked a second vodka martini, and there was wine to come – although luckily they had a good selection in half-bottles. We'd ordered scallops in some sauce or other that Rosie had known about and approved, then duck with spinach and sautéed potatoes; a half of Sancerre with the scallops – remembering how she'd gone for that – and a good claret with the duck. Well – she was giving me

324

whole damn book! In fact had been working at it like a beaver – and on top of that was extremely good company. On top of *that* – well, this was Rosie Quarry, the one and only, who in my wildest dreams I'd never thought I'd have the luck and privilege to meet. Telling me when we were settled at the table, 'Really *will* get us to Banyuls now, I promise.'

She'd got back into the car with the transceiver in its case but not properly packed up, had then separated the various parts and transferred the case to the floor with the jumble loose in it, and Jake had stopped or slowed at various points – rivers mainly – until she'd got rid of all of it.

Now as far as London was concerned they were *perdus* – lost, deaf and dumb. She told him, 'I'm out of a job', and his answer was, 'I'm sure they'll find alternative employment for you in due course.'

'Then let's say for both of us.'

'But perhaps not together, d'you think?'

'Not in the field together, you mean.'

'Could have its complications, couldn't it?'

'Yes, well, bugger *them*. The essential, I'd say, would be to have the home base secure – would you go along with that?'

'You mean *us*.'

'Surely. *Seriously*, Suzie. In fact –'

'Let's get there, *then* get serious?'

Getting there by way of the outskirts of Perpignan, then Canet-en-Roussillon where they dumped the Buick on the edge of a builder's yard, and the long, far from enjoyable trek back into town and to the station. Jake's limp had become a lot more noticeable by the time they got there, although it worried her more than it seemed to worry him: he wasn't so much limping as hobbling, assuring her from time to time that it didn't hurt, only sort of stiffened when used harder than it was used to: and declining to take her arm or let her take his suitcase as well as hers: what did she think he was – a cripple?

Certainly was not a mountaineer.

But having told herself that, had to recognise that he might well *become* one.

The station was already crowded before it was fully daylight, and the queue at the *guichet*, where everyone had to show their papers, was more than half an hour long. The clerks selling tickets were supervised by gendarmerie and *Funkabwehr* – not all the time, but constantly enough to ensure they were scrupulous in the double-checking of identities. Jake had given Rosie about half the wad of francs he'd collected from his apartment – in case they should somehow become separated, she had to be able to carry on alone if necessary: and at Banyuls the bar-keeper Gérard – Marc's friend – was going to want cash for his *passeur* or *passeurs* – despite which he bought her train ticket as well as his own, in the belief that this looked more natural.

He'd told her before they'd joined the queue, 'Older man, much younger woman, after all –'

'Not *that* much younger.'

'Go on with you. Anyone'd think I should be in a wheel-chair!'

'Accidents in the hunting field have nothing to do with age.'

'Forget the hunting field. I had a smash-up in a Renault – in Lille, that was. When you were barely out of your pram!'

He'd paid for the tickets anyway, after they'd identified themselves – papers which had been forged in London being accepted after careful examination, identities and ticket details then entered in a register. Hardly surprising the queue was slow-moving. Nowhere to sit, of course

326

while waiting – and further delay when the train steamed in, finally, and the place filled up with passengers from Narbonne. Boche military were by now around in greater numbers – uniformed, not Gestapo, a lot of them mere boys. Jake didn't get the weight off his knee until finally they were allowed to board, and crowded into the box-like carriage with its hard benches and dirty windows; their travelling companions were initially a mother with three young daughters, an old man sucking an empty clay pipe and two labourers – vineyard workers, might be. A few nods and mutters of bonjour . . . Jake got their suitcases up into the rack, steered Rosie into a corner seat, sank down beside her, stuck that leg out straight and let out a long, hard breath.

'Better?'

Actually of course, 'Va mieux?'

He smiled at her. 'You've no idea.'

Perpignan to Argelès twenty kilometres, Argelès to Collioure six and a half: about an hour's run. In the course of it, soon after leaving Perpignan they had a visit from a ticket inspector who looked a bit like a weasel and had two other civilians – plain clothes, not railway uniforms like his, but Frenchmen and as like as not DST or Gestapo. Then at Argelès three Germans, an NCO and two corporals pushed in; they'd been standing in the corridor and now replaced the two labourers who were getting out, but being three in a space previously occupied by two necessitated the two smaller children crowding on to their mother's lap, the older one standing close up against them. The mother had engaged Jake in conversation just as they'd been pulling into the station, asking him, 'Are you and the young lady taking a little holiday, monsieur?' and he'd told her, 'Little honeymoon.' Elaborating with 'Four days is all we have. Back in Toulouse Monday. We were married a few weeks ago, these are the first days we could get away together.'

'Precious days, then!'

'Precious *hours*, madame!'

'A shame to have so little time.' She smiled sympathetically at Rosie. 'May I ask what sort of an employer won't allow you at least two weeks off for a honeymoon?'

'I'm a nurse, at a hospital outside Toulouse. We're shorthanded at the moment.' She was thinking of the hospital at Fonsorbes where Déclan's wife worked, didn't name it in case the woman turned out to be a matron there. A million to one against, but coincidences did happen – why risk them when you didn't need to? The woman asking then – wriggling irritably as the Boches pushed up still further – 'Collioure, you're going to?' and Jake took over again, saying yes, but they'd not had time to book at an hotel, only *hoped* –

'You'll be all right, I'm sure. My daughters and I are going to Banyuls – I have an uncle there who's ill, that's how we've had permission. Entry is strictly controlled, you know – on account of its proximity to the border, some such reason –'

A whistle shrilled and the train lurched, got going. Rosie leant her head back, closed her eyes; the woman said, 'Twenty minutes is all you've got, young lady.'

'Just a few minutes helps.' Smiling at the children, then meeting the eyes of the Boche NCO – Feldwebel, something of that kind – eyes like wet stones under greying brows – malicious, unblinking. She shut her eyes again, wondered where *they*'d be getting out. If at Collioure, might be awkward: the station was at some height above the town, apparently, Jake wasn't intending to go down into it if they could avoid doing so. You'd only have to climb another steep hill to get out of it and continue southward – shanks's pony over the high ground inland of Port Vendres – four kilometres to get to Port Vendres, then another six to Banyuls.

She'd opened her eyes again, found the German *still* staring. It was – disconcerting. A hard, even penetrative stare: simply to embarrass, frighten – or provoke reaction?

Jake asked her quietly, 'All right?'

'Except the one keeps staring.'

'Is a bit sinister. But if I objected –'

'No, don't do that. It's intended to intimidate, I think.' A smile. 'Does, too.'

'They never have been the nicest of people, Suzie pet. It won't be for much longer now, anyway.'

'As long as they aren't getting out where we are.'

'They'd most likely have transport meeting them. Did I mention that I love you?'

'Not in so many words. Implied it once or twice.'

'Take it as fact?'

'Well, well, well.'

'Do better than that, surely?'

'How about "snap"?'

'*Much* better, Suzie. Unbelievably so.'

'I'm looking forward to having you use my *real* name. We're going to have a lot to look back on, aren't we?'

'As of now, plenty to look forward to.'

'Yes – well . . .'

'If I were you, I wouldn't look at that sod again.'

'I won't. He's a sadist, isn't he. I'll fade on you now, then shut-eye until we're there.'

'Then don't look at him or get near him. When we move I'll try to keep myself between you.'

'I really am *quite* keen on you, Jake.'

★ ★ ★

329

Old Rosie said, 'That kind of dialogue.'

'Keeping each other's morale up in whispers under the fishy eye of an evil-minded Kraut.'

'More lizard-like than fishy. Quite hateful. Evil, yes. The effect of it exaggerated I dare say because one wasn't exactly riding high in any case. You're right, would have been the value of the exchange with Jake. His notion too, of course. But we had a ten-kilometre hike ahead of us over country patrolled by goons who actually did shoot on sight – although we didn't run into any – and I was worried for Jake with his gammy knee. We'd *find* Banyuls all right, just by following the railway and / or the coast road, but how it'd be when we got there, actually getting into the town – entry being so restricted, that woman had said – well, spin of a coin . . .'

'*And* Marc and his new friends on your tail.'

'Oh, they were. As I'll be telling you in a moment.'

Dwelling a pause at this stage because the *sommelier* was favouring us with his attentions. I asked her, 'Your Feldwebel admirer and his friends stayed on the train, did they?'

'Yes. OK for the time being – didn't want them getting out at Collioure, obviously, but preferably no reunion in Banyuls either. After all, it wasn't much more than a fishing village at that time, not a town with parking problems like it is now, odds were you *would* have run into anyone you'd ever met before. One's hope was they might be going to Port Vendres – and maybe they were. Real creep, that one.'

Watching the *sommelier* half-fill her glass with Graves – which happened to be one I knew, and closely related to nectar.

'Here's to you, Rosie. Wouldn't have missed a minute of this for anything on earth.'

'You mean tonight?'

'I mean the whole thing, these few days.'

'How nice. Especially as I wouldn't either. You know, when I wrote you that letter I damn near didn't post it? I asked myself why am I doing this, what's the *point*? Well, there *is* a point – one we haven't got to yet, *hell* of a point in fact –'

'What are you talking about?'

'No.' Both hands up, as if to ward me off. '*Not* talking about any of that yet. Banyuls first. Get you there in one leap – actually a ten-kilometre slog over varied terrain, lumping our suitcases. Jake I was sure in bloody agony from that knee – which *wasn't* exactly propitious, for crossing mountains . . . But there they were, a beautiful distant mass with Banyuls somewhere this side of it – and we just – well, from the station at Collioure we started downhill, eastward, towards the harbour and that old castle and a patch of sea in sight, taking it easy until others had outdistanced us, then getting off-road in a southerly direction, I think over public gardens or allotments of some kind and up again over that hill's rounded shoulder – in full view of some kind of lookout tower, which gave one another go of the heebie-jeebies . . . Going into detail again, having sworn I wouldn't. All that matters is we made it – I guess, in something like four hours. Jake hobbling and me – well, not finding it exactly a lark. Anything that moved, we got out of its sight – a couple of trains, some *gazos* now and then, the odd horse and cart. No patrols or strongpoints, that was the vital thing. I think patrols might only have been out at night – either that or on the other side of Banyuls, the mountain side. Oh, this is a fantastic wine . . .'

On their way into the town they'd found themselves passing a house that had a notice in a window saying 'Rooms', and had booked in for two nights – separate rooms, Rosie allegedly being Jake's sister – Jake's idea, no prior discussion and neither of them had mentioned it since – then sluiced off in cold water, changed some clothes, and set out to find l'Etoile, which was easy enough after first locating l'Hôtel des Pyrénées. The hotel faced the sea across a road and a crescent-shaped beach about a kilometre from end to end; following Marc's instructions they went down an alleyway at the side of the hotel to a triangular cobbled area, and there was the bar *en face*.

They stopped on the cobbles, looking at it.

'Might have booked into the hotel, if we'd thought.'

Jake leant with a hand on a lamp-post. 'Better off where we are, I'd say – not right in Marc's likely zone of operations. Come to think of it, if we could find ourselves a *passeur* Marc wouldn't know of – maybe *not* use this Gérard . . .'

'Making it a bit easy for Marc otherwise, I suppose.'

'Except if Gérard can get us away quickly, a chance worth taking? We know he's reliable, whereas one's heard a lot of them are crooks – take your money and leave you stranded –'

'Taking Gérard on trust on *Marc's* recommendation?'

'Well – yes. With the escape-line, he used him and got people out – same man, *he's* not turned.'

'But this is where Marc'll come – if he *is* coming.'

'But if we've cleared out by then –'

'Should we see what we think of Gérard and how soon he'd reckon to get us away?'

'Yes. That's *it*.' He patted her arm. 'Twenty-four hours maximum – to be gone by this time tomorrow, say.'

'Or sooner. Alternatively if he could produce a *passeur* Marc *wouldn't* know of – we'd have to pay him whatever he'd have made using one of his own lot?'

'Yes. Yes . . .' An arm tight around her shoulders for a moment. 'But I'll see him first on my own. If we have to go elsewhere, the less he knows about us the better, so –'

'All right.'

'So. Go back to the front there, have a look at the sea, then come back, I'll meet you hereabouts. Ten minutes, say?'

'What'll I be when you introduce me – your sister again?'

'How about wife?'

'Oh – I think I'd buy that . . .'

'You *mean* it?'

'Time being, make it fiancée?'

It was a vivid seascape beyond the long, surf-washed crescent of beach. Cloud had been breaking up in recent hours, allowing for periods of sunshine like this one, with a brisk wind smashing the tops off the rollers that were powering slantwise into the bay from the north and / or north-west, smashing themselves white against the headlands, racing on into the bay in a welter of white and green – bottle-green when the sun was covered, emerald when it all lit up again, as now . . .

Not a sail or anything else in sight. Fishing-boats at the far end there, inside an arc of sea-wall sheltering them. She wondered if she'd just become engaged: rather thought she *had*. In which case, better tell him her real name and start calling him James instead of Jake. Ending up, if they did actually go through with it, as Mrs James Kinnear. Not a bad name, she thought – in fact it would be one of the best she'd had. Having started life as Rosalie de Bosque, then become Rosie Ewing – wife of Squadron Leader Ewing, whom she'd come to dislike quite strongly, had only not walked out on because at about the time she'd realised there was nothing else for it, he'd saved her the trouble by getting himself shot down into the Channel by a Messerschmidt 109.

Which was when she'd offered herself to SOE for training as a field agent, been turned down for some silly reason and that same evening got plastered with the Australian, ending up in bed with him at the Savoy. Savoy, not the Charing Cross Hotel, as had been alleged.

'Suzie. *Suzie* . . .'

Jake – taking her by surprise – taking her arm, turning with her towards the Etoile. 'I think he's probably OK. Any case the best chance we've got.'

Rosie said, telling it fast now – with a target in sight, I surmised, a point she wanted to reach in this session – 'Gérard as he called himself had never heard of anyone called Marc Voreux, but when I described him and Jake mentioned the Jewish couple who'd been the last ones he'd sent through – putting a rough date on it too – there was no doubt he knew who we were talking about. Jake then gave him the background: Marc having been turned and in cahoots with the Gestapo, which was why we were in a hurry to get out. Whether this might deter Gérard from helping us as we'd like him to – with an introduction to a *passeur* – was obviously up to him, and if so we'd have to find someone else. This was bullshit, but obviously we *would* have had to – that was how it was, what we were up against. Presumably his tracks were covered, though – and Voreux wasn't going to inform on *him* because he'd be incriminating himself. There'd have been other angles I dare say, but the upshot was Gérard said if the money could be agreed, he could handle it. All he was really interested in was money. If a *passeur* of good repute were by chance to be available at such alarmingly short notice, what *about* finance? Regrettably, only cash would be acceptable. *Passeurs* took their own lives in their hands, in the course of saving others, and like anyone else had families dependent on them. And so forth. Jake assured him we had cash. As long as he wasn't (a) holding us to ransom, and (b) could have us on our way by tomorrow noon. That caused a bit of an eruption, but it simmered down when Jake made it clear we'd pay in advance and well over the odds, agreeing a figure right away if Gérard would get his man here this evening – tonight. He thought that might be possible: but another point now, what about equipment? Backpacks, boots, outer protective clothing – and rations, water-bottles – all absolute necessities: *could* in fact be provided, at a certain cost . . .'

I broke in with 'What did Gérard look like?'

'Stocky, fiftyish, foxy-looking. He was French, all right, although his wife was Spanish and the young waiter, Andrés, was her nephew. Nice lad, we got on well right from the start. He was about nineteen and his father had been killed in their civil war, shot after being taken prisoner. He was smallish with curly dark hair and eyes like brown buttons. You think I'm waffling, but it so happens he saved my life, d'you *mind* if I tell you what he looked like?'

'Sorry, Rosie . . .'

'I should think so. Where was I . . . Oh, the *passeur* turned out to be his uncle, the woman's brother. Eladio, his name was. So – basics – there are your characters, Gérard would have his brother-in-law at the Etoile to meet us later that evening – eight o'clock, say, eight-thirty – yes, *guaranteed*, if we'd produce the cash, have it there this evening, uh? The morning would be soon enough to discuss the gear and price it: we could see it, here in Banyuls. Boots no good if they don't fit, eh? And Andrés would convey all this to his uncle: he – Andrés – was so fortunate as to possess a *petrolette*, motor-scooter.

'And so on. Price agreed. Just as well we *were* really loaded. Madame incidentally was in on all of it – not conversationally, but ears and eyes, crikey . . . You could have fun with this scene. Actually it *wasn't* fun, for us, too

335

many uncertainties and all we could do was accept them. A complete chance we were taking, if they turned out to be crooks we were in their hands. And the Noé action might have failed – no way of knowing, we were both fairly agonised for Déclan. Jake was hoping to talk to the tobacconist again, get him to pass on a message about the Pau *réseau*; he'd thought of doing it from the Etoile, but decided there was too much risk of a tap on the line, if Marc had put the Gestapo on to Gérard, which he might have. He made the call – on the way back to our digs, from a phone in the Hôtel des Pyrenées: the tobacconist said he'd given him the first message, and would *try* to get this one to him.'

'At least Déclan did know the worst of it.'

'Yes. And to have been in a position to have spoken with the tobacconist he'd obviously survived Noé, so maybe that had gone to plan. We both felt better for it.'

'Think *we*'d feel better for a kümmel now?'

'Well . . .' Slight frown: fingertips to one of the ruby studs. Then: 'How would *you* feel about a cognac?'

She gave me the rest of it over that cognac. In other words, made it last. Which wasn't such a bad idea. Tonight though she was *really* singing for her supper – needing from her own point of view to get on with it, get it over – I wasn't having to keep her to the point, only listen and occasionally put a question.

They'd gone back to their rooming house, and rested – slept maybe, and found the water warm enough to bath in. They'd have taken in sustenance of some kind before leaving the Etoile, I think. Rosie wasn't bothering with trivialities though, jumped straight to eight, eight-thirty or thereabouts when they were to have supper – paella made with – oh, mussels and – anchovies, it might have been, Madame had promised them? – and to be introduced to Eladio, and give Gérard half the money.

Eladio hadn't arrived when they got there, but Andrés had seen him earlier and was certain he was coming. The place was quite full, and Madame had kept a table for them at the kitchen end of the darkish, low-ceilinged, lamp-lit room, a table big enough for six in the angle between the left-hand wall and that end of the counter. She asked whether they'd like to have their meal right away and they opted for this – to be finished before Eladio turned up seemed a good idea. Gérard appeared while they were eating it, and brought them a bottle of wine they hadn't asked for; they'd had a glass when they'd first arrived, but wanted to be clear-headed in their negotiations with Eladio.

They finished the paella, which was very good, and Andrés brought coffee, to all intents and purposes joined them, having to go off a couple of times but both times returning. There was a waitress-cum-kitchenmaid – French, local girl – and several tables were unoccupied by this time, so there was no great pressure on him. This must have been when he told them about the Fascists having murdered his father, his hatred of them and of their German buddies; he was surprised Franco hadn't yet joined in *this* war – presumably wasn't *quite* sure the Boches were going to win it. He asked Rosie was she by any chance English; then, 'SOE, maybe?' She gave him somewhat vague answers, including the fact her father had been French, and he said he'd like nothing better than to do something of that kind: how could he apply to be considered for such employment? Rosie had been about to suggest that BCRA might be a better bet, on account of his not having a word of English, when Eladio arrived – Andrés leaping to his feet to perform the introductions, and Gérard then joining them.

Eladio was a man of about forty, dark-skinned like his sister and nephew, curly-haired like Andrés too, but heavily-built and ponderous in his movements. He spoke French slowly with a Spanish accent.

Terms were agreed. They'd see to the provision of gear in the morning: at Aristide's *grenier*, say 0930? *Grenier* meaning loft or attic. It would take a little time: and rations for the journey could be prepared in the kitchen here, also in the morning? Gérard agreed, no problem. Jake had already given him half the passage-money, would bring the rest of it to this loft – which was actually an artist's studio, one of them had mentioned – in the morning. Come *here*, Gérard suggested, and either he or Andrés would take them along. It was actually no distance. Better bring such gear as they had, although they might have to leave some of it behind – essentials only, no more than fitted in the back-packs.

That was about that. Eladio finished the wine. They'd start the journey in a donkey-cart, he said. Only a few kilometres, to a place where they'd spend the night, setting off before daylight next morning. Jake hadn't liked the sound of that, would have preferred to be putting more distance behind them, but all of this was in Eladio's hands, obviously had to be. And at least they'd be out of Banyuls. While Rosie thought a pause before the marathon mightn't be a bad thing at all. Jake was looking distinctly under par after the hike from Collioure, and she wasn't looking forward to three days of foot-slogging over mountains.

Eladio had departed then, and Andrés had gone to see him on his way. Jake got up and moved to the counter to pay the bill, having seen that madame did not bring bills to tables, and Rosie decided to visit the ladies' WC before departure. She'd seen where it was: you went along to the end of the counter and around it to the left, the entrance to the kitchen was then on your left, there was a staircase just past it on the right, staff entry / exit just beyond that, and beyond *that* a door marked *Dames*.

Jake would make it all right, she told herself in the flyblown mirror. Simply because he knew he had to. She'd told herself this before, and believed it, but also realised it was going to be hellish for him. Maybe when it got *really* bad, Eladio would lend a hand. He was big enough, strong enough by the look of him.

She came out of the *toilette*, turned left past the back door and then around the foot of the stairs, was on her way through to the bar when the crash of Jake's 9-millimetre – double crash, two fast shots – came near to stopping her heart, did of course stop her in her tracks – seeing through a whole lot of movement a group of men at the end of the room just inside the door, Marc going down with Jake's bullets in him and a German in a trench coat with a Schmeisser snarling deafeningly in gloved hands, Jake there to her right crumpling, toppling where he'd been at the counter chatting with madame – who'd ducked down behind it, screaming. There was a lot of screaming as the Schmeisser's racket ceased, and arms around her from behind, a shout in her ear of '*Viens* – come!' Andrés – dragging her back towards the staircase. Estelle the waitress this side of the kitchen doorway, screaming, also blocking Rosie's view of whatever else was happening in there, offering help to madame who was there with her. Rosie had had a glimpse of a second German, she thought, but only momentarily: her impulse was to get back to Jake – useless and fatal as that would have been – and in any case Andrés had her at the back door, urging, 'Quick, quick, you'll be all right, if only –'

Dark alleyway, a step down into it. Racket of shouts and screams subdued by the closing of the door. Jake dead. *Dead*.

339

Half a clip of 9-millimetre out of that Schmeisser which she could still see juddering, flaming – you didn't walk or even limp away from *that*. Marc dead too, but –

'Christ. Oh, *Christ . . .*'

18

Sunday breakfast at the Brasserie des Aviateurs. I'd had coffee at my own hotel before setting out – needing it, having spent some time at the laptop after seeing Rosie home last night, and then been blasted out of sleep by the *coup de téléphone* I'd requested, in order to meet her here at nine. Early enough, for a Sunday morning after a very late Saturday night, in any case necessitated by this shindig's guest of honour being due to put in an appearance, at last. I can't say I was exactly tingling with excitement at the prospect of seeing, hearing or even meeting him, but Rosie *was*, in her own quiet way, and as much as anything out of politeness to her one was bound to show a bit of interest.

The brasserie was fuller than I'd seen it until now – and noisier than one might have expected. They couldn't by any means all have been former agents: I vaguely remembered Rosie having mentioned that a good few were actually relatives, siblings or offspring who kept in touch out of family pride or loyalty. And it wasn't difficult to see where the centre of attraction was – in the middle there, grey, white and bald-headed delegates clustered like bees round honey. Trying to spot Rosie, I was beginning to think she might be in that swarm – in which case I'd wait until she came out of it – when I saw her waving to me from a table off to the right, close to the door people used when coming or going from / to the hotel itself. She was wearing a charcoal-grey jacket and skirt, white blouse, and had with her a woman to whom she'd introduced me a few days ago. Tall, white-headed, a BCRA widow – not all that jolly-looking, more what you might call a *commanding presence*. Reaching them, I shook hands with her, after kissing Rosie.

And *that* was something to be proud of. They could keep their André Brussauds et al – to be on kissing terms with Rosie Quarry knocked any of that stuff into the proverbial cocked hat. This friend of hers – Rosie had reminded me that her name was Amélie Viernet – was leaving us, seemingly making for centre-stage, where there was some reshuffling in progress – had been camera flashes, two pressmen with cameras shouldering their way out. Rosie told me, 'Brussaud's only been here about ten minutes. Look, this is your coffee, and it's getting cold – you're a little late, you know. The rest of it's yours too.'

'*Very* kind, Rosie. But listen – while we have time – I was sorting my notes last night, and if you wouldn't mind, one thing's not as clear as it might be – your escape route, after they'd smuggled you out of Banyuls –'

'Go into it later, shall we? What you need to know about now – I do mean *now* – is Ben and events in Australia. Here – sugar?'

For my cold coffee. 'No, thanks. But just to get this out of the way – please – you spent three days in Aristide's loft were then moved by donkey-cart – inland, westward, to that other place – combined efforts of Gérard, Andrés and Aristide – town still being searched, all that . . . Rosie?'

She'd sighed. 'All right. But just *very* briefly.'

342

'Bless you. I guarantee, less than two minutes. The puzzle is that when Eladio joined you, instead of making a beeline for the border and the mountains you went quite a long way west. Hadn't realised until early this morning, looking it up on the map. You were actually being hunted, but still –'

'In the *Zone Interdite* we were being hunted, yes – in so far as every intruder was. But after that long night's march we were out of it – in open country south of Ceret, right? It *was* a longish haul. There'd been an easier, shorter way the *passeurs* used until then, but the Boches had got on to that right away. That's one thing, the other is that normally we'd have started from Perpignan – over the River Tech and through the *Zone Interdite* south-westward. Long, long way, but none of that railway business. Would have brought us to the same point south of Ceret, from where in fact we did make your beeline for the frontier – crossed it in daylight and set course for Figueras. I was actually the first escaper Eladio took that way. Once in Spain the problem was the Gardia Civil and *their* bloody concentration camp. I forget what it was called, but escapees could disappear into it for years. Anyway, Eladio knew his onions, and as I must have told you I ended up in Barcelona, eventually Gibraltar.'

'Ah. That's another thing I was going to mention – I have a note that your friend Marilyn said something about Portugal, and I'd taken that to mean a ship or flight from Lisbon.'

'Marilyn was slightly up the pole on this one, wasn't she. Would you like fresh coffee?'

'No – really –'

'Not doing much with that croissant, either.'

'Well –'

'Hard day's night, eh? Tell you about Ben now, may I?'

'Yes. Please.'

'Brisbane 1957, then. Ben in the timber business, his father's deputy. Bare facts only now, because when this crowd thins a bit, or Brussaud makes a move –'

'Madame Viernet hasn't got anywhere near him yet.'

'Our president's with him, controlling it or trying to. So many of them want to be seen and if possible photographed with him. And BCRA naturally have priority, it's their show, so –'

'Isn't she a BCRA widow?'

'No. Daughter. She's a lot younger than we are.' A smile. 'Believe it or not. Her father survived Buchenvald, poor devil. I met her at the last reunion – the one Brussaud did *not* attend – although we'd been in touch before that. But now listen. Brisbane – Middle Harbour Yacht Club. Ben and I were lunching there – we did quite often . . . Oh, d'you remember at one time he was set on becoming a painter? Living before the war in Paris, washing dishes in hotels while – well, chasing girls as much as painting pictures – actually sold *one* canvas in all that time, to a pie-eyed Yank on a cross-Channel steamer. Anyway he'd persevered with it, off and on – even when he was at sea in his beloved motor gunboats – never got anywhere much with it, but then about the time we got married he found he had a real talent for just sketching – you know, pencil sketches?'

'Did he sell them?'

'Didn't try to, that I knew of. More of a parlour trick, dash one off and surprise a friend with it. Anyway – MHYC, the two of us on our own, place crowded, and suddenly old genius is at it again – on the back of a menu, pencil flying around, then it's stopped and he's telling me, "Rosie, don't look round, don't look anywhere except at me. *Important* you don't, OK?"

'I nod, he swivels the thing around flat on the table and pushes it at me, asks me does it ring any bells.'

'Does it?'

344

'My head's spinning and I feel a bit sick. I'm looking at what's unquestionably the face of a man I saw shot dead twenty-five years earlier. In the same visual memory I'm seeing Jake riddled, crumpling – and Ben's seeing from my expression something's – amiss. Haywire. I'm managing to keep my eyes on *his* face all right because in an odd way I *dread* seeing the man himself – if he's there, *could* be – and Ben seeing I'm in a state, telling me quietly, "He's not keen to have you see *him*, either. Near had a fit when he spotted you. Foreigner, I guess – funny way of handling his knife and fork."

'I whispered to him, "Ben, I saw this guy shot. Frenchman, name of Marc Voreux."'

I cut in with 'Rosie, this story has gone weird!'

'How about weirder still – name also André Brussaud?'

Pause. Noise in the brasserie unabated, but between us a silence while my brain coped with it. Finally I tried her with 'So your hero there – for starters, the man you saw shot wasn't killed.'

Small shrug. 'Might say the name just went out of circulation. Jake's two slugs had knocked him flat, I'd had no doubt it was a dead man falling. And neither Gérard nor Andrés said anything to suggest otherwise, one simply took it for granted. I was delighted he was dead but it wasn't him I was mostly thinking about.'

'No. Of course. Jake . . . But – Voreux's Boche chums must have carted him off, and in due course – some hospital got him back on his feet?'

'And he'd then got away from them. If they were holding him, that is. Supposed to have been working for them, maybe, ratted on *them*, resurfaced as aide to Jean Moulin and then Resistance leader / hero in his own right. Going after Gestapo was his speciality, gunning them down as often as not in broad daylight, well-planned operations but with a high degree of personal exposure. That's the legend anyway what makes him so famous. Back to Ben, though – Brussaud and another Frenchman had come up to Brisbane from Sydney in a Nicholson 65 owned by some Trade Department official. They were part of a mission from the Quai d'Orsay promoting a big trade deal – armaments or aircraft, might have been. There was a lot of PR angle on it, this famous war hero now political big cheese – and Ben and I stirring things in Canberra through contacts of my well-connected father-in-law – me knowing said war hero to have been a traitor who'd tried to sell me to the Gestapo, had Jake killed – oh, and Déclan –'

'You're saying *Déclan* was –'

'Poor Alain got himself caught – arrested, and – usual thing. He'd have had a good chance of making it over the Pyrenees if he'd just run for it, but he tried to take his wife with him, went back for her. No reason to think she shopped him – Marc must have done that.' A hand flipping out, pointing across the room – 'I mean *that* thing. Alain would have just walked into it. They – *La Geste* – had him in Paris, Rue des Saussaies, we got to know of it later through a woman agent who was there at the time and actually survived.'

'As you did, on a later occasion.'

She grimaced. 'Come to think of it, so I did. But – *poor* old Déclan. He was such a good fellow. Terrific, actually. Hardball really cost us, didn't it . . . Look – *must* finish this – from my own point of view it's really what I got you here for. Brussaud had seen me in the club, and he knew I'd seen him. Ben's father had these connections, and within days we were badgering X, Y and Z – caused a lot of trouble, weren't popular – and the French withdrew him pronto – maybe at his own request. Likely *would* have been. So it was all out of Canberra's hair – you'd think migh have proved something to them, but they still as good as told us to get lost. And Brussaud really *wanted* me lost – dead – and he or his employers put out a contract on me – left that behind him, you might say. Three times – well, the one I had no doubt at all was an attempted hit, I was leaving my hairdresser's in Brisbane and a car damn near ran me down, I knew it had been deliberate, but – no proof, police didn't believe me. Either that time or the others. Even Ben began to wonder – commiserating looks and – what I'd been through in my SOE deployments, then the shock of seeing that bastard bringing it all back . . . And not long after, they got *him*. I mean Ben. As I told you, didn't I. Early '58. A business trip he had to make every couple of months – I'd always gone with him, we had friends nearby we'd stay with – but I had a bad go of flu, last-minute decision he'd go on his own – well, vicinity of Mount Lindesay, that's not far south of Brisbane, a heavy truck knocked him off the road, sent his Chev bouncing down the hillside – burst into flame. It was my side, front passenger seat, the truck had hit. Not being all that tall in the saddle, they wouldn't have expected to see much of me – especially if I'd nodded off, as I might have – long trip and oven-hot. There was a witness but she was a moron – no identification, police got nowhere.'

Movement of the hands. 'Just goodbye Ben.'

'Dreadful, Rosie.'

'Bad enough.' A nod. 'As bad as it could have been, actually.'

She'd part-risen from her chair to get a sight of the Viernet woman, who was at a table with some other people now; she saw Rosie and raised her hands in a despairing motion. Obviously they had something going together. Mutual interest in getting to close quarters with that creature, I supposed. But with what in mind . . . She'd turned back to me: 'Brussaud had left the French government's service by the time I moved here from Australia. He wasn't the reason I made the move – long before that I'd had a Brisbane lawyer consult people in Paris on what if anything might be done – like suing for criminal damage, or whatever, but – see, for Ben's murder, *how* – no shred of evidence there in Aussie even – and for 1942–43 there was damnall either. No Marc Voreux on any record or in any memory, let alone linked to the famous Brussaud. *He'd* simply appeared on the scene out of the Resistance milieu in '43, no one knew anything of his origins. Parisian was all, mightn't have *had* a childhood. And having quit the Foreign Service he'd settled in Réunion. BCRA records were as sparse as SOE's – sparser, even – and of course there were no survivors. Hell – Jake, Déclan . . . I mean, who else, where else?'

'Germany?'

'Tried there. Not *much* of a try, but . . .' Shake of the head. 'Tried SIS, of course. The Hardball team had got von Schleben out, I knew that, but believe it or not *they* didn't, they'd never heard of him. As for SOE, you must know from your own researches that most of Section F's records were shredded or burnt when they shut us down at the end of it.'

'Yes. Coming back to you and Ben, though – presumably by the time you moved to Paris they'd given up trying to kill you?'

She nodded 'Two things, as I see it. No – three. One, I'd become harmless. Efforts getting absolutely nowhere told me that. Two, if they'd had another shot at me and bungled it, light might have been thrown on Ben's murder. And three –'

I'd put a hand on one of hers: 'Looks like they're moving Rosie.'

348

'Well, at long last . . .'

General movement – that nucleus in the centre shifting, breaking up. And the Viernet woman on her feet, looking this way. Rosie slid her chair back. 'Stay with me, will you?'

'Of course. But what are we—'

A hand lightly on my arm: 'Could be I'm not *entirely* harmless.' She'd said that as I came round to her side of the table – and caught my first sight of André Brussaud. Asking her, 'That him with the yellow face?'

'And the other one's our conference president, Armand Ruillaud.'

'The heavyweight.'

'Not exactly slim-line, is he. But my God, Brussaud has *not* weathered well!'

He certainly had not. Parchment-yellow, scrawny, stooped, leaning left-handed on a stick; thin, slack lips smirking at whatever Ruillaud was saying. Lizard-like – but by his manner enjoying the guest-of-honour rôle, limping along-side the burly president with his silver chain and medallion of some kind dangling on his rather prominent *poitrine*. They were heading for the glass door leading to the hotel foyer, so we were well placed to intercept them – Rosie I guessed having had that intention all along: and Amélie Viernet, I saw, closing up fast from somewhere on our port quarter.

Rosie had raised a hand to Ruillaud, who'd seen it, focused on her cautiously but now smiled, touched Brussaud's arm: Brussaud had also noticed her, and instantly lost his smirk. Ruillaud said with a hand out towards her, 'Madame Quarry, Brussaud, a very welcome guest-delegate from SOE. She has generously agreed to follow your address with a brief one of her own, on behalf of our former British colleagues. Still so minded I hope, madame?'

'With your permission.' Smiling at Brussaud's frozen,

349

mask-like stare. 'A tribute from those of us who knew the incomparable André Brussaud in his heyday.' She added – to *him*, with no smile, 'Those of us who survived it, that is.'

'You didn't think to mention this, Ruillaud?'

'Oh, a surprise for you, I thought – as well as a pleasure for the rest of us. I mean to say, a tribute from our Britannic allies?'

'And who's this?'

Asking who Amélie was. I was rather in the background – not a member of the club, so to speak. Rosie telling Ruillaud, 'Madame Viernet is the daughter of one of your most distinguished BCRA field agents – the late Clément Fonquéreuil, author and historian.'

'Clément Fonquéreuil, no less?' Ruillaud was visibly impressed. 'We're honoured indeed, madame! Brussaud, d'you realise –'

'Heard of him, but –'

Amélie said, 'You met him on a December night in 1942 on Canet-Plage near Perpignan and drove him in your van to Narbonne. His field name at that time was Gérone.'

'Forty-*two*.' Dismissive gesture. 'I've no recollection of *any*—'

'My father later survived the extermination camp at Buchenwald.'

Ruillaud was wide-eyed: 'Why, I do remember there was a biographical note in his famous *Charlemagne et les Franks* to the effect that he had done so. *What* a man he was. But I'm ashamed, not to have realised –'

Rosie put in, 'The thing is, monsieur, Madame Viernet would like your approval of her adding a few words to my own address. The fact is, I was on Canet-Plage myself that night, and I think your delegates might find the conjoined memories intriguing – if we keep it short and to the point?'

350

'I'm sure they'd be fascinated – irrespective of how long or short.' Pausing, looking at Brussaud, who wasn't showing much enthusiasm. Adding then diplomatically, 'But perhaps a prior discussion between the three of you – to avoid possible conflicts of memory? You could allow yourselves say half an hour, before we make our way to St-Sernin's?'

For the Memorial Mass, which was scheduled for ten forty-five. Brussaud checked the time: 'If that's really necessary –'

'I think it's a first-class idea.' Rosie said. 'I'd be mortified to include anything that conflicted with your own recollections.'

'Excellent.' Ruillaud beamed. 'The only thing is, in here you'd be constantly interrupted.' Glancing round at delegates still waiting for a chance to horn in. 'And I have the answer to that – there's a small *salon privé* adjacent to the manager's office, which –'

'Who's this?'

Brussaud was looking suspiciously at *me* now. Rosie began – to Ruillaud more than to him – 'My private guest, and long-time companion –'

'I'm a writer.' Shaking hands with Ruillaud. 'I've written four books about her various deployments, and now there's to be a fifth.' Brussaud had started towards the glass door, Ruillaud calling after him, 'I'll show you where it is, then leave you to it.' Standing back for Rosie, Amélie and I to precede him; people were coming through from the foyer and Brussaud was having to wait, to let them through. They weren't delegates, didn't give him a second glance.

I'd asked her in a whisper, 'What are we up to, Rosie?' and she'd whispered back, 'Method in one's madness, I hope. I think we've got him. When he sees it, though, God knows –' Looking round at Amélie, who'd nudged her, murmured,

351

'Shush': then we were in this rather smart little *salon* that the hotel had placed at Ruillaud's disposal – off-white, with a soft-blue carpet, and comfortable chairs around an oblong glass table. Brussaud placed himself at the table's head, surprisingly dropped his stick on it, then took some time lighting himself a black cheroot that he'd no doubt have brought with him from Réunion.

Flicking the spent match away. 'So what's the meaning of this charade?'

'Meaning . . .' Rosie shrugged, with a smile across the table at Amélie. 'Meaning, Marc –'

'My name is not Marc, it's André Brussaud.'

'Meaning, Marc, that if you address the conference after this lunch, then so will we. Our subject would be "Marc Voreux, traitor to France and her allies and his own former colleagues".'

'I don't believe I ever heard of him.' Staring at her for a moment: cheroot-smoke leaking from the loose lips. Eyes behind the thick-lensed, wire-framed glasses shifting to Amélie then. 'You, I certainly never heard of.'

'How about my father, whom you delivered to the Abwehr?'

'You're clearly deranged. Both of you. Oh – is it blackmail?' A glance at me: 'Writer, you said?'

'This'll be the fifth book in what we're calling the Rosie Saga. Rosie being Madame Quarry's given name. You as Marc Voreux knew her by her SOE field name Suzette Treniard, in a *réseau* they called "Countryman". You allowed yourself to be turned by the Gestapo.'

Amélie corrected me: 'By the Abwehr, to be precise.' She told Brussaud, 'My father left a memoir – in typescript, not for publication, just for the family. I've had some copies made. He describes how you were supposed to have driven him and two others to some safe-house beyond Narbonne but left him and one of the others in the town – at his request, he had old friends there – took the third to the safe-house where Abwehr were expecting you to deliver all three – so they were put to the trouble of arresting them next morning at the station. You were there to identify them. I should explain, he wrote this memoir only for private circulation because he felt it would hardly fit in with the main body of his work. His three-volume *History of the Hundred Years' War*, for instance. But as I say I've had copies made – following the decease of my husband, whose instincts were strongly against our becoming involved in such controversy – in *any* controversy, in fact. But I've little doubt that today it would attract a great deal of interest. And incidentally I have a copy with me, with passages marked for reading to them at this banquet.'

She looked from Brussaud to me. Having effectively shattered him – left him one might say foundering. I was surprised how quickly – *instantly* . . . I suppose the shock – from certainty that there could be no sustainable evidence against him, to – well, effectively instant devastation as it were in one single broadside . . . Telling me, 'Gestapo came into it *after* that. Although apparently they'd been in it anyway, in the background somehow.'

Brussaud said thinly, 'They had my sister.'

Looking at Rosie, who was on his left. I was on *her* left, and Amélie was facing us, on Brussaud's right. Rosie told us, 'His sister's name was Denise.'

'You know that, uh?'

'Jake – Jean Samblat as you knew him – told me about her when I joined the *réseau*. And I *think* you and I talked about her, at one stage. She'd started the escape-line you worked in – to which you'd been released by BCRA, were then taken on by Countryman, SOE, after the escape-line was blown and amongst other problems you had no access

353

to a pianist. But you were saying – because they held your sister hostage, was it, that you betrayed us?'

'Denise had been a mother to me. From infancy, I was devoted to her. It was through me they tracked her down. A woman by name Gabrielle Vérisoin with whom I was in contact – had made friends with – I'd told her about Denise, how desperately concerned I was for her – and Gabrielle offered to act as post-office. She was – I thought, and she may have thought so too – inviolate. Married to a rich man with friends in high places, Vichy loyalist – in fact he was nothing of the sort, but –'

'Gestapo traced your sister through your approach to her?'

'And back the other way. I think she was already being watched. They arrested her – in Paris. Abwehr had been hunting both of us – it was Abwehr who'd broken into the escape-line.'

'So Abwehr turned you, Gestapo were holding *her*.'

'They said unless I gave them what they wanted they'd send me pieces of her – at first, fingers with her rings on them, then—'

'Jesus.' Amélie had whispered it, flinching. She and Rosie exchanging glances, and Brussaud continuing, '– then whole hands, or –'

'What did they want, exactly?'

'Oh – details of what you were calling Operation Hardball –'

'Details you didn't have.'

'– and the identity of Countryman's new pianist.'

'Me.'

'Yes.' He'd stubbed out the cheroot. 'But – believe me – *please* – I resisted, tried to stall them, play for time – honestly, I swear it, I –'

'Eventually gave them the lot – or all you *had* –'

354

'To save my sister. One couldn't stall for ever. Try to understand? I know it's – difficult, on the face of it I was – I mean,
it's like speaking of another person – myself, but under such
enormous strain – *and* anguish for *her* – and they were in a
hurry, weren't going to –'

'Were they going to release her? Straight swap for *us*?'

'They were bringing her down to Castres, the prison there.
Said they were. Then release her to me, and when they did
so we'd have made a run for it. I *thought* . . .' Looking Rosie
in the face now, his own eyes like bruised, wet slits behind
those lenses . . . 'What will you do with this – apart from
destroy me this afternoon? Oh, his book –'

'That's one thing. The others he wrote were fiction, this
can be for real. Are you going to address the conference?'

'If you could only see – comprehend – how it was with
my sister, how I couldn't *possibly* have –'

'*Did* they release her to you? When you recovered from
wounds you should have died of?'

'She was dead before that. The first time they had me in
– at the *préfecture* at Narbonne, when they told me the Gestapo
had her, I could save her if I played ball – she was dead *then*.
The Abwehr told me Gestapo had fooled *them*.'

'D'you think that was the case?'

'All I know for sure is it marked the birth of André
Brussaud.'

Rosie thought about it, and nodded. 'That's – under-
standable.'

Amélie had concurred. A gesture, murmur of assent.
Sympathy, even? Rosie looked queryingly at me now: I said
something like 'Damn-all to do with having Ben murdered
fifteen or sixteen years later.'

'No. Certainly is not. And whoever it was he hired . . .'

Staring at him. Could hardly have expected an answer –
and didn't look like getting one. He was gripping his

355

walking-stick horizontally in front of him in both hands: maybe to stop them shaking. She reminded him, 'It was me they were trying to kill, and you must have paid them to do it. *You* wanting me dead – you the instigator, my husband's murderer. The only others concerned would be the ones you hired. Your colleagues – bosses, fellow diplomats, whatever – wouldn't have known about Voreux, your treachery, any of that – how could they? You'd hardly have told them, would you?'

'If I withdraw – that's to say, the indication was, if I withdraw – *don't* speak at this luncheon, don't attend it – then you don't speak either?'

I said – her glance had invited comment – 'Letting you just run off home to Réunion – reputation unsullied?'

He'd shut his eyes. 'I have a wife in Réunion.'

'I did have a husband in Australia.' Insisting, then: 'I'm right, aren't I, solely *your* decision to take out a contract on me – couple of bosh shots then the one that misfired, killed my husband?'

'I'm sorry. Terribly, genuinely – I mean yes – *yes*, I –'

Amélie said, 'If we're going to this Memorial Mass – *I* certainly am –'

Rosie asked Brussaud, 'Are you?'

Hands over his face. Yellowish putty-colour streaked with ivory and sweat- or tear-damp. He looked, truly, like death. Shaking of the head and jowls more like trembling. Grasping the stick again, knuckles white; a croak of 'I will not attend either Mass or the lunch. I'm not a *well* man, I –'

'Well, in that case . . .' Rosie had pulled back a little from the table, was reaching down for her bag. 'Remember once asking me to get you one of these?'

Small screw of paper. Untwisting it, and its contents spilling out on the table-top – a gelatine capsule two-thirds of an inch long, the gelatine itself clouded with age.

356

'Didn't have one for you then. This was of a much later vintage, one I kept as a souvenir.' Poking at it with her fore-finger. 'We were told they were extremely quick-acting – one's teeth wouldn't even get to meet, they said. Might have some use for it now, Marc?'

He'd been staring at it, now met Rosie's surprisingly calm gaze. Calm, but deeply interested. Brussaud's eyes returning to the capsule lying ten centimetres from his left hand – that hand's fingers having loosened themselves from the stick. He was, clearly, considering the offer. Looking at Rosie again now, though, and I heard him mutter, 'You see – my wife –'

'Yes.' A double nod. 'Yes, well.' A small sigh. 'You'll just go, then.' Her fingers retrieving the capsule – rewrapping it in what might have been a toffee-paper, twisting its ends to close it before dropping it in her bag. Looking at me then, and across at Amélie: 'St-Sernin's for us now, and we'd better –'

'But – excuse me –'

Eyes screwed up and seeping, that left hand clawing in her direction – towards her bag. The bag, not her, he was looking at. 'If I may change my mind, I –'

'What?'

She'd got as far as turning her chair my way, in the course of getting to her feet, was looking at him sharply, surpris-edly, as if – well, my impression, this – as if she'd to all intents and purposes finished with him, been thinking only of getting as quickly as possible to the Memorial Mass and had been almost startled – irritated, maybe – by this reminder of his presence, continued existence even. Amélie and I were already up from the table, Amélie on her way round to this side of it, hissing, 'Have you any idea of the time? We'll never –'

'Saying you *would* have a use for it?'

Affirmative grunt. Breath coming in short, urgent gasps. 'If you'd – beg you, be so kind –'

'No.' She was with us, heading for the door, wasn't bothering even to look back at him. 'No, Marc. I won't. I think you just have to live with it. All of it. Alain Déclan, for instance – remember him? Excuse us now . . .'

IN AT THE KILL

France, 1944. SOE agent Rosie Ewing has been shot by the Gestapo on her way to a death camp, having run off as a decoy so that her fellow agent Lise can make an escape. One of them must survive in order to tell London of double agent Andre Marcheval's activities. Left for dead, Rosie is rescued by two men of the Maquis and taken to a safe house. Here, as she recuperates, she begins to form her own plans to reduce the threat posed by Marcheval and, more immediately, to get in touch with London and inform them of her current situation. She learns that Marcheval's father has a factory some way away in which rocket casings are being manufactured. Now she must not only find Marcheval and eliminate him if necessary, but also stop these potential bombs from being made . . .

978 0 7515 2846 6

SINGLE TO PARIS

France, August 1945. When two agents are arrested in Paris, it is SOE operative Rosie Ewing who is sent in to rescue them. Also in Paris is a woman by the name of Jacqueline with whom Rosie has had previous dealings and who is now the live-in girlfriend of a highly-placed SD officer. Rosie's brief is to find Jacqueline, then through her and her lover discover where the two agents are being held, then get them out before they either talk or die under torture.

But get them out how?

The only way has to be with French Resistance help. In the chaos prevailing at this time, both Gaullist and Communist resistance groups are stirring – and at each other's throats. There are also several pro-Nazi groups – including one quite exceptionally vicious lot. Rosie is going solo and virtually blind into the middle of all that . . .

978 0 7515 3234 0

Other bestselling titles available by mail:

The prices shown above are correct at time of going to press. However, the publishers reserve the right to increase prices on covers from those previously advertised, without further notice.

——————————————— sphere ———————————————

SPHERE
PO Box 121, Kettering, Northants, NN14 4ZQ
Tel: 01832 737525, Fax: 01832 733076
Email: aspenhouse@FSBDial.co.uk

POST AND PACKING:
Payments can be made as follows: cheque, postal order (payable to Sphere), credit card or Switch Card. Do not send cash or currency.

| All UK Orders | **FREE OF CHARGE** |
| EC & Overseas | 25% of order value |

Name (BLOCK LETTERS) . . . .

Address . . . .

. . . .

Post/zip code: . . . .

☐ Please keep me in touch with future Sphere publications

☐ I enclose my remittance £ . . . .

☐ I wish to pay by Visa/Access/Mastercard/Eurocard/Switch Card

```
┌─┬─┬─┬─┬─┬─┬─┬─┬─┬─┬─┬─┬─┬─┬─┬─┐
│ │ │ │ │ │ │ │ │ │ │ │ │ │ │ │ │
└─┴─┴─┴─┴─┴─┴─┴─┴─┴─┴─┴─┴─┴─┴─┴─┘
```

Card Expiry Date ☐☐☐☐   Switch Issue No. ☐☐